ONYVILLE MYSTERI

Facebook: **facebook.com/idwpublishing**
Twitter: **@idwpublishing**
YouTube: **youtube.com/idwpublishing**
Tumblr: **tumblr.idwpublishing.com**
Instagram: **instagram.com/idwpublishing**

COVER ART BY
BRENDA HICKEY

SERIES EDITS BY
BOBBY CURNOW

COLLECTION EDITS BY
JUSTIN EISINGER
AND ALONZO SIMON

COLLECTION DESIGN BY
SHAWN LEE

PUBLISHER
GREG GOLDSTEIN

Licensed By:
Hasbro

ISBN: 978-1-68405-393-3   22 21 20 19   1 2 3 4

Originally published as MY LITTLE PONY: PONYVILLE MYSTERIES issues #1–5.

Greg Goldstein, President & Publisher
John Barber, Editor-In-Chief
Robbie Robbins, EVP/Sr. Art Director
Cara Morrison, Chief Financial Officer
Matthew Ruzicka, Chief Accounting Officer
Anita Frazier, SVP of Sales and Marketing
David Hedgecock, Associate Publisher
Jerry Bennington, VP of New Product Development
Lorelei Bunjes, VP of Digital Services
Justin Eisinger, Editorial Director, Graphic Novels & Collections
Eric Moss, Sr. Director, Licensing & Business Development

Ted Adams, IDW Founder

Special thanks to Meghan McCarthy, Eliza Hart, Ed Lane, Beth Artale, and Michael Kelly.

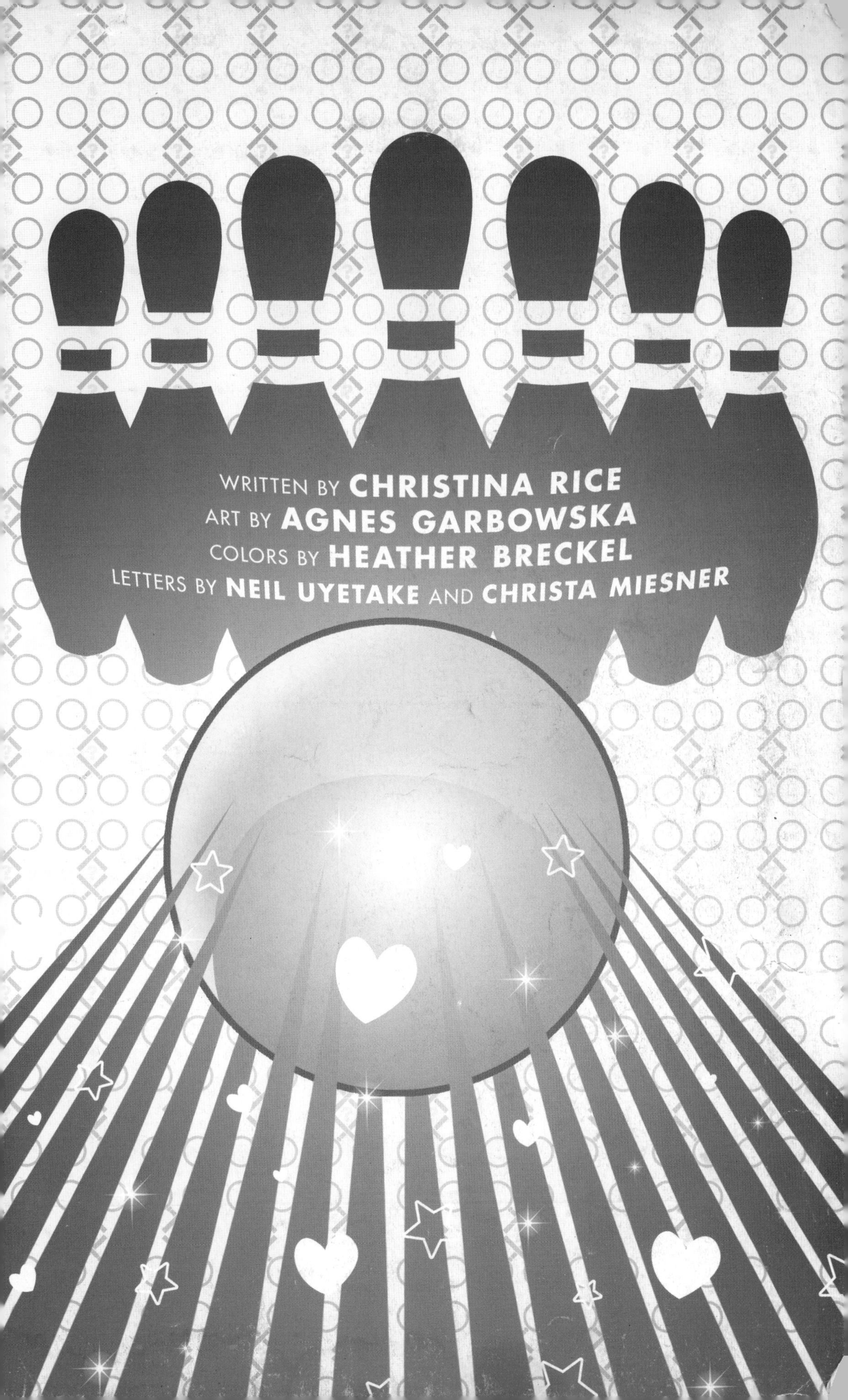

WRITTEN BY **CHRISTINA RICE**
ART BY **AGNES GARBOWSKA**
COLORS BY **HEATHER BRECKEL**
LETTERS BY **NEIL UYETAKE** AND **CHRISTA MIESNER**

1

ART BY **AGNES GARBOWSKA**

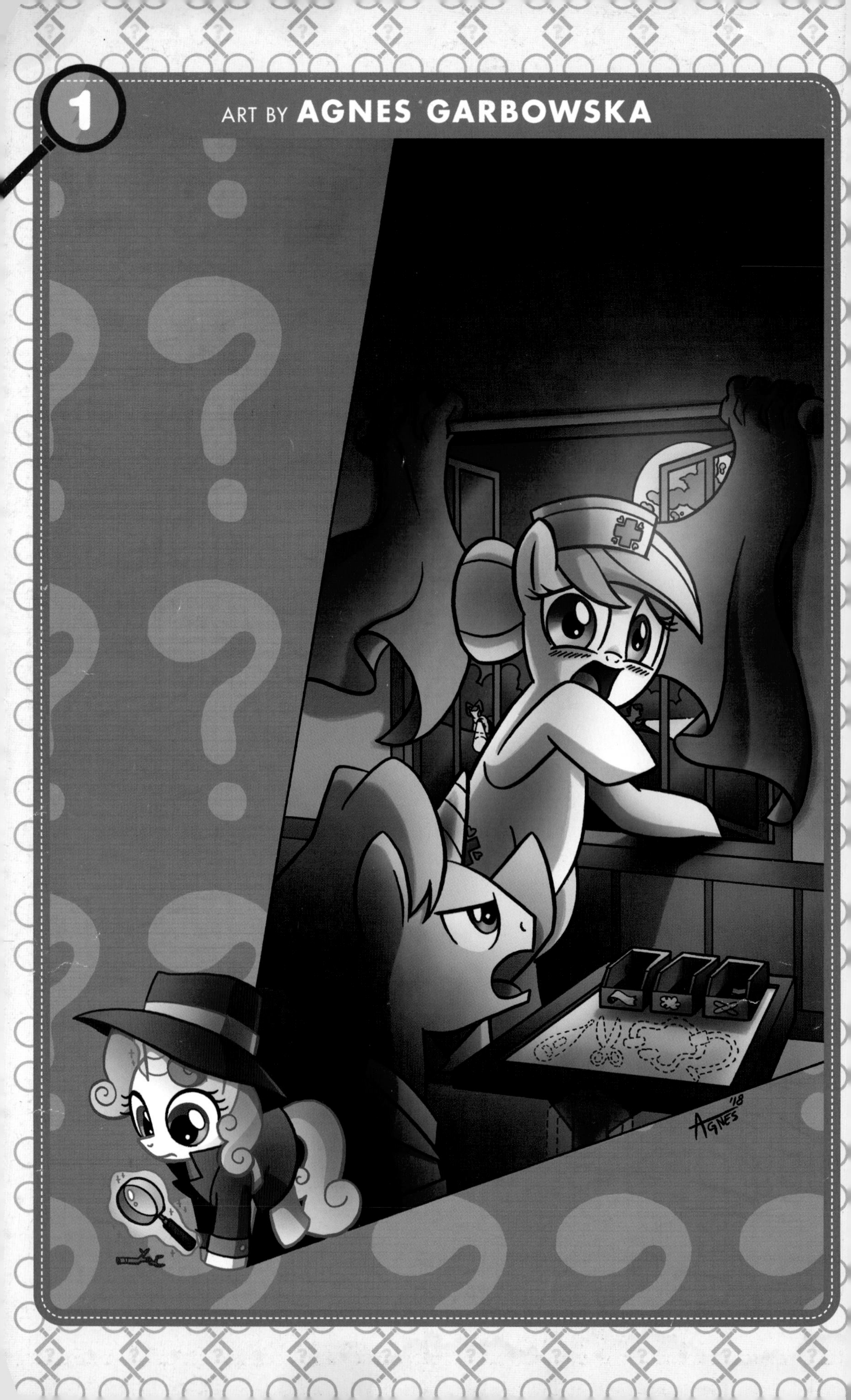
AGNES '18

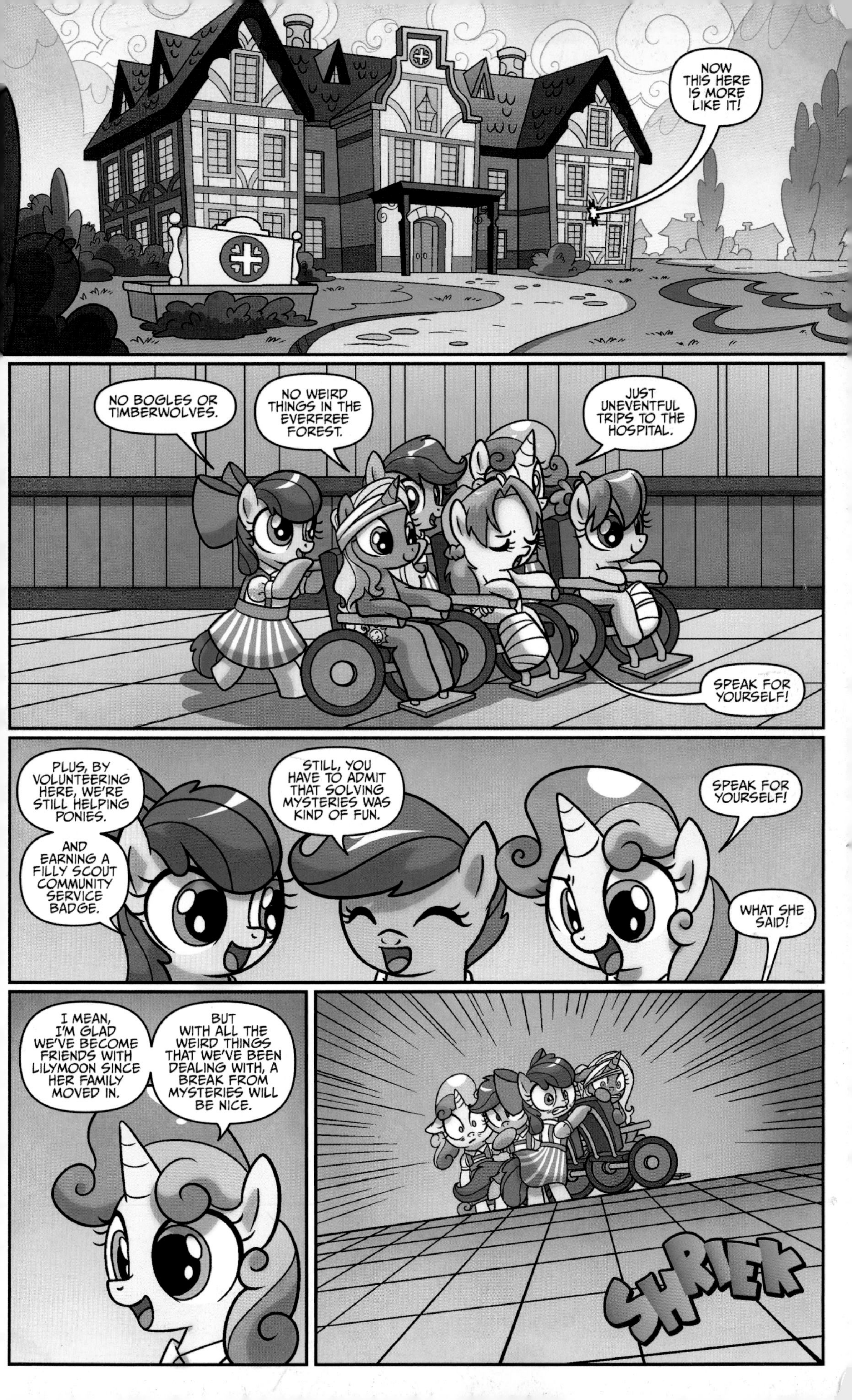
NOW THIS HERE IS MORE LIKE IT!
NO BOGLES OR TIMBERWOLVES.
NO WEIRD THINGS IN THE EVERFREE FOREST.
JUST UNEVENTFUL TRIPS TO THE HOSPITAL.
SPEAK FOR YOURSELF!
PLUS, BY VOLUNTEERING HERE, WE'RE STILL HELPING PONIES.
AND EARNING A FILLY SCOUT COMMUNITY SERVICE BADGE.
STILL, YOU HAVE TO ADMIT THAT SOLVING MYSTERIES WAS KIND OF FUN.
SPEAK FOR YOURSELF!
WHAT SHE SAID!
I MEAN, I'M GLAD WE'VE BECOME FRIENDS WITH LILYMOON SINCE HER FAMILY MOVED IN.
BUT WITH ALL THE WEIRD THINGS THAT WE'VE BEEN DEALING WITH, A BREAK FROM MYSTERIES WILL BE NICE.
SHRIEK

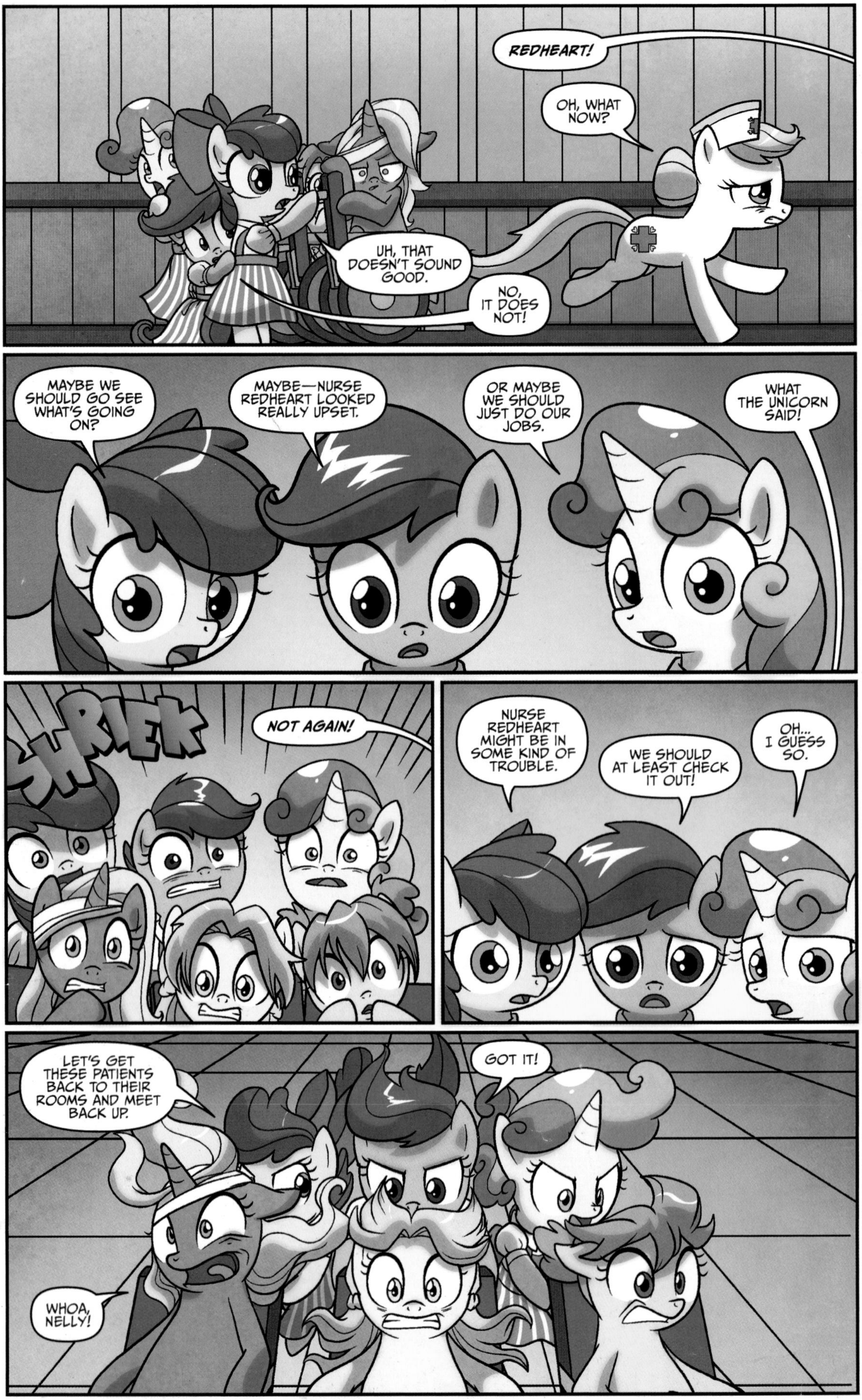
REDHEART!
OH, WHAT NOW?
UH, THAT DOESN'T SOUND GOOD.
NO, IT DOES NOT!
MAYBE WE SHOULD GO SEE WHAT'S GOING ON?
MAYBE—NURSE REDHEART LOOKED REALLY UPSET.
OR MAYBE WE SHOULD JUST DO OUR JOBS.
WHAT THE UNICORN SAID!
SHRIEK
NOT AGAIN!
NURSE REDHEART MIGHT BE IN SOME KIND OF TROUBLE.
WE SHOULD AT LEAST CHECK IT OUT!
OH... I GUESS SO.
LET'S GET THESE PATIENTS BACK TO THEIR ROOMS AND MEET BACK UP.
GOT IT!
WHOA, NELLY!

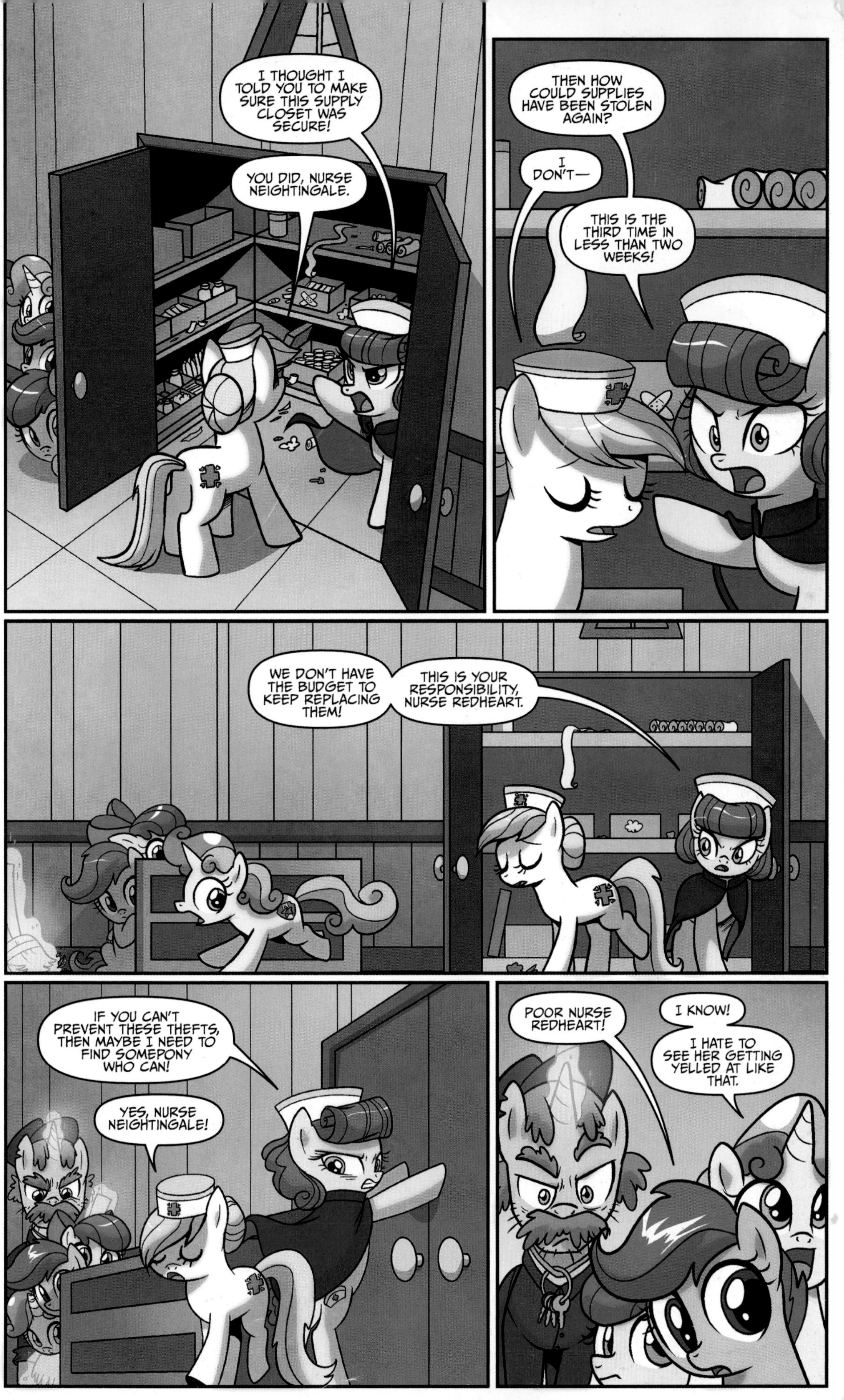

I THOUGHT I TOLD YOU TO MAKE SURE THIS SUPPLY CLOSET WAS SECURE!
YOU DID, NURSE NEIGHTINGALE.
THEN HOW COULD SUPPLIES HAVE BEEN STOLEN AGAIN?
I DON'T—
THIS IS THE THIRD TIME IN LESS THAN TWO WEEKS!
WE DON'T HAVE THE BUDGET TO KEEP REPLACING THEM!
THIS IS YOUR RESPONSIBILITY, NURSE REDHEART.
IF YOU CAN'T PREVENT THESE THEFTS, THEN MAYBE I NEED TO FIND SOMEPONY WHO CAN!
YES, NURSE NEIGHTINGALE!
POOR NURSE REDHEART!
I KNOW!
I HATE TO SEE HER GETTING YELLED AT LIKE THAT.

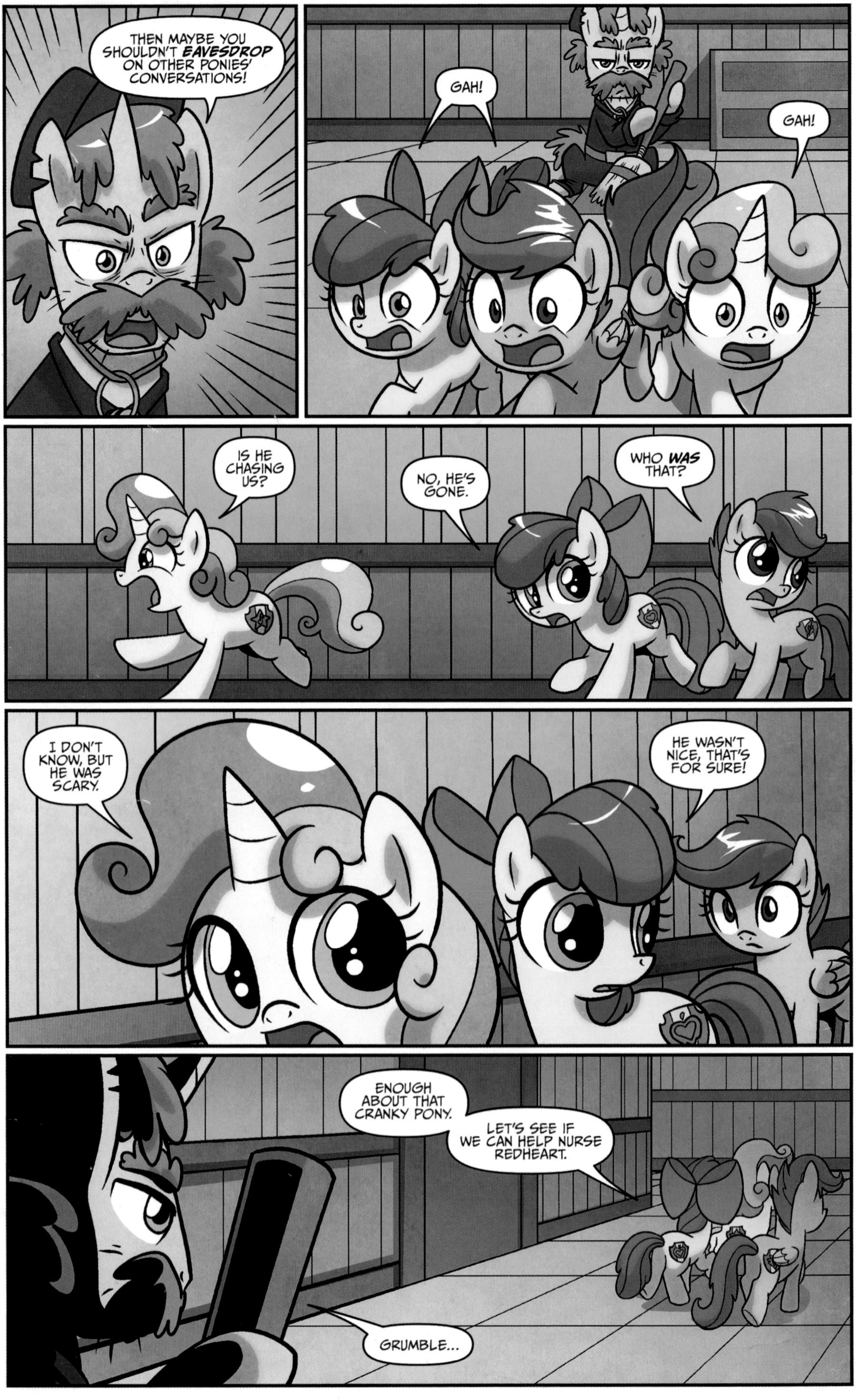
THEN MAYBE YOU SHOULDN'T EAVESDROP ON OTHER PONIES' CONVERSATIONS!
GAH!
GAH!
IS HE CHASING US?
NO, HE'S GONE.
WHO WAS THAT?
I DON'T KNOW, BUT HE WAS SCARY.
HE WASN'T NICE, THAT'S FOR SURE!
ENOUGH ABOUT THAT CRANKY PONY.
LET'S SEE IF WE CAN HELP NURSE REDHEART.
GRUMBLE...

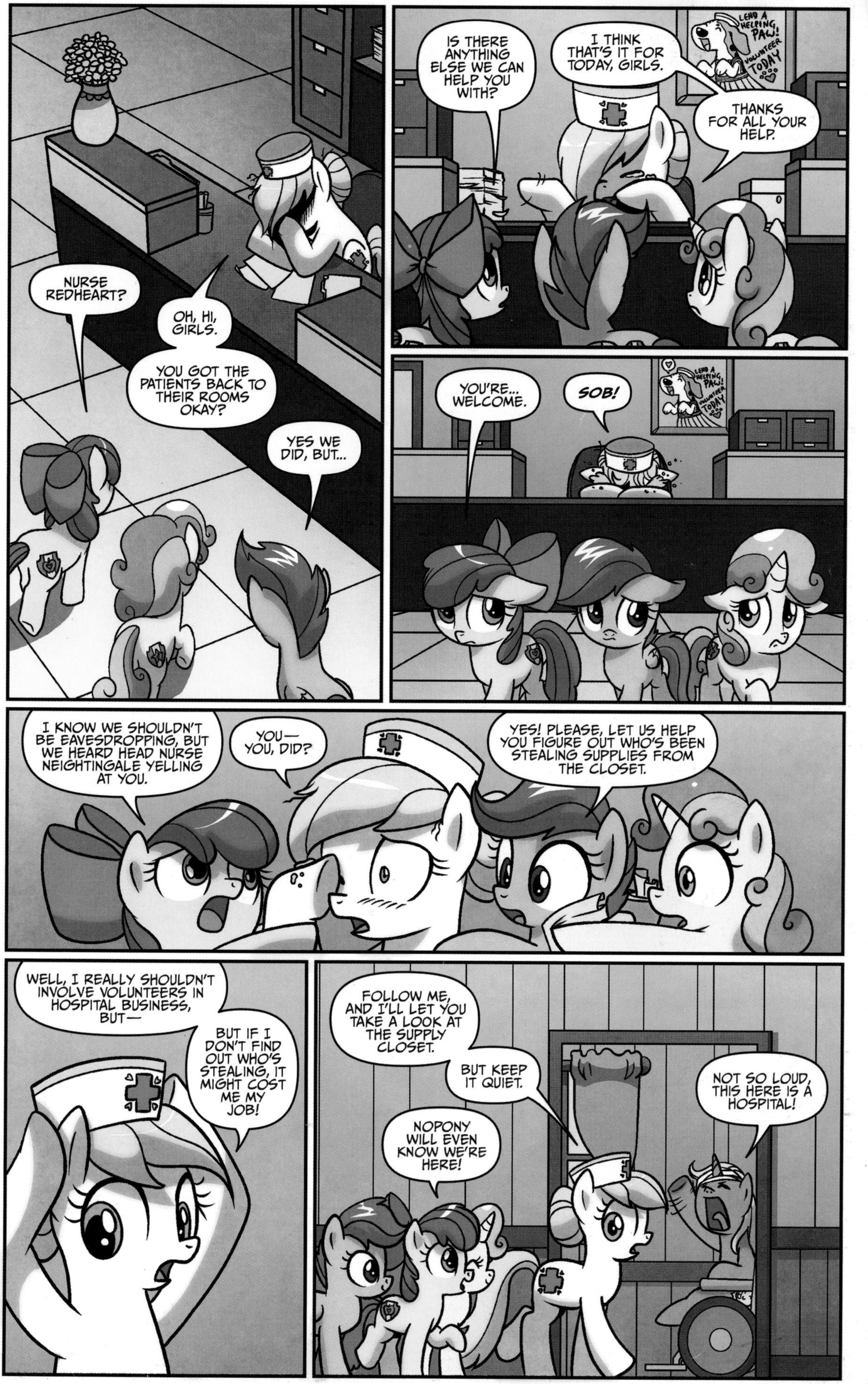
NURSE REDHEART?
OH, HI, GIRLS.
YOU GOT THE PATIENTS BACK TO THEIR ROOMS OKAY?
YES WE DID, BUT...
IS THERE ANYTHING ELSE WE CAN HELP YOU WITH?
I THINK THAT'S IT FOR TODAY, GIRLS.
LEND A HELPING PAW! VOLUNTEER TODAY
THANKS FOR ALL YOUR HELP.
YOU'RE... WELCOME.
SOB!
LEND A HELPING PAW! VOLUNTEER TODAY
I KNOW WE SHOULDN'T BE EAVESDROPPING, BUT WE HEARD HEAD NURSE NEIGHTINGALE YELLING AT YOU.
YOU— YOU, DID?
YES! PLEASE, LET US HELP YOU FIGURE OUT WHO'S BEEN STEALING SUPPLIES FROM THE CLOSET.
WELL, I REALLY SHOULDN'T INVOLVE VOLUNTEERS IN HOSPITAL BUSINESS, BUT—
BUT IF I DON'T FIND OUT WHO'S STEALING, IT MIGHT COST ME MY JOB!
FOLLOW ME, AND I'LL LET YOU TAKE A LOOK AT THE SUPPLY CLOSET.
BUT KEEP IT QUIET.
NOPONY WILL EVEN KNOW WE'RE HERE!
NOT SO LOUD, THIS HERE IS A HOSPITAL!

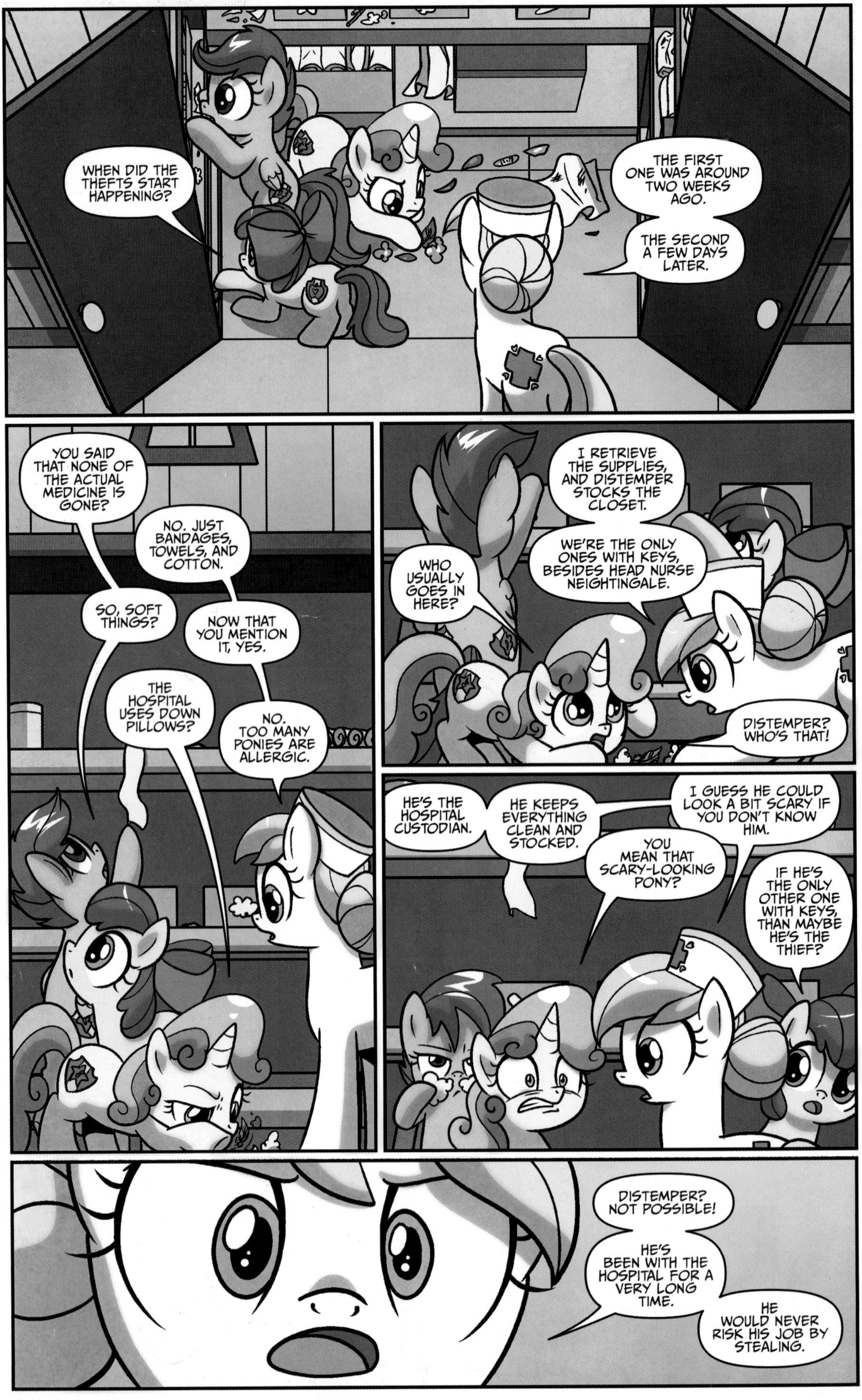
WHEN DID THE THEFTS START HAPPENING?
THE FIRST ONE WAS AROUND TWO WEEKS AGO.
THE SECOND A FEW DAYS LATER.
YOU SAID THAT NONE OF THE ACTUAL MEDICINE IS GONE?
NO. JUST BANDAGES, TOWELS, AND COTTON.
SO, SOFT THINGS?
NOW THAT YOU MENTION IT, YES.
THE HOSPITAL USES DOWN PILLOWS?
NO. TOO MANY PONIES ARE ALLERGIC.
I RETRIEVE THE SUPPLIES, AND DISTEMPER STOCKS THE CLOSET.
WHO USUALLY GOES IN HERE?
WE'RE THE ONLY ONES WITH KEYS, BESIDES HEAD NURSE NEIGHTINGALE.
DISTEMPER? WHO'S THAT!
HE'S THE HOSPITAL CUSTODIAN.
HE KEEPS EVERYTHING CLEAN AND STOCKED.
I GUESS HE COULD LOOK A BIT SCARY IF YOU DON'T KNOW HIM.
YOU MEAN THAT SCARY-LOOKING PONY?
IF HE'S THE ONLY OTHER ONE WITH KEYS, THAN MAYBE HE'S THE THIEF?
DISTEMPER? NOT POSSIBLE!
HE'S BEEN WITH THE HOSPITAL FOR A VERY LONG TIME.
HE WOULD NEVER RISK HIS JOB BY STEALING.

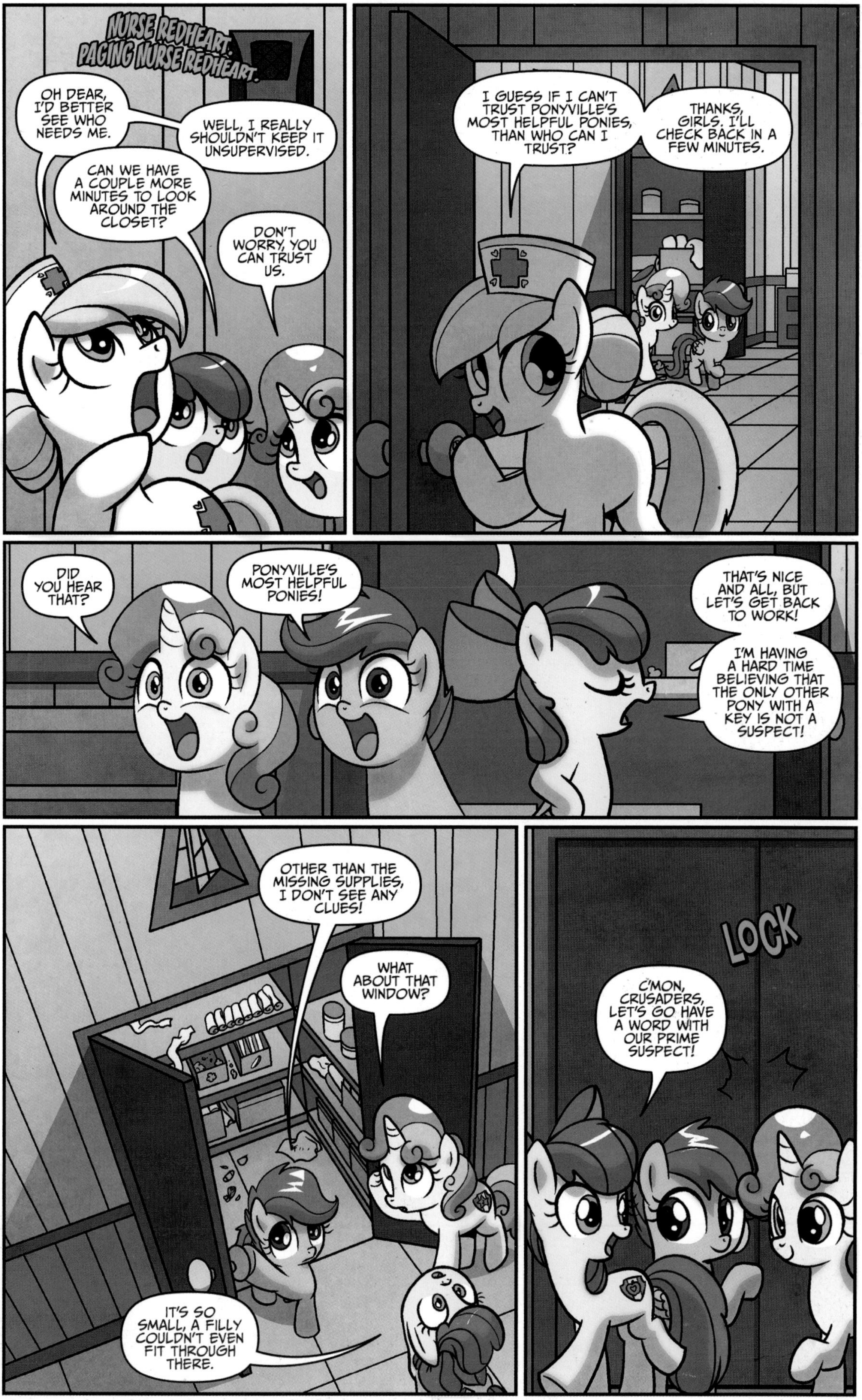
NURSE REDHEART. PAGING NURSE REDHEART.
OH DEAR, I'D BETTER SEE WHO NEEDS ME.
WELL, I REALLY SHOULDN'T KEEP IT UNSUPERVISED.
CAN WE HAVE A COUPLE MORE MINUTES TO LOOK AROUND THE CLOSET?
DON'T WORRY, YOU CAN TRUST US.
I GUESS IF I CAN'T TRUST PONYVILLE'S MOST HELPFUL PONIES, THAN WHO CAN I TRUST?
THANKS, GIRLS. I'LL CHECK BACK IN A FEW MINUTES.
DID YOU HEAR THAT?
PONYVILLE'S MOST HELPFUL PONIES!
THAT'S NICE AND ALL, BUT LET'S GET BACK TO WORK!
I'M HAVING A HARD TIME BELIEVING THAT THE ONLY OTHER PONY WITH A KEY IS NOT A SUSPECT!
OTHER THAN THE MISSING SUPPLIES, I DON'T SEE ANY CLUES!
WHAT ABOUT THAT WINDOW?
IT'S SO SMALL, A FILLY COULDN'T EVEN FIT THROUGH THERE.
LOCK
C'MON, CRUSADERS, LET'S GO HAVE A WORD WITH OUR PRIME SUSPECT!

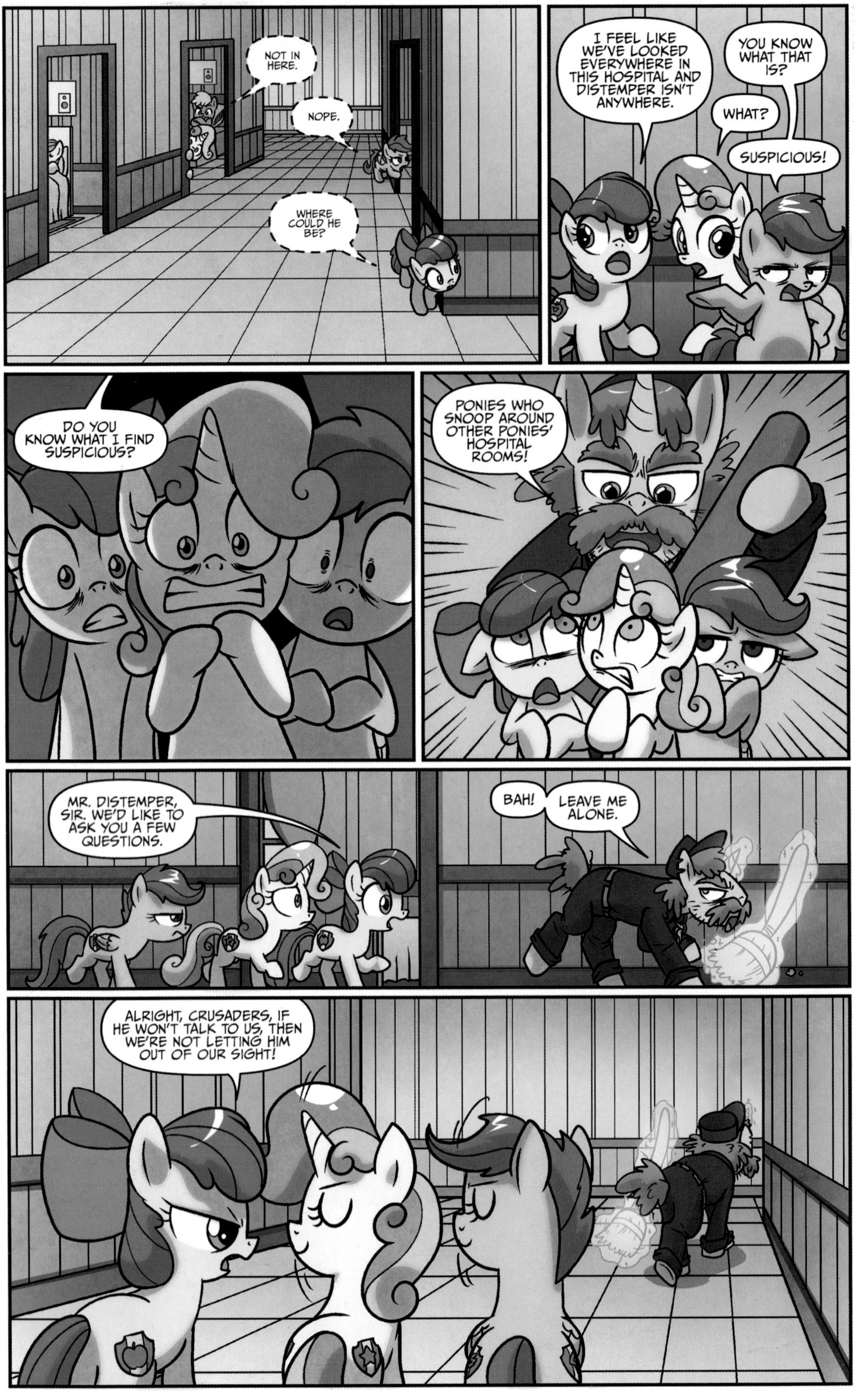
NOT IN HERE.
NOPE.
WHERE COULD HE BE?
I FEEL LIKE WE'VE LOOKED EVERYWHERE IN THIS HOSPITAL AND DISTEMPER ISN'T ANYWHERE.
YOU KNOW WHAT THAT IS?
WHAT?
SUSPICIOUS!
DO YOU KNOW WHAT I FIND SUSPICIOUS?
PONIES WHO SNOOP AROUND OTHER PONIES' HOSPITAL ROOMS!
MR. DISTEMPER, SIR. WE'D LIKE TO ASK YOU A FEW QUESTIONS.
BAH!
LEAVE ME ALONE.
ALRIGHT, CRUSADERS, IF HE WON'T TALK TO US, THEN WE'RE NOT LETTING HIM OUT OF OUR SIGHT!

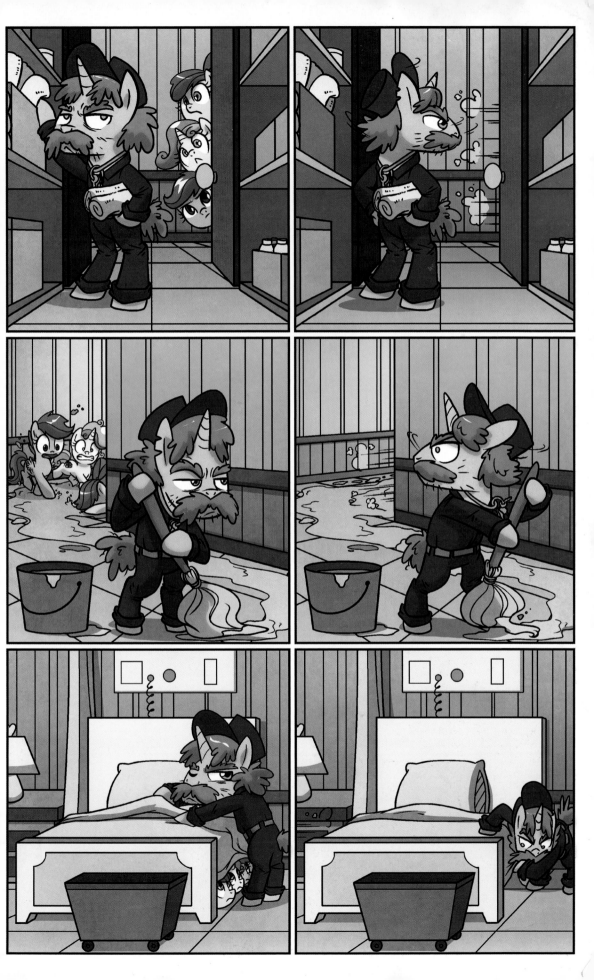

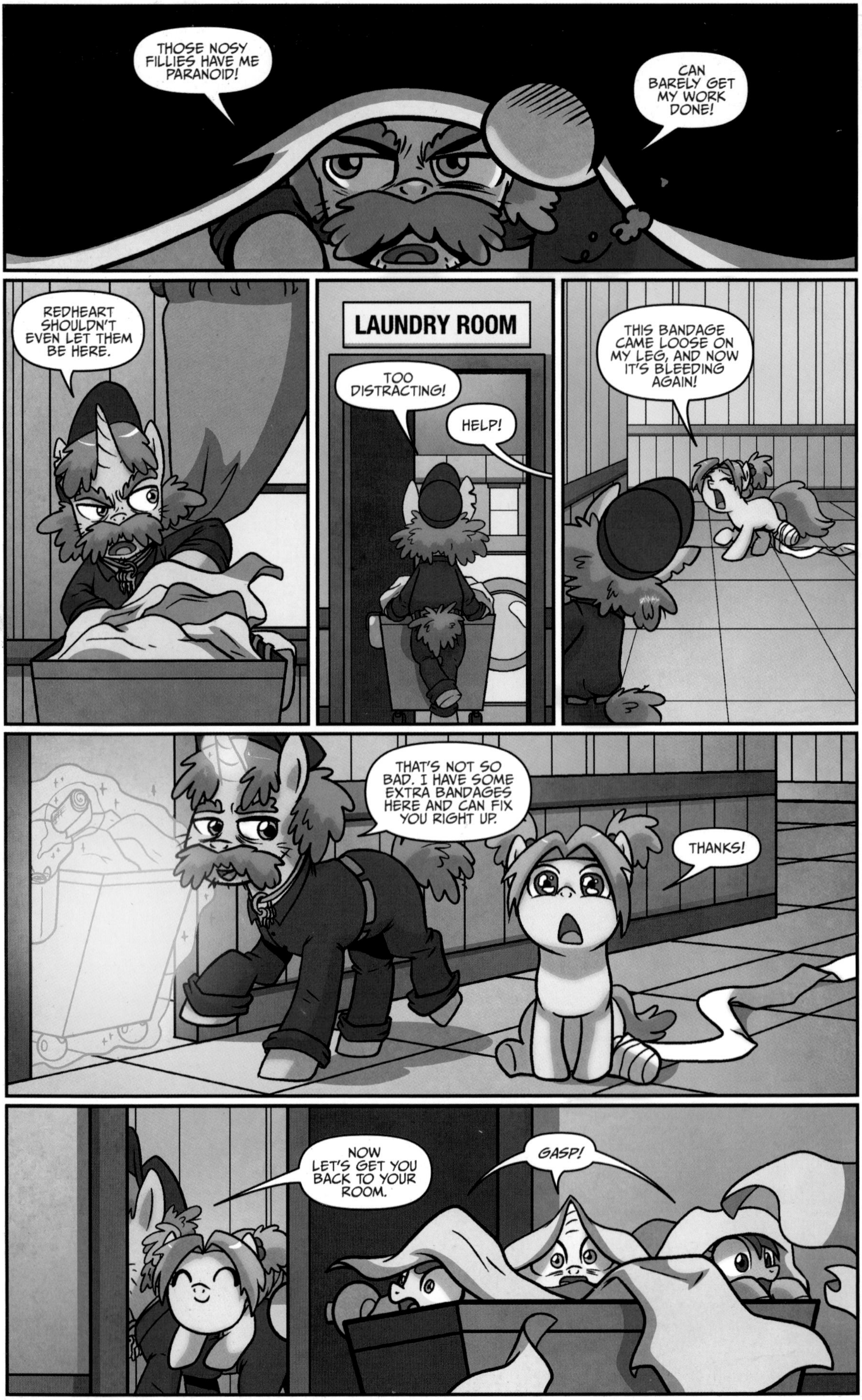
THOSE NOSY FILLIES HAVE ME PARANOID!
CAN BARELY GET MY WORK DONE!
REDHEART SHOULDN'T EVEN LET THEM BE HERE.
LAUNDRY ROOM
TOO DISTRACTING!
HELP!
THIS BANDAGE CAME LOOSE ON MY LEG, AND NOW IT'S BLEEDING AGAIN!
THAT'S NOT SO BAD. I HAVE SOME EXTRA BANDAGES HERE AND CAN FIX YOU RIGHT UP.
THANKS!
NOW LET'S GET YOU BACK TO YOUR ROOM.
GASP!

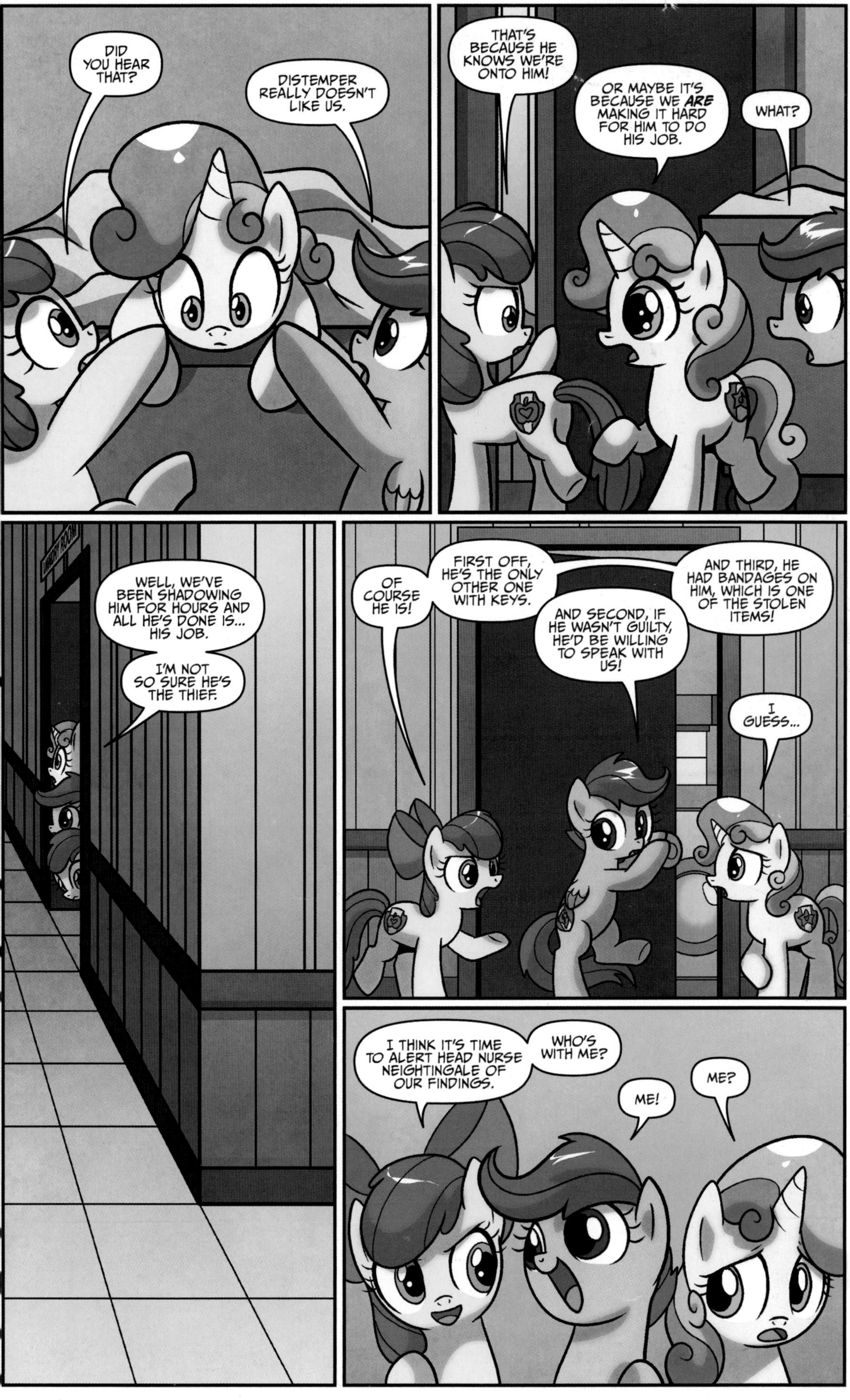
DID YOU HEAR THAT?
DISTEMPER REALLY DOESN'T LIKE US.
THAT'S BECAUSE HE KNOWS WE'RE ONTO HIM!
OR MAYBE IT'S BECAUSE WE ***ARE*** MAKING IT HARD FOR HIM TO DO HIS JOB.
WHAT?
WELL, WE'VE BEEN SHADOWING HIM FOR HOURS AND ALL HE'S DONE IS... HIS JOB.
I'M NOT SO SURE HE'S THE THIEF.
OF COURSE HE IS!
FIRST OFF, HE'S THE ONLY OTHER ONE WITH KEYS.
AND SECOND, IF HE WASN'T GUILTY, HE'D BE WILLING TO SPEAK WITH US!
AND THIRD, HE HAD BANDAGES ON HIM, WHICH IS ONE OF THE STOLEN ITEMS!
I GUESS...
I THINK IT'S TIME TO ALERT HEAD NURSE NEIGHTINGALE OF OUR FINDINGS.
WHO'S WITH ME?
ME!
ME?

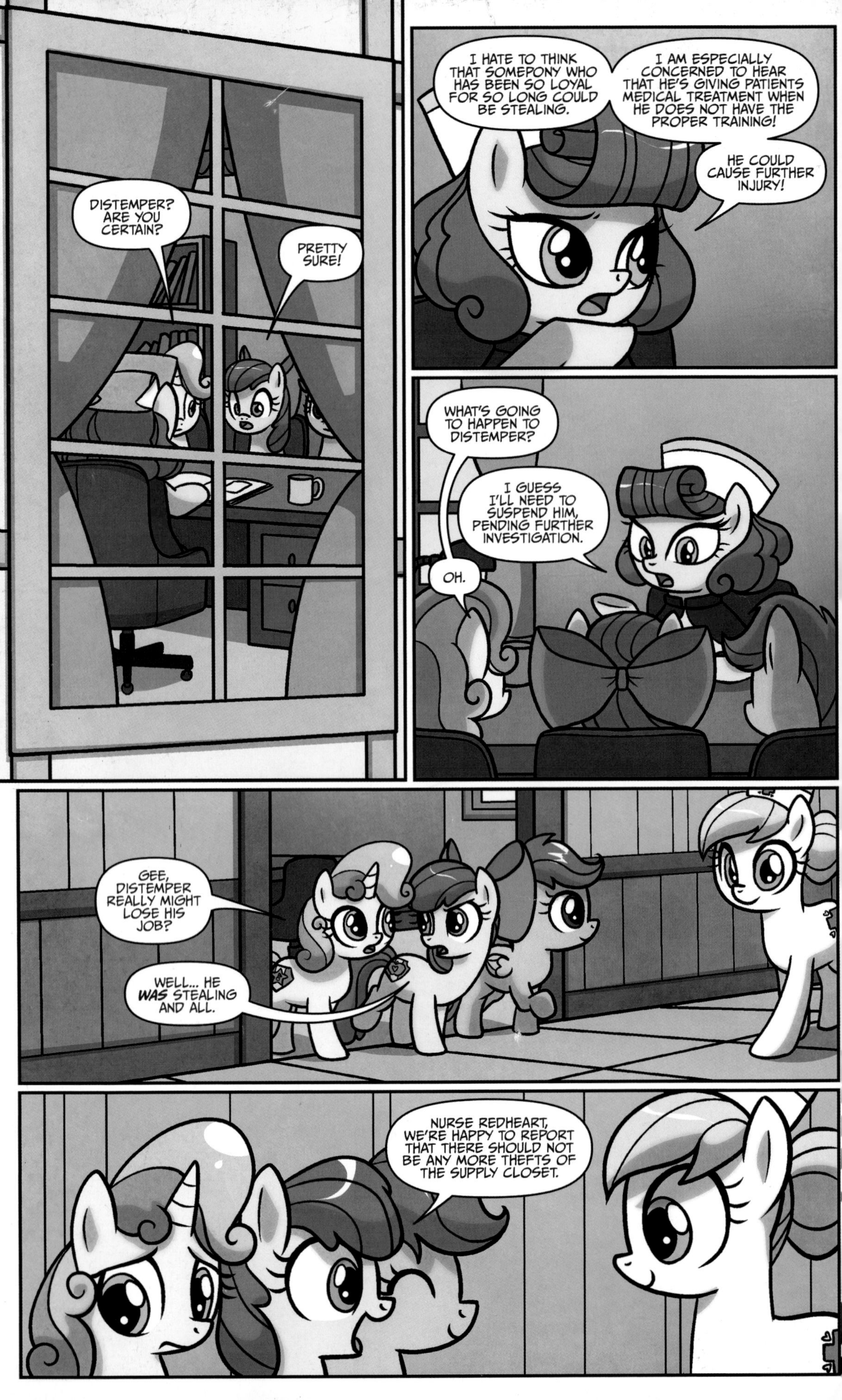

DISTEMPER? ARE YOU CERTAIN?
PRETTY SURE!
I HATE TO THINK THAT SOMEPONY WHO HAS BEEN SO LOYAL FOR SO LONG COULD BE STEALING.
I AM ESPECIALLY CONCERNED TO HEAR THAT HE'S GIVING PATIENTS MEDICAL TREATMENT WHEN HE DOES NOT HAVE THE PROPER TRAINING!
HE COULD CAUSE FURTHER INJURY!
WHAT'S GOING TO HAPPEN TO DISTEMPER?
I GUESS I'LL NEED TO SUSPEND HIM, PENDING FURTHER INVESTIGATION.
OH.
GEE, DISTEMPER REALLY MIGHT LOSE HIS JOB?
WELL... HE *WAS* STEALING AND ALL.
NURSE REDHEART, WE'RE HAPPY TO REPORT THAT THERE SHOULD NOT BE ANY MORE THEFTS OF THE SUPPLY CLOSET.

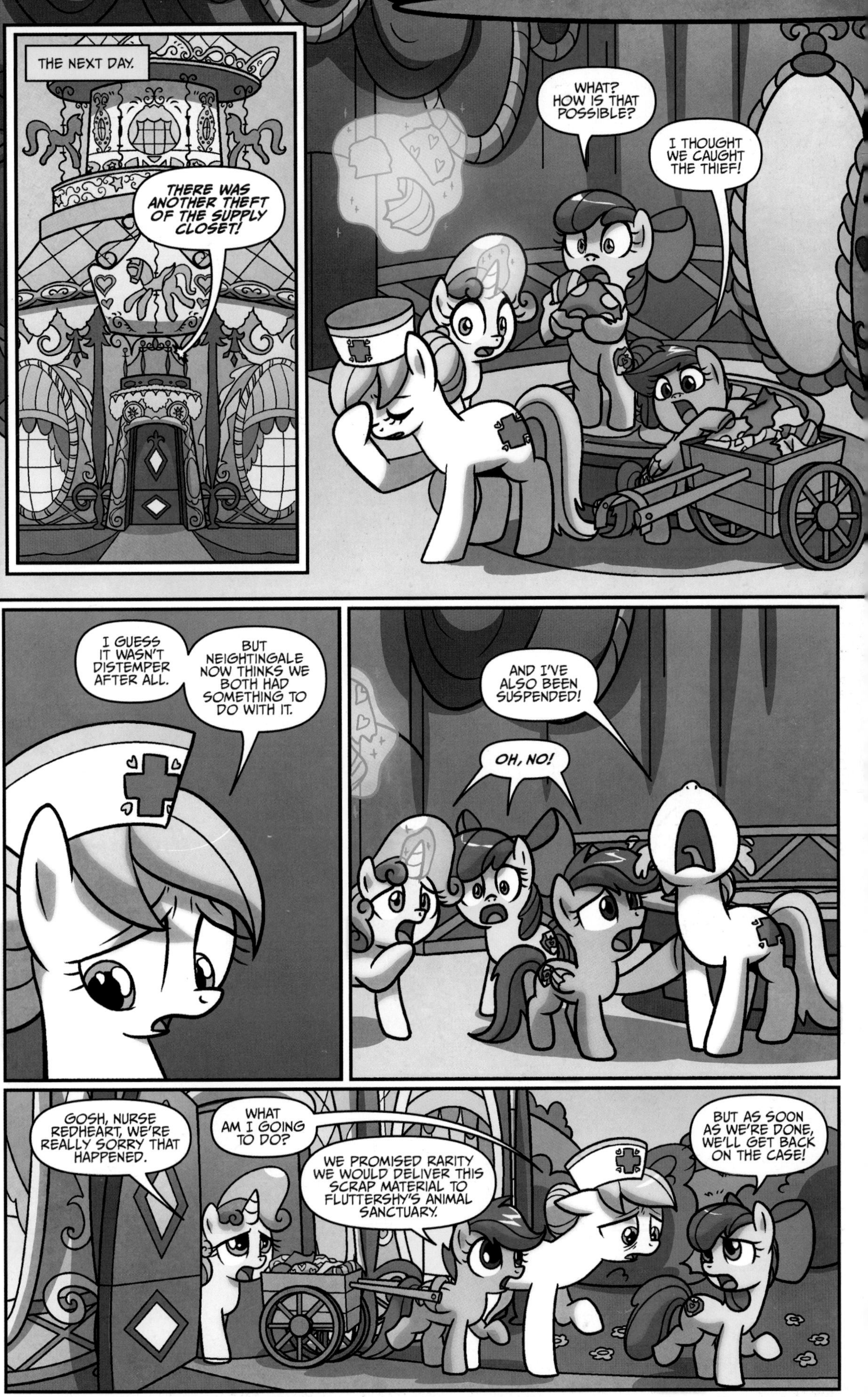
THE NEXT DAY.
THERE WAS ANOTHER THEFT OF THE SUPPLY CLOSET!
WHAT? HOW IS THAT POSSIBLE?
I THOUGHT WE CAUGHT THE THIEF!
I GUESS IT WASN'T DISTEMPER AFTER ALL.
BUT NEIGHTINGALE NOW THINKS WE BOTH HAD SOMETHING TO DO WITH IT.
AND I'VE ALSO BEEN SUSPENDED!
OH, NO!
GOSH, NURSE REDHEART, WE'RE REALLY SORRY THAT HAPPENED.
WHAT AM I GOING TO DO?
WE PROMISED RARITY WE WOULD DELIVER THIS SCRAP MATERIAL TO FLUTTERSHY'S ANIMAL SANCTUARY.
BUT AS SOON AS WE'RE DONE, WE'LL GET BACK ON THE CASE!

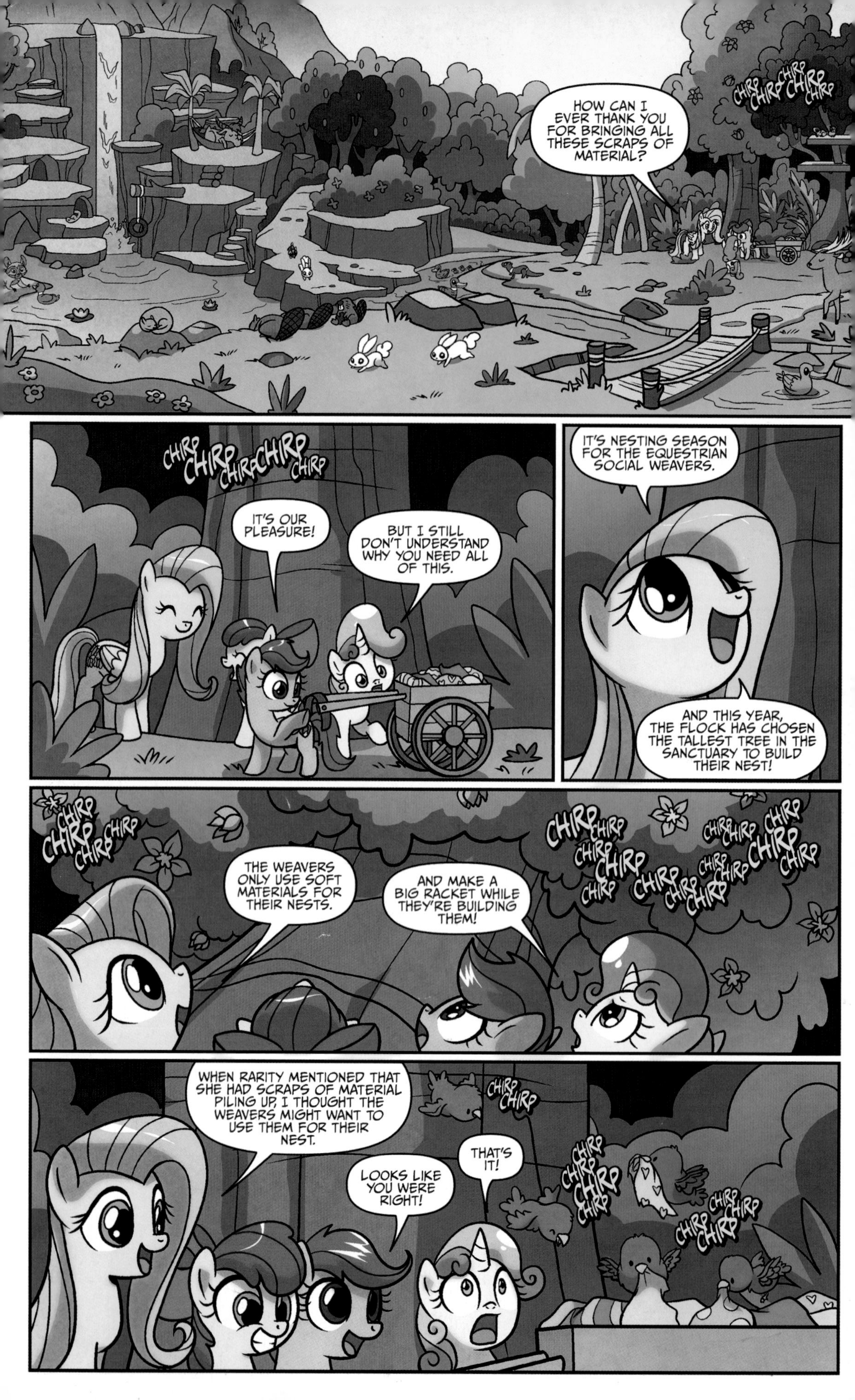
HOW CAN I EVER THANK YOU FOR BRINGING ALL THESE SCRAPS OF MATERIAL?
CHIRP CHIRP CHIRP CHIRP CHIRP
CHIRP CHIRP CHIRP CHIRP CHIRP
IT'S OUR PLEASURE!
BUT I STILL DON'T UNDERSTAND WHY YOU NEED ALL OF THIS.
IT'S NESTING SEASON FOR THE EQUESTRIAN SOCIAL WEAVERS.
AND THIS YEAR, THE FLOCK HAS CHOSEN THE TALLEST TREE IN THE SANCTUARY TO BUILD THEIR NEST!
CHIRP CHIRP CHIRP CHIRP
THE WEAVERS ONLY USE SOFT MATERIALS FOR THEIR NESTS.
AND MAKE A BIG RACKET WHILE THEY'RE BUILDING THEM!
CHIRP CHIRP CHIRP CHIRP CHIRP CHIRP CHIRP CHIRP CHIRP CHIRP CHIRP CHIRP CHIRP CHIRP CHIRP CHIRP
WHEN RARITY MENTIONED THAT SHE HAD SCRAPS OF MATERIAL PILING UP, I THOUGHT THE WEAVERS MIGHT WANT TO USE THEM FOR THEIR NEST.
CHIRP CHIRP
LOOKS LIKE YOU WERE RIGHT!
THAT'S IT!
CHIRP CHIRP CHIRP CHIRP
CHIRP CHIRP CHIRP CHIRP

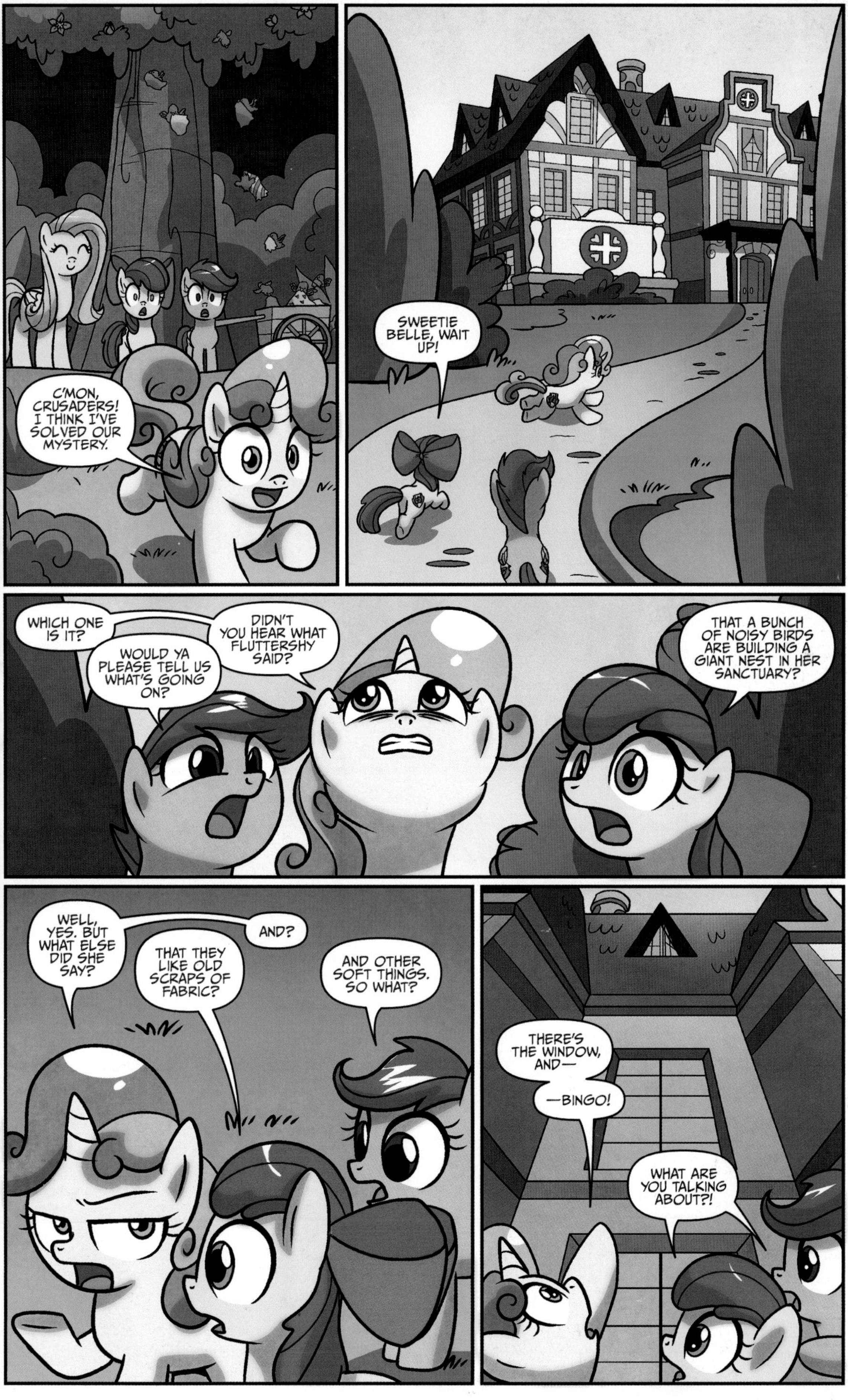
C'MON, CRUSADERS! I THINK I'VE SOLVED OUR MYSTERY.
SWEETIE BELLE, WAIT UP!
WHICH ONE IS IT?
WOULD YA PLEASE TELL US WHAT'S GOING ON?
DIDN'T YOU HEAR WHAT FLUTTERSHY SAID?
THAT A BUNCH OF NOISY BIRDS ARE BUILDING A GIANT NEST IN HER SANCTUARY?
WELL, YES. BUT WHAT ELSE DID SHE SAY?
AND?
THAT THEY LIKE OLD SCRAPS OF FABRIC?
AND OTHER SOFT THINGS. SO WHAT?
THERE'S THE WINDOW, AND—
—BINGO!
WHAT ARE YOU TALKING ABOUT?!

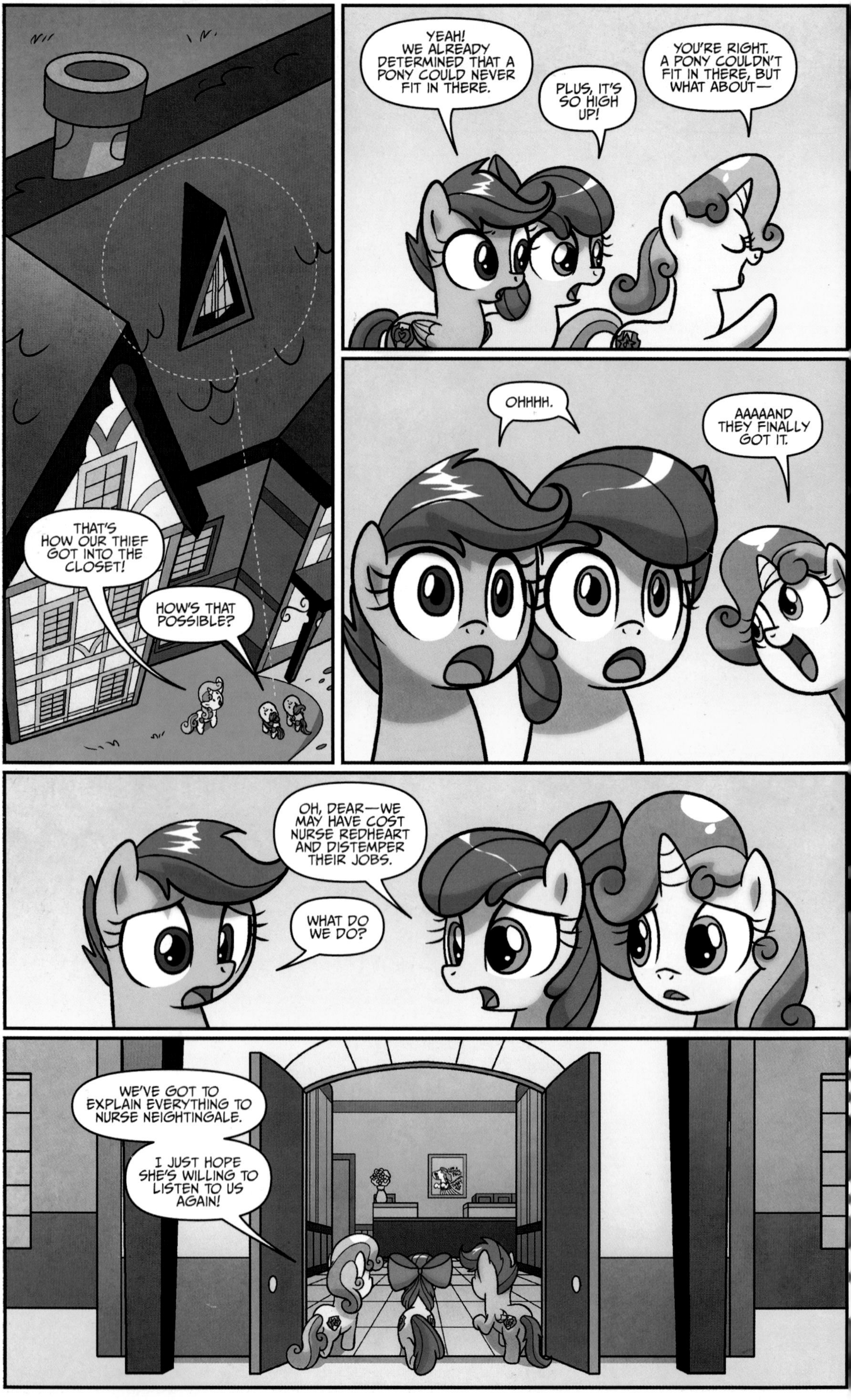
THAT'S HOW OUR THIEF GOT INTO THE CLOSET!
HOW'S THAT POSSIBLE?
YEAH! WE ALREADY DETERMINED THAT A PONY COULD NEVER FIT IN THERE.
PLUS, IT'S SO HIGH UP!
YOU'RE RIGHT. A PONY COULDN'T FIT IN THERE, BUT WHAT ABOUT—
OHHHH.
AAAAAND THEY FINALLY GOT IT.
OH, DEAR—WE MAY HAVE COST NURSE REDHEART AND DISTEMPER THEIR JOBS.
WHAT DO WE DO?
WE'VE GOT TO EXPLAIN EVERYTHING TO NURSE NEIGHTINGALE.
I JUST HOPE SHE'S WILLING TO LISTEN TO US AGAIN!

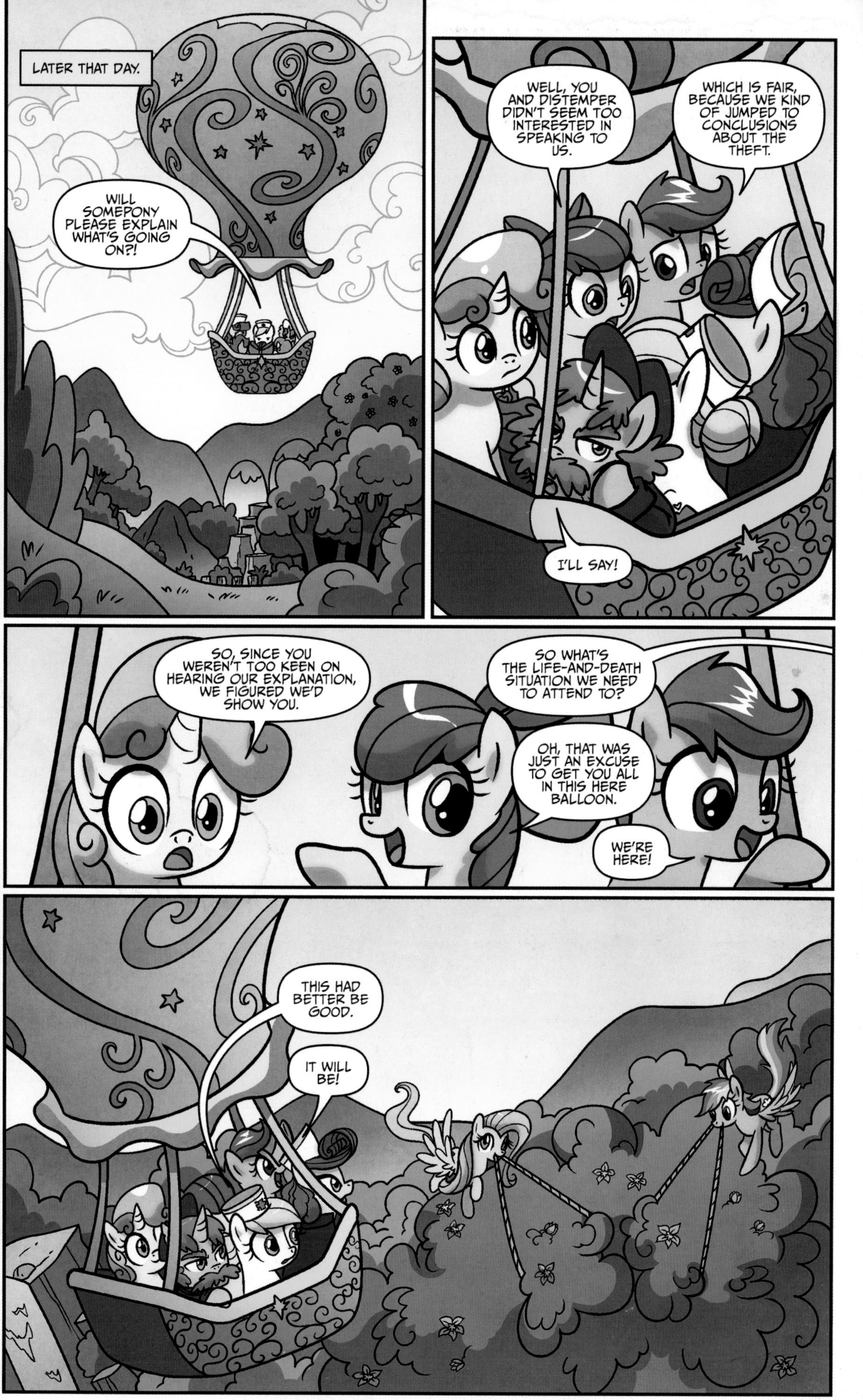
LATER THAT DAY.
WILL SOMEPONY PLEASE EXPLAIN WHAT'S GOING ON?!
WELL, YOU AND DISTEMPER DIDN'T SEEM TOO INTERESTED IN SPEAKING TO US.
WHICH IS FAIR, BECAUSE WE KIND OF JUMPED TO CONCLUSIONS ABOUT THE THEFT.
I'LL SAY!
SO, SINCE YOU WEREN'T TOO KEEN ON HEARING OUR EXPLANATION, WE FIGURED WE'D SHOW YOU.
SO WHAT'S THE LIFE-AND-DEATH SITUATION WE NEED TO ATTEND TO?
OH, THAT WAS JUST AN EXCUSE TO GET YOU ALL IN THIS HERE BALLOON.
WE'RE HERE!
THIS HAD BETTER BE GOOD.
IT WILL BE!

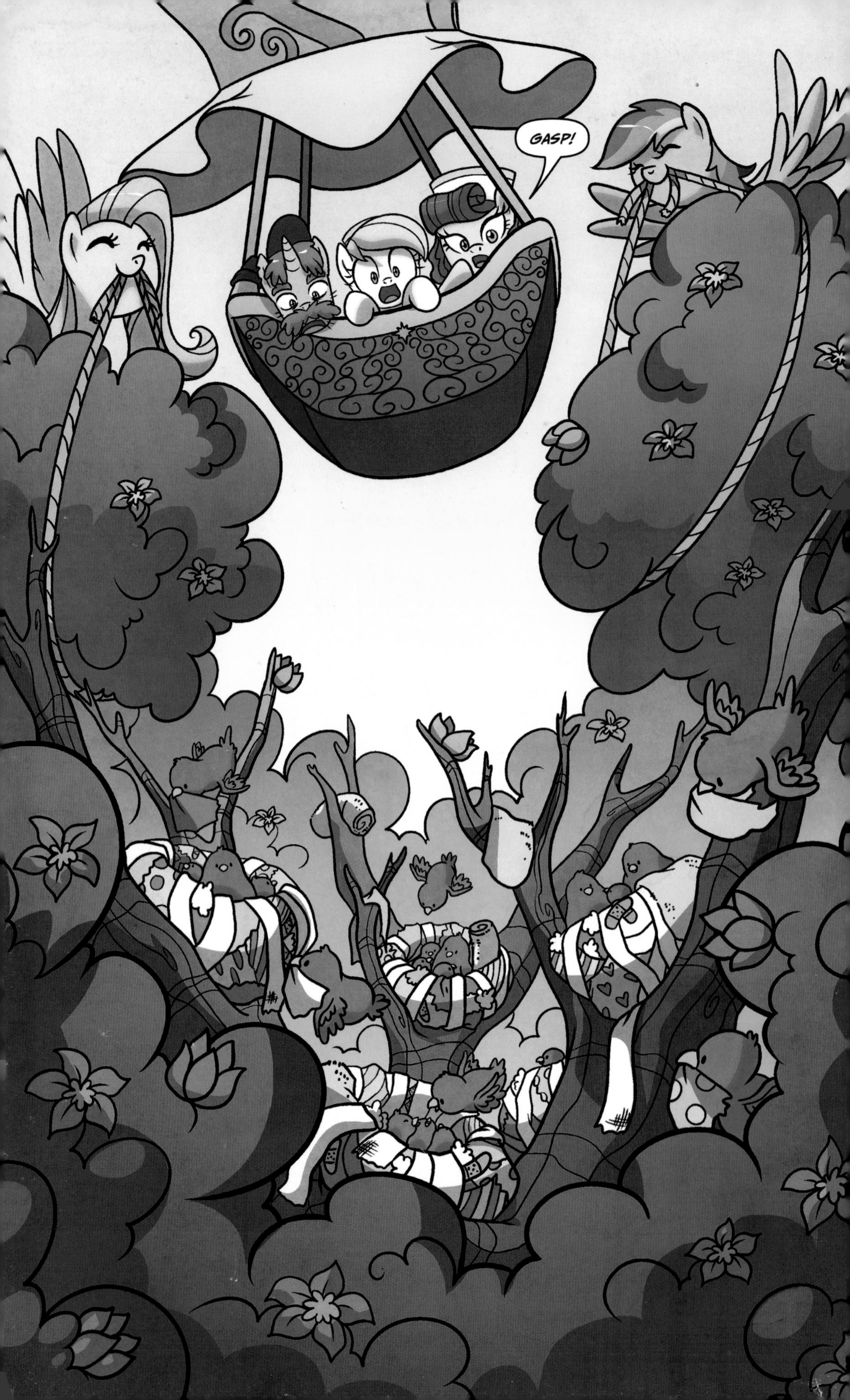
GASP!

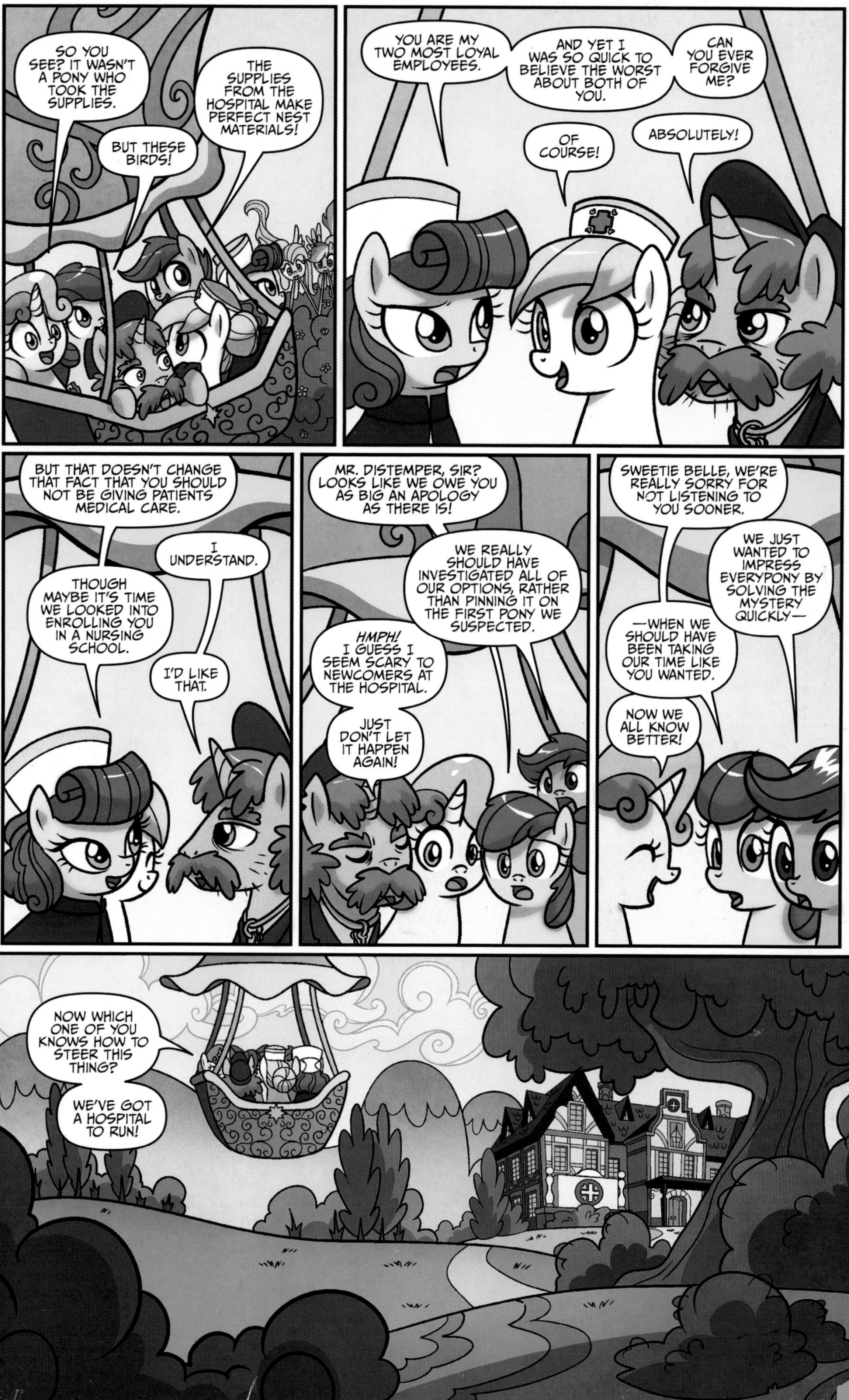
SO YOU SEE? IT WASN'T A PONY WHO TOOK THE SUPPLIES.
BUT THESE BIRDS!
THE SUPPLIES FROM THE HOSPITAL MAKE PERFECT NEST MATERIALS!
YOU ARE MY TWO MOST LOYAL EMPLOYEES.
AND YET I WAS SO QUICK TO BELIEVE THE WORST ABOUT BOTH OF YOU.
CAN YOU EVER FORGIVE ME?
OF COURSE!
ABSOLUTELY!
BUT THAT DOESN'T CHANGE THAT FACT THAT YOU SHOULD NOT BE GIVING PATIENTS MEDICAL CARE.
I UNDERSTAND.
THOUGH MAYBE IT'S TIME WE LOOKED INTO ENROLLING YOU IN A NURSING SCHOOL.
I'D LIKE THAT.
MR. DISTEMPER, SIR? LOOKS LIKE WE OWE YOU AS BIG AN APOLOGY AS THERE IS!
WE REALLY SHOULD HAVE INVESTIGATED ALL OF OUR OPTIONS, RATHER THAN PINNING IT ON THE FIRST PONY WE SUSPECTED.
HMPH! I GUESS I SEEM SCARY TO NEWCOMERS AT THE HOSPITAL.
JUST DON'T LET IT HAPPEN AGAIN!
SWEETIE BELLE, WE'RE REALLY SORRY FOR NOT LISTENING TO YOU SOONER.
WE JUST WANTED TO IMPRESS EVERYPONY BY SOLVING THE MYSTERY QUICKLY—
—WHEN WE SHOULD HAVE BEEN TAKING OUR TIME LIKE YOU WANTED.
NOW WE ALL KNOW BETTER!
NOW WHICH ONE OF YOU KNOWS HOW TO STEER THIS THING?
WE'VE GOT A HOSPITAL TO RUN!

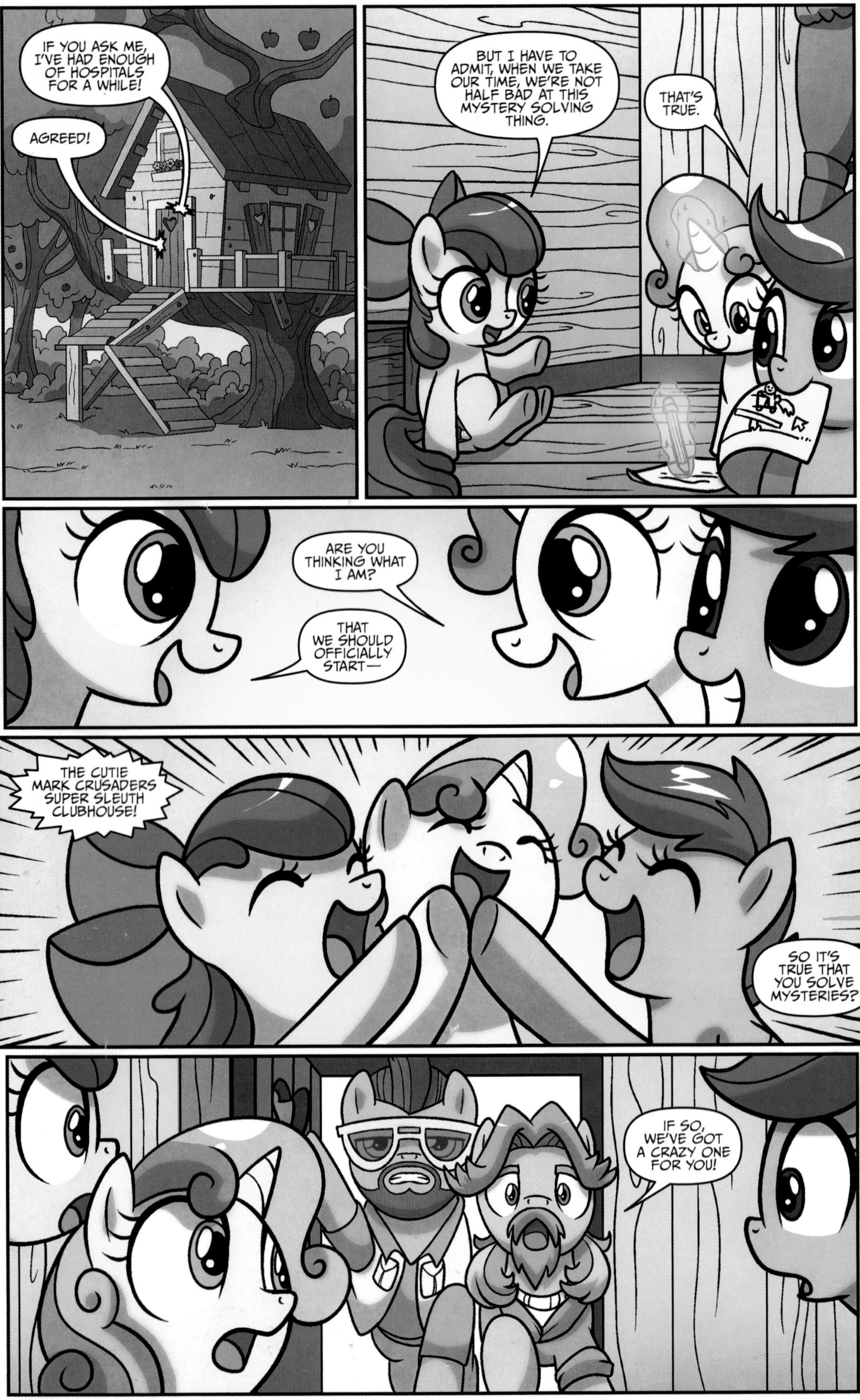
IF YOU ASK ME, I'VE HAD ENOUGH OF HOSPITALS FOR A WHILE!
AGREED!
BUT I HAVE TO ADMIT, WHEN WE TAKE OUR TIME, WE'RE NOT HALF BAD AT THIS MYSTERY SOLVING THING.
THAT'S TRUE.
ARE YOU THINKING WHAT I AM?
THAT WE SHOULD OFFICIALLY START—
THE CUTIE MARK CRUSADERS SUPER SLEUTH CLUBHOUSE!
SO IT'S TRUE THAT YOU SOLVE MYSTERIES?
IF SO, WE'VE GOT A CRAZY ONE FOR YOU!

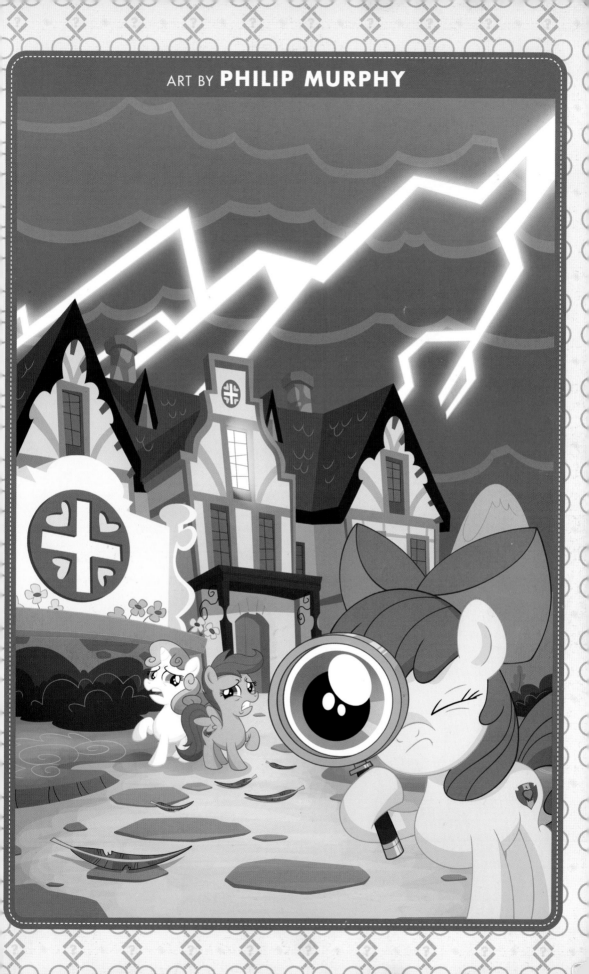

ART BY **PHILIP MURPHY**

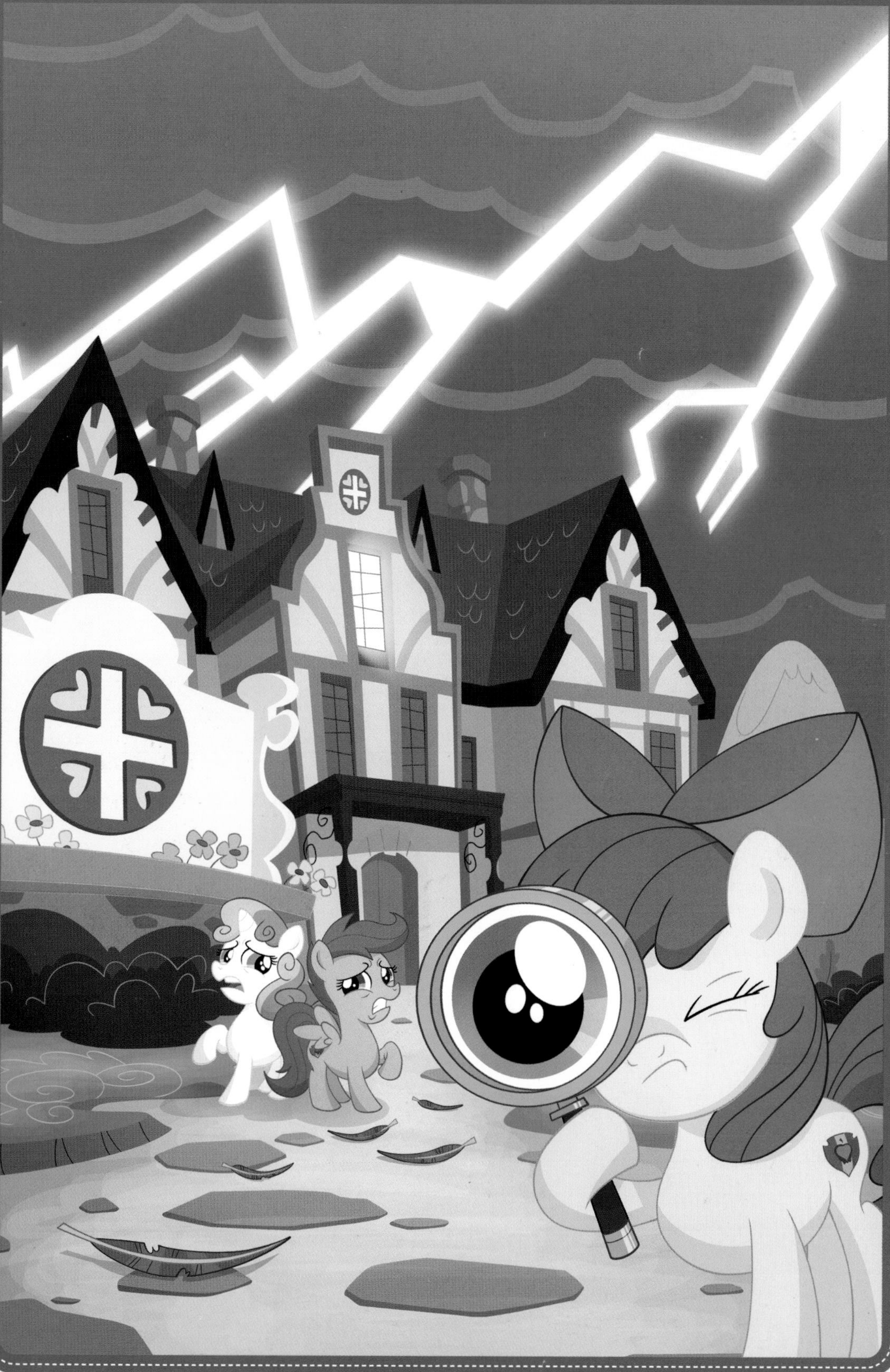

2 ART BY AGNES GARBOWSKA

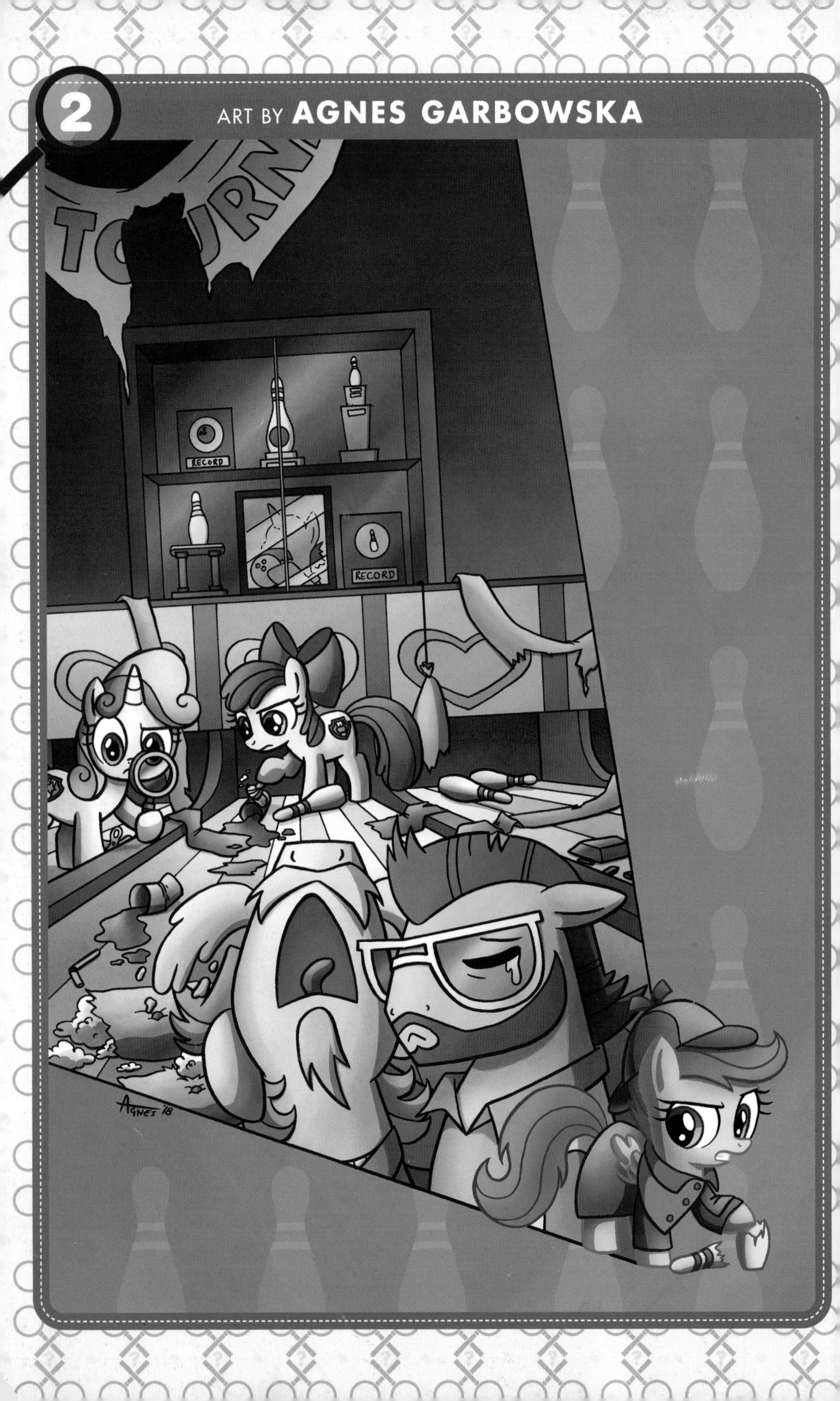
TO URN
RECORD
RECORD
Agnes '18

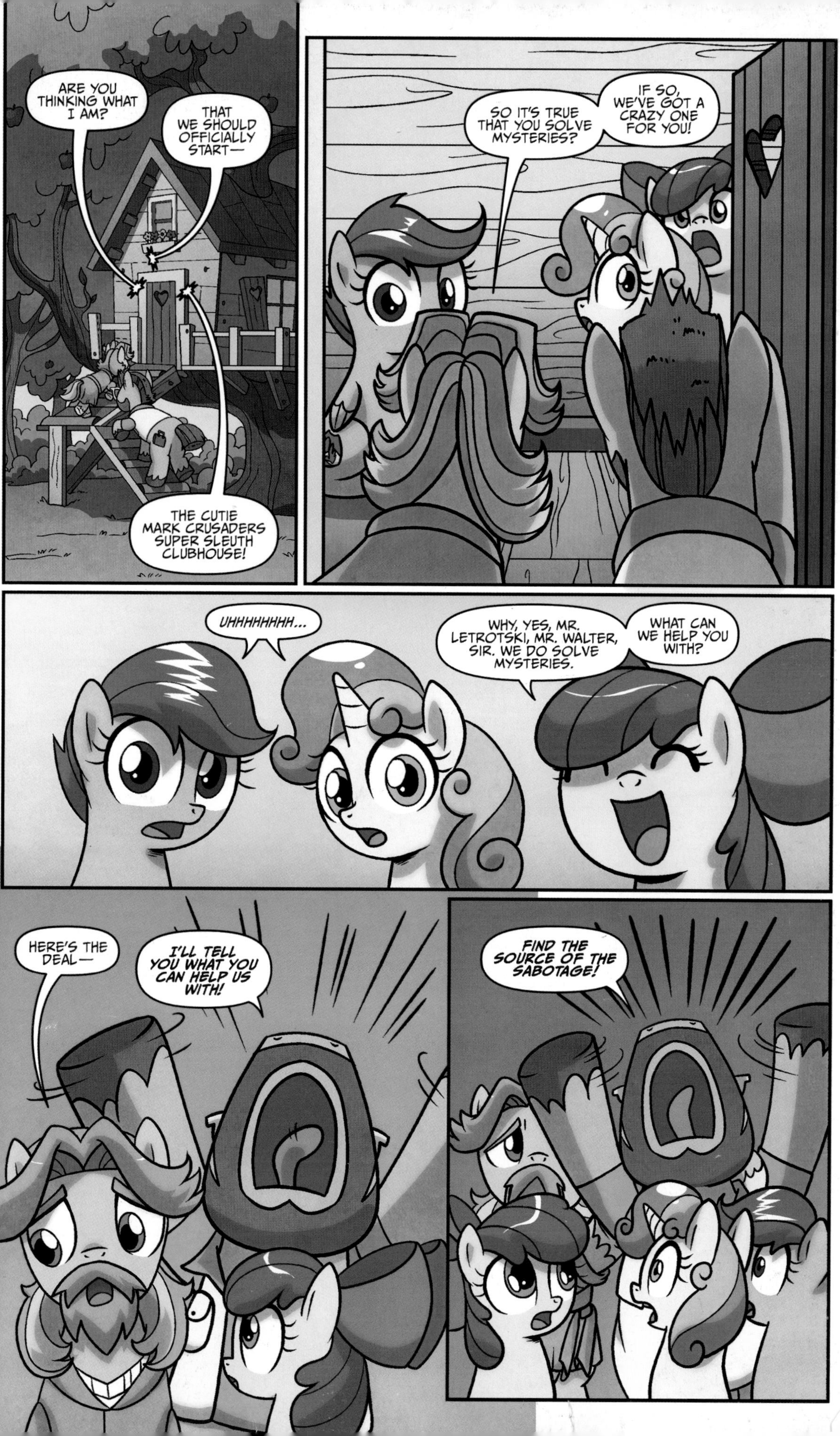
ARE YOU THINKING WHAT I AM?
THAT WE SHOULD OFFICIALLY START—
THE CUTIE MARK CRUSADERS SUPER SLEUTH CLUBHOUSE!
SO IT'S TRUE THAT YOU SOLVE MYSTERIES?
IF SO, WE'VE GOT A CRAZY ONE FOR YOU!
UHHHHHHHH...
WHY, YES, MR. LETROTSKI, MR. WALTER, SIR. WE DO SOLVE MYSTERIES.
WHAT CAN WE HELP YOU WITH?
HERE'S THE DEAL—
I'LL TELL YOU WHAT YOU CAN HELP US WITH!
FIND THE SOURCE OF THE SABOTAGE!

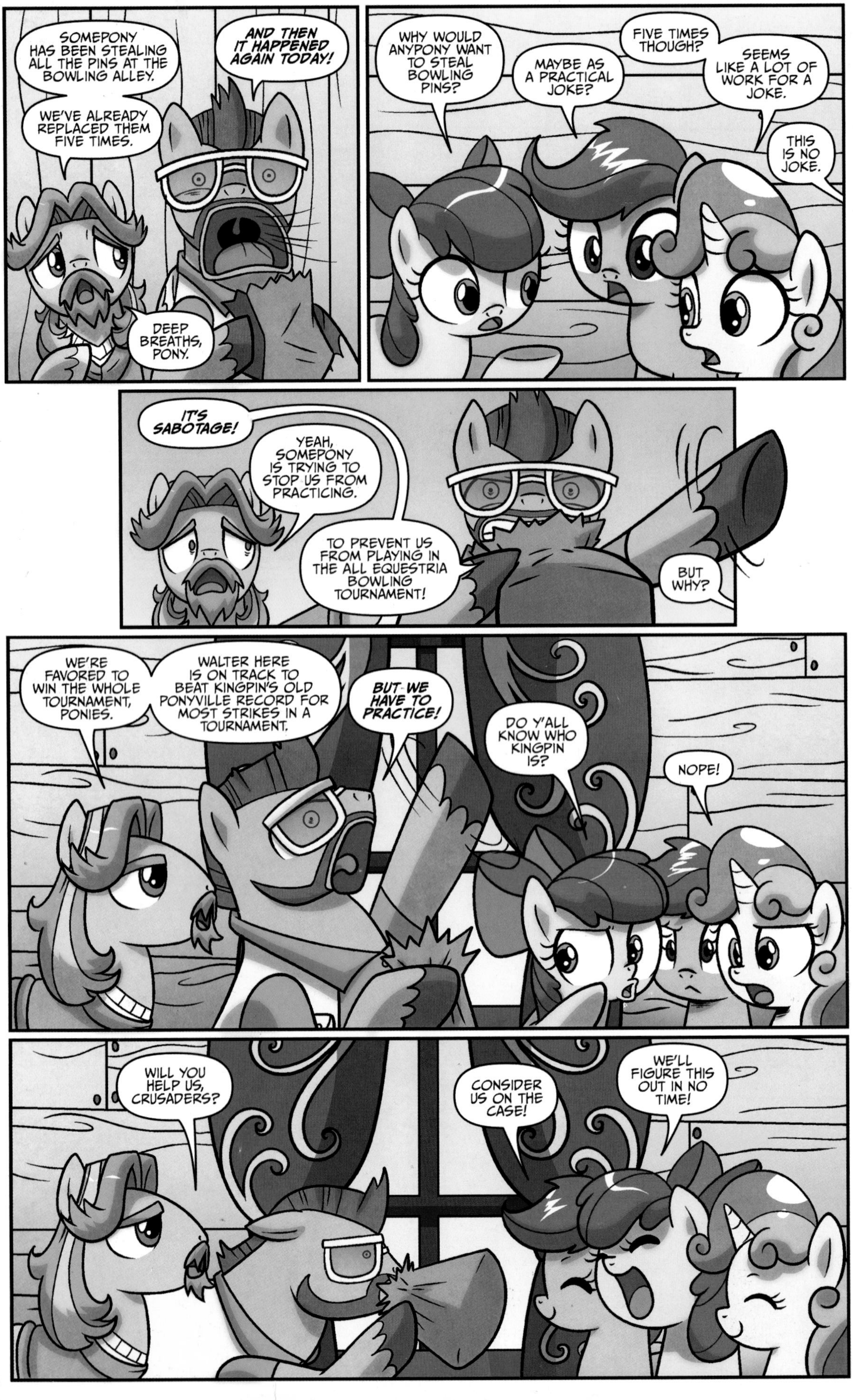
SOMEPONY HAS BEEN STEALING ALL THE PINS AT THE BOWLING ALLEY.
WE'VE ALREADY REPLACED THEM FIVE TIMES.
AND THEN IT HAPPENED AGAIN TODAY!
DEEP BREATHS, PONY.
WHY WOULD ANYPONY WANT TO STEAL BOWLING PINS?
MAYBE AS A PRACTICAL JOKE?
FIVE TIMES THOUGH?
SEEMS LIKE A LOT OF WORK FOR A JOKE.
THIS IS NO JOKE.
IT'S SABOTAGE!
YEAH, SOMEPONY IS TRYING TO STOP US FROM PRACTICING.
TO PREVENT US FROM PLAYING IN THE ALL EQUESTRIA BOWLING TOURNAMENT!
BUT WHY?
WE'RE FAVORED TO WIN THE WHOLE TOURNAMENT, PONIES.
WALTER HERE IS ON TRACK TO BEAT KINGPIN'S OLD PONYVILLE RECORD FOR MOST STRIKES IN A TOURNAMENT.
BUT WE HAVE TO PRACTICE!
DO Y'ALL KNOW WHO KINGPIN IS?
NOPE!
WILL YOU HELP US, CRUSADERS?
CONSIDER US ON THE CASE!
WE'LL FIGURE THIS OUT IN NO TIME!

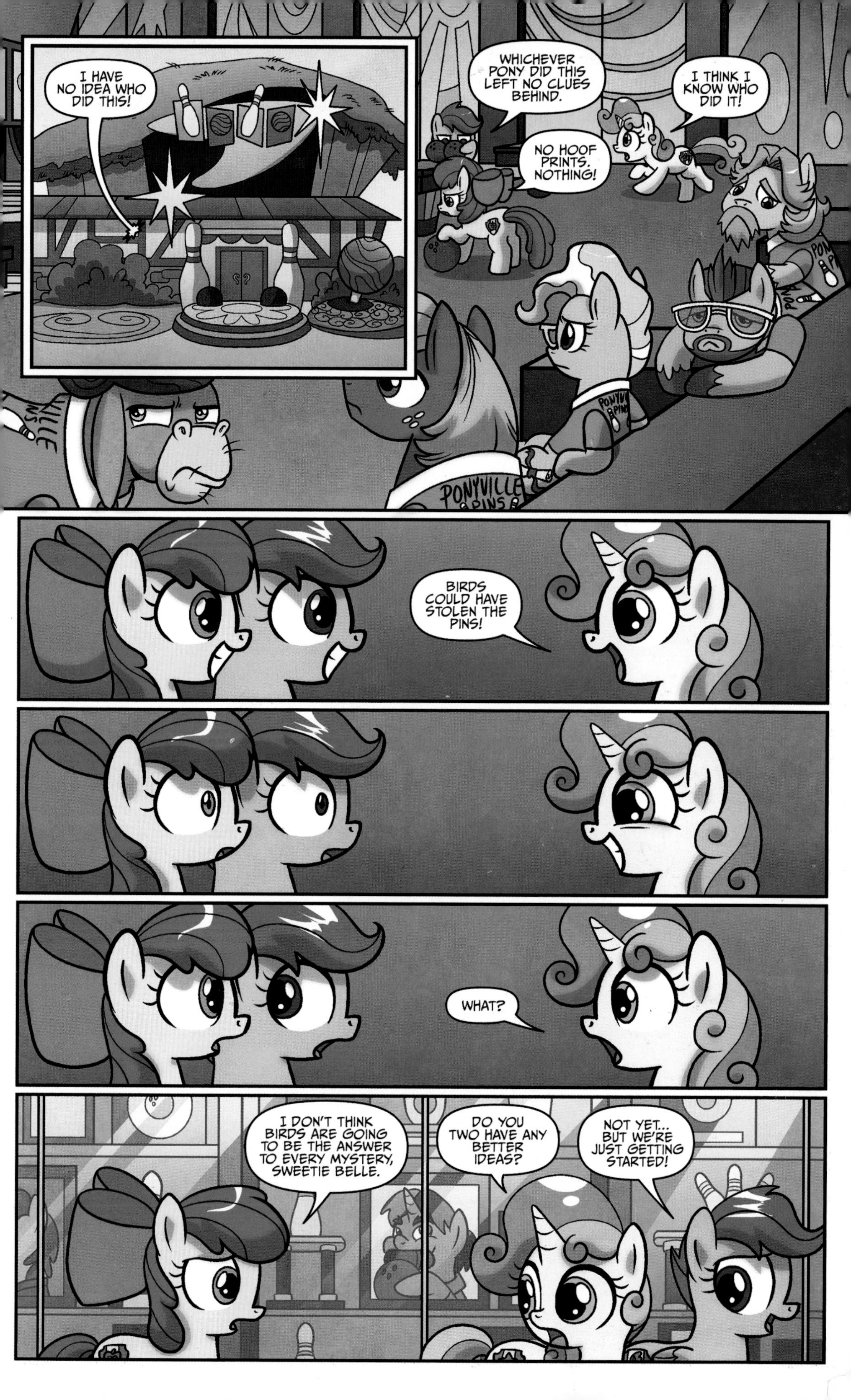
I HAVE NO IDEA WHO DID THIS!
WHICHEVER PONY DID THIS LEFT NO CLUES BEHIND.
NO HOOF PRINTS. NOTHING!
I THINK I KNOW WHO DID IT!
PONYVILLE PINS
BIRDS COULD HAVE STOLEN THE PINS!
WHAT?
I DON'T THINK BIRDS ARE GOING TO BE THE ANSWER TO EVERY MYSTERY, SWEETIE BELLE.
DO YOU TWO HAVE ANY BETTER IDEAS?
NOT YET... BUT WE'RE JUST GETTING STARTED!

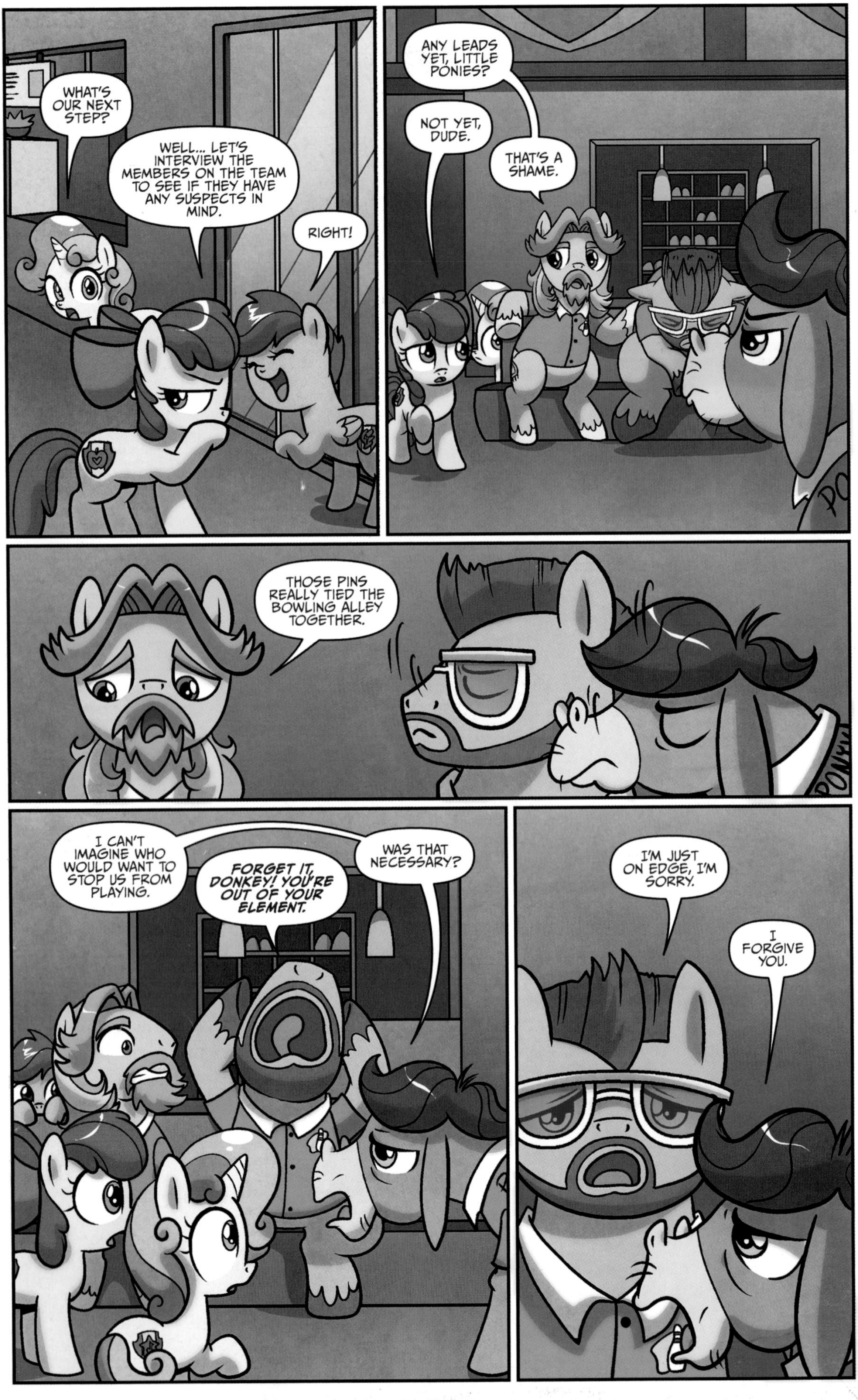
WHAT'S OUR NEXT STEP?
WELL... LET'S INTERVIEW THE MEMBERS ON THE TEAM TO SEE IF THEY HAVE ANY SUSPECTS IN MIND.
RIGHT!
ANY LEADS YET, LITTLE PONIES?
NOT YET, DUDE.
THAT'S A SHAME.
THOSE PINS REALLY TIED THE BOWLING ALLEY TOGETHER.
I CAN'T IMAGINE WHO WOULD WANT TO STOP US FROM PLAYING.
FORGET IT, DONKEY! YOU'RE OUT OF YOUR ELEMENT.
WAS THAT NECESSARY?
I'M JUST ON EDGE, I'M SORRY.
I FORGIVE YOU.

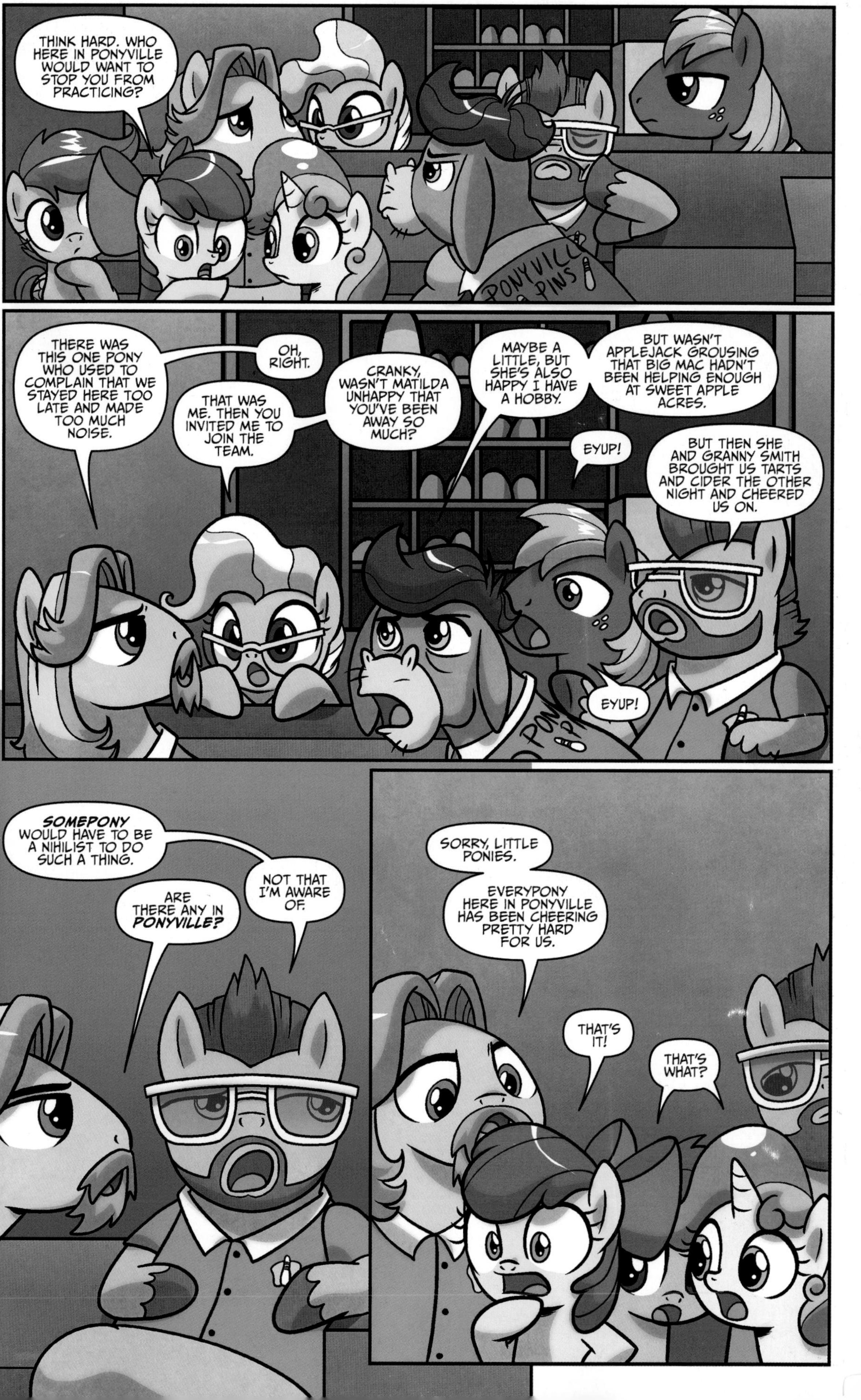
THINK HARD. WHO HERE IN PONYVILLE WOULD WANT TO STOP YOU FROM PRACTICING?
PONYVILLE PINS
THERE WAS THIS ONE PONY WHO USED TO COMPLAIN THAT WE STAYED HERE TOO LATE AND MADE TOO MUCH NOISE.
OH, RIGHT.
THAT WAS ME. THEN YOU INVITED ME TO JOIN THE TEAM.
CRANKY, WASN'T MATILDA UNHAPPY THAT YOU'VE BEEN AWAY SO MUCH?
MAYBE A LITTLE, BUT SHE'S ALSO HAPPY I HAVE A HOBBY.
BUT WASN'T APPLEJACK GROUSING THAT BIG MAC HADN'T BEEN HELPING ENOUGH AT SWEET APPLE ACRES.
EYUP!
BUT THEN SHE AND GRANNY SMITH BROUGHT US TARTS AND CIDER THE OTHER NIGHT AND CHEERED US ON.
EYUP!
SOMEPONY WOULD HAVE TO BE A NIHILIST TO DO SUCH A THING.
ARE THERE ANY IN *PONYVILLE?*
NOT THAT I'M AWARE OF.
SORRY, LITTLE PONIES.
EVERYPONY HERE IN PONYVILLE HAS BEEN CHEERING PRETTY HARD FOR US.
THAT'S IT!
THAT'S WHAT?

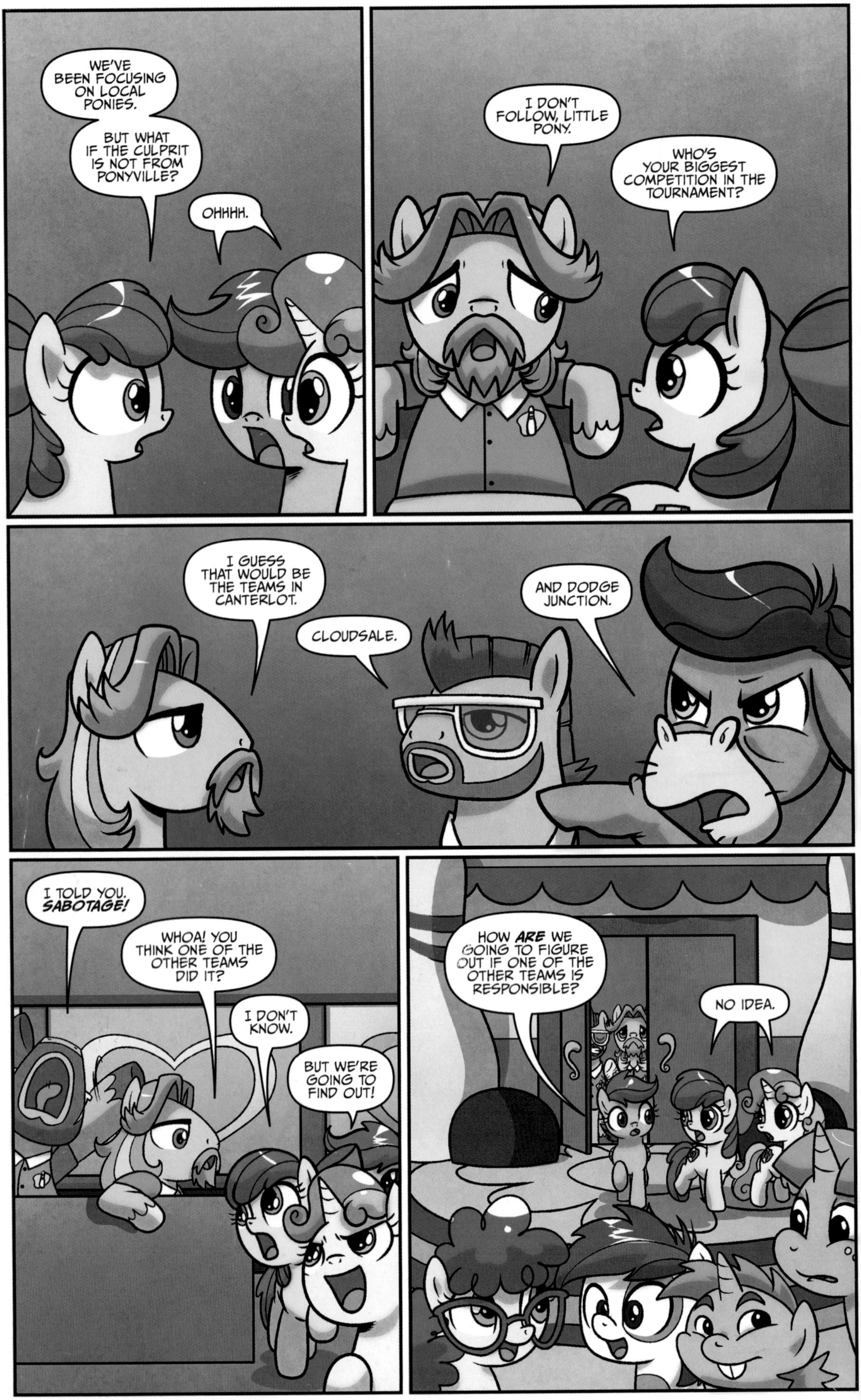
WE'VE BEEN FOCUSING ON LOCAL PONIES.
BUT WHAT IF THE CULPRIT IS NOT FROM PONYVILLE?
OHHHH.
I DON'T FOLLOW, LITTLE PONY.
WHO'S YOUR BIGGEST COMPETITION IN THE TOURNAMENT?
I GUESS THAT WOULD BE THE TEAMS IN CANTERLOT.
CLOUDSALE.
AND DODGE JUNCTION.
I TOLD YOU. ***SABOTAGE!***
WHOA! YOU THINK ONE OF THE OTHER TEAMS DID IT?
I DON'T KNOW.
BUT WE'RE GOING TO FIND OUT!
HOW ***ARE*** WE GOING TO FIGURE OUT IF ONE OF THE OTHER TEAMS IS RESPONSIBLE?
NO IDEA.

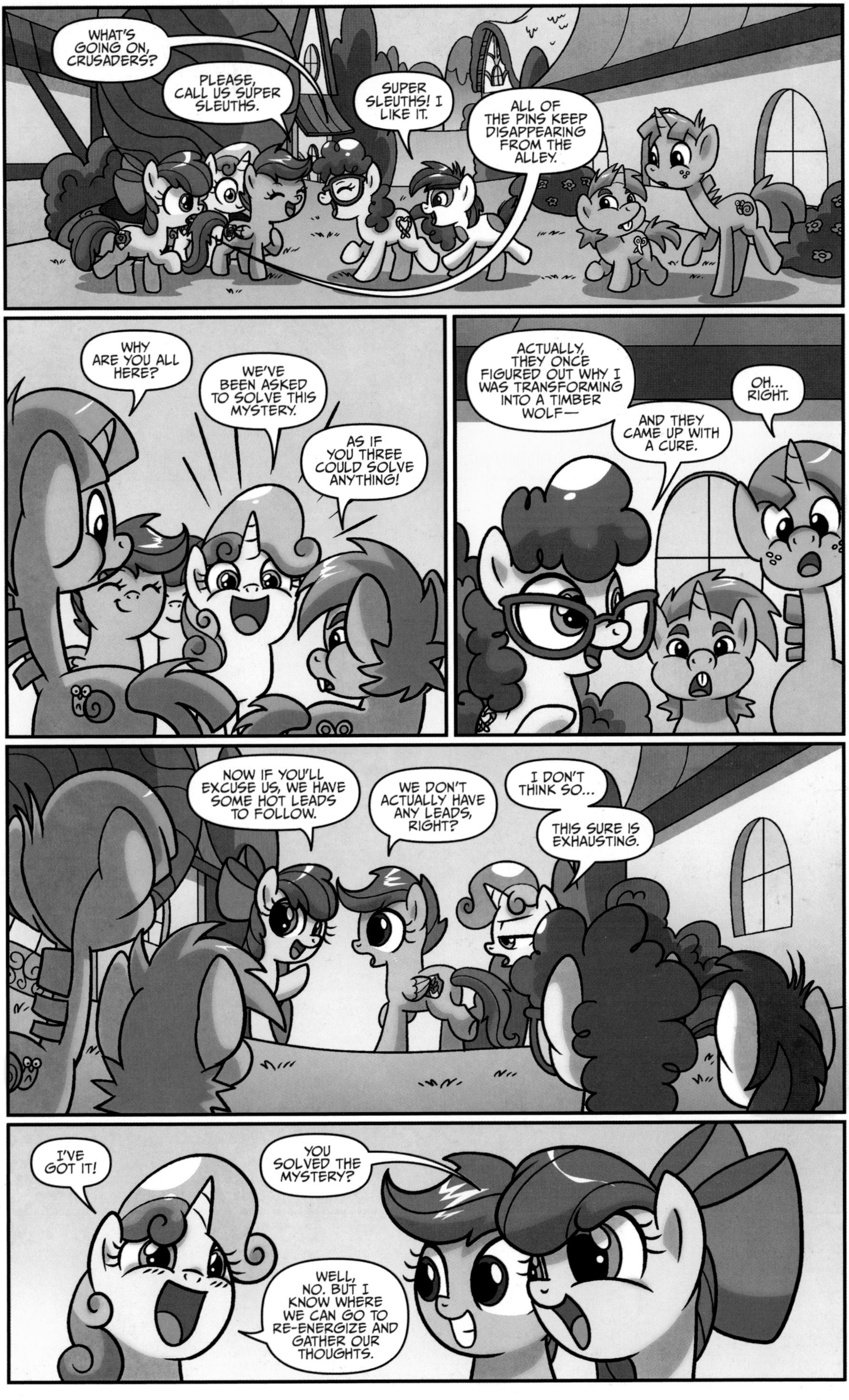
WHAT'S GOING ON, CRUSADERS?
PLEASE, CALL US SUPER SLEUTHS.
SUPER SLEUTHS! I LIKE IT.
ALL OF THE PINS KEEP DISAPPEARING FROM THE ALLEY.
WHY ARE YOU ALL HERE?
WE'VE BEEN ASKED TO SOLVE THIS MYSTERY.
AS IF YOU THREE COULD SOLVE ANYTHING!
ACTUALLY, THEY ONCE FIGURED OUT WHY I WAS TRANSFORMING INTO A TIMBER WOLF—
AND THEY CAME UP WITH A CURE.
OH... RIGHT.
NOW IF YOU'LL EXCUSE US, WE HAVE SOME HOT LEADS TO FOLLOW.
WE DON'T ACTUALLY HAVE ANY LEADS, RIGHT?
I DON'T THINK SO...
THIS SURE IS EXHAUSTING.
I'VE GOT IT!
YOU SOLVED THE MYSTERY?
WELL, NO. BUT I KNOW WHERE WE CAN GO TO RE-ENERGIZE AND GATHER OUR THOUGHTS.

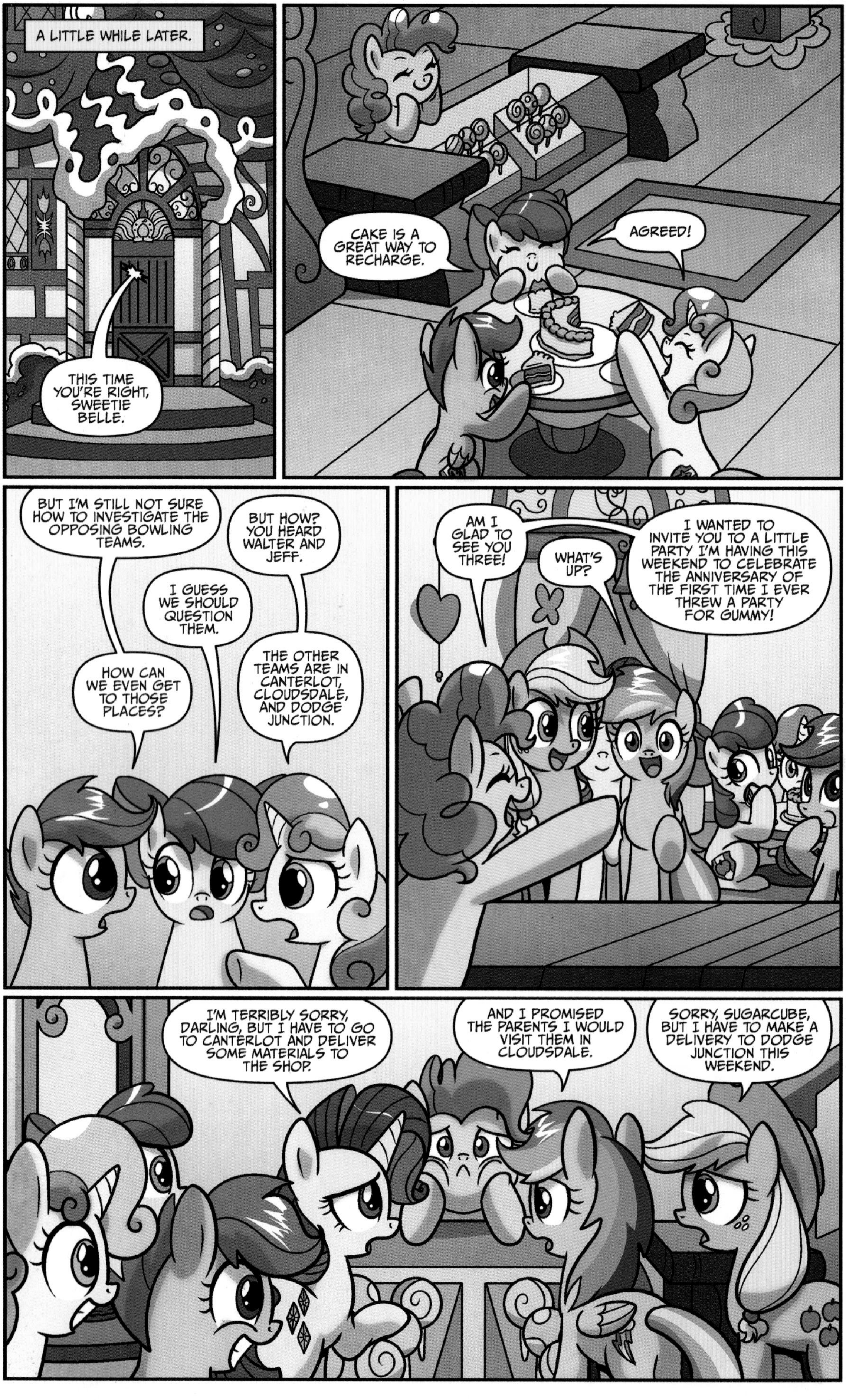
A LITTLE WHILE LATER.
THIS TIME YOU'RE RIGHT, SWEETIE BELLE.
CAKE IS A GREAT WAY TO RECHARGE.
AGREED!
BUT I'M STILL NOT SURE HOW TO INVESTIGATE THE OPPOSING BOWLING TEAMS.
HOW CAN WE EVEN GET TO THOSE PLACES?
I GUESS WE SHOULD QUESTION THEM.
BUT HOW? YOU HEARD WALTER AND JEFF.
THE OTHER TEAMS ARE IN CANTERLOT, CLOUDSDALE, AND DODGE JUNCTION.
AM I GLAD TO SEE YOU THREE!
WHAT'S UP?
I WANTED TO INVITE YOU TO A LITTLE PARTY I'M HAVING THIS WEEKEND TO CELEBRATE THE ANNIVERSARY OF THE FIRST TIME I EVER THREW A PARTY FOR GUMMY!
I'M TERRIBLY SORRY, DARLING, BUT I HAVE TO GO TO CANTERLOT AND DELIVER SOME MATERIALS TO THE SHOP.
AND I PROMISED THE PARENTS I WOULD VISIT THEM IN CLOUDSDALE.
SORRY, SUGARCUBE, BUT I HAVE TO MAKE A DELIVERY TO DODGE JUNCTION THIS WEEKEND.

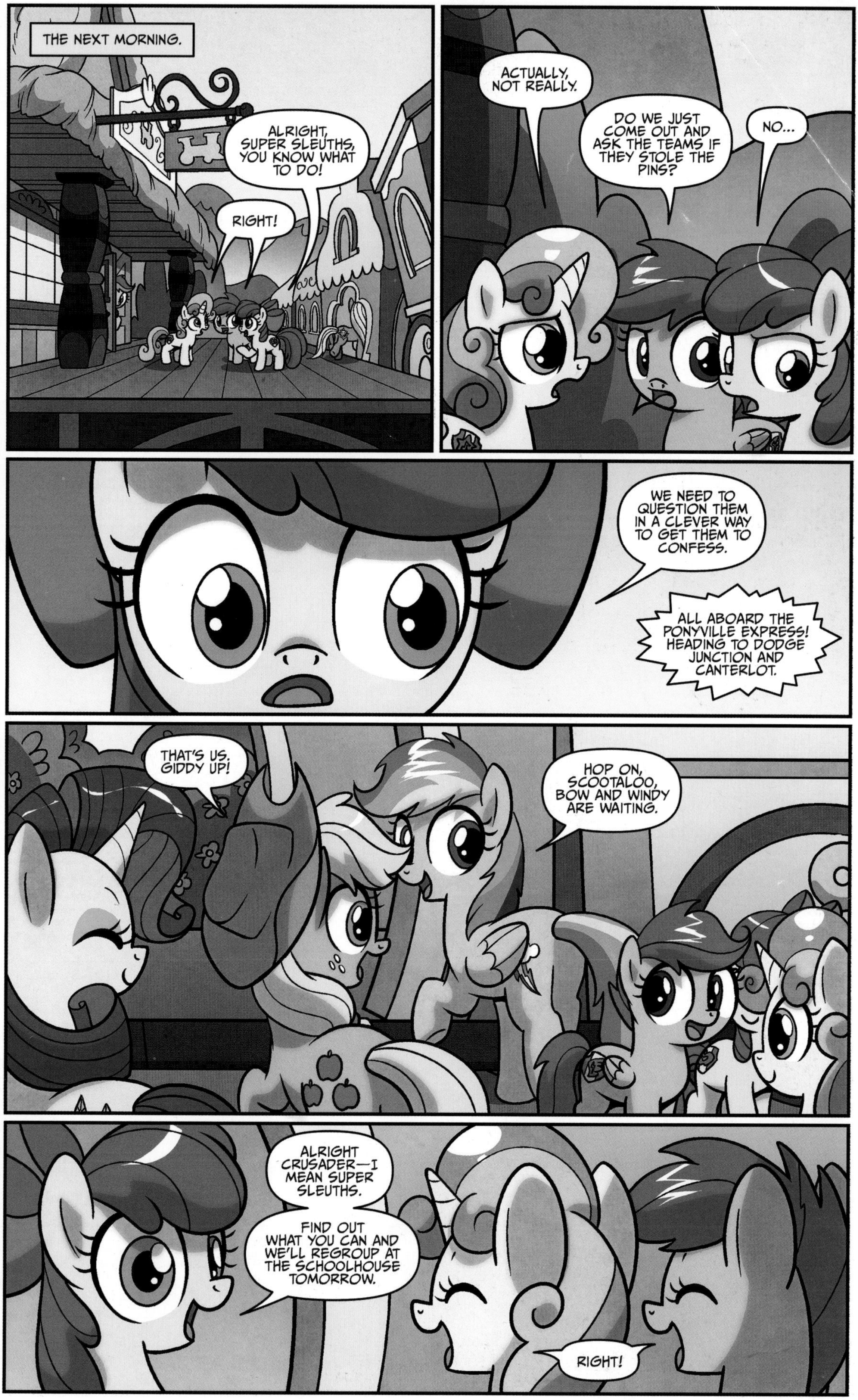
THE NEXT MORNING.
ALRIGHT, SUPER SLEUTHS, YOU KNOW WHAT TO DO!
RIGHT!
ACTUALLY, NOT REALLY.
DO WE JUST COME OUT AND ASK THE TEAMS IF THEY STOLE THE PINS?
NO...
WE NEED TO QUESTION THEM IN A CLEVER WAY TO GET THEM TO CONFESS.
ALL ABOARD THE PONYVILLE EXPRESS! HEADING TO DODGE JUNCTION AND CANTERLOT.
THAT'S US. GIDDY UP!
HOP ON, SCOOTALOO, BOW AND WINDY ARE WAITING.
ALRIGHT CRUSADER—I MEAN SUPER SLEUTHS.
FIND OUT WHAT YOU CAN AND WE'LL REGROUP AT THE SCHOOLHOUSE TOMORROW.
RIGHT!

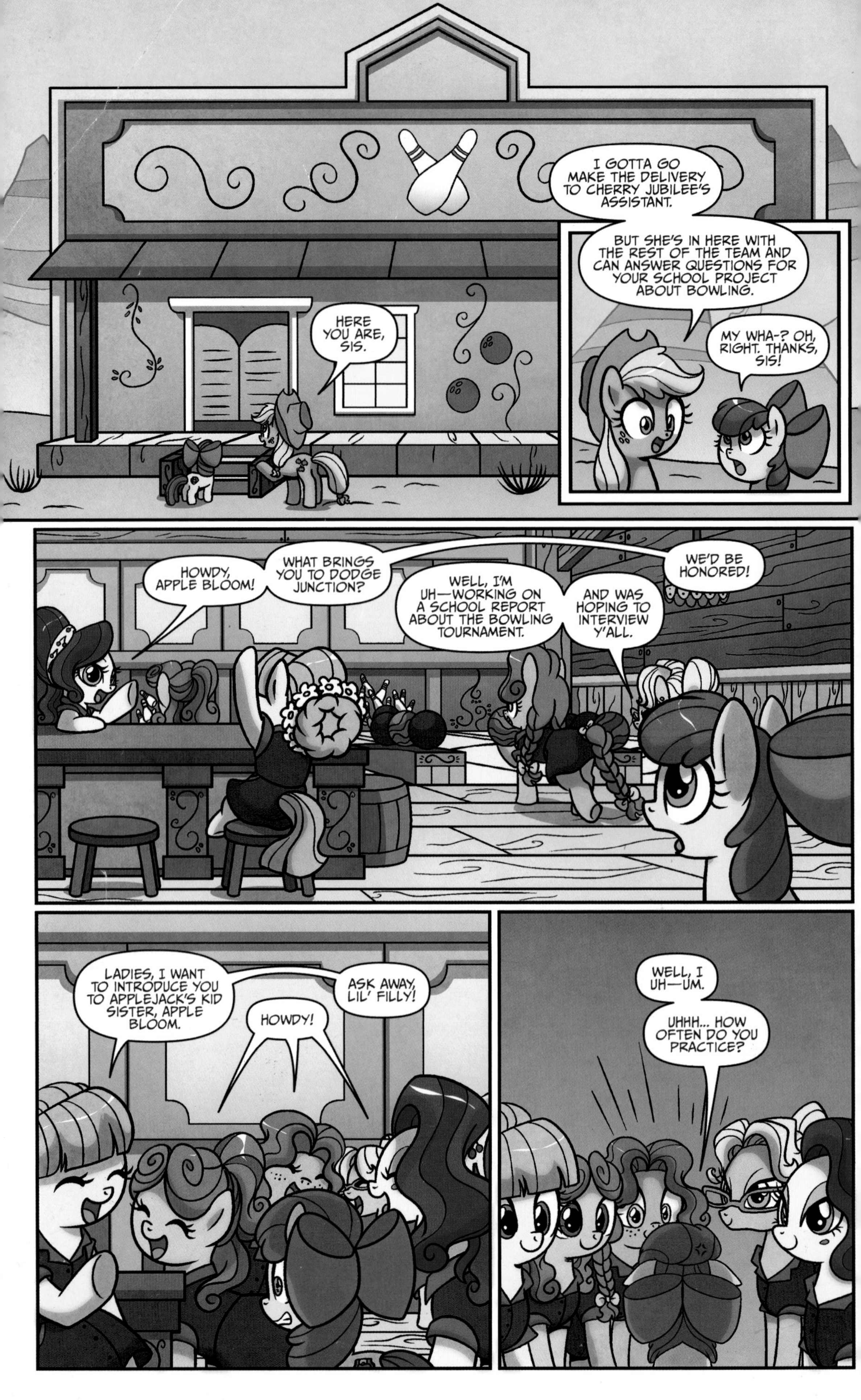
HERE YOU ARE, SIS.
I GOTTA GO MAKE THE DELIVERY TO CHERRY JUBILEE'S ASSISTANT.
BUT SHE'S IN HERE WITH THE REST OF THE TEAM AND CAN ANSWER QUESTIONS FOR YOUR SCHOOL PROJECT ABOUT BOWLING.
MY WHA-? OH, RIGHT. THANKS, SIS!
HOWDY, APPLE BLOOM!
WHAT BRINGS YOU TO DODGE JUNCTION?
WELL, I'M UH—WORKING ON A SCHOOL REPORT ABOUT THE BOWLING TOURNAMENT.
AND WAS HOPING TO INTERVIEW Y'ALL.
WE'D BE HONORED!
LADIES, I WANT TO INTRODUCE YOU TO APPLEJACK'S KID SISTER, APPLE BLOOM.
HOWDY!
ASK AWAY, LIL' FILLY!
WELL, I UH—UM.
UHHH... HOW OFTEN DO YOU PRACTICE?

RIGHT NOW, WE'RE PRACTICING NON-STOP.

PONYVILLE IS THE TEAM TO BEAT THIS YEAR!

WE NEED TO GET AS MANY PRACTICE GAMES IN AS POSSIBLE!

HAS ANYPONY ON THE TEAM DONE ANY TRAVELING LATELY?

TRAVELING? GOSH, NO!

WE'VE PRACTICALLY BEEN SLEEPING IN THIS HERE BOWLING ALLEY. AIN'T THAT RIGHT, MARIAN?

INDEED! I DON'T THINK I'VE BEEN ANYWHERE BUT HERE AND THE LIBRARY FOR THE LAST FEW WEEKS!

THE LAST FEW WEEKS?

YUP! WE WANT TO WIN THIS TOURNAMENT FAIR AND SQUARE, SO THERE'S NOT MUCH TIME FOR ANYTHING ELSE.

WHAT OTHER QUESTIONS DO YOU HAVE?

I GUESS THAT'S IT...

YOU SURE DIDN'T HAVE TOO MANY QUESTION—

STIIIIRIKE!

HOORAY!

GOSH, THEY'RE ALL SO NICE AND ARE WORKING SO HARD.

THEY'RE NOT ACTING SUSPICIOUS AT ALL.

I DON'T THINK ANY OF THEM DID IT.

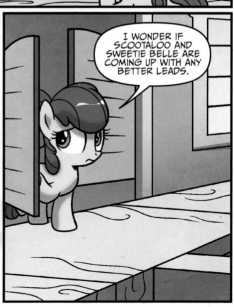

I WONDER IF SCOOTALOO AND SWEETIE BELLE ARE COMING UP WITH ANY BETTER LEADS.

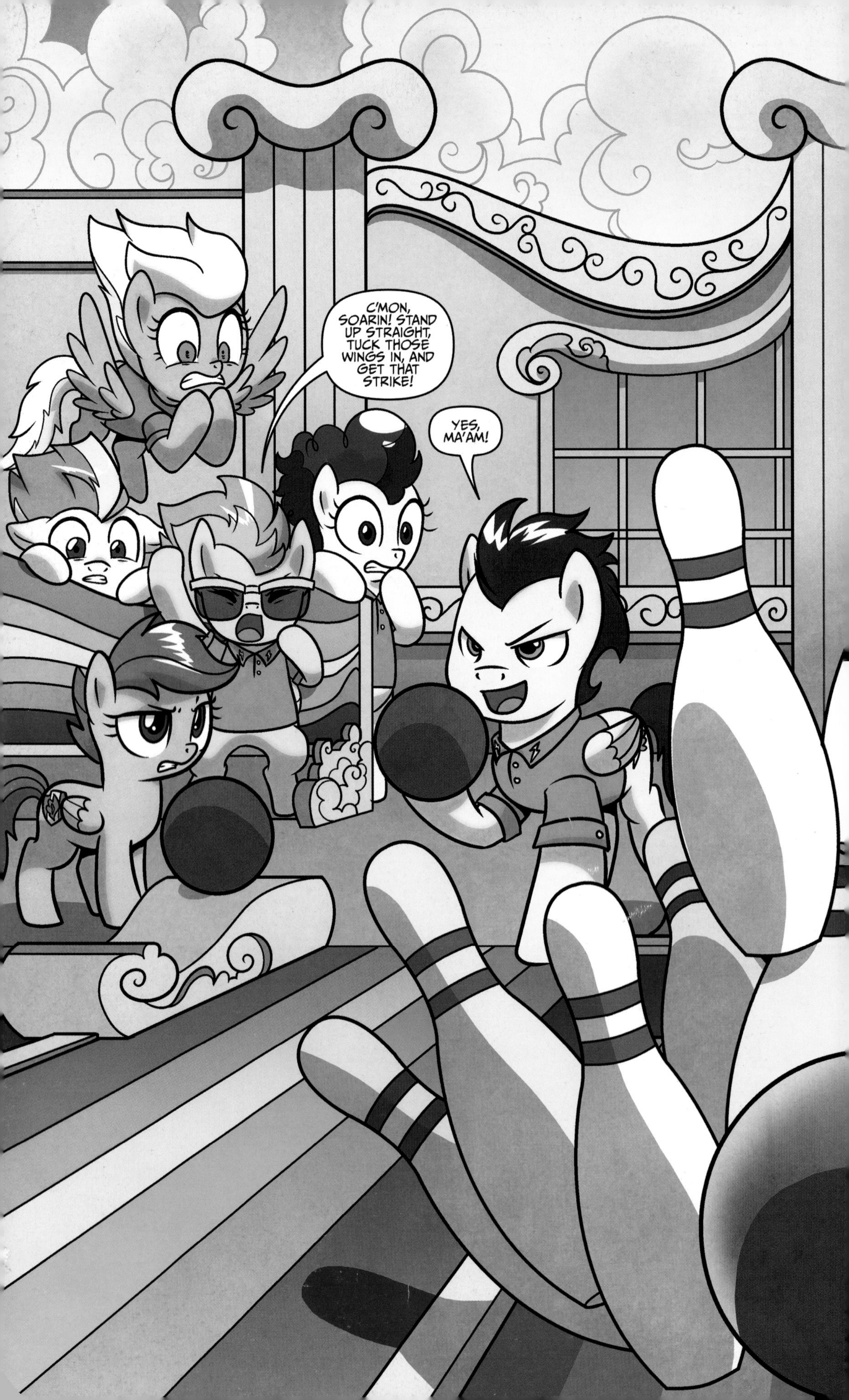
C'MON, SOARIN! STAND UP STRAIGHT, TUCK THOSE WINGS IN, AND GET THAT STRIKE!
YES, MA'AM!

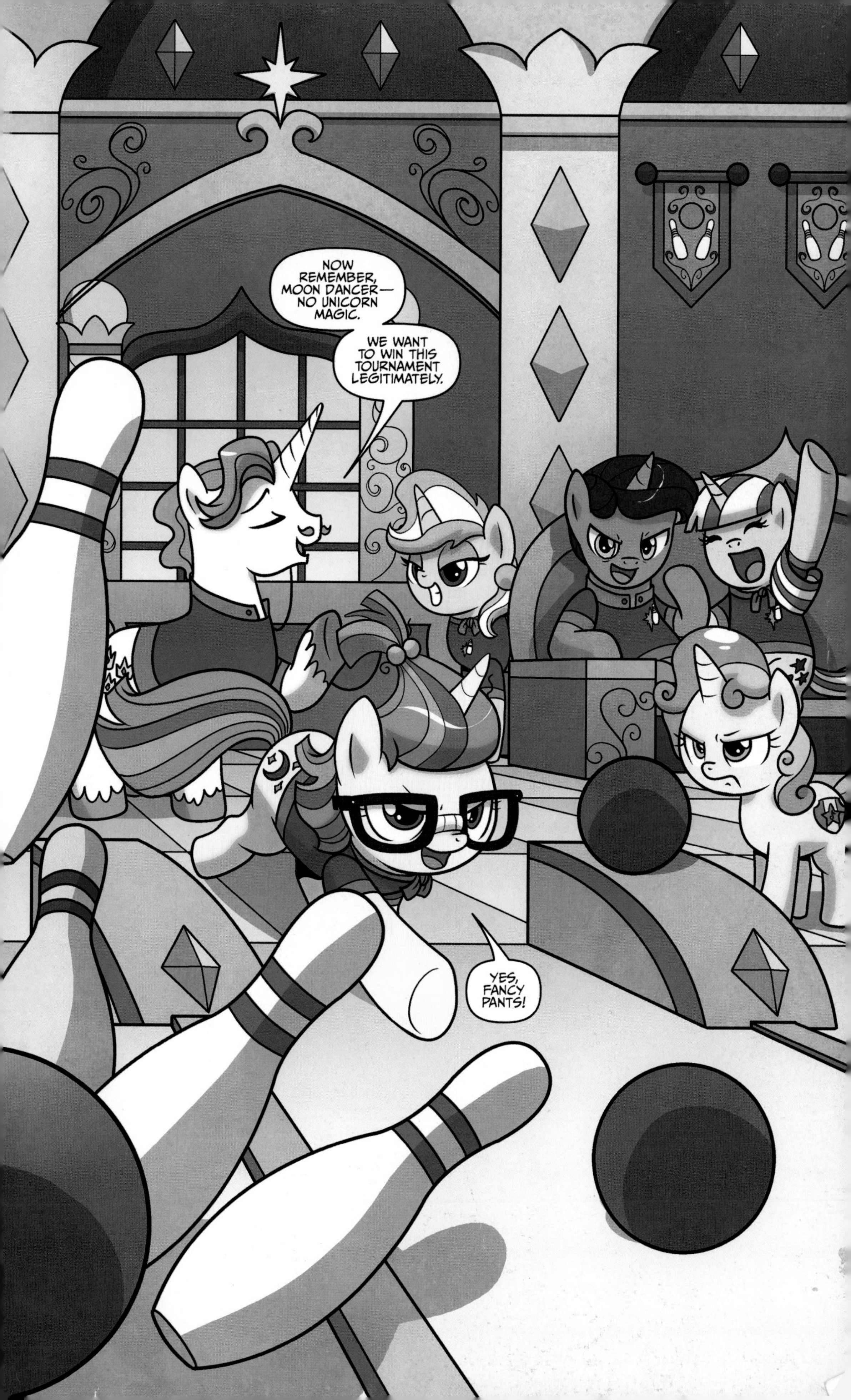
NOW REMEMBER, MOON DANCER— NO UNICORN MAGIC.
WE WANT TO WIN THIS TOURNAMENT LEGITIMATELY.
YES, FANCY PANTS!

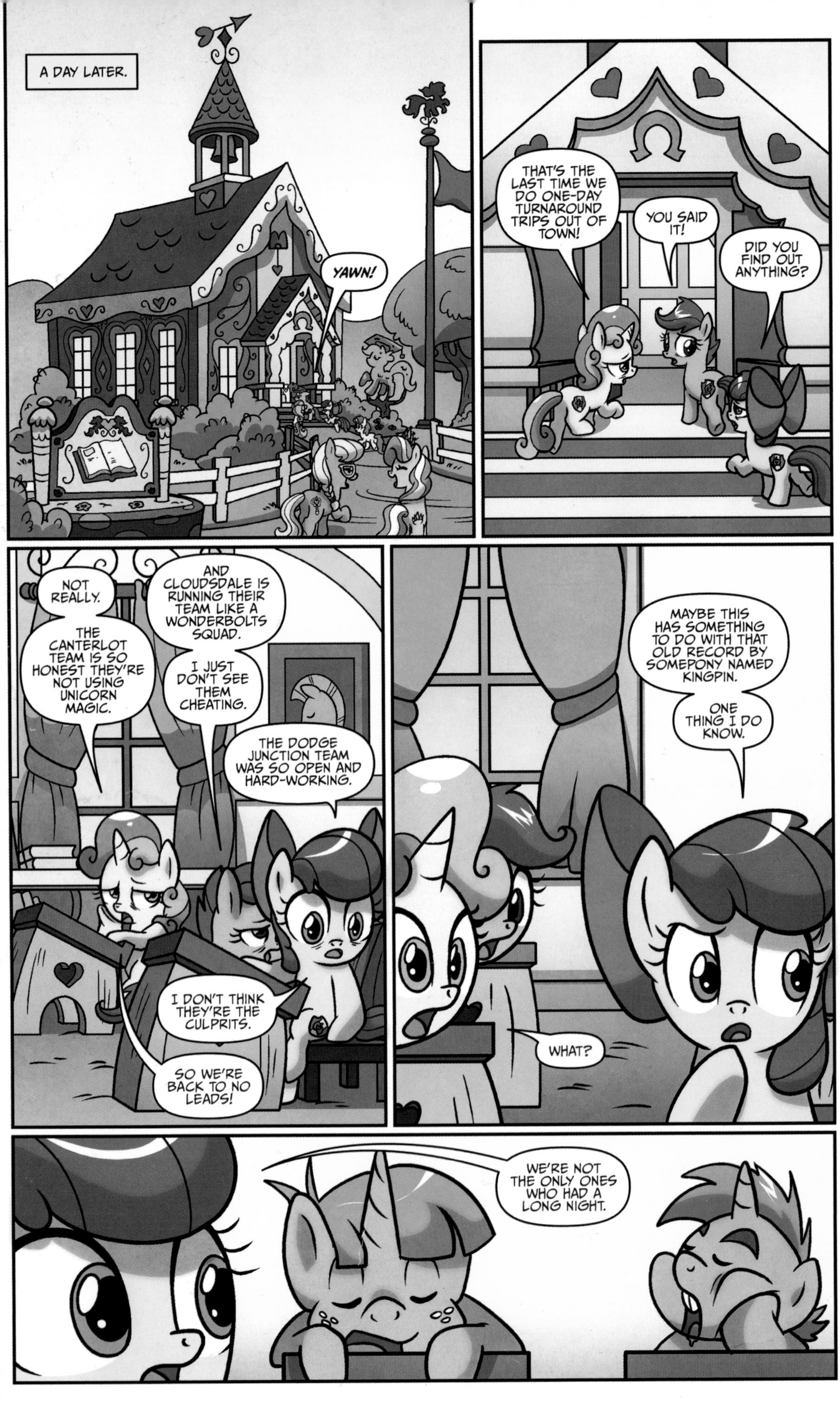
A DAY LATER.
YAWN!
THAT'S THE LAST TIME WE DO ONE-DAY TURNAROUND TRIPS OUT OF TOWN!
YOU SAID IT!
DID YOU FIND OUT ANYTHING?
NOT REALLY.
THE CANTERLOT TEAM IS SO HONEST THEY'RE NOT USING UNICORN MAGIC.
AND CLOUDSDALE IS RUNNING THEIR TEAM LIKE A WONDERBOLTS SQUAD.
I JUST DON'T SEE THEM CHEATING.
THE DODGE JUNCTION TEAM WAS SO OPEN AND HARD-WORKING.
I DON'T THINK THEY'RE THE CULPRITS.
SO WE'RE BACK TO NO LEADS!
MAYBE THIS HAS SOMETHING TO DO WITH THAT OLD RECORD BY SOMEPONY NAMED KINGPIN.
ONE THING I DO KNOW.
WHAT?
WE'RE NOT THE ONLY ONES WHO HAD A LONG NIGHT.

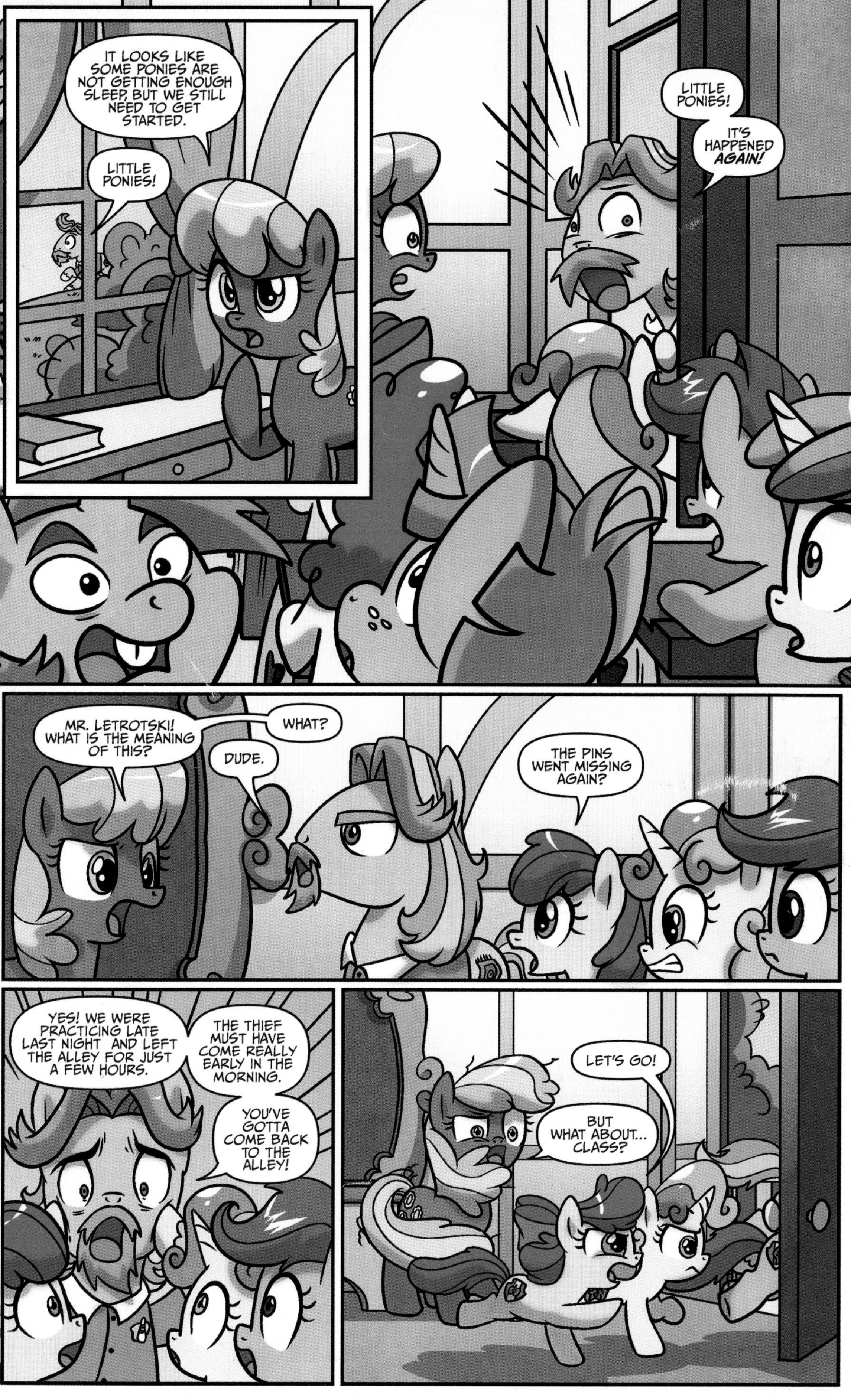
IT LOOKS LIKE SOME PONIES ARE NOT GETTING ENOUGH SLEEP, BUT WE STILL NEED TO GET STARTED.
LITTLE PONIES!
LITTLE PONIES!
IT'S HAPPENED **AGAIN!**
MR. LETROTSKI! WHAT IS THE MEANING OF THIS?
WHAT?
DUDE.
THE PINS WENT MISSING AGAIN?
YES! WE WERE PRACTICING LATE LAST NIGHT AND LEFT THE ALLEY FOR JUST A FEW HOURS.
THE THIEF MUST HAVE COME REALLY EARLY IN THE MORNING.
YOU'VE GOTTA COME BACK TO THE ALLEY!
LET'S GO!
BUT WHAT ABOUT... CLASS?

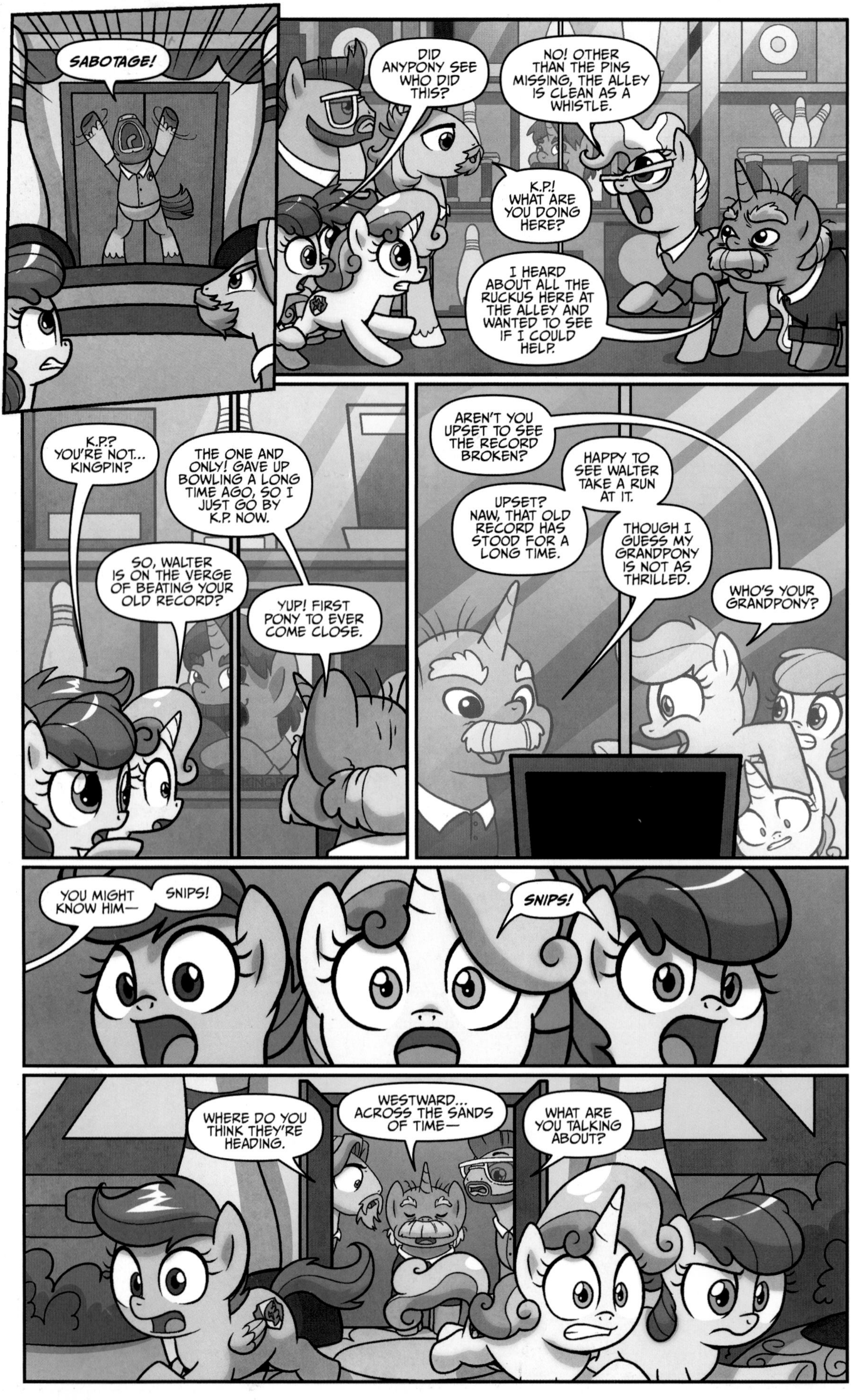
SABOTAGE!
DID ANYPONY SEE WHO DID THIS?
NO! OTHER THAN THE PINS MISSING, THE ALLEY IS CLEAN AS A WHISTLE.
K.P.! WHAT ARE YOU DOING HERE?
I HEARD ABOUT ALL THE RUCKUS HERE AT THE ALLEY AND WANTED TO SEE IF I COULD HELP.
K.P.? YOU'RE NOT... KINGPIN?
THE ONE AND ONLY! GAVE UP BOWLING A LONG TIME AGO, SO I JUST GO BY K.P. NOW.
SO, WALTER IS ON THE VERGE OF BEATING YOUR OLD RECORD?
YUP! FIRST PONY TO EVER COME CLOSE.
AREN'T YOU UPSET TO SEE THE RECORD BROKEN?
UPSET? NAW, THAT OLD RECORD HAS STOOD FOR A LONG TIME.
HAPPY TO SEE WALTER TAKE A RUN AT IT.
THOUGH I GUESS MY GRANDPONY IS NOT AS THRILLED.
WHO'S YOUR GRANDPONY?
YOU MIGHT KNOW HIM—
SNIPS!
SNIPS!
WHERE DO YOU THINK THEY'RE HEADING.
WESTWARD... ACROSS THE SANDS OF TIME—
WHAT ARE YOU TALKING ABOUT?

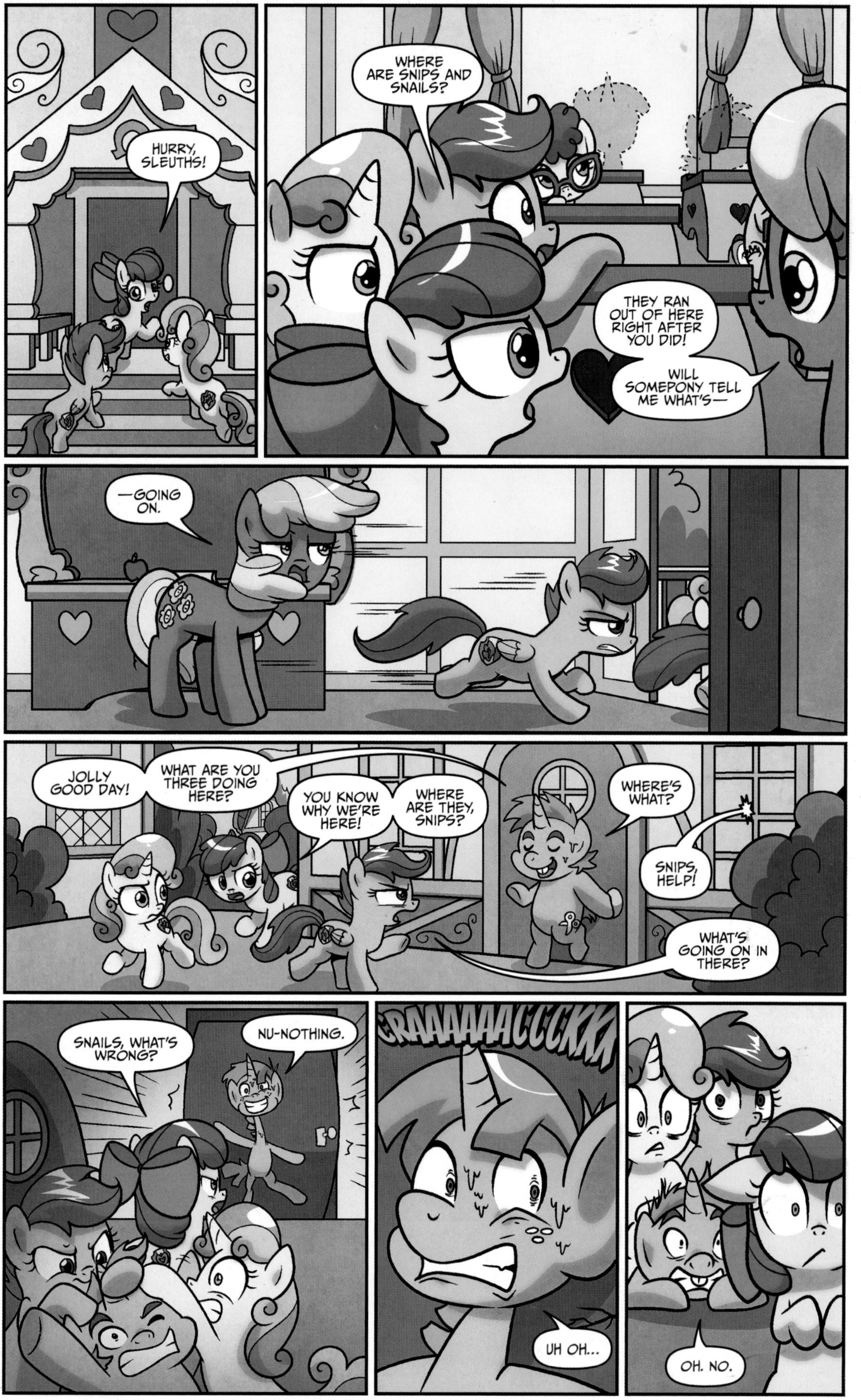
HURRY, SLEUTHS!
WHERE ARE SNIPS AND SNAILS?
THEY RAN OUT OF HERE RIGHT AFTER YOU DID!
WILL SOMEPONY TELL ME WHAT'S—
—GOING ON.
JOLLY GOOD DAY!
WHAT ARE YOU THREE DOING HERE?
YOU KNOW WHY WE'RE HERE!
WHERE ARE THEY, SNIPS?
WHERE'S WHAT?
SNIPS, HELP!
WHAT'S GOING ON IN THERE?
SNAILS, WHAT'S WRONG?
NU-NOTHING.
CRAAAAAACCCKKK
UH OH...
OH. NO.

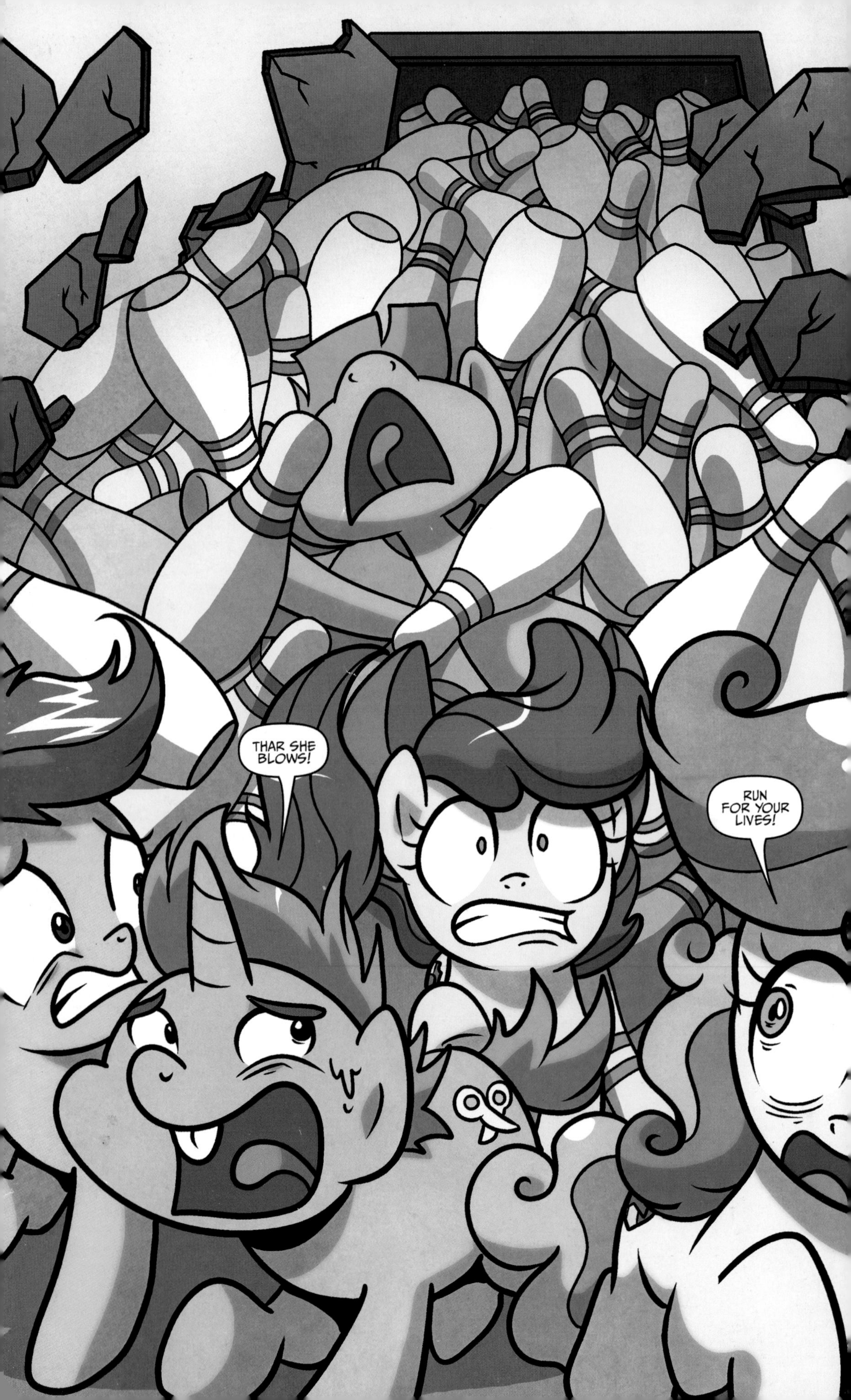
THAR SHE BLOWS!
RUN FOR YOUR LIVES!

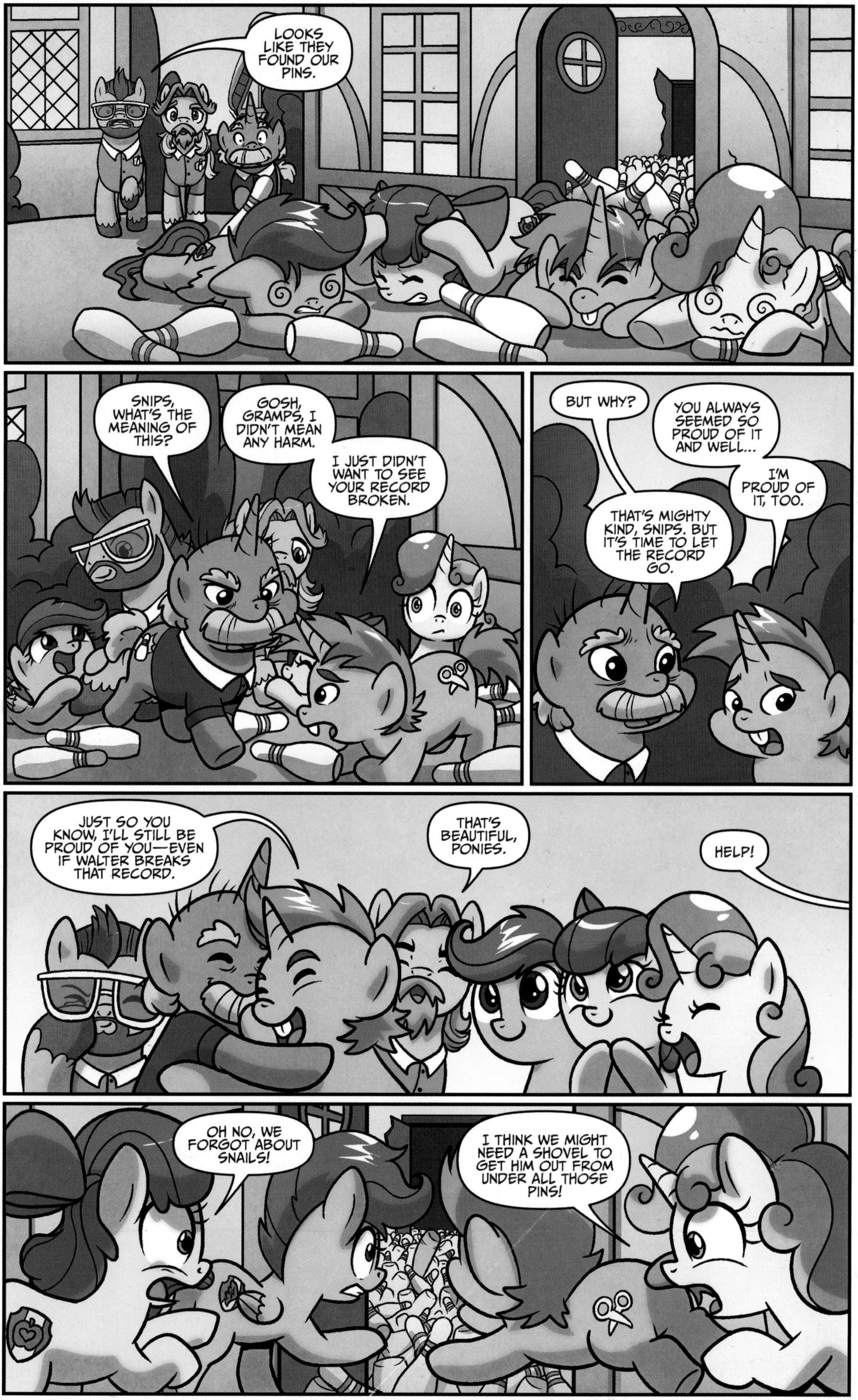
LOOKS LIKE THEY FOUND OUR PINS.
SNIPS, WHAT'S THE MEANING OF THIS?
GOSH, GRAMPS, I DIDN'T MEAN ANY HARM.
I JUST DIDN'T WANT TO SEE YOUR RECORD BROKEN.
BUT WHY?
YOU ALWAYS SEEMED SO PROUD OF IT AND WELL...
I'M PROUD OF IT, TOO.
THAT'S MIGHTY KIND, SNIPS. BUT IT'S TIME TO LET THE RECORD GO.
JUST SO YOU KNOW, I'LL STILL BE PROUD OF YOU—EVEN IF WALTER BREAKS THAT RECORD.
THAT'S BEAUTIFUL, PONIES.
HELP!
OH NO, WE FORGOT ABOUT SNAILS!
I THINK WE MIGHT NEED A SHOVEL TO GET HIM OUT FROM UNDER ALL THOSE PINS!

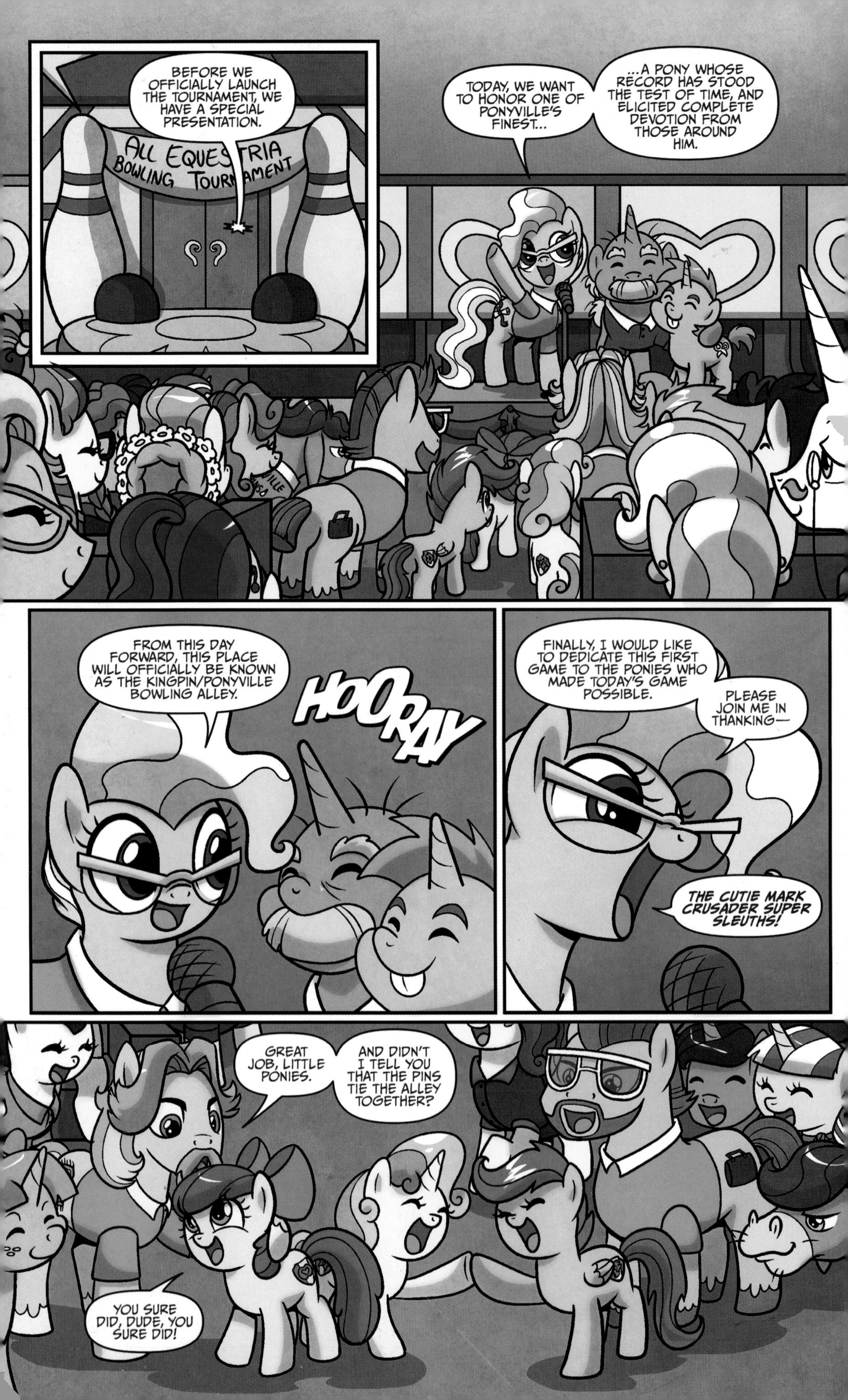
BEFORE WE OFFICIALLY LAUNCH THE TOURNAMENT, WE HAVE A SPECIAL PRESENTATION.
ALL EQUESTRIA BOWLING TOURNAMENT
TODAY, WE WANT TO HONOR ONE OF PONYVILLE'S FINEST...
...A PONY WHOSE RECORD HAS STOOD THE TEST OF TIME, AND ELICITED COMPLETE DEVOTION FROM THOSE AROUND HIM.
FROM THIS DAY FORWARD, THIS PLACE WILL OFFICIALLY BE KNOWN AS THE KINGPIN/PONYVILLE BOWLING ALLEY.
HOORAY
FINALLY, I WOULD LIKE TO DEDICATE THIS FIRST GAME TO THE PONIES WHO MADE TODAY'S GAME POSSIBLE.
PLEASE JOIN ME IN THANKING—
THE CUTIE MARK CRUSADER SUPER SLEUTHS!
GREAT JOB, LITTLE PONIES.
AND DIDN'T I TELL YOU THAT THE PINS TIE THE ALLEY TOGETHER?
YOU SURE DID, DUDE, YOU SURE DID!

ART BY **PHILIP MURPHY**

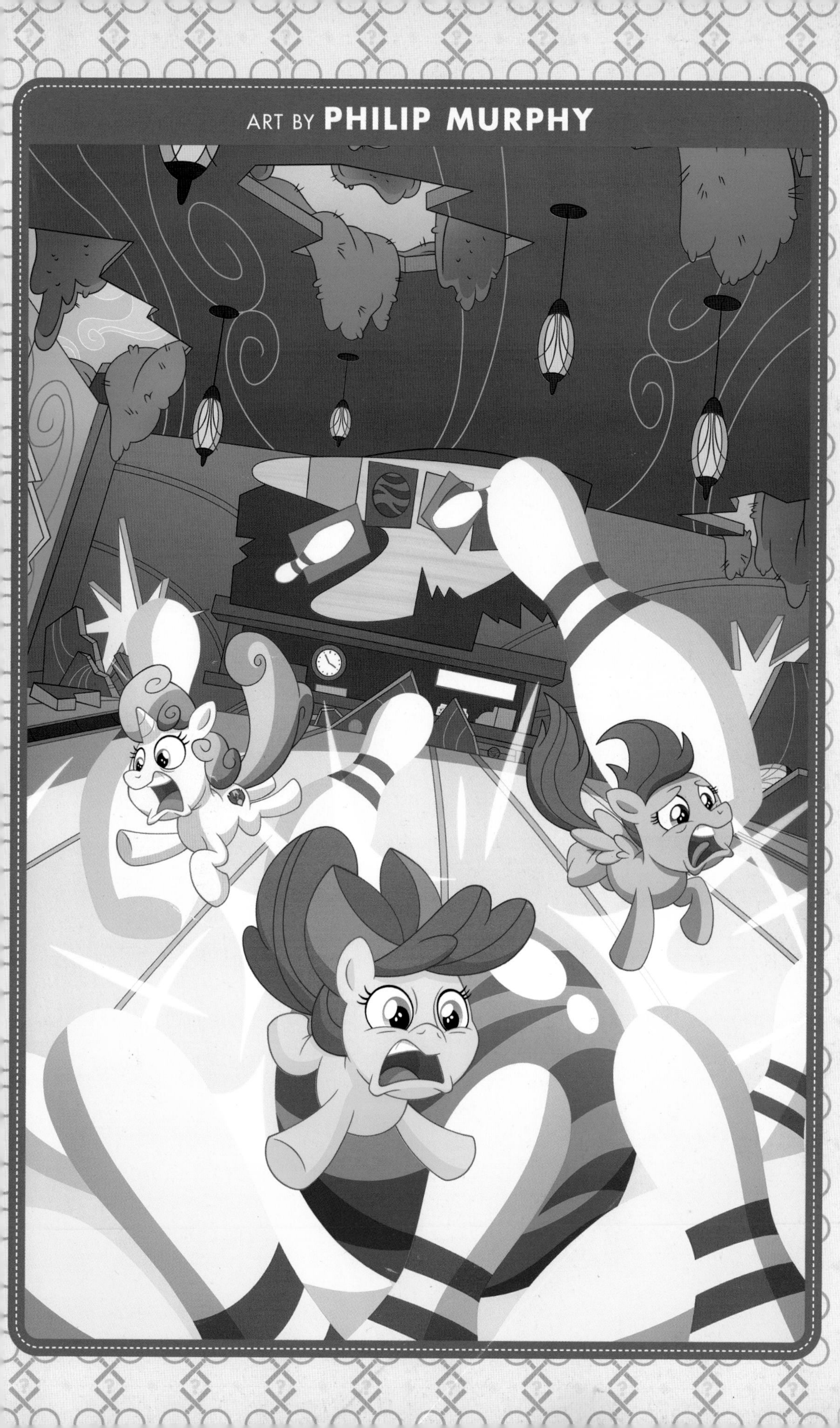

3 ART BY **AGNES GARBOWSKA**

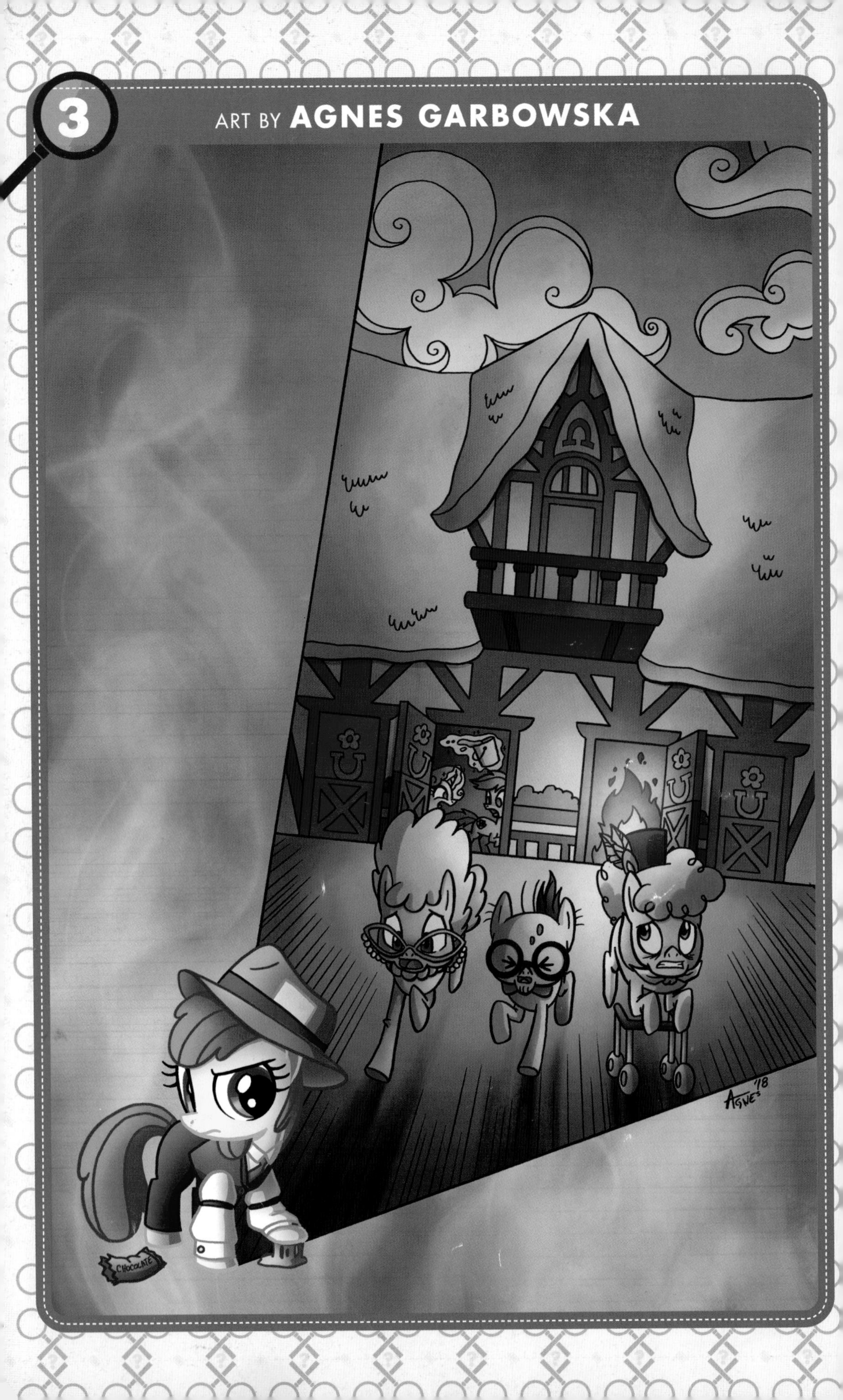

CHOCOLATE
Agnes '18

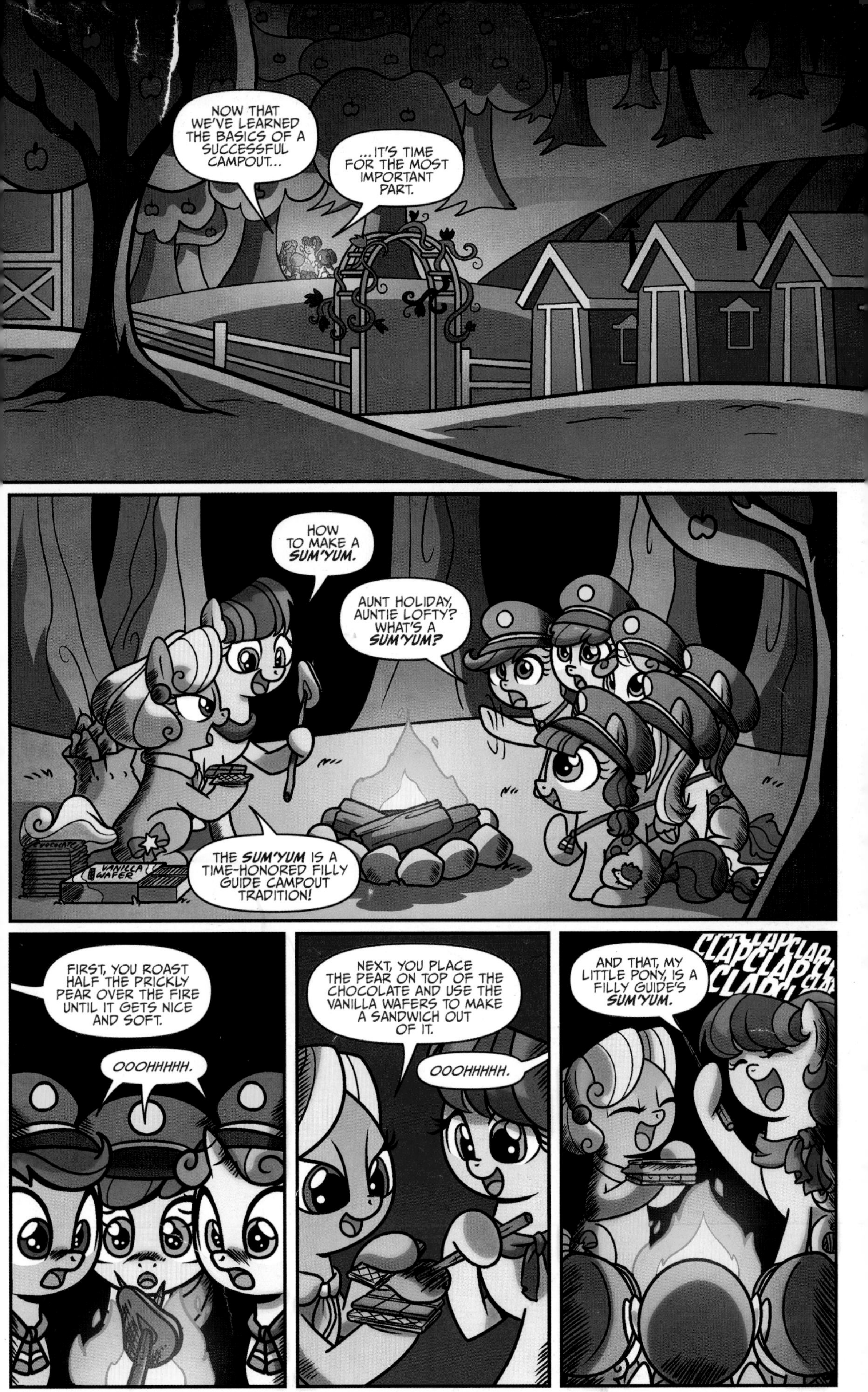
NOW THAT WE'VE LEARNED THE BASICS OF A SUCCESSFUL CAMPOUT...
...IT'S TIME FOR THE MOST IMPORTANT PART.
HOW TO MAKE A *SUM'YUM.*
AUNT HOLIDAY, AUNTIE LOFTY? WHAT'S A *SUM'YUM?*
THE *SUM'YUM* IS A TIME-HONORED FILLY GUIDE CAMPOUT TRADITION!
VANILLA WAFER
FIRST, YOU ROAST HALF THE PRICKLY PEAR OVER THE FIRE UNTIL IT GETS NICE AND SOFT.
OOOHHHHH.
NEXT, YOU PLACE THE PEAR ON TOP OF THE CHOCOLATE AND USE THE VANILLA WAFERS TO MAKE A SANDWICH OUT OF IT.
OOOHHHHH.
CLAPCLAPCL
AND THAT, MY LITTLE PONY, IS A FILLY GUIDE'S *SUM'YUM.*

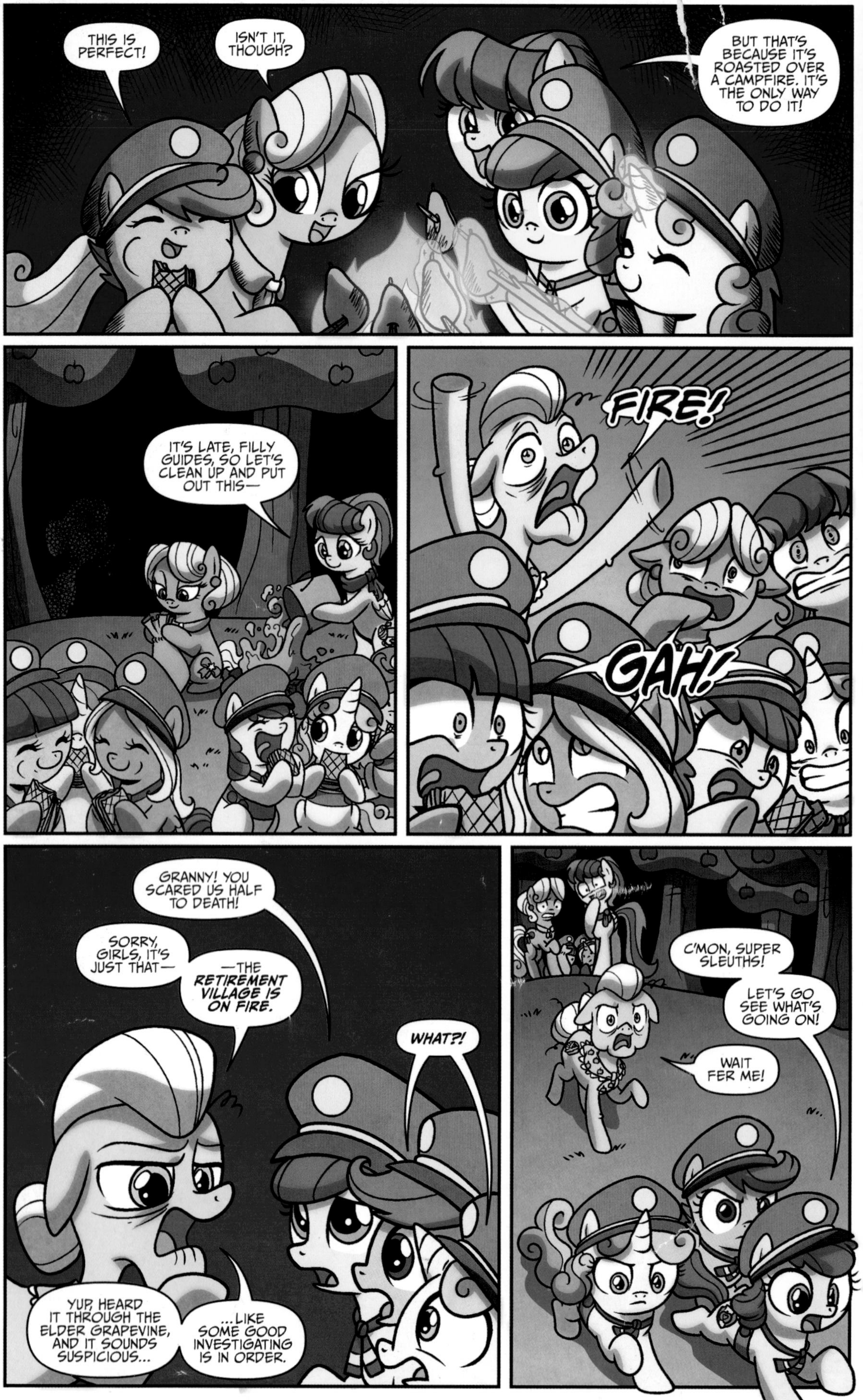
THIS IS PERFECT!
ISN'T IT, THOUGH?
BUT THAT'S BECAUSE IT'S ROASTED OVER A CAMPFIRE. IT'S THE ONLY WAY TO DO IT!
IT'S LATE, FILLY GUIDES, SO LET'S CLEAN UP AND PUT OUT THIS—
FIRE!
GAH!
GRANNY! YOU SCARED US HALF TO DEATH!
SORRY, GIRLS, IT'S JUST THAT—
—THE RETIREMENT VILLAGE IS ON FIRE.
WHAT?!
YUP, HEARD IT THROUGH THE ELDER GRAPEVINE, AND IT SOUNDS SUSPICIOUS...
...LIKE SOME GOOD INVESTIGATING IS IN ORDER.
C'MON, SUPER SLEUTHS!
LET'S GO SEE WHAT'S GOING ON!
WAIT FER ME!

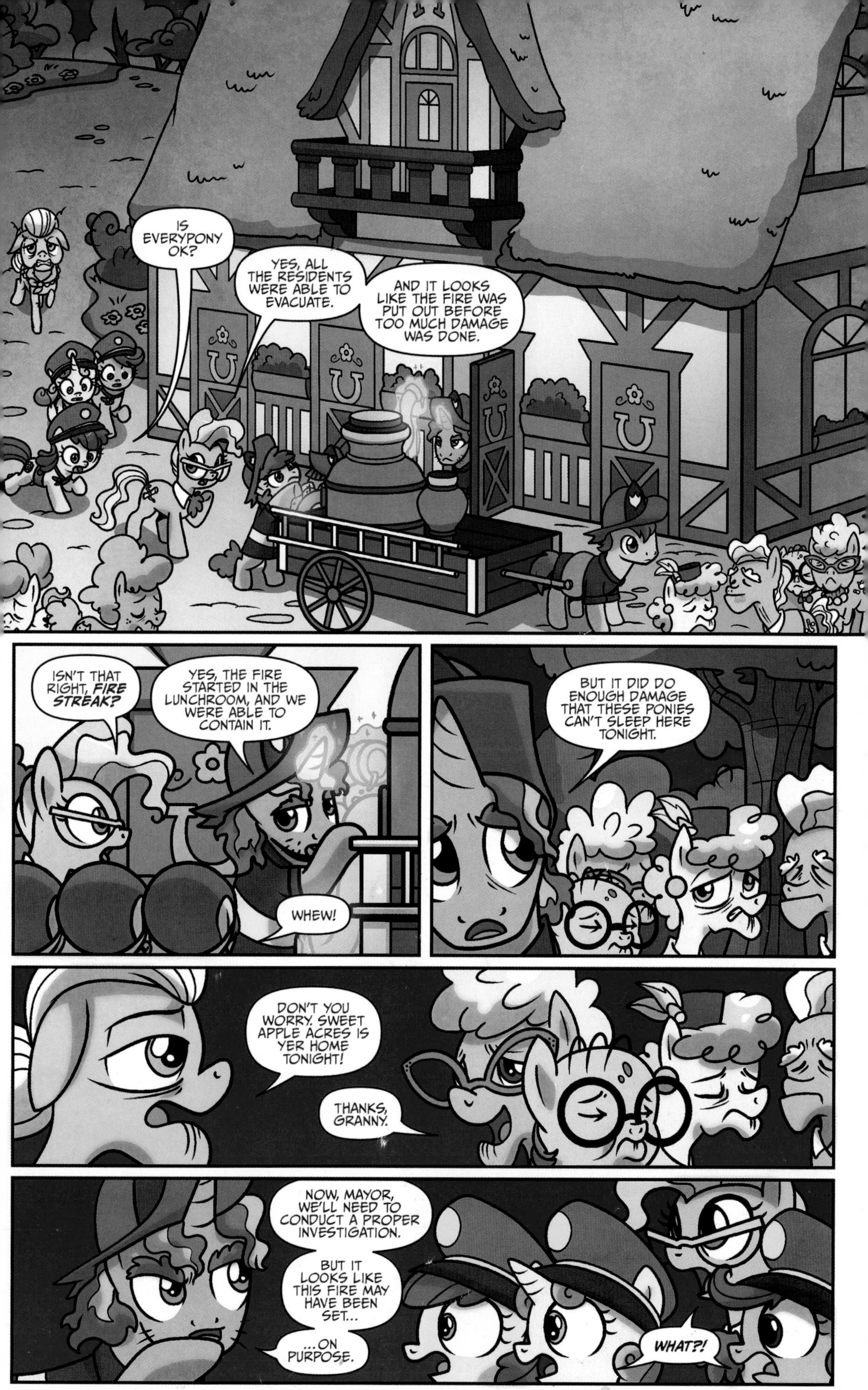
IS EVERYPONY OK?
YES, ALL THE RESIDENTS WERE ABLE TO EVACUATE.
AND IT LOOKS LIKE THE FIRE WAS PUT OUT BEFORE TOO MUCH DAMAGE WAS DONE.
ISN'T THAT RIGHT, *FIRE STREAK?*
YES, THE FIRE STARTED IN THE LUNCHROOM, AND WE WERE ABLE TO CONTAIN IT.
WHEW!
BUT IT DID DO ENOUGH DAMAGE THAT THESE PONIES CAN'T SLEEP HERE TONIGHT.
DON'T YOU WORRY. SWEET APPLE ACRES IS YER HOME TONIGHT!
THANKS, GRANNY.
NOW, MAYOR, WE'LL NEED TO CONDUCT A PROPER INVESTIGATION.
BUT IT LOOKS LIKE THIS FIRE MAY HAVE BEEN SET...
...ON PURPOSE.
WHAT?!

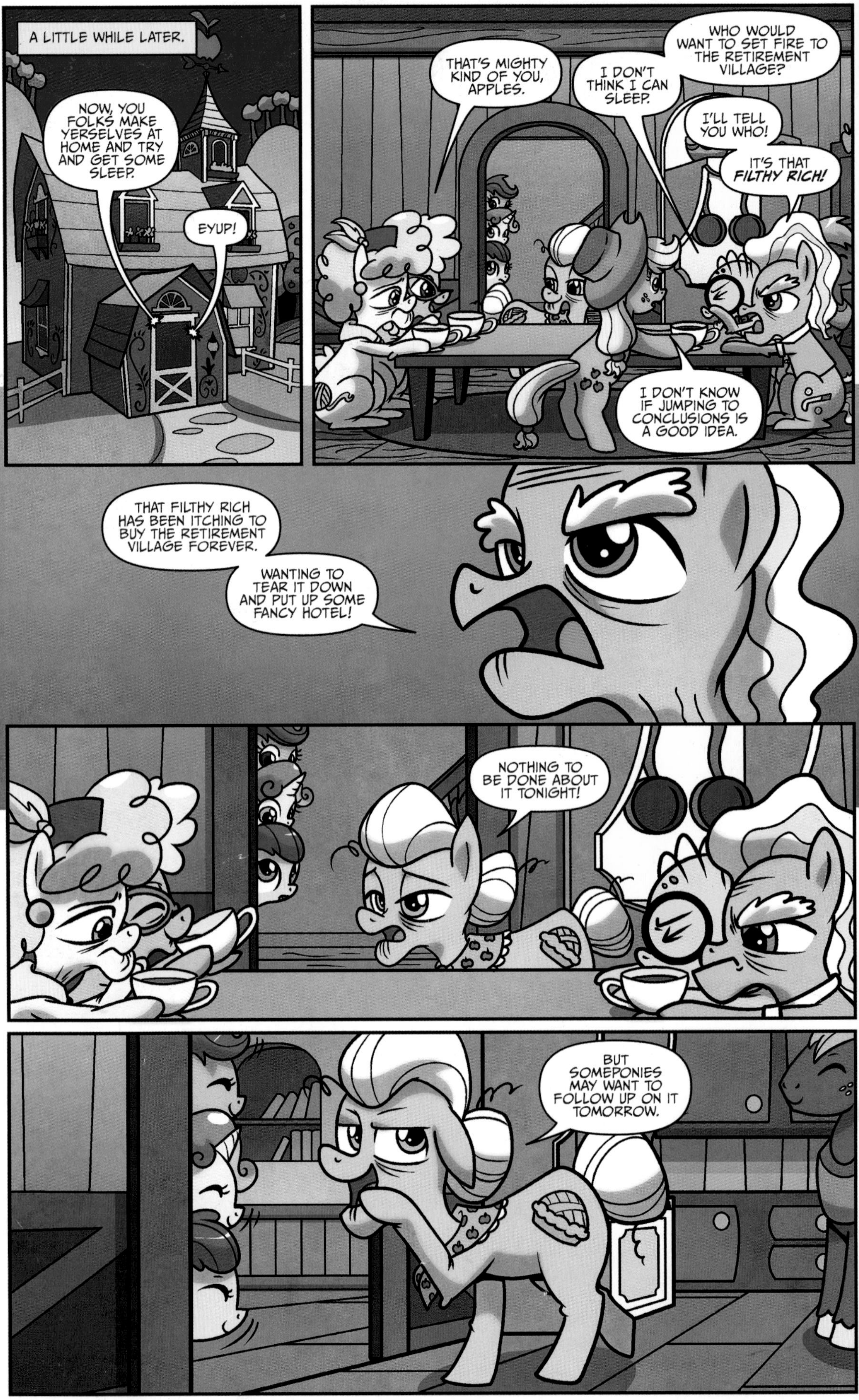

A LITTLE WHILE LATER.
NOW, YOU FOLKS MAKE YERSELVES AT HOME AND TRY AND GET SOME SLEEP.
EYUP!
THAT'S MIGHTY KIND OF YOU, APPLES.
I DON'T THINK I CAN SLEEP.
WHO WOULD WANT TO SET FIRE TO THE RETIREMENT VILLAGE?
I'LL TELL YOU WHO!
IT'S THAT FILTHY RICH!
I DON'T KNOW IF JUMPING TO CONCLUSIONS IS A GOOD IDEA.
THAT FILTHY RICH HAS BEEN ITCHING TO BUY THE RETIREMENT VILLAGE FOREVER.
WANTING TO TEAR IT DOWN AND PUT UP SOME FANCY HOTEL!
NOTHING TO BE DONE ABOUT IT TONIGHT!
BUT SOMEPONIES MAY WANT TO FOLLOW UP ON IT TOMORROW.

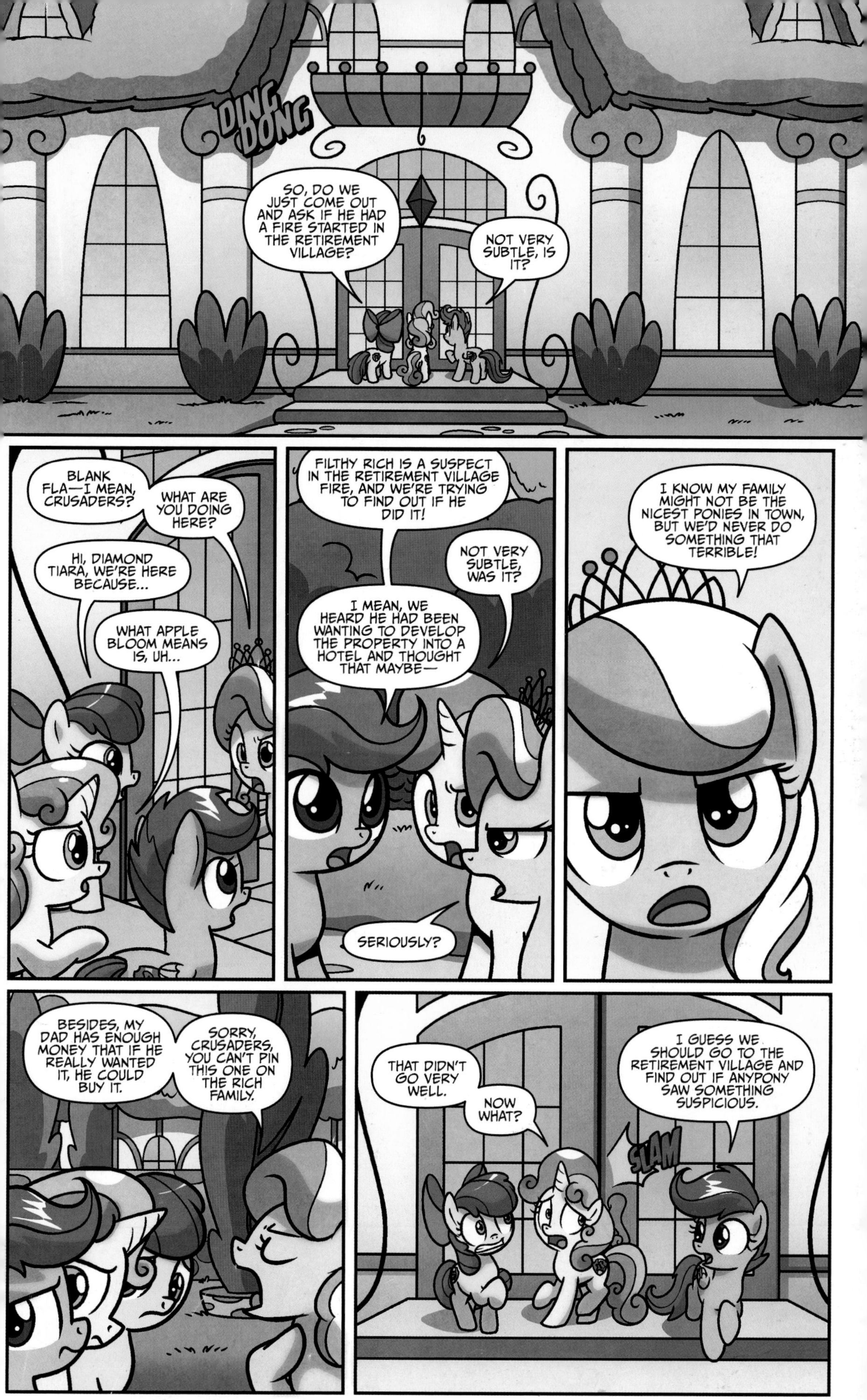
DING DONG
SO, DO WE JUST COME OUT AND ASK IF HE HAD A FIRE STARTED IN THE RETIREMENT VILLAGE?
NOT VERY SUBTLE, IS IT?
BLANK FLA—I MEAN, CRUSADERS?
WHAT ARE YOU DOING HERE?
HI, DIAMOND TIARA, WE'RE HERE BECAUSE...
WHAT APPLE BLOOM MEANS IS, UH...
FILTHY RICH IS A SUSPECT IN THE RETIREMENT VILLAGE FIRE, AND WE'RE TRYING TO FIND OUT IF HE DID IT!
NOT VERY SUBTLE, WAS IT?
I MEAN, WE HEARD HE HAD BEEN WANTING TO DEVELOP THE PROPERTY INTO A HOTEL AND THOUGHT THAT MAYBE—
SERIOUSLY?
I KNOW MY FAMILY MIGHT NOT BE THE NICEST PONIES IN TOWN, BUT WE'D NEVER DO SOMETHING THAT TERRIBLE!
BESIDES, MY DAD HAS ENOUGH MONEY THAT IF HE REALLY WANTED IT, HE COULD BUY IT.
SORRY, CRUSADERS, YOU CAN'T PIN THIS ONE ON THE RICH FAMILY.
SLAM
THAT DIDN'T GO VERY WELL.
NOW WHAT?
I GUESS WE SHOULD GO TO THE RETIREMENT VILLAGE AND FIND OUT IF ANYPONY SAW SOMETHING SUSPICIOUS.

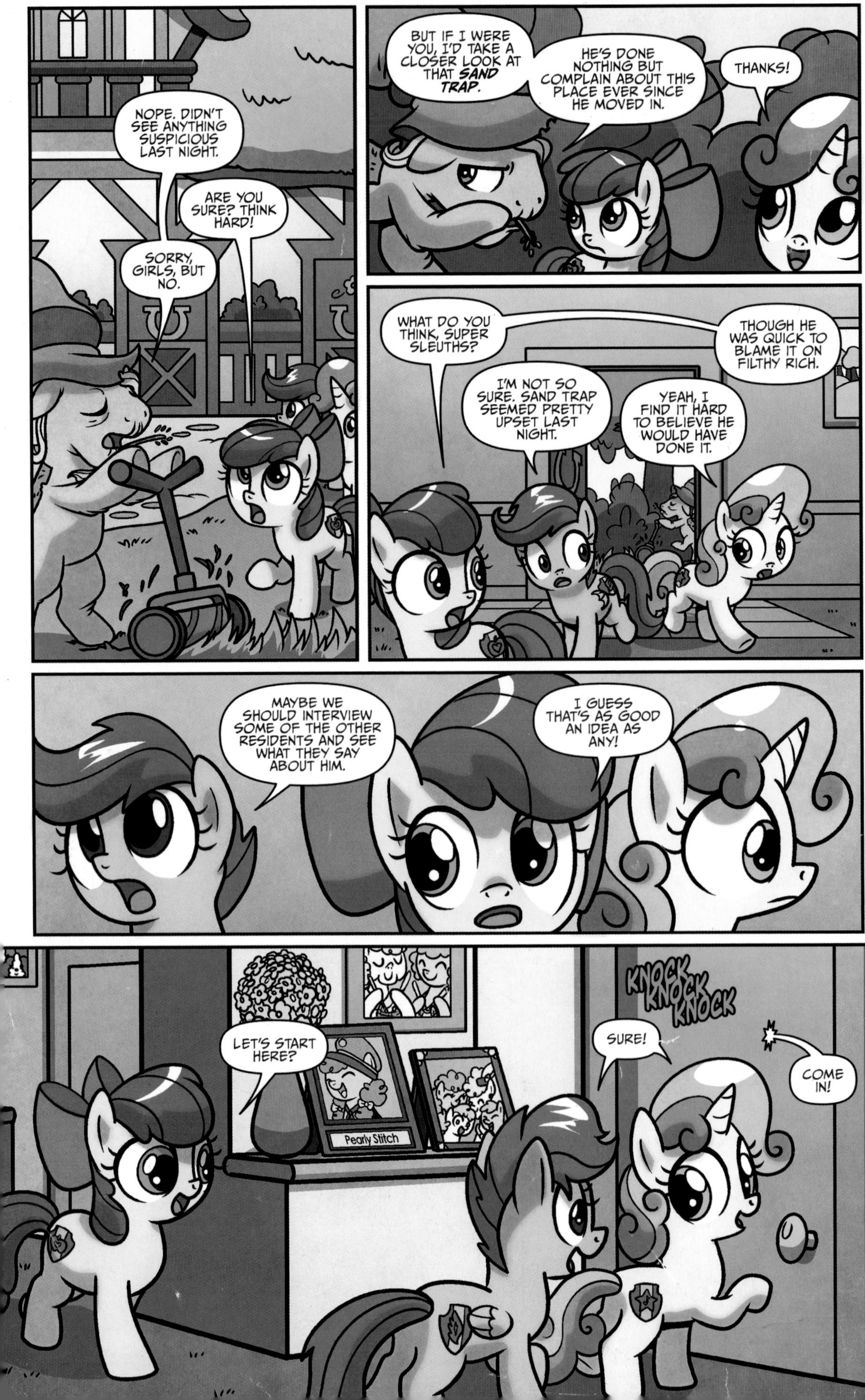
NOPE. DIDN'T SEE ANYTHING SUSPICIOUS LAST NIGHT.
ARE YOU SURE? THINK HARD!
SORRY, GIRLS, BUT NO.
BUT IF I WERE YOU, I'D TAKE A CLOSER LOOK AT THAT SAND TRAP.
HE'S DONE NOTHING BUT COMPLAIN ABOUT THIS PLACE EVER SINCE HE MOVED IN.
THANKS!
WHAT DO YOU THINK, SUPER SLEUTHS?
THOUGH HE WAS QUICK TO BLAME IT ON FILTHY RICH.
I'M NOT SO SURE. SAND TRAP SEEMED PRETTY UPSET LAST NIGHT.
YEAH, I FIND IT HARD TO BELIEVE HE WOULD HAVE DONE IT.
MAYBE WE SHOULD INTERVIEW SOME OF THE OTHER RESIDENTS AND SEE WHAT THEY SAY ABOUT HIM.
I GUESS THAT'S AS GOOD AN IDEA AS ANY!
LET'S START HERE?
Pearly Stitch
KNOCK KNOCK KNOCK
SURE!
COME IN!

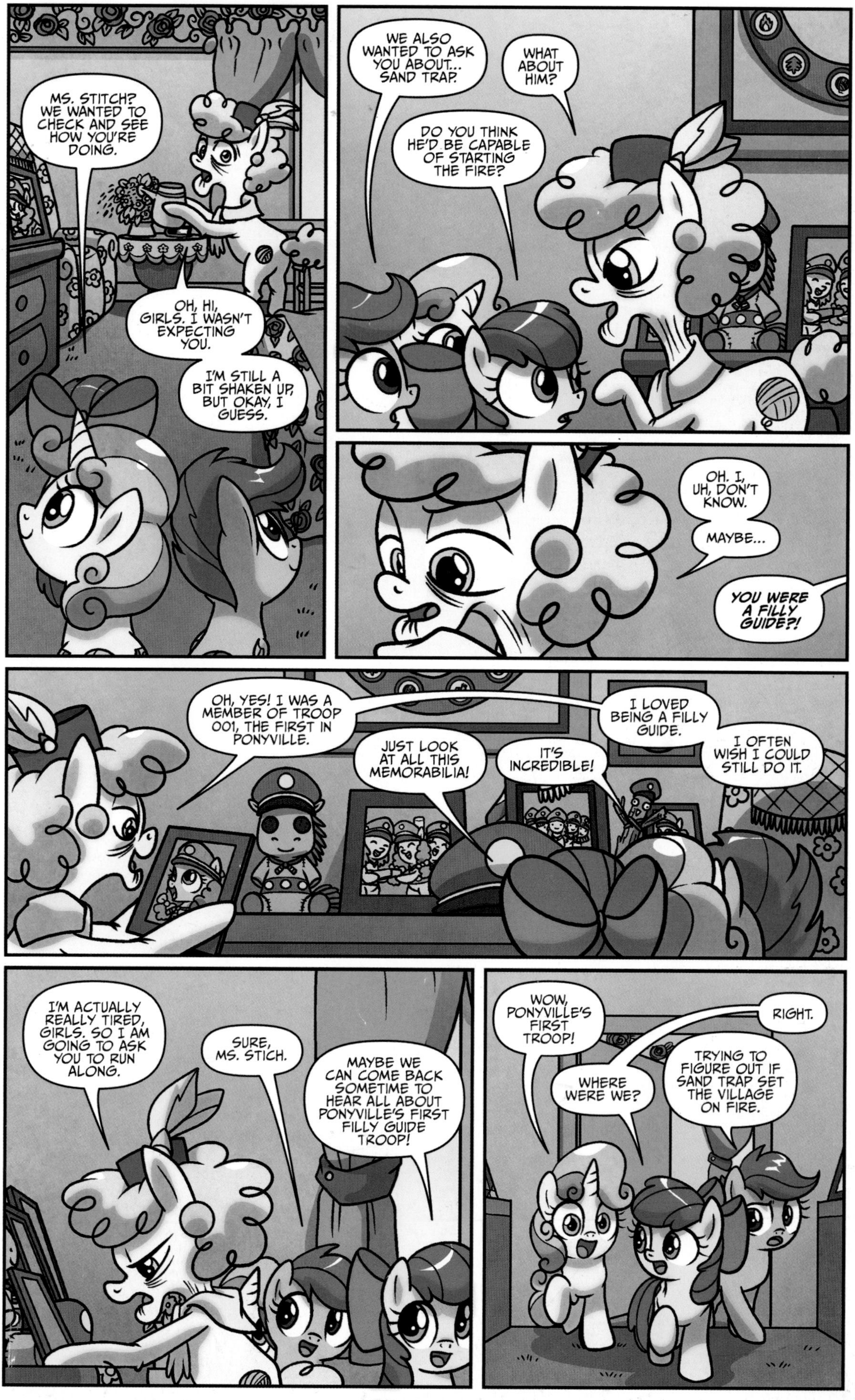
MS. STITCH? WE WANTED TO CHECK AND SEE HOW YOU'RE DOING.
OH, HI, GIRLS. I WASN'T EXPECTING YOU.
I'M STILL A BIT SHAKEN UP, BUT OKAY, I GUESS.
WE ALSO WANTED TO ASK YOU ABOUT... SAND TRAP.
WHAT ABOUT HIM?
DO YOU THINK HE'D BE CAPABLE OF STARTING THE FIRE?
OH. I, UH, DON'T KNOW.
MAYBE...
YOU WERE A FILLY GUIDE?!
OH, YES! I WAS A MEMBER OF TROOP 001, THE FIRST IN PONYVILLE.
I LOVED BEING A FILLY GUIDE.
I OFTEN WISH I COULD STILL DO IT.
JUST LOOK AT ALL THIS MEMORABILIA!
IT'S INCREDIBLE!
I'M ACTUALLY REALLY TIRED, GIRLS. SO I AM GOING TO ASK YOU TO RUN ALONG.
SURE, MS. STICH.
MAYBE WE CAN COME BACK SOMETIME TO HEAR ALL ABOUT PONYVILLE'S FIRST FILLY GUIDE TROOP!
WOW, PONYVILLE'S FIRST TROOP!
WHERE WERE WE?
RIGHT.
TRYING TO FIGURE OUT IF SAND TRAP SET THE VILLAGE ON FIRE.

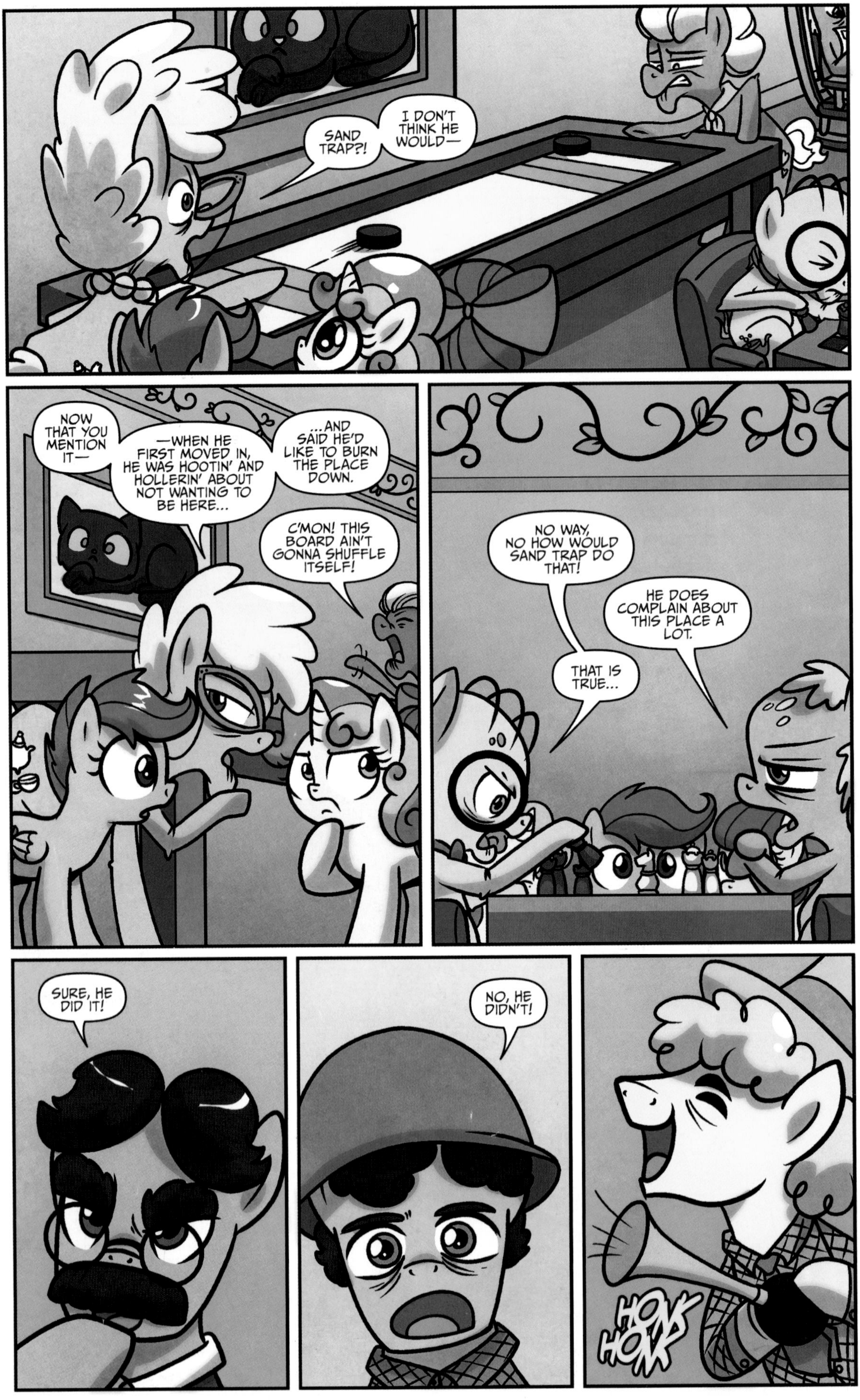
I DON'T THINK HE WOULD—
SAND TRAP?!
NOW THAT YOU MENTION IT—
—WHEN HE FIRST MOVED IN, HE WAS HOOTIN' AND HOLLERIN' ABOUT NOT WANTING TO BE HERE...
...AND SAID HE'D LIKE TO BURN THE PLACE DOWN.
C'MON! THIS BOARD AIN'T GONNA SHUFFLE ITSELF!
NO WAY, NO HOW WOULD SAND TRAP DO THAT!
THAT IS TRUE...
HE DOES COMPLAIN ABOUT THIS PLACE A LOT.
SURE, HE DID IT!
NO, HE DIDN'T!
HONK HONK

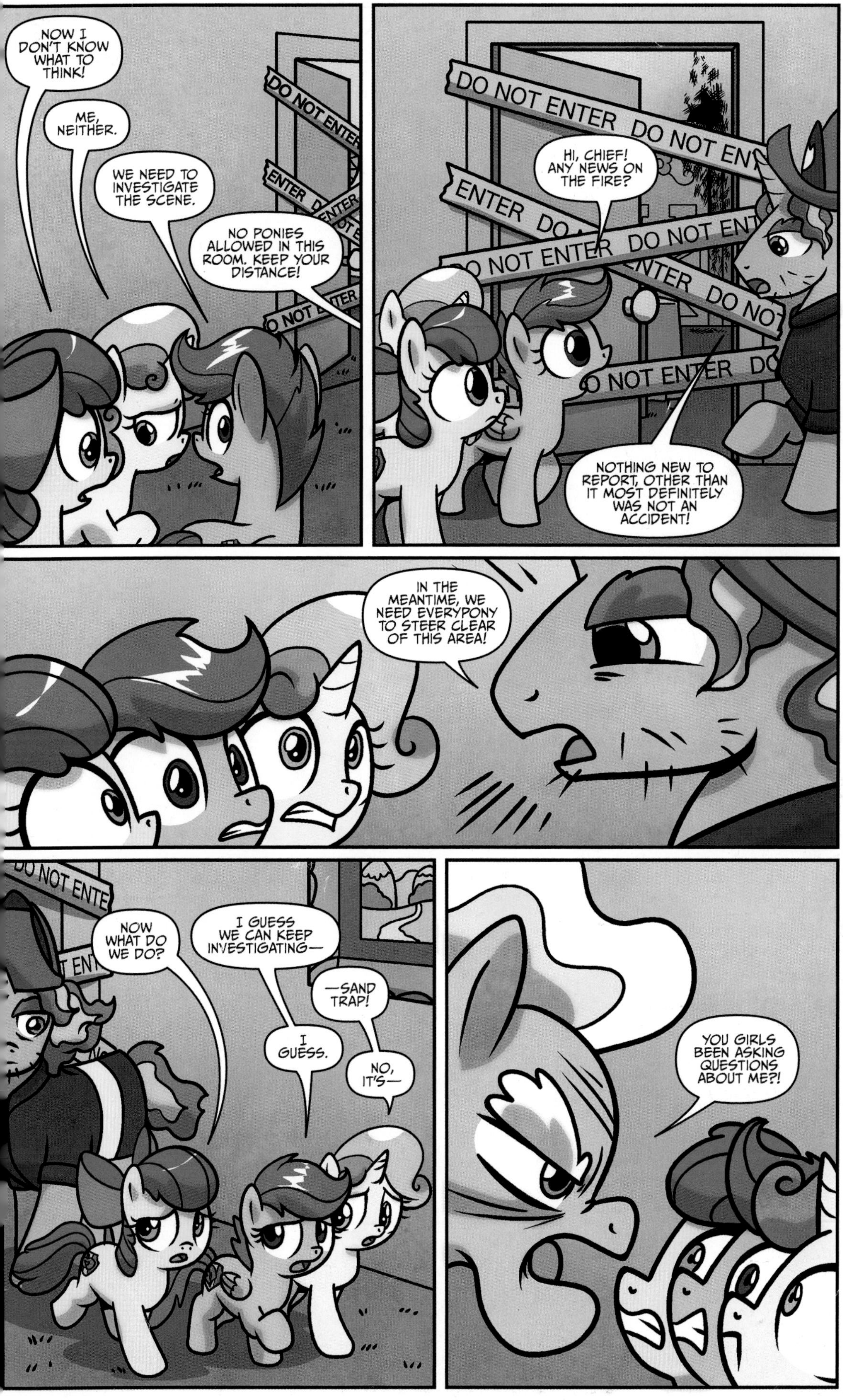
NOW I DON'T KNOW WHAT TO THINK!
ME, NEITHER.
WE NEED TO INVESTIGATE THE SCENE.
NO PONIES ALLOWED IN THIS ROOM. KEEP YOUR DISTANCE!
DO NOT ENTER
HI, CHIEF! ANY NEWS ON THE FIRE?
NOTHING NEW TO REPORT, OTHER THAN IT MOST DEFINITELY WAS NOT AN ACCIDENT!
IN THE MEANTIME, WE NEED EVERYPONY TO STEER CLEAR OF THIS AREA!
NOW WHAT DO WE DO?
I GUESS WE CAN KEEP INVESTIGATING—
—SAND TRAP!
I GUESS.
NO, IT'S—
YOU GIRLS BEEN ASKING QUESTIONS ABOUT ME?!

WELL, SOME OF THE RESIDENTS THOUGHT THAT YOU MIGHT HAVE HAD SOMETHING TO DO WITH THE FIRE.

IS THAT RIGHT?

BUT NOT ALL OF THEM.

YOU KNOW WHAT I THINK?

YOU SHOULD MIND YOUR OWN BUSINESS!

MR. SAND TRAP, WAIT!

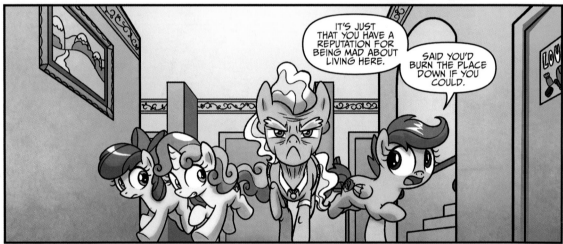

IT'S JUST THAT YOU HAVE A REPUTATION FOR BEING MAD ABOUT LIVING HERE.

SAID YOU'D BURN THE PLACE DOWN IF YOU COULD.

I GUESS I DID SAY THAT ONCE.

IT'S TRUE I DIDN'T WANT TO MOVE HERE.

IT WAS REALLY DIFFICULT AT FIRST.

BUT THIS PLACE HAS BECOME MY HOME.

THE OTHER RESIDENTS MY FAMILY.

I COULD NEVER DO ANYTHING TO JEOPARDIZE THAT.

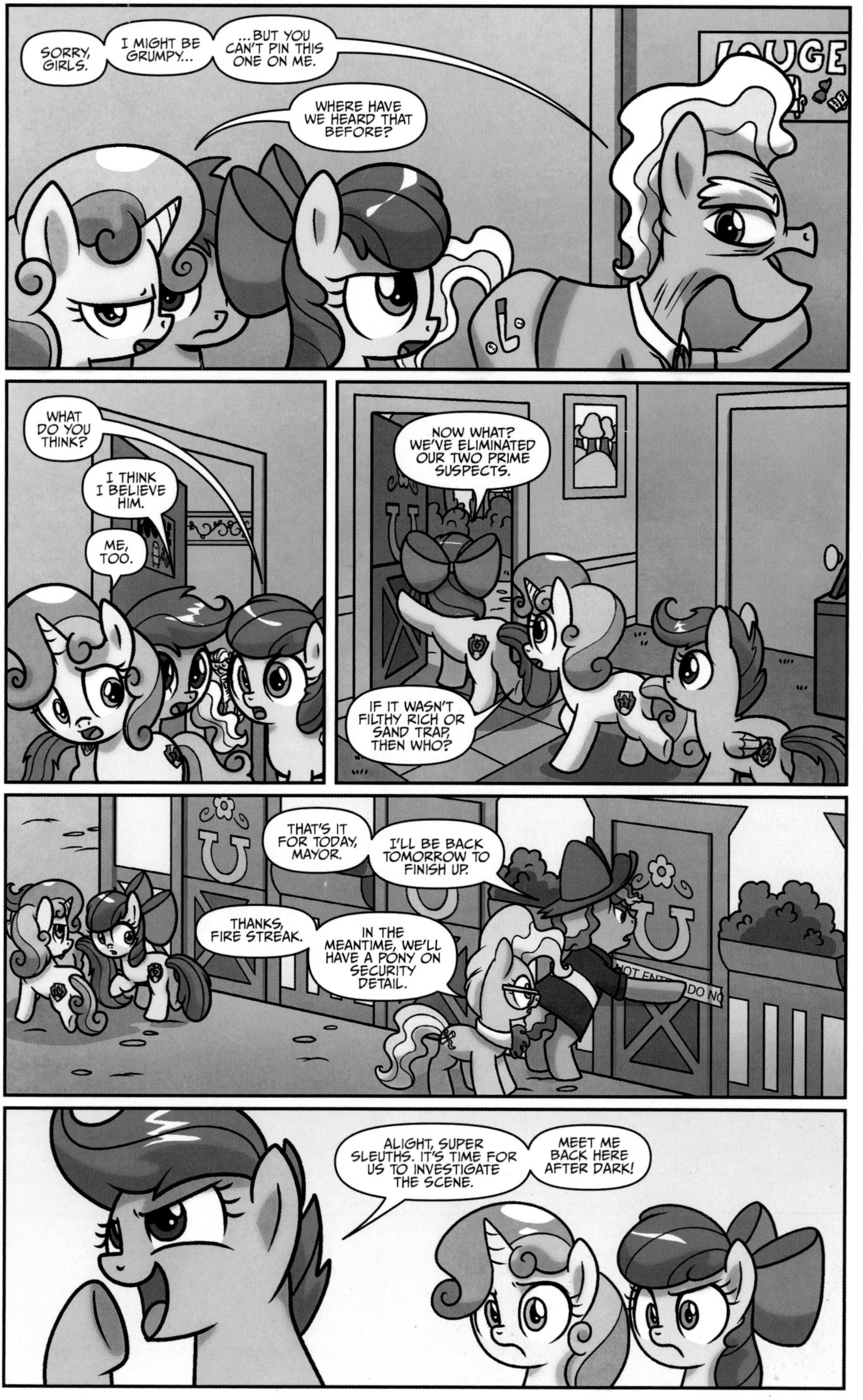
SORRY, GIRLS.
I MIGHT BE GRUMPY...
...BUT YOU CAN'T PIN THIS ONE ON ME.
WHERE HAVE WE HEARD THAT BEFORE?
WHAT DO YOU THINK?
I THINK I BELIEVE HIM.
ME, TOO.
NOW WHAT? WE'VE ELIMINATED OUR TWO PRIME SUSPECTS.
IF IT WASN'T FILTHY RICH OR SAND TRAP, THEN WHO?
THAT'S IT FOR TODAY, MAYOR.
I'LL BE BACK TOMORROW TO FINISH UP.
THANKS, FIRE STREAK.
IN THE MEANTIME, WE'LL HAVE A PONY ON SECURITY DETAIL.
ALIGHT, SUPER SLEUTHS. IT'S TIME FOR US TO INVESTIGATE THE SCENE.
MEET ME BACK HERE AFTER DARK!

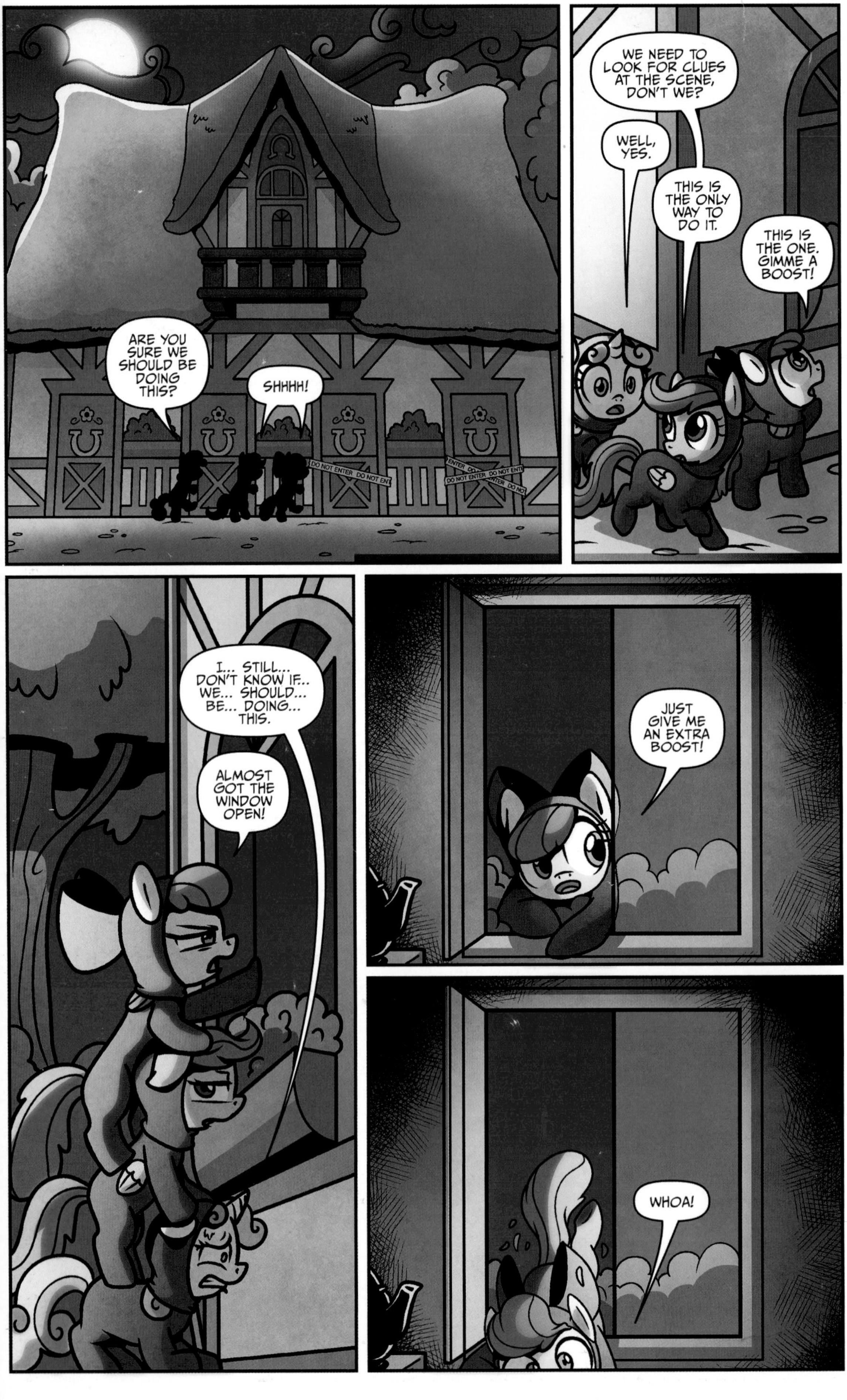
ARE YOU SURE WE SHOULD BE DOING THIS?
SHHHH!
DO NOT ENTER DO NOT ENT
ENTER DO NOT ENTER DO NOT ENTER DO NOT ENTER DO
WE NEED TO LOOK FOR CLUES AT THE SCENE, DON'T WE?
WELL, YES.
THIS IS THE ONLY WAY TO DO IT.
THIS IS THE ONE. GIMME A BOOST!
I... STILL... DON'T KNOW IF... WE... SHOULD... BE... DOING... THIS.
ALMOST GOT THE WINDOW OPEN!
JUST GIVE ME AN EXTRA BOOST!
WHOA!

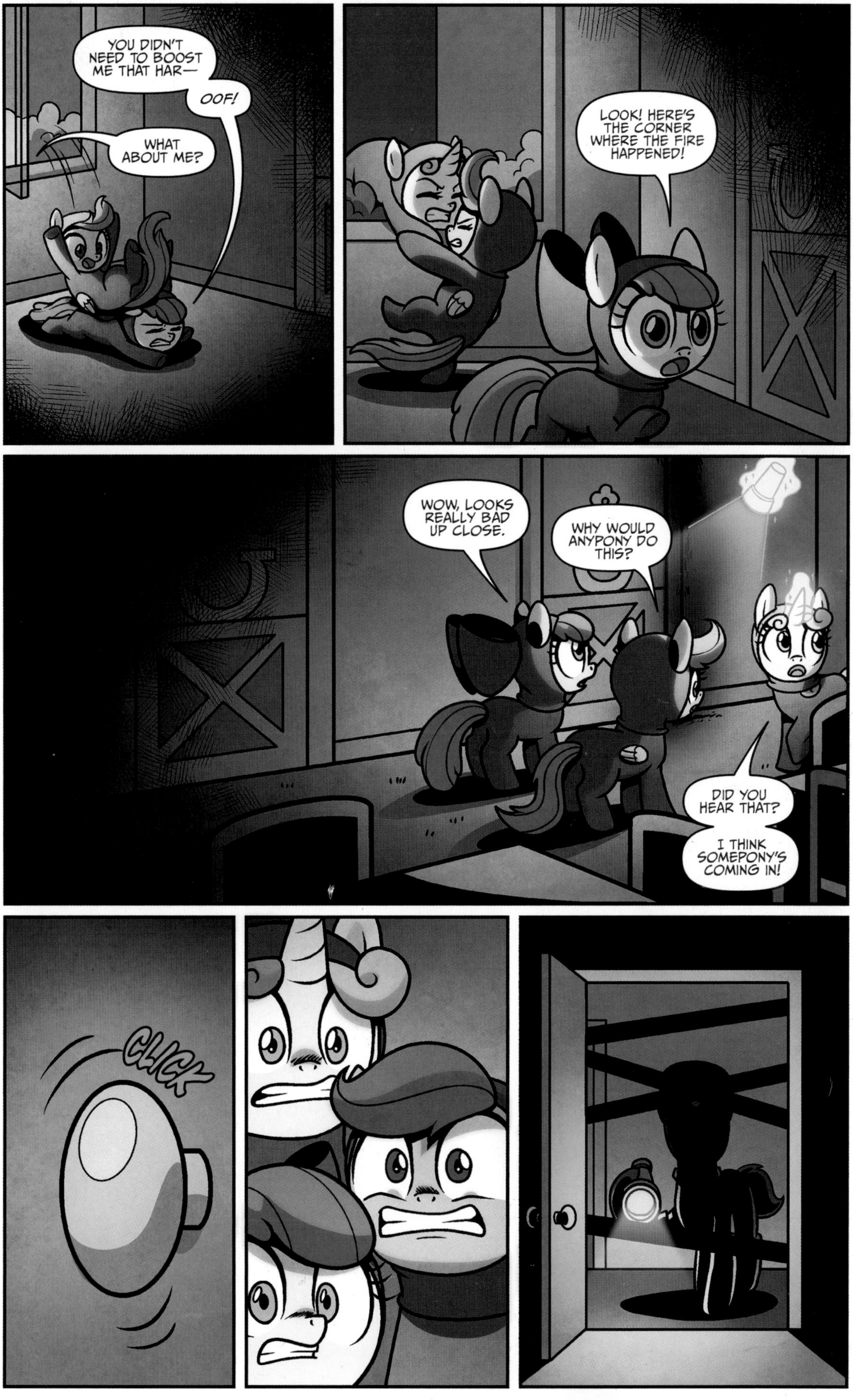
YOU DIDN'T NEED TO BOOST ME THAT HAR—
OOF!
WHAT ABOUT ME?
LOOK! HERE'S THE CORNER WHERE THE FIRE HAPPENED!
WOW, LOOKS REALLY BAD UP CLOSE.
WHY WOULD ANYPONY DO THIS?
DID YOU HEAR THAT?
I THINK SOMEPONY'S COMING IN!
CLICK

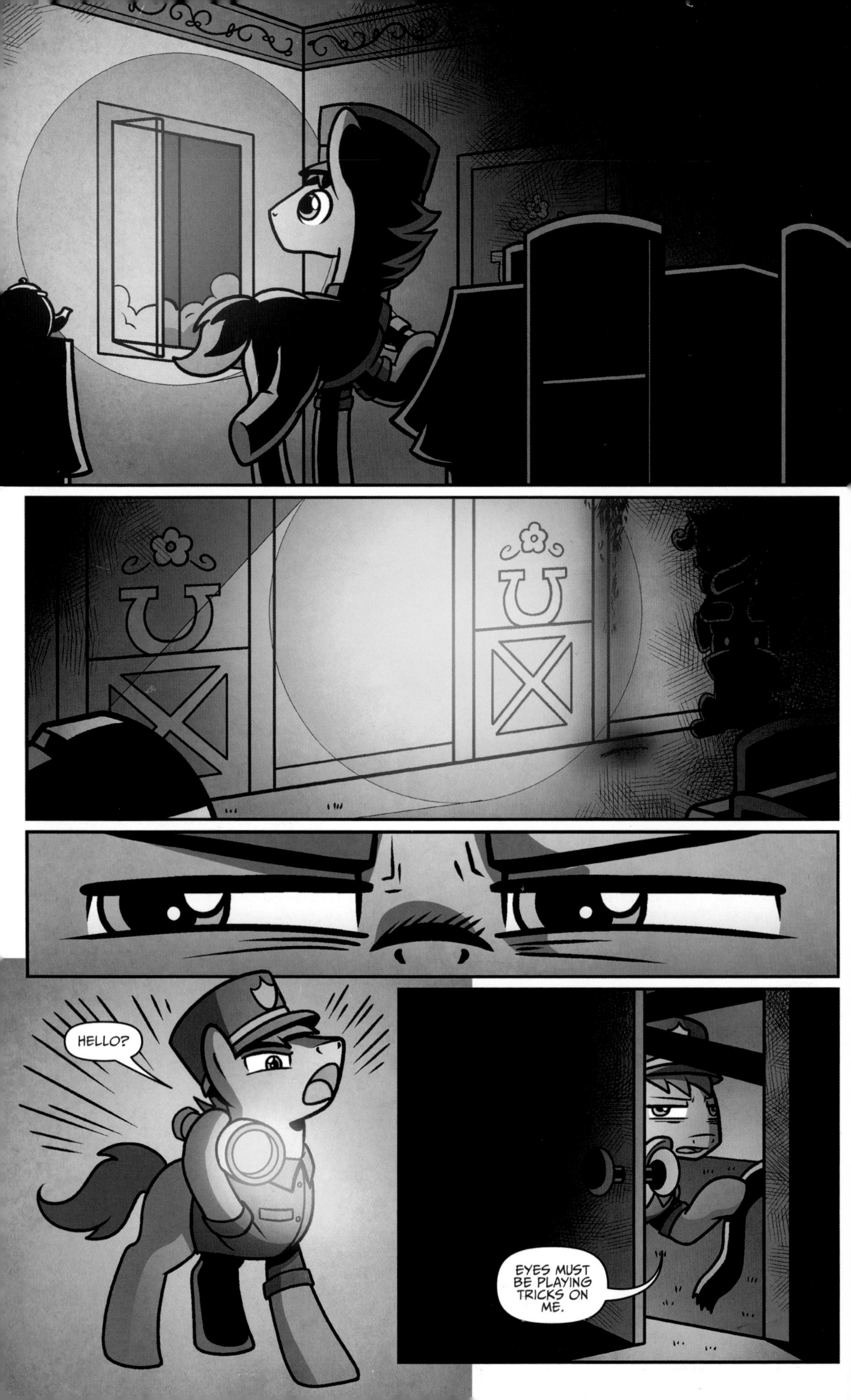
HELLO?
EYES MUST BE PLAYING TRICKS ON ME.

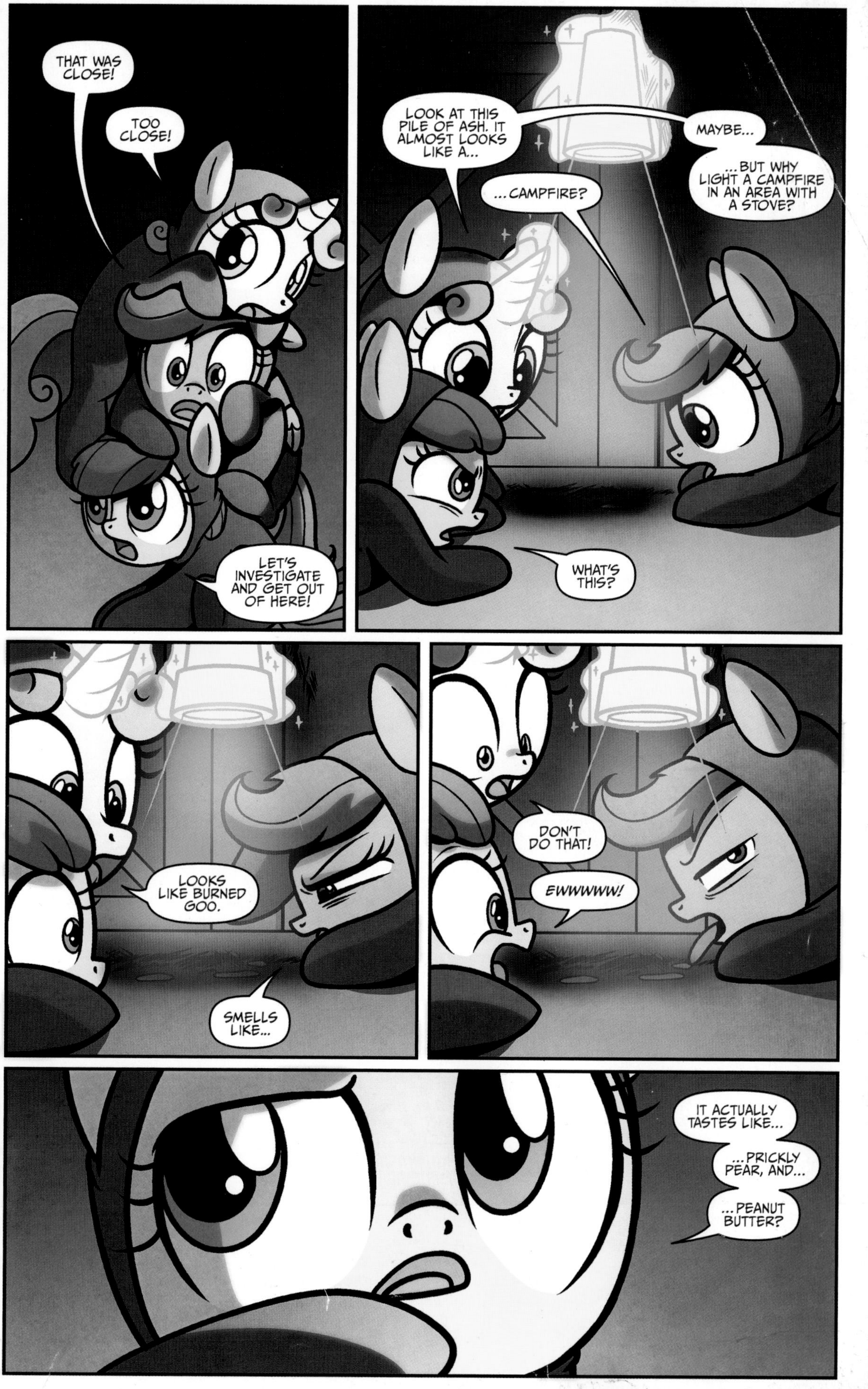
THAT WAS CLOSE!
TOO CLOSE!
LET'S INVESTIGATE AND GET OUT OF HERE!
WHAT'S THIS?
LOOK AT THIS PILE OF ASH. IT ALMOST LOOKS LIKE A...
...CAMPFIRE?
MAYBE...
...BUT WHY LIGHT A CAMPFIRE IN AN AREA WITH A STOVE?
LOOKS LIKE BURNED GOO.
SMELLS LIKE...
DON'T DO THAT!
EWWWWW!
IT ACTUALLY TASTES LIKE...
...PRICKLY PEAR, AND...
...PEANUT BUTTER?

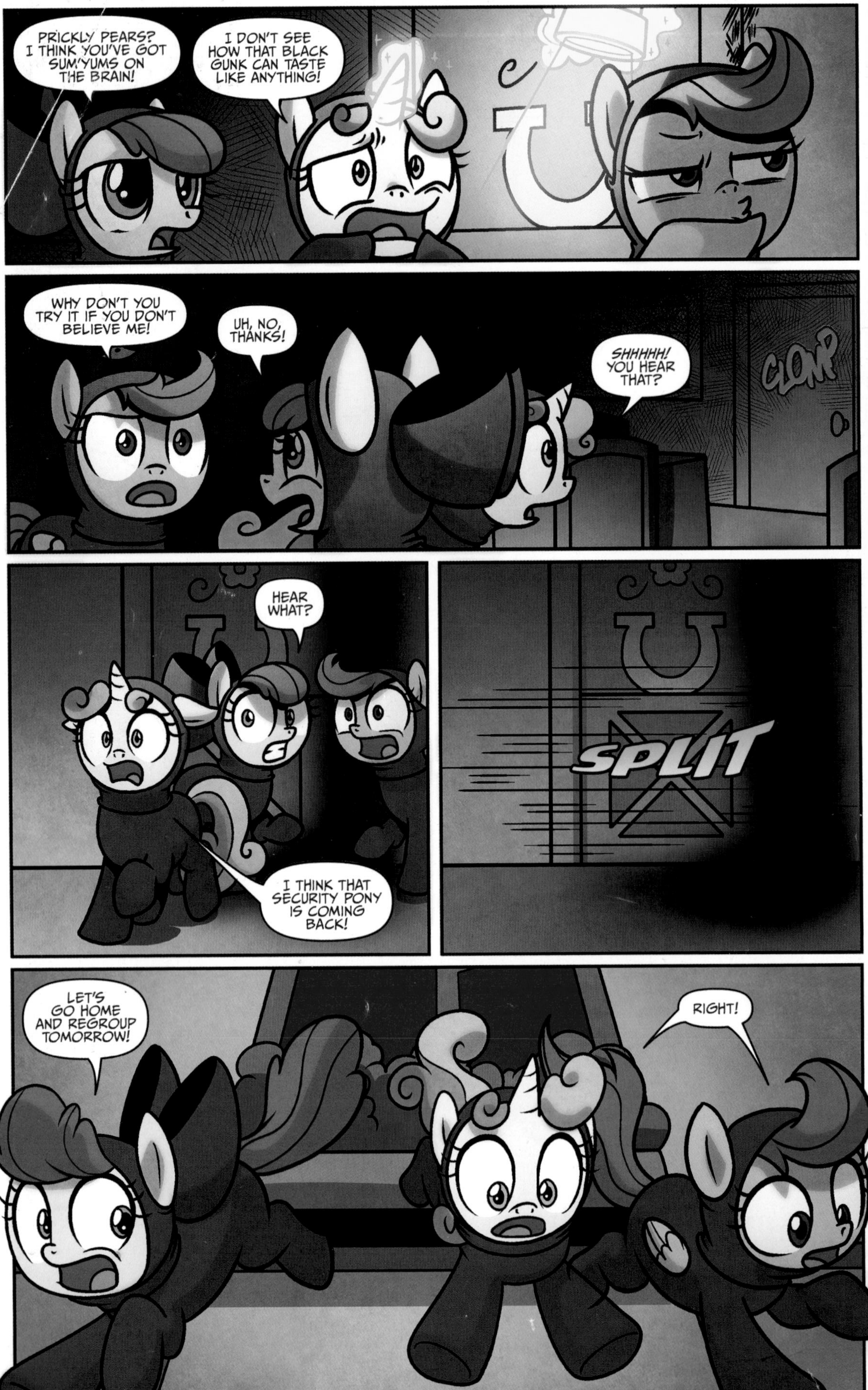
PRICKLY PEARS? I THINK YOU'VE GOT SUM'YUMS ON THE BRAIN!
I DON'T SEE HOW THAT BLACK GUNK CAN TASTE LIKE ANYTHING!
WHY DON'T YOU TRY IT IF YOU DON'T BELIEVE ME!
UH, NO, THANKS!
SHHHHH! YOU HEAR THAT?
CLONP
HEAR WHAT?
I THINK THAT SECURITY PONY IS COMING BACK!
SPLIT
LET'S GO HOME AND REGROUP TOMORROW!
RIGHT!

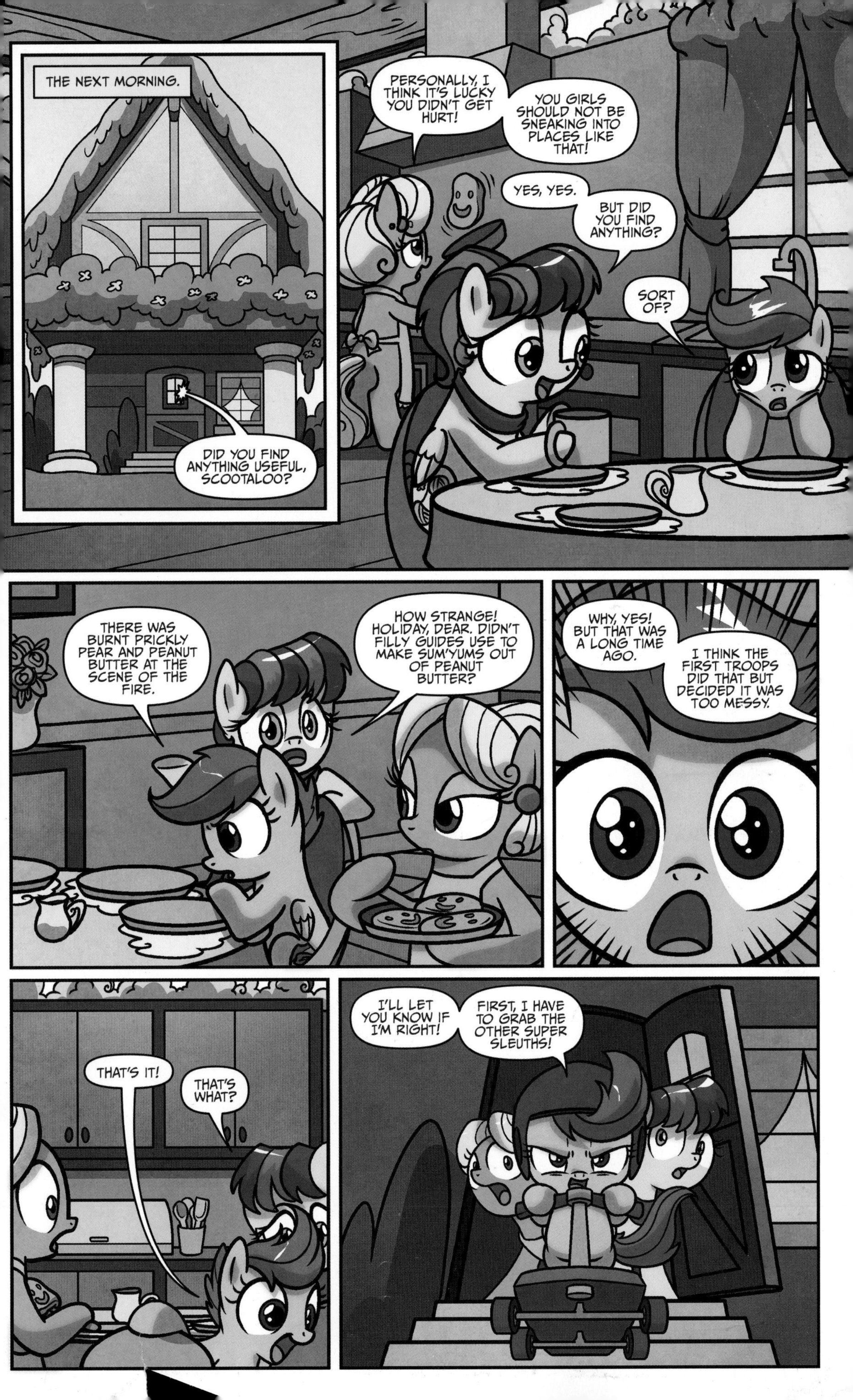
THE NEXT MORNING.
DID YOU FIND ANYTHING USEFUL, SCOOTALOO?
PERSONALLY, I THINK IT'S LUCKY YOU DIDN'T GET HURT!
YOU GIRLS SHOULD NOT BE SNEAKING INTO PLACES LIKE THAT!
YES, YES.
BUT DID YOU FIND ANYTHING?
SORT OF?
THERE WAS BURNT PRICKLY PEAR AND PEANUT BUTTER AT THE SCENE OF THE FIRE.
HOW STRANGE! HOLIDAY, DEAR. DIDN'T FILLY GUIDES USE TO MAKE SUM'YUMS OUT OF PEANUT BUTTER?
WHY, YES! BUT THAT WAS A LONG TIME AGO.
I THINK THE FIRST TROOPS DID THAT BUT DECIDED IT WAS TOO MESSY.
THAT'S IT!
THAT'S WHAT?
I'LL LET YOU KNOW IF I'M RIGHT!
FIRST, I HAVE TO GRAB THE OTHER SUPER SLEUTHS!

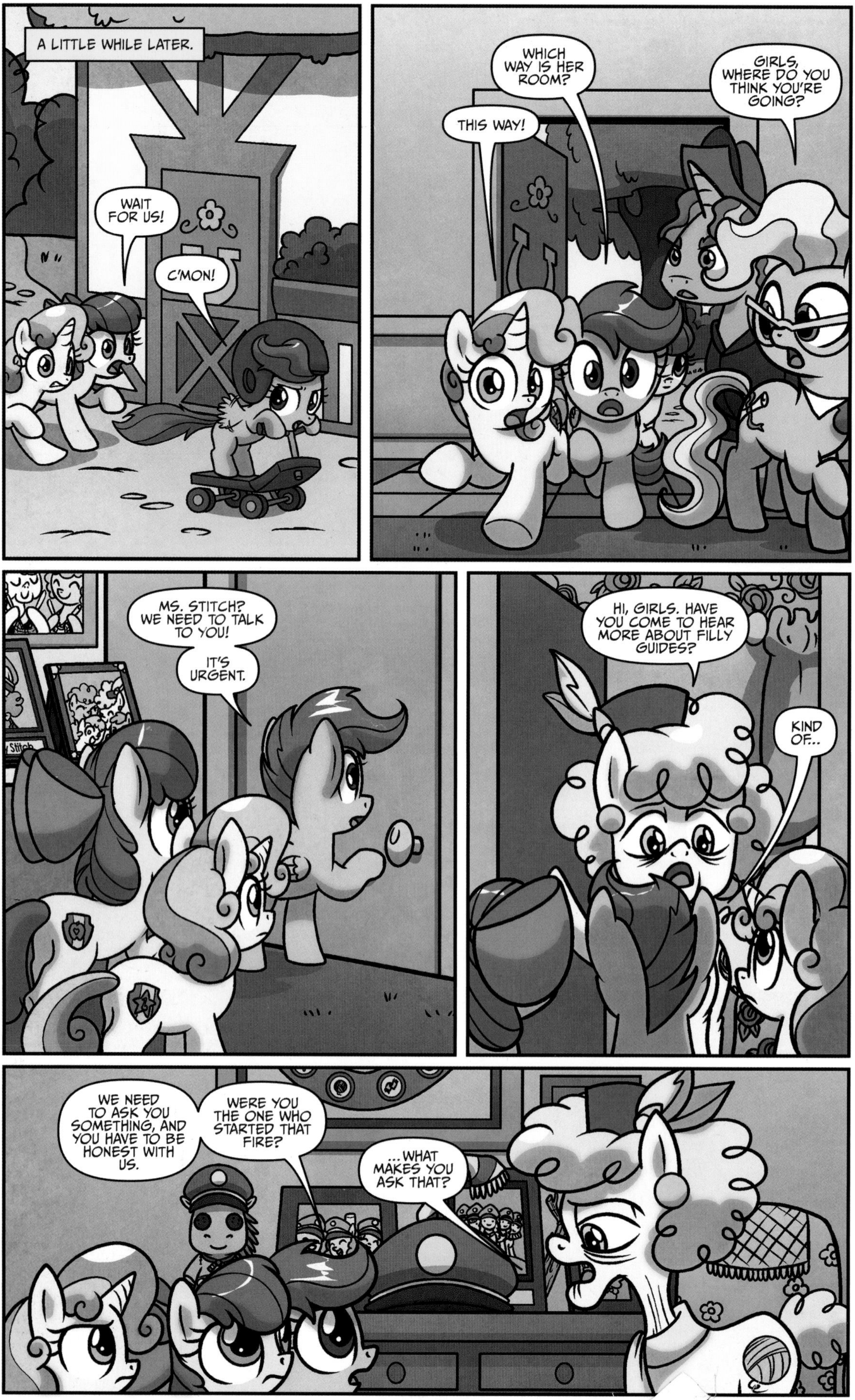
A LITTLE WHILE LATER.
WAIT FOR US!
C'MON!
WHICH WAY IS HER ROOM?
THIS WAY!
GIRLS, WHERE DO YOU THINK YOU'RE GOING?
MS. STITCH? WE NEED TO TALK TO YOU!
IT'S URGENT.
HI, GIRLS. HAVE YOU COME TO HEAR MORE ABOUT FILLY GUIDES?
KIND OF...
WE NEED TO ASK YOU SOMETHING, AND YOU HAVE TO BE HONEST WITH US.
WERE YOU THE ONE WHO STARTED THAT FIRE?
...WHAT MAKES YOU ASK THAT?

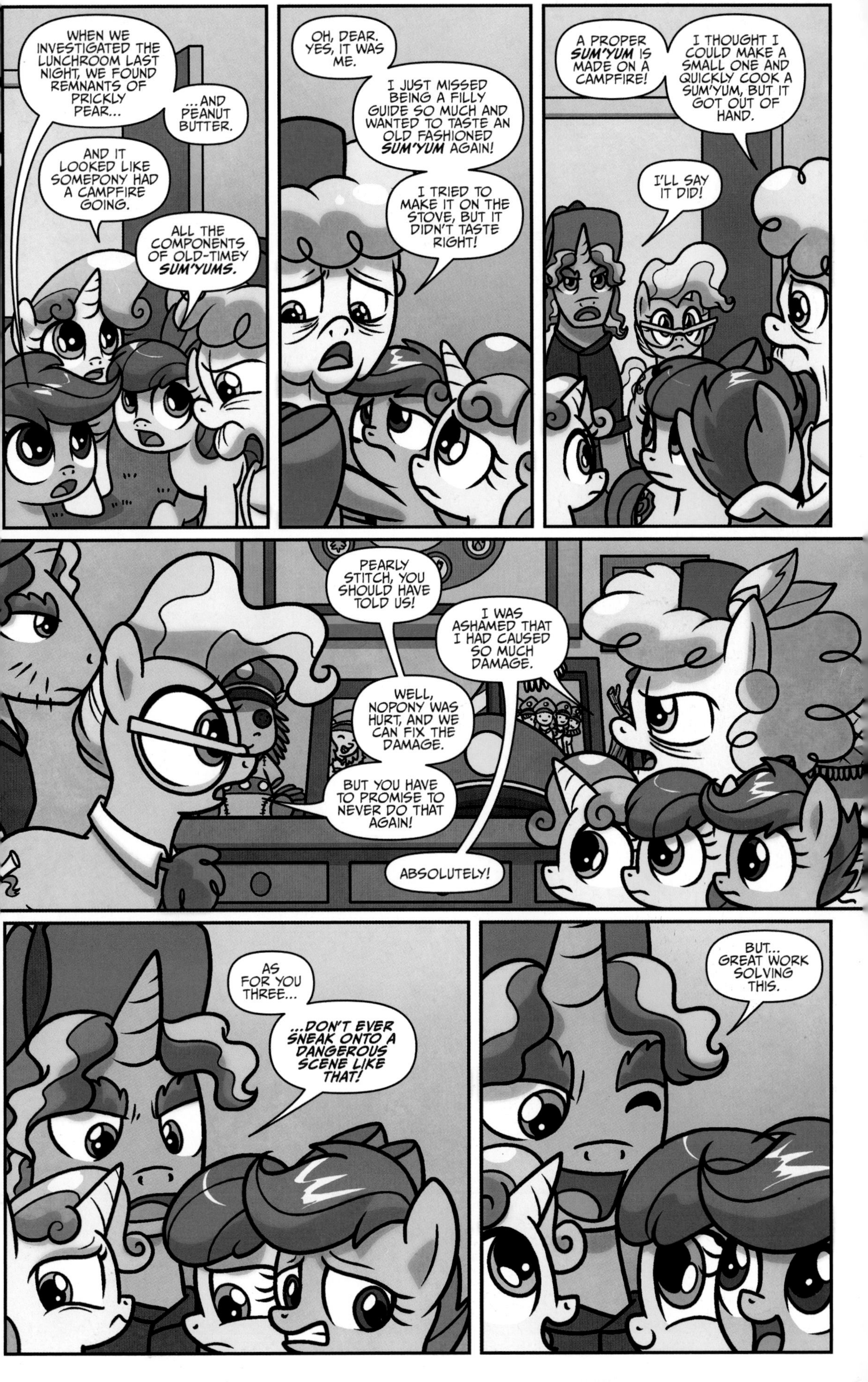
WHEN WE INVESTIGATED THE LUNCHROOM LAST NIGHT, WE FOUND REMNANTS OF PRICKLY PEAR...
...AND PEANUT BUTTER.
AND IT LOOKED LIKE SOMEPONY HAD A CAMPFIRE GOING.
ALL THE COMPONENTS OF OLD-TIMEY SUM'YUMS.
OH, DEAR. YES, IT WAS ME.
I JUST MISSED BEING A FILLY GUIDE SO MUCH AND WANTED TO TASTE AN OLD FASHIONED SUM'YUM AGAIN!
I TRIED TO MAKE IT ON THE STOVE, BUT IT DIDN'T TASTE RIGHT!
A PROPER SUM'YUM IS MADE ON A CAMPFIRE!
I THOUGHT I COULD MAKE A SMALL ONE AND QUICKLY COOK A SUM'YUM, BUT IT GOT OUT OF HAND.
I'LL SAY IT DID!
PEARLY STITCH, YOU SHOULD HAVE TOLD US!
I WAS ASHAMED THAT I HAD CAUSED SO MUCH DAMAGE.
WELL, NOPONY WAS HURT, AND WE CAN FIX THE DAMAGE.
BUT YOU HAVE TO PROMISE TO NEVER DO THAT AGAIN!
ABSOLUTELY!
AS FOR YOU THREE...
...DON'T EVER SNEAK ONTO A DANGEROUS SCENE LIKE THAT!
BUT... GREAT WORK SOLVING THIS.

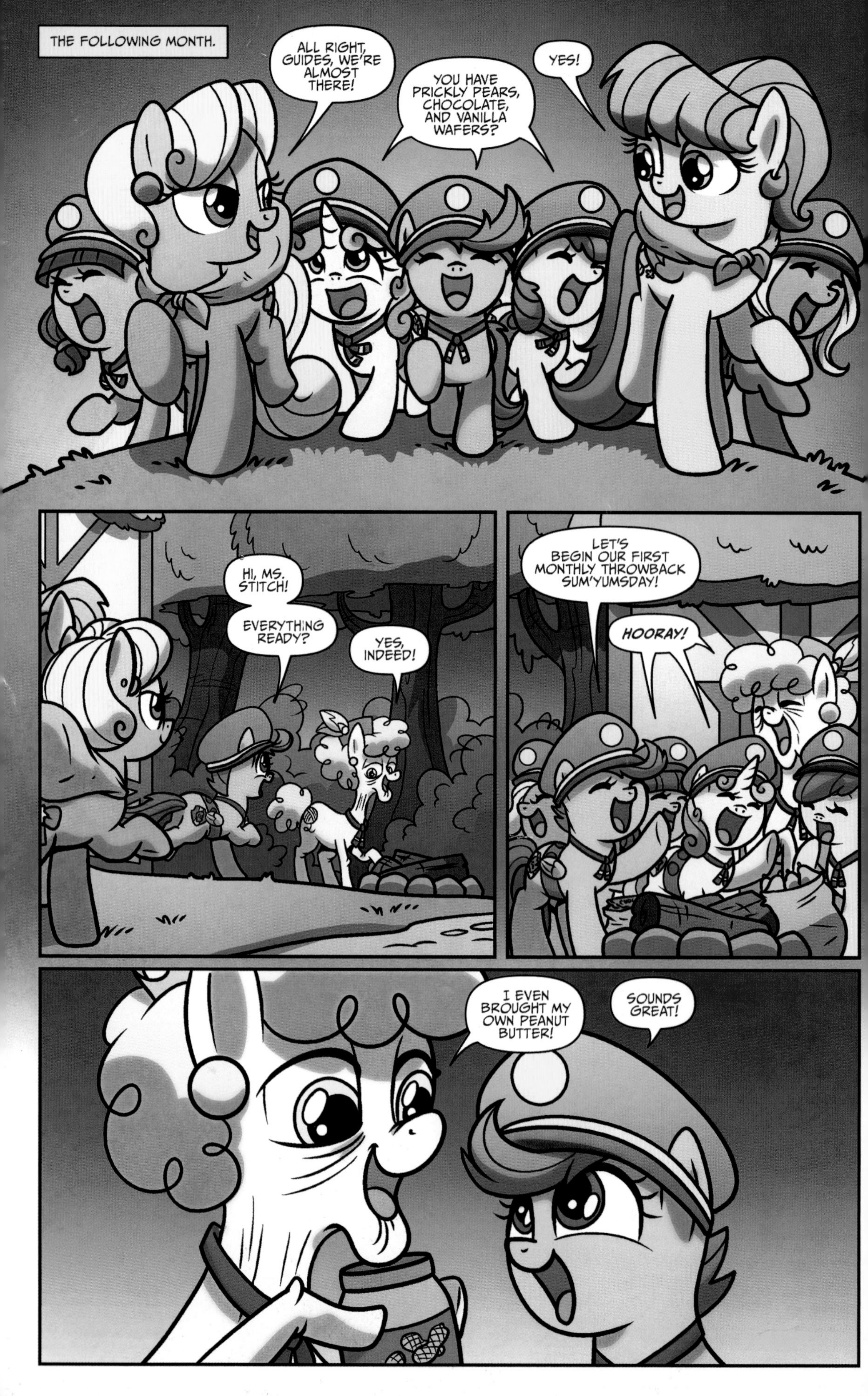
THE FOLLOWING MONTH.
ALL RIGHT, GUIDES, WE'RE ALMOST THERE!
YOU HAVE PRICKLY PEARS, CHOCOLATE, AND VANILLA WAFERS?
YES!
HI, MS. STITCH!
EVERYTHING READY?
YES, INDEED!
LET'S BEGIN OUR FIRST MONTHLY THROWBACK SUM'YUMSDAY!
HOORAY!
I EVEN BROUGHT MY OWN PEANUT BUTTER!
SOUNDS GREAT!

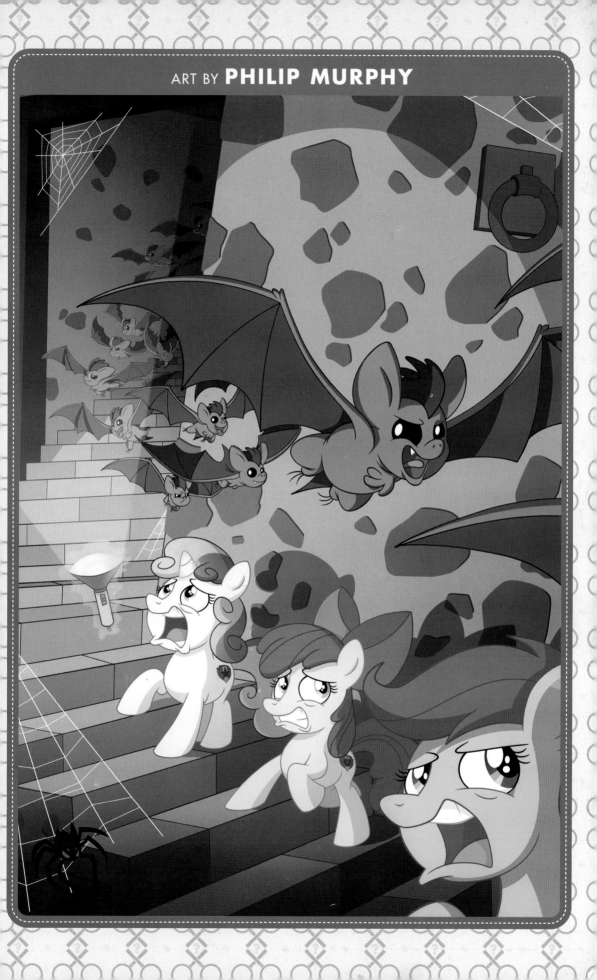

ART BY **PHILIP MURPHY**

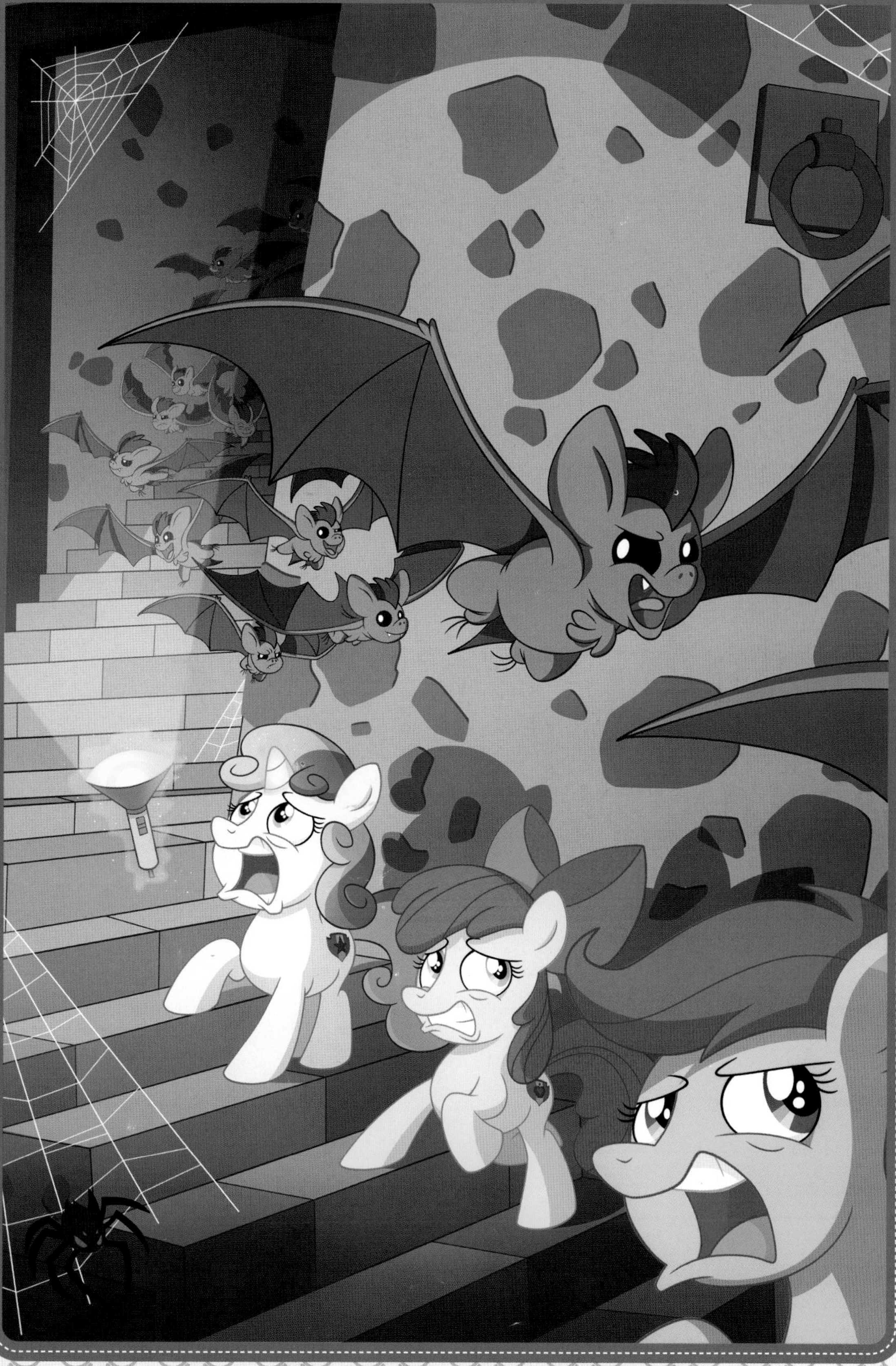

4

ART BY **AGNES GARBOWSKA**

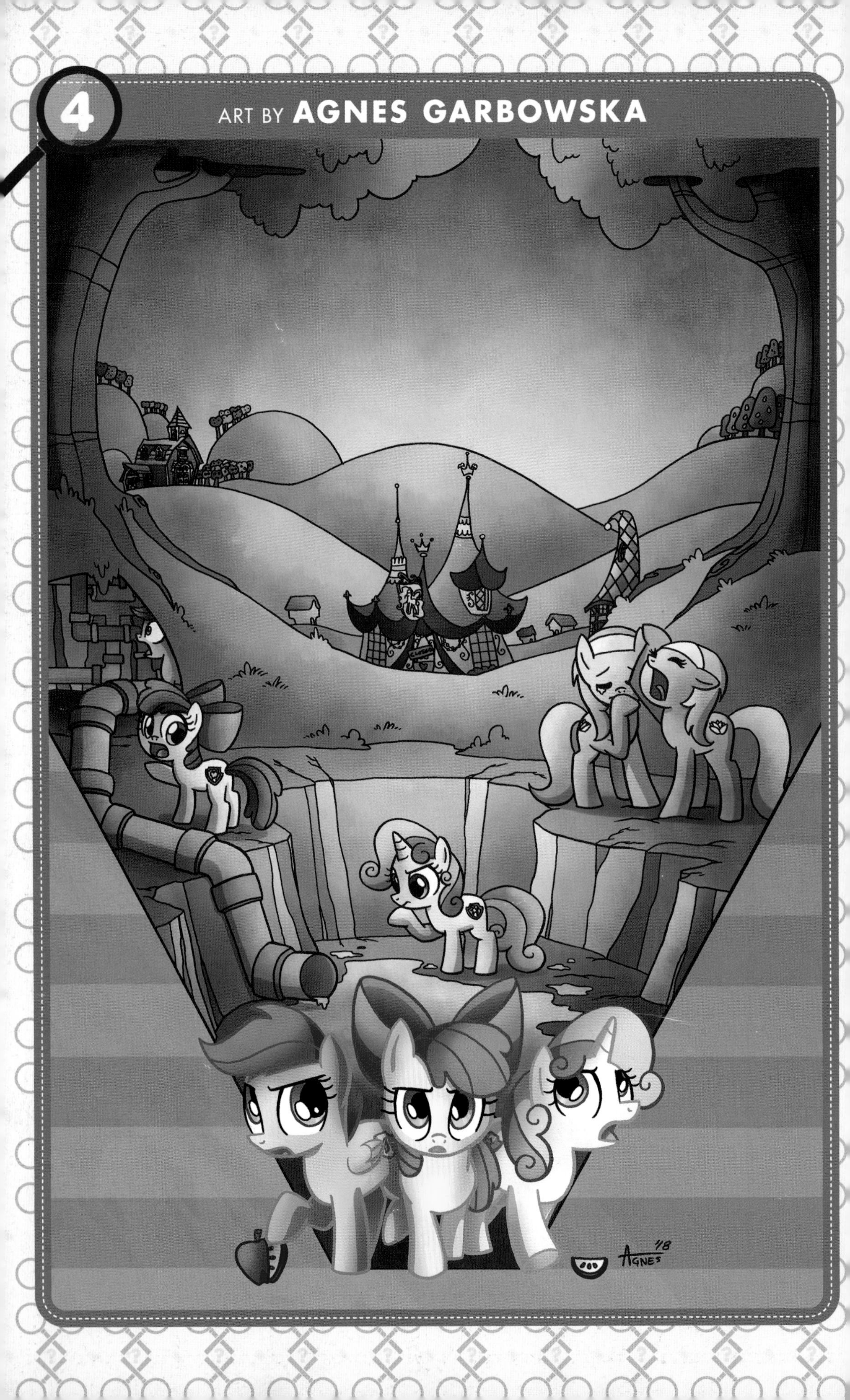
AGNES '18

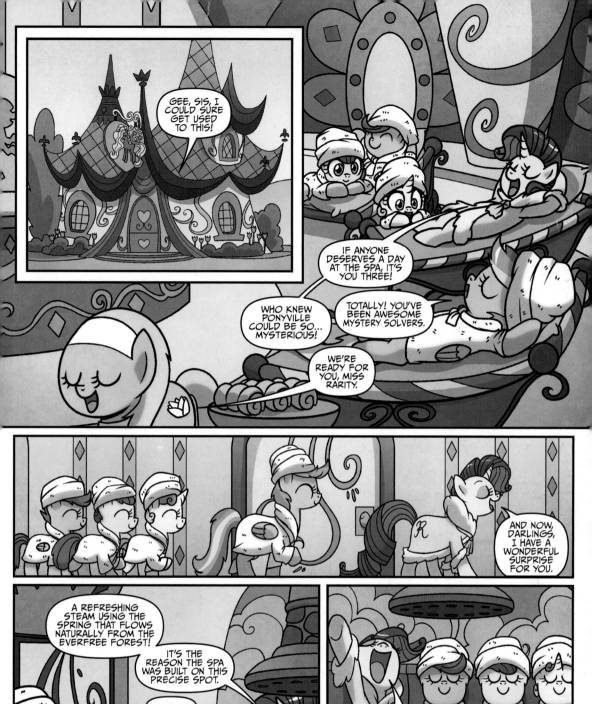

GEE, SIS, I COULD SURE GET USED TO THIS!

IF ANYONE DESERVES A DAY AT THE SPA, IT'S YOU THREE!

WHO KNEW PONYVILLE COULD BE SO... MYSTERIOUS!

TOTALLY! YOU'VE BEEN AWESOME MYSTERY SOLVERS.

WE'RE READY FOR YOU, MISS RARITY.

AND NOW, DARLINGS, I HAVE A WONDERFUL SURPRISE FOR YOU.

A REFRESHING STEAM USING THE SPRING THAT FLOWS NATURALLY FROM THE EVERFREE FOREST!

IT'S THE REASON THE SPA WAS BUILT ON THIS PRECISE SPOT.

OHHHHH!

RELEASE THE SPRING AND LET THE STEAMING BEGIN!

THAT'S ODD...

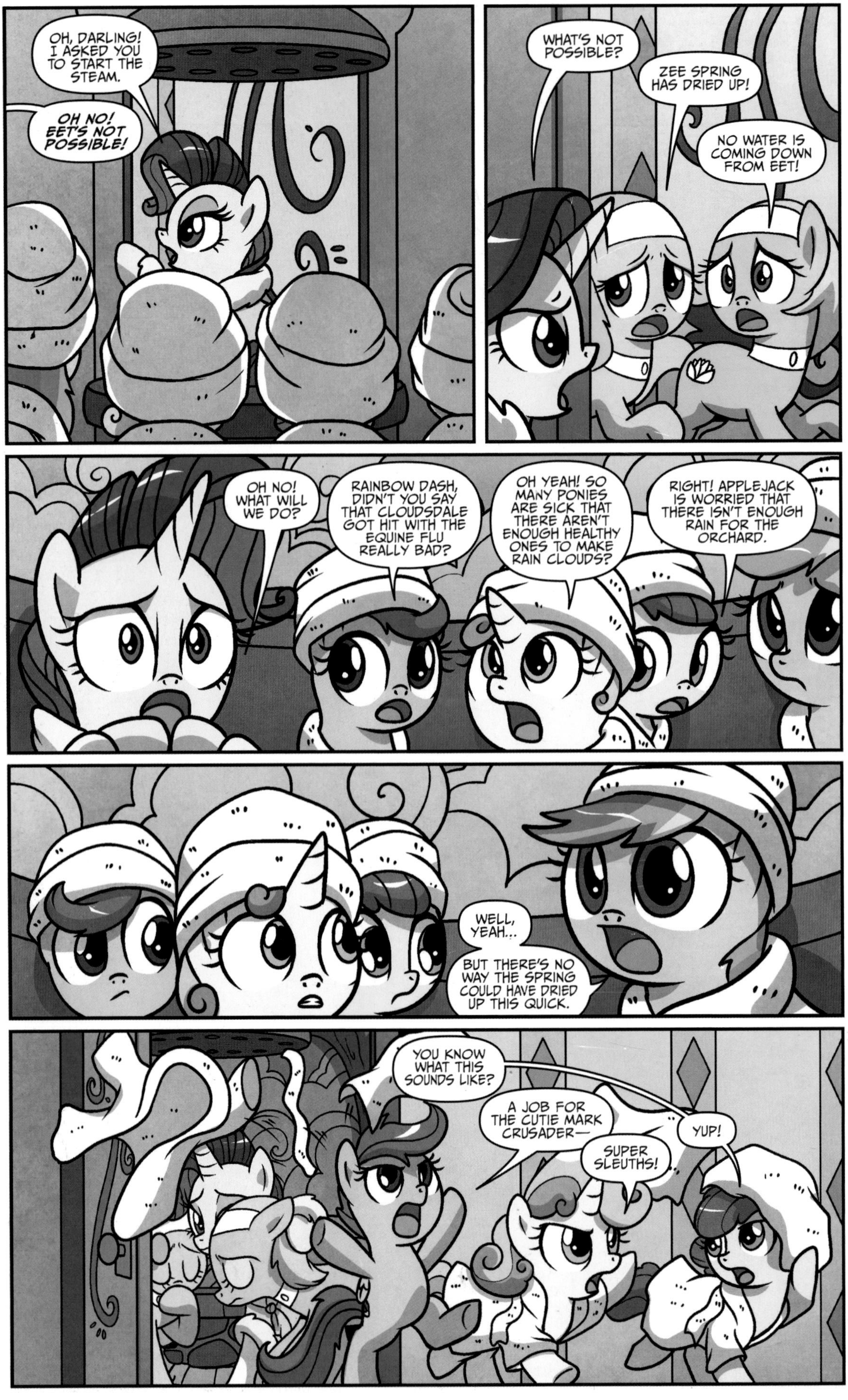
OH, DARLING! I ASKED YOU TO START THE STEAM.
OH NO! EET'S NOT POSSIBLE!
WHAT'S NOT POSSIBLE?
ZEE SPRING HAS DRIED UP!
NO WATER IS COMING DOWN FROM EET!
OH NO! WHAT WILL WE DO?
RAINBOW DASH, DIDN'T YOU SAY THAT CLOUDSDALE GOT HIT WITH THE EQUINE FLU REALLY BAD?
OH YEAH! SO MANY PONIES ARE SICK THAT THERE AREN'T ENOUGH HEALTHY ONES TO MAKE RAIN CLOUDS?
RIGHT! APPLEJACK IS WORRIED THAT THERE ISN'T ENOUGH RAIN FOR THE ORCHARD.
WELL, YEAH...
BUT THERE'S NO WAY THE SPRING COULD HAVE DRIED UP THIS QUICK.
YOU KNOW WHAT THIS SOUNDS LIKE?
A JOB FOR THE CUTIE MARK CRUSADER—
SUPER SLEUTHS!
YUP!

WHICH WAY TO THE SPRING?

THAT WAY!

ARE YOU SURE?

...NO.

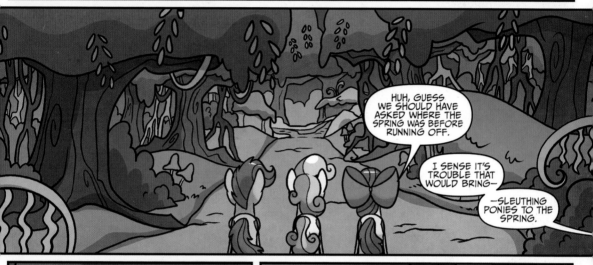

HUH, GUESS WE SHOULD HAVE ASKED WHERE THE SPRING WAS BEFORE RUNNING OFF.

I SENSE IT'S TROUBLE THAT WOULD BRING—

—SLEUTHING PONIES TO THE SPRING.

ZECORA! ARE WE GLAD TO SEE YOU!

SO YOU KNOW THE WAY TO THE NATURAL SPRING?

THE NATURAL WONDER OF WHICH YOU SPEAK—

—WILL SHOW ITSELF BEYOND THE CREEK.

THANK YOU, BYE!

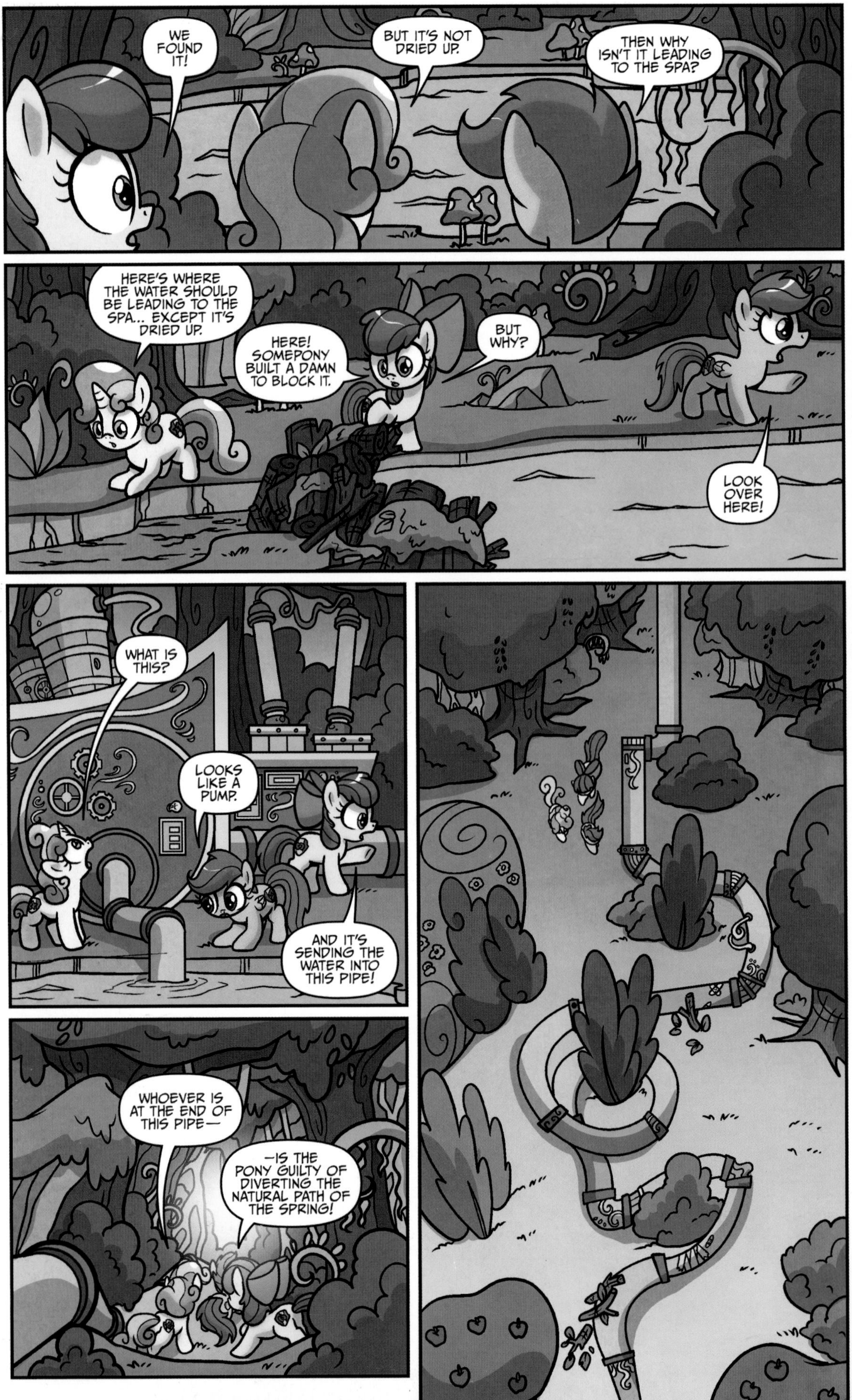
WE FOUND IT!
BUT IT'S NOT DRIED UP.
THEN WHY ISN'T IT LEADING TO THE SPA?
HERE'S WHERE THE WATER SHOULD BE LEADING TO THE SPA... EXCEPT IT'S DRIED UP.
HERE! SOMEPONY BUILT A DAMN TO BLOCK IT.
BUT WHY?
LOOK OVER HERE!
WHAT IS THIS?
LOOKS LIKE A PUMP.
AND IT'S SENDING THE WATER INTO THIS PIPE!
WHOEVER IS AT THE END OF THIS PIPE—
—IS THE PONY GUILTY OF DIVERTING THE NATURAL PATH OF THE SPRING!

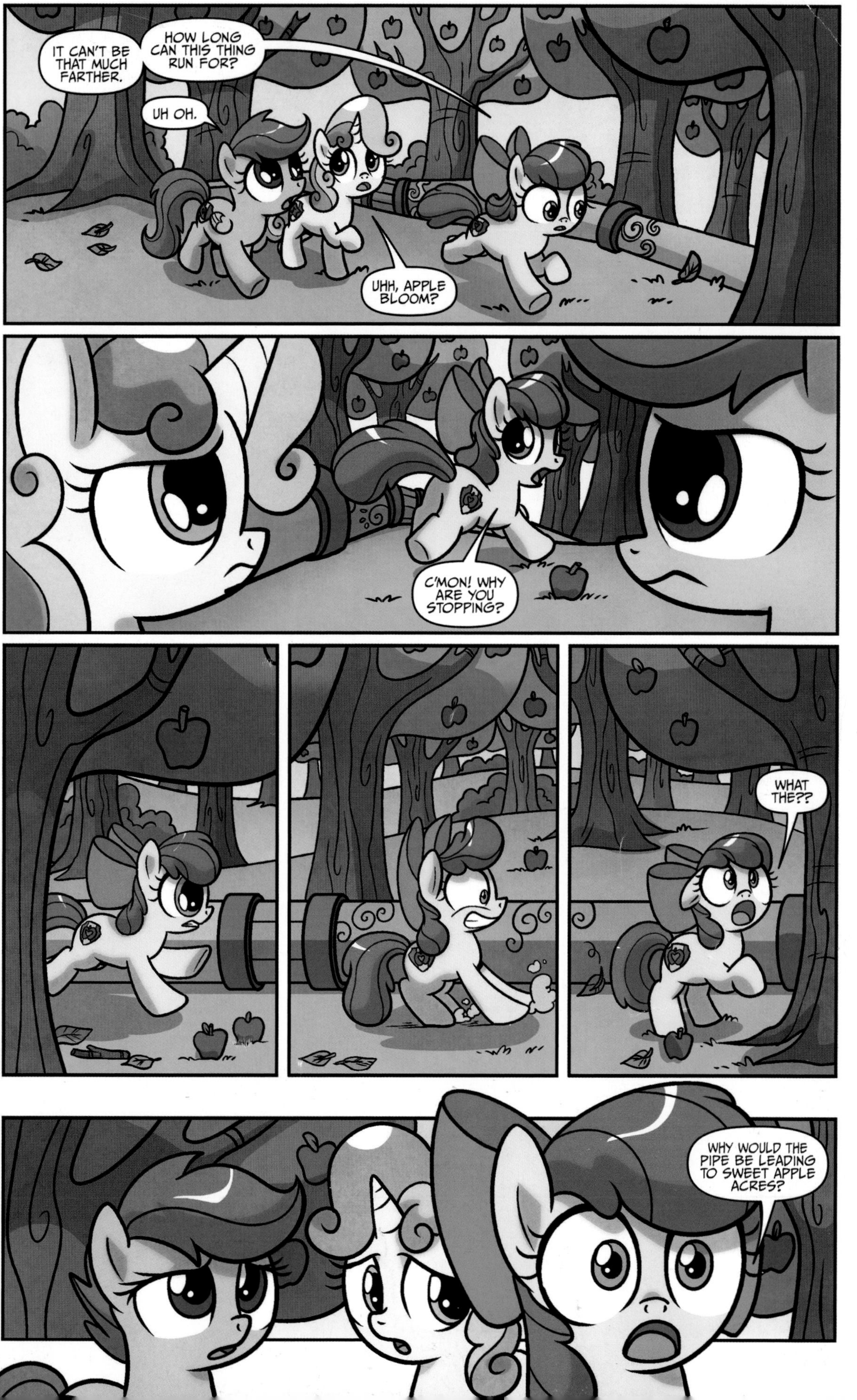
IT CAN'T BE THAT MUCH FARTHER.
HOW LONG CAN THIS THING RUN FOR?
UH OH.
UHH, APPLE BLOOM?
C'MON! WHY ARE YOU STOPPING?
WHAT THE??
WHY WOULD THE PIPE BE LEADING TO SWEET APPLE ACRES?

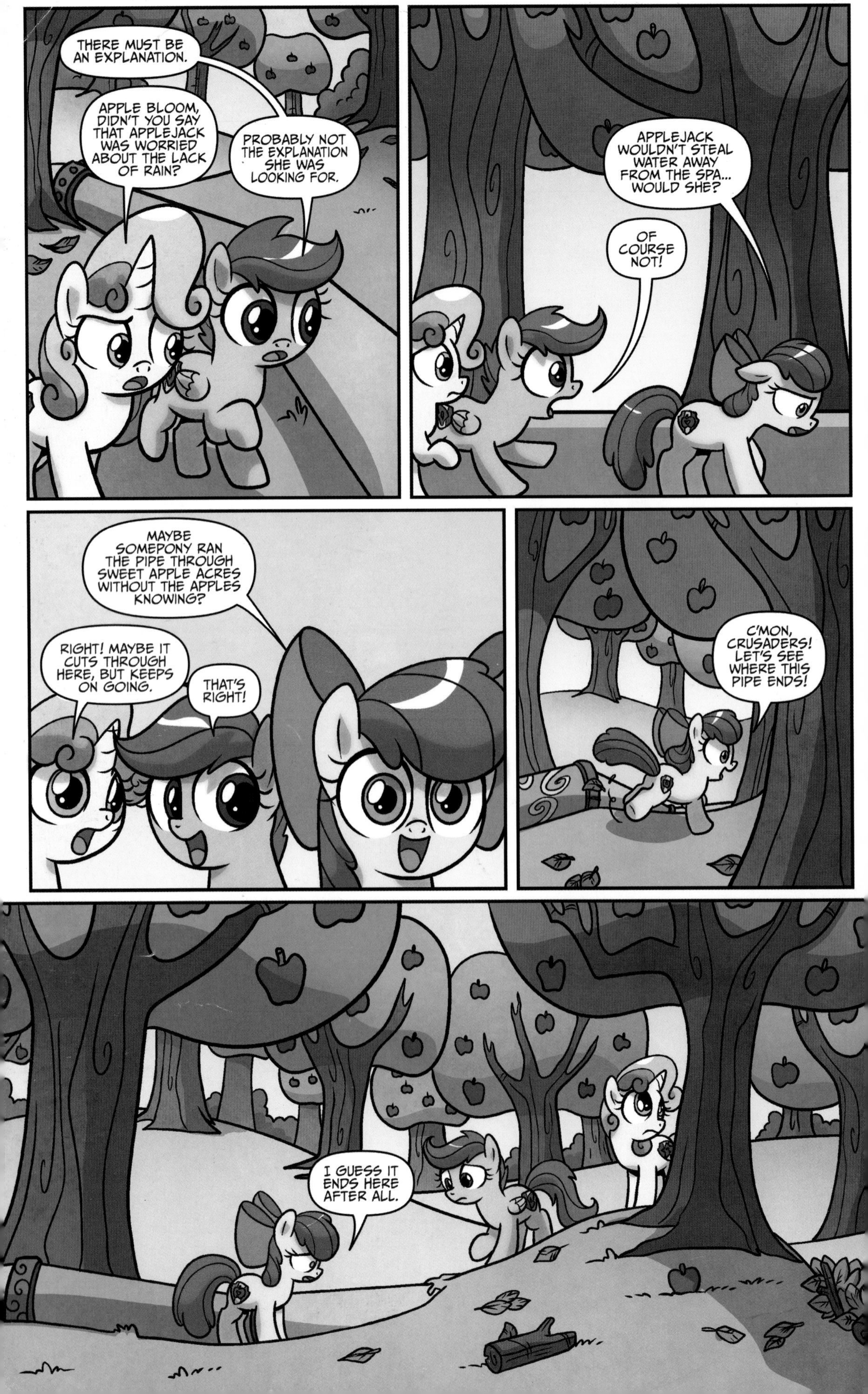
THERE MUST BE AN EXPLANATION.
APPLE BLOOM, DIDN'T YOU SAY THAT APPLEJACK WAS WORRIED ABOUT THE LACK OF RAIN?
PROBABLY NOT THE EXPLANATION SHE WAS LOOKING FOR.
APPLEJACK WOULDN'T STEAL WATER AWAY FROM THE SPA... WOULD SHE?
OF COURSE NOT!
MAYBE SOMEPONY RAN THE PIPE THROUGH SWEET APPLE ACRES WITHOUT THE APPLES KNOWING?
RIGHT! MAYBE IT CUTS THROUGH HERE, BUT KEEPS ON GOING.
THAT'S RIGHT!
C'MON, CRUSADERS! LET'S SEE WHERE THIS PIPE ENDS!
I GUESS IT ENDS HERE AFTER ALL.

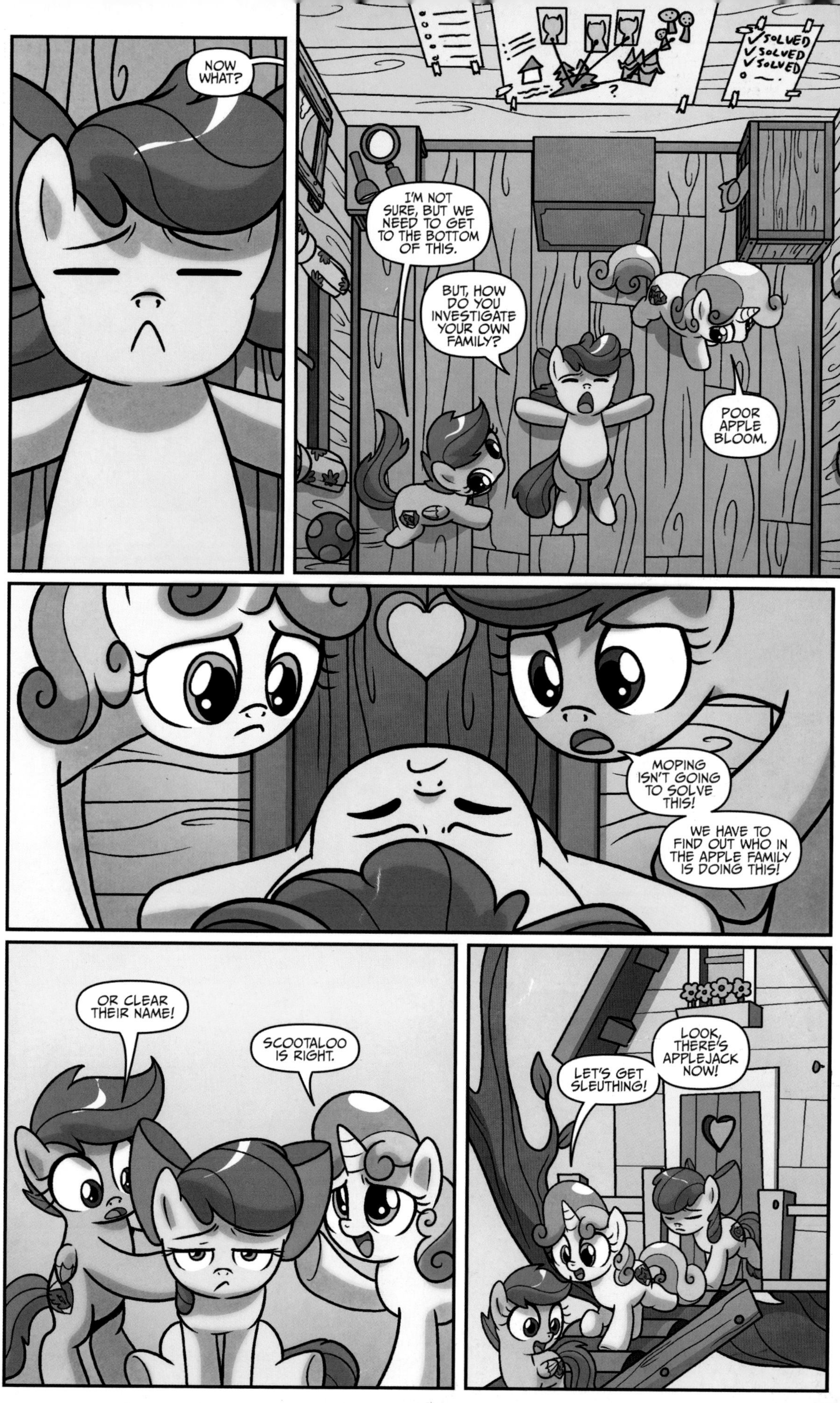

NOW WHAT?
✓SOLVED
✓SOLVED
✓SOLVED
I'M NOT SURE, BUT WE NEED TO GET TO THE BOTTOM OF THIS.
BUT, HOW DO YOU INVESTIGATE YOUR OWN FAMILY?
POOR APPLE BLOOM.
MOPING ISN'T GOING TO SOLVE THIS!
WE HAVE TO FIND OUT WHO IN THE APPLE FAMILY IS DOING THIS!
OR CLEAR THEIR NAME!
SCOOTALOO IS RIGHT.
LOOK, THERE'S APPLEJACK NOW!
LET'S GET SLEUTHING!

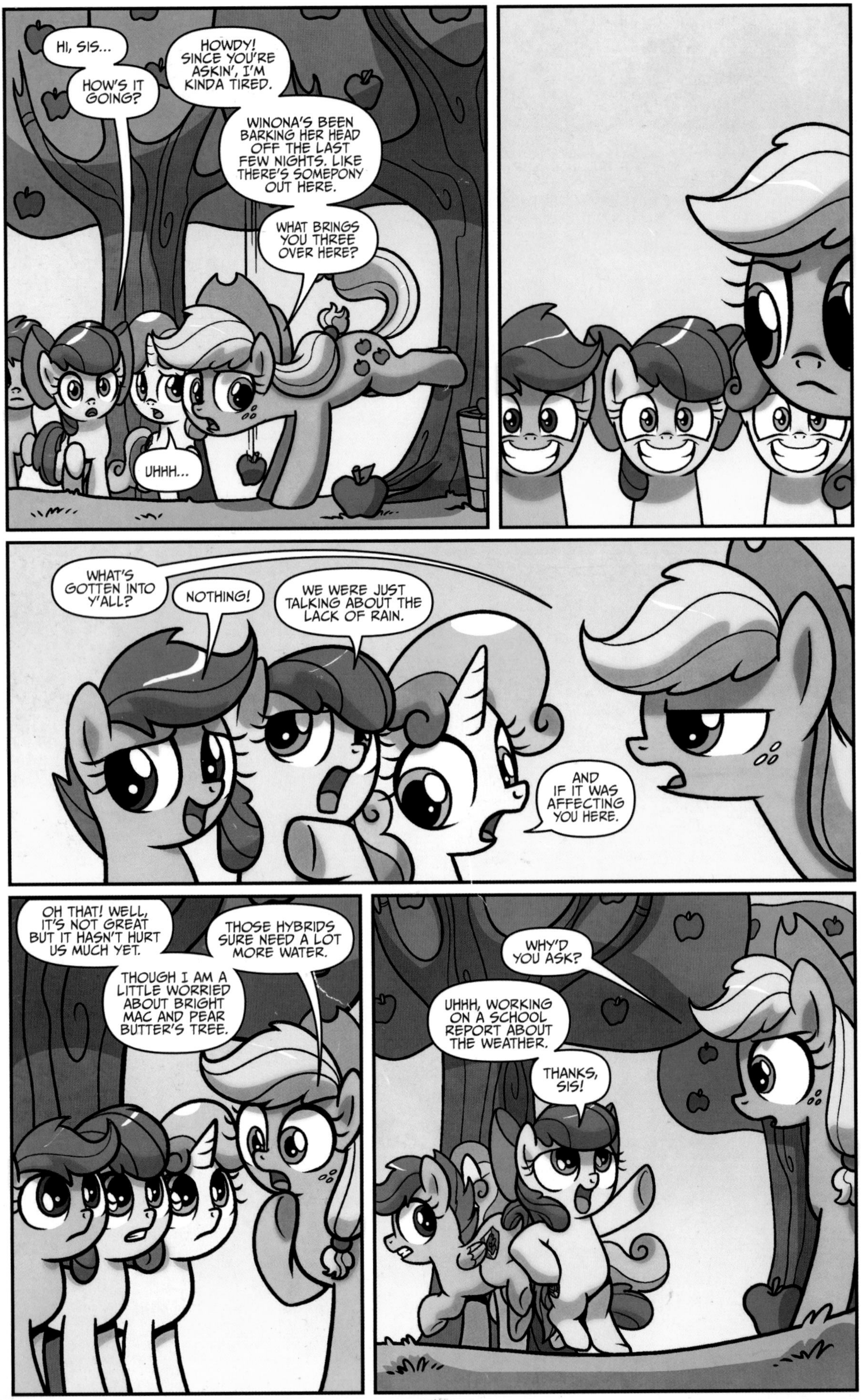
HI, SIS...
HOW'S IT GOING?
HOWDY! SINCE YOU'RE ASKIN', I'M KINDA TIRED.
WINONA'S BEEN BARKING HER HEAD OFF THE LAST FEW NIGHTS. LIKE THERE'S SOMEPONY OUT HERE.
WHAT BRINGS YOU THREE OVER HERE?
UHHH...
WHAT'S GOTTEN INTO Y'ALL?
NOTHING!
WE WERE JUST TALKING ABOUT THE LACK OF RAIN.
AND IF IT WAS AFFECTING YOU HERE.
OH THAT! WELL, IT'S NOT GREAT BUT IT HASN'T HURT US MUCH YET.
THOSE HYBRIDS SURE NEED A LOT MORE WATER.
THOUGH I AM A LITTLE WORRIED ABOUT BRIGHT MAC AND PEAR BUTTER'S TREE.
WHY'D YOU ASK?
UHHH, WORKING ON A SCHOOL REPORT ABOUT THE WEATHER.
THANKS, SIS!

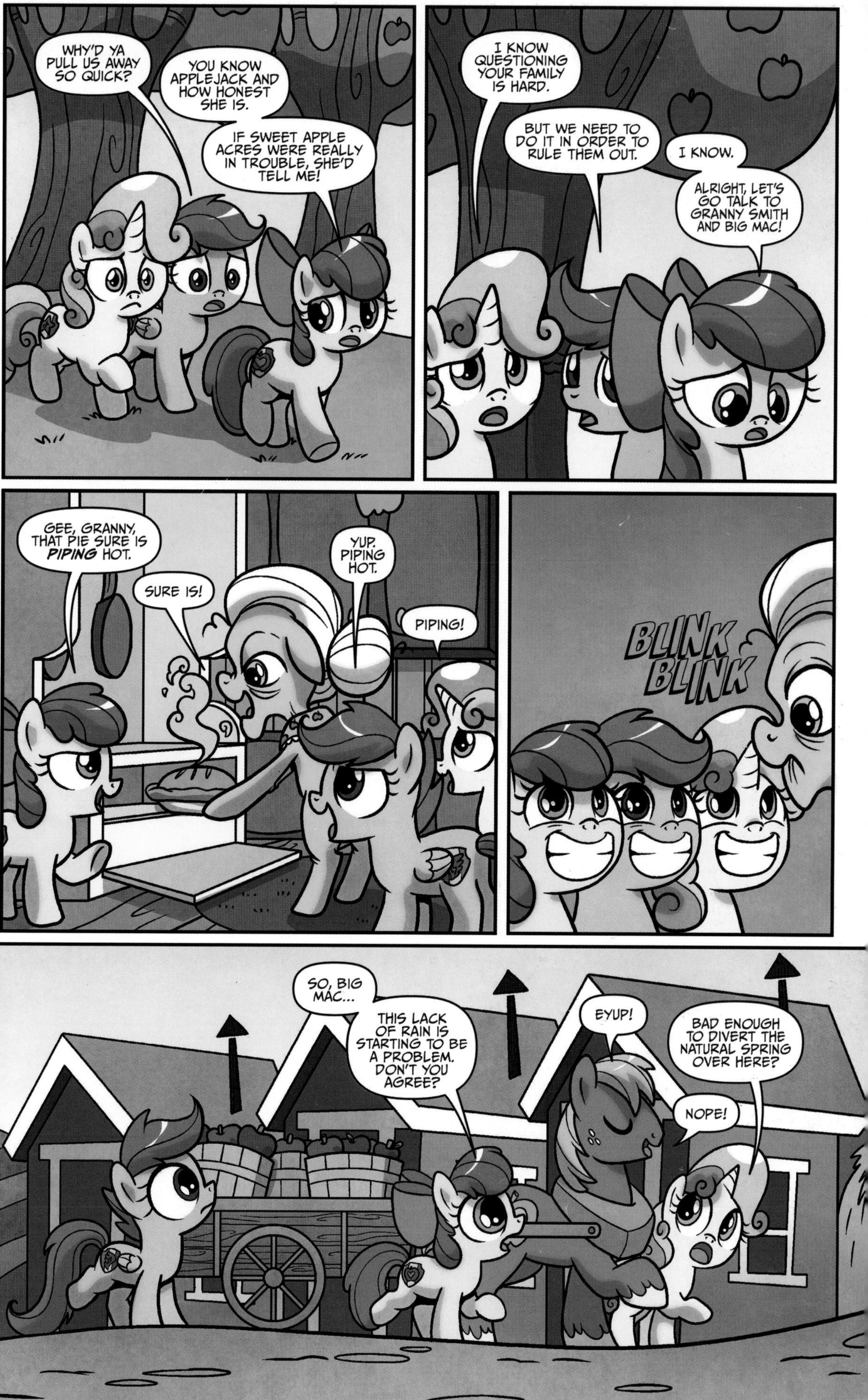
WHY'D YA PULL US AWAY SO QUICK?
YOU KNOW APPLEJACK AND HOW HONEST SHE IS.
IF SWEET APPLE ACRES WERE REALLY IN TROUBLE, SHE'D TELL ME!
I KNOW QUESTIONING YOUR FAMILY IS HARD.
BUT WE NEED TO DO IT IN ORDER TO RULE THEM OUT.
I KNOW.
ALRIGHT, LET'S GO TALK TO GRANNY SMITH AND BIG MAC!
GEE, GRANNY, THAT PIE SURE IS PIPING HOT.
SURE IS!
YUP. PIPING HOT.
PIPING!
BLINK BLINK
SO, BIG MAC...
THIS LACK OF RAIN IS STARTING TO BE A PROBLEM. DON'T YOU AGREE?
EYUP!
BAD ENOUGH TO DIVERT THE NATURAL SPRING OVER HERE?
NOPE!

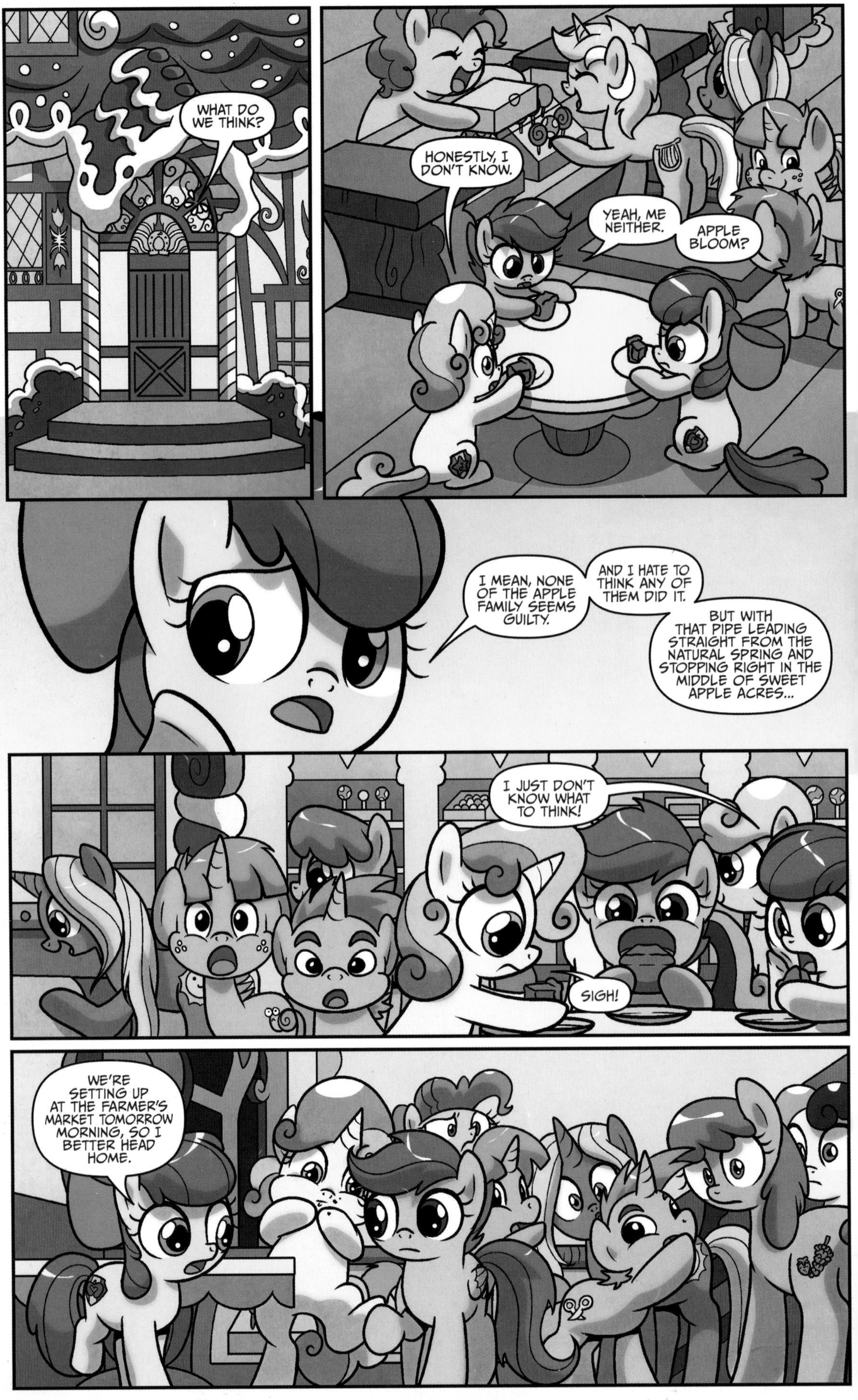
WHAT DO WE THINK?
HONESTLY, I DON'T KNOW.
YEAH, ME NEITHER.
APPLE BLOOM?
I MEAN, NONE OF THE APPLE FAMILY SEEMS GUILTY.
AND I HATE TO THINK ANY OF THEM DID IT.
BUT WITH THAT PIPE LEADING STRAIGHT FROM THE NATURAL SPRING AND STOPPING RIGHT IN THE MIDDLE OF SWEET APPLE ACRES...
I JUST DON'T KNOW WHAT TO THINK!
SIGH!
WE'RE SETTING UP AT THE FARMER'S MARKET TOMORROW MORNING, SO I BETTER HEAD HOME.

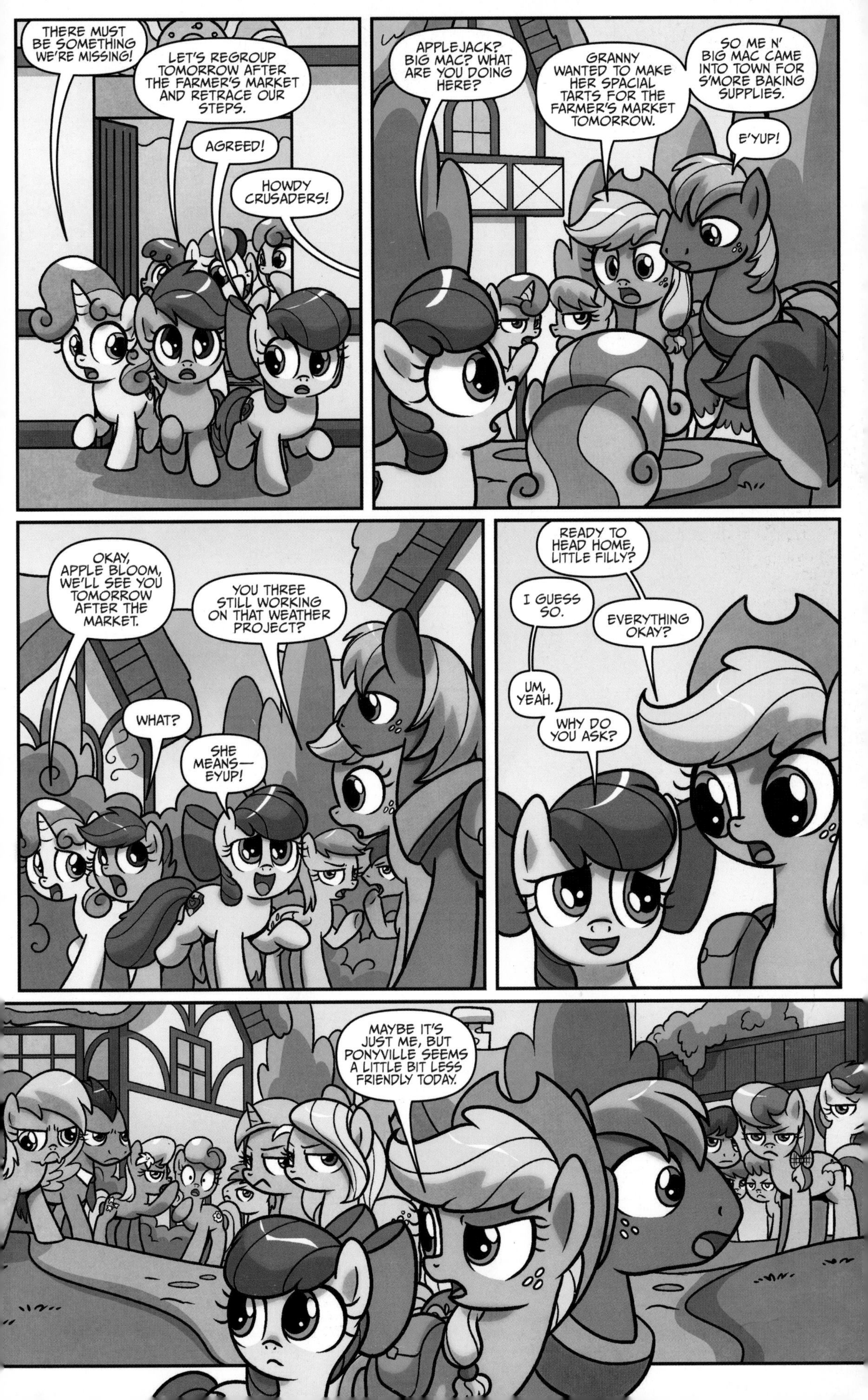
THERE MUST BE SOMETHING WE'RE MISSING!
LET'S REGROUP TOMORROW AFTER THE FARMER'S MARKET AND RETRACE OUR STEPS.
AGREED!
HOWDY CRUSADERS!
APPLEJACK? BIG MAC? WHAT ARE YOU DOING HERE?
GRANNY WANTED TO MAKE HER SPACIAL TARTS FOR THE FARMER'S MARKET TOMORROW.
SO ME N' BIG MAC CAME INTO TOWN FOR S'MORE BAKING SUPPLIES.
E'YUP!
OKAY, APPLE BLOOM, WE'LL SEE YOU TOMORROW AFTER THE MARKET.
YOU THREE STILL WORKING ON THAT WEATHER PROJECT?
WHAT?
SHE MEANS— EYUP!
READY TO HEAD HOME, LITTLE FILLY?
I GUESS SO.
EVERYTHING OKAY?
UM, YEAH.
WHY DO YOU ASK?
MAYBE IT'S JUST ME, BUT PONYVILLE SEEMS A LITTLE BIT LESS FRIENDLY TODAY.

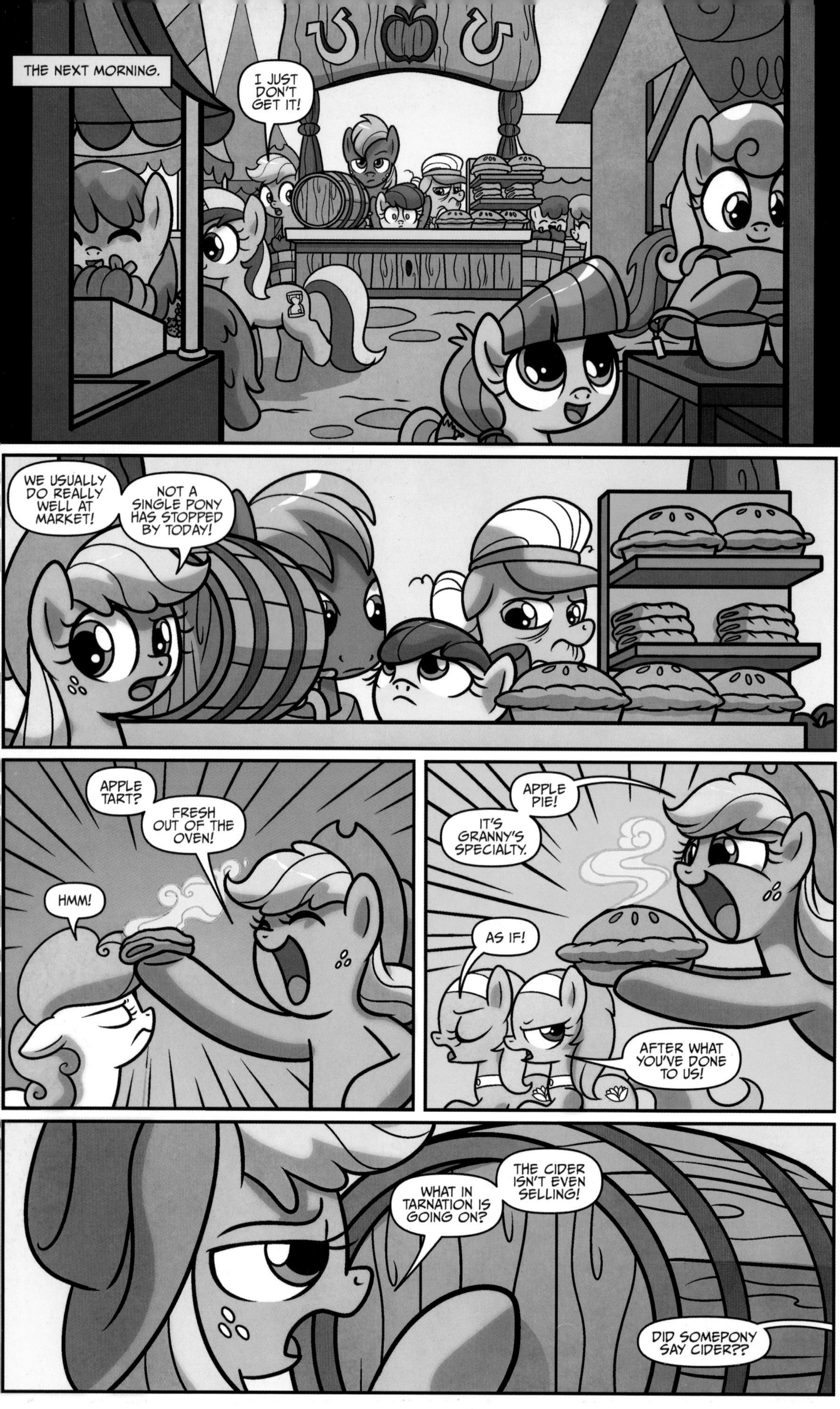
THE NEXT MORNING.
I JUST DON'T GET IT!
WE USUALLY DO REALLY WELL AT MARKET!
NOT A SINGLE PONY HAS STOPPED BY TODAY!
APPLE TART?
FRESH OUT OF THE OVEN!
HMM!
APPLE PIE!
IT'S GRANNY'S SPECIALTY.
AS IF!
AFTER WHAT YOU'VE DONE TO US!
WHAT IN TARNATION IS GOING ON?
THE CIDER ISN'T EVEN SELLING!
DID SOMEPONY SAY CIDER??

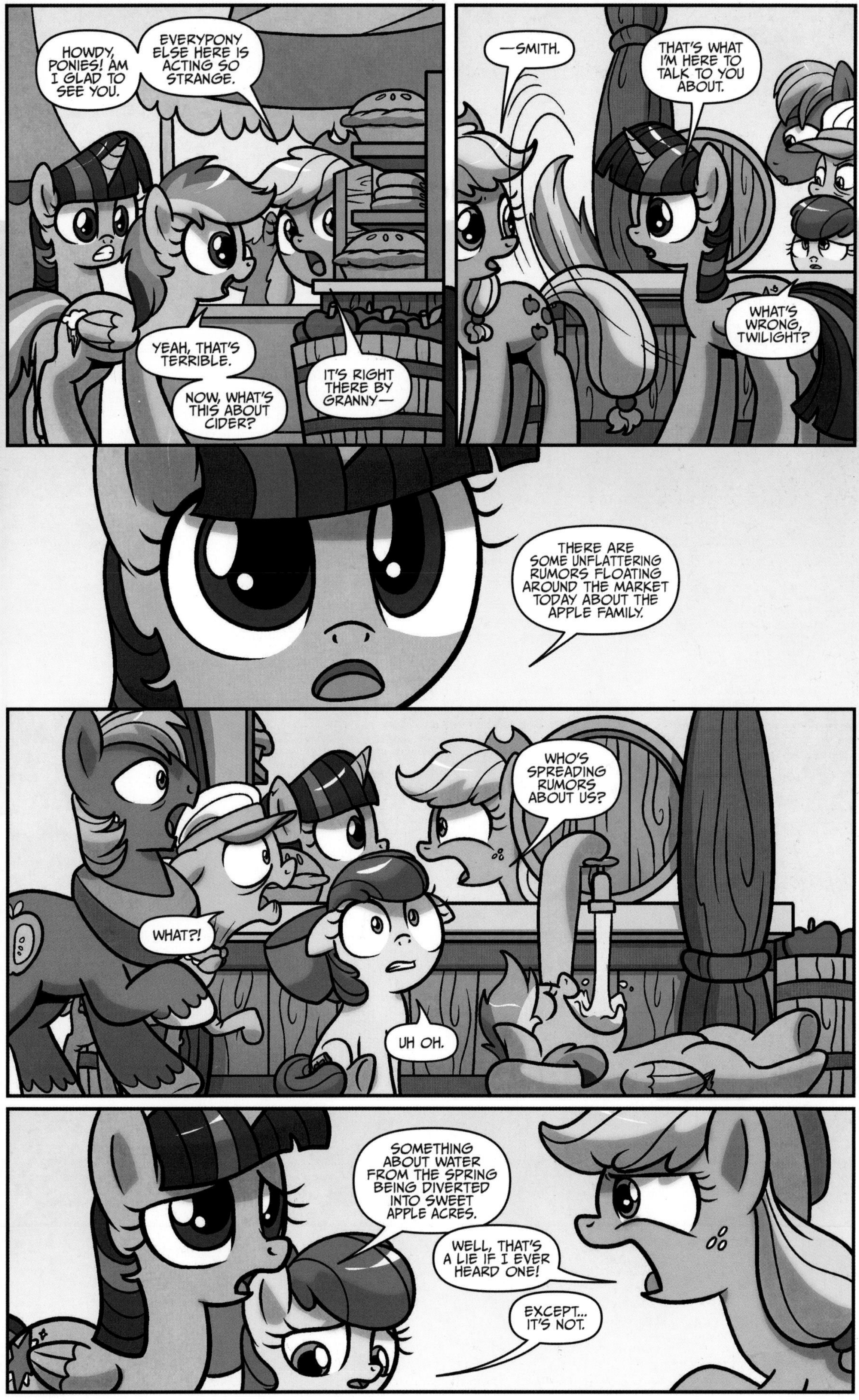
HOWDY, PONIES! AM I GLAD TO SEE YOU.
EVERYPONY ELSE HERE IS ACTING SO STRANGE.
YEAH, THAT'S TERRIBLE.
NOW, WHAT'S THIS ABOUT CIDER?
IT'S RIGHT THERE BY GRANNY—
—SMITH.
THAT'S WHAT I'M HERE TO TALK TO YOU ABOUT.
WHAT'S WRONG, TWILIGHT?
THERE ARE SOME UNFLATTERING RUMORS FLOATING AROUND THE MARKET TODAY ABOUT THE APPLE FAMILY.
WHO'S SPREADING RUMORS ABOUT US?
WHAT?!
UH OH.
SOMETHING ABOUT WATER FROM THE SPRING BEING DIVERTED INTO SWEET APPLE ACRES.
WELL, THAT'S A LIE IF I EVER HEARD ONE!
EXCEPT... IT'S NOT.

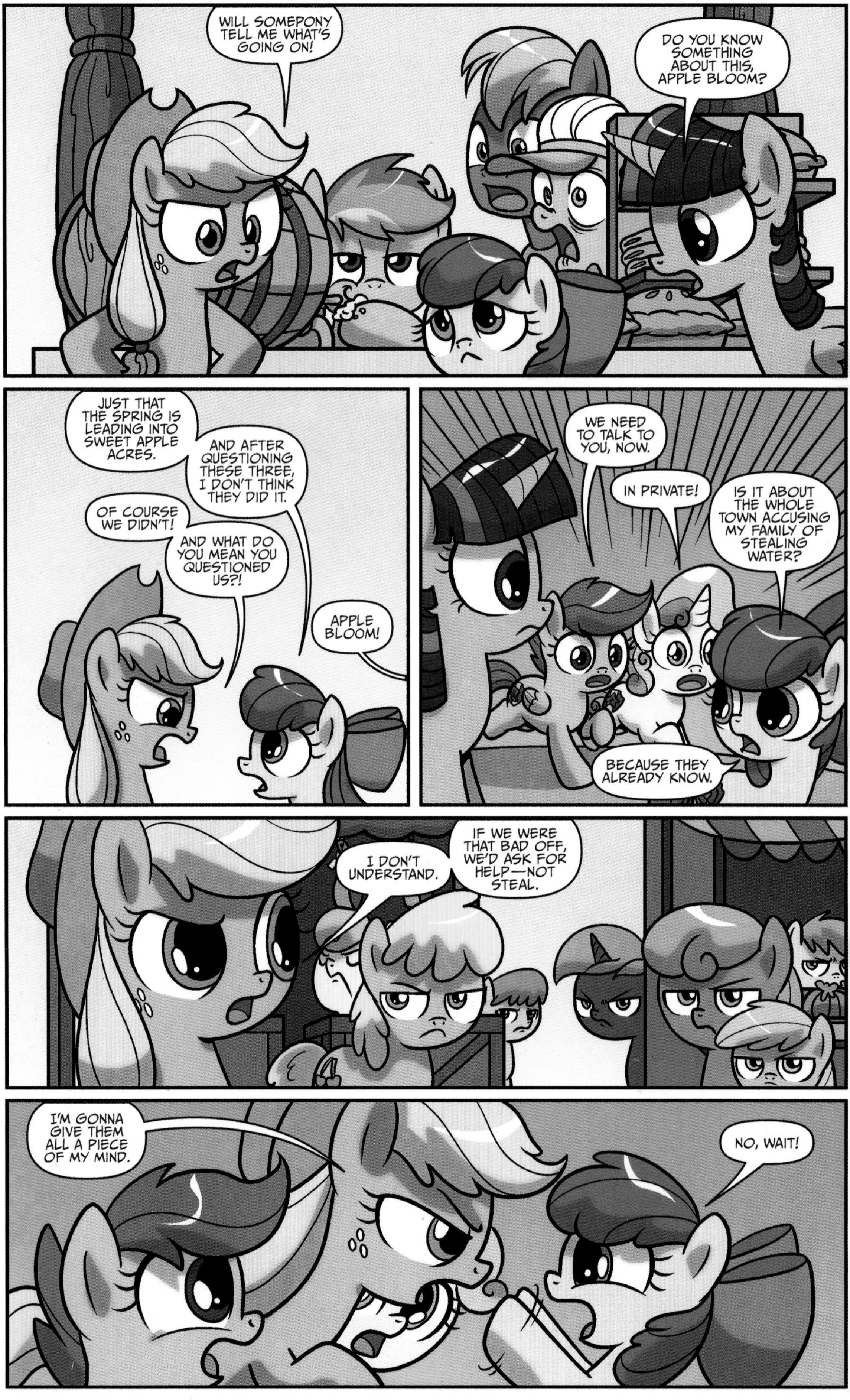
WILL SOMEPONY TELL ME WHAT'S GOING ON!
DO YOU KNOW SOMETHING ABOUT THIS, APPLE BLOOM?
JUST THAT THE SPRING IS LEADING INTO SWEET APPLE ACRES.
AND AFTER QUESTIONING THESE THREE, I DON'T THINK THEY DID IT.
OF COURSE WE DIDN'T!
AND WHAT DO YOU MEAN YOU QUESTIONED US?!
APPLE BLOOM!
WE NEED TO TALK TO YOU, NOW.
IN PRIVATE!
IS IT ABOUT THE WHOLE TOWN ACCUSING MY FAMILY OF STEALING WATER?
BECAUSE THEY ALREADY KNOW.
I DON'T UNDERSTAND.
IF WE WERE THAT BAD OFF, WE'D ASK FOR HELP—NOT STEAL.
I'M GONNA GIVE THEM ALL A PIECE OF MY MIND.
NO, WAIT!

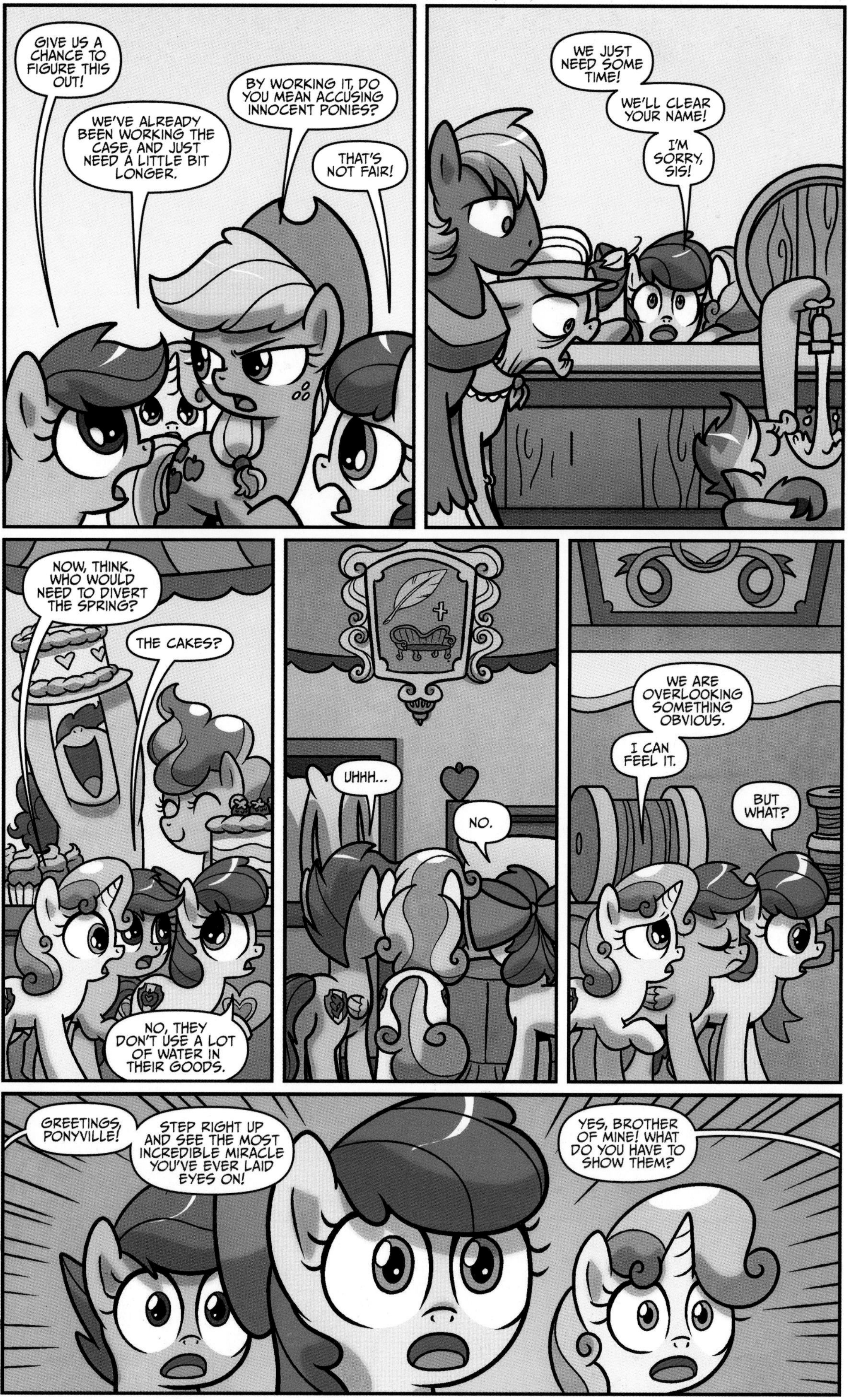

GIVE US A CHANCE TO FIGURE THIS OUT!
WE'VE ALREADY BEEN WORKING THE CASE, AND JUST NEED A LITTLE BIT LONGER.
BY WORKING IT, DO YOU MEAN ACCUSING INNOCENT PONIES?
THAT'S NOT FAIR!
WE JUST NEED SOME TIME!
WE'LL CLEAR YOUR NAME!
I'M SORRY, SIS!
NOW, THINK. WHO WOULD NEED TO DIVERT THE SPRING?
THE CAKES?
NO, THEY DON'T USE A LOT OF WATER IN THEIR GOODS.
UHHH...
NO.
WE ARE OVERLOOKING SOMETHING OBVIOUS.
I CAN FEEL IT.
BUT WHAT?
GREETINGS, PONYVILLE!
STEP RIGHT UP AND SEE THE MOST INCREDIBLE MIRACLE YOU'VE EVER LAID EYES ON!
YES, BROTHER OF MINE! WHAT DO YOU HAVE TO SHOW THEM?

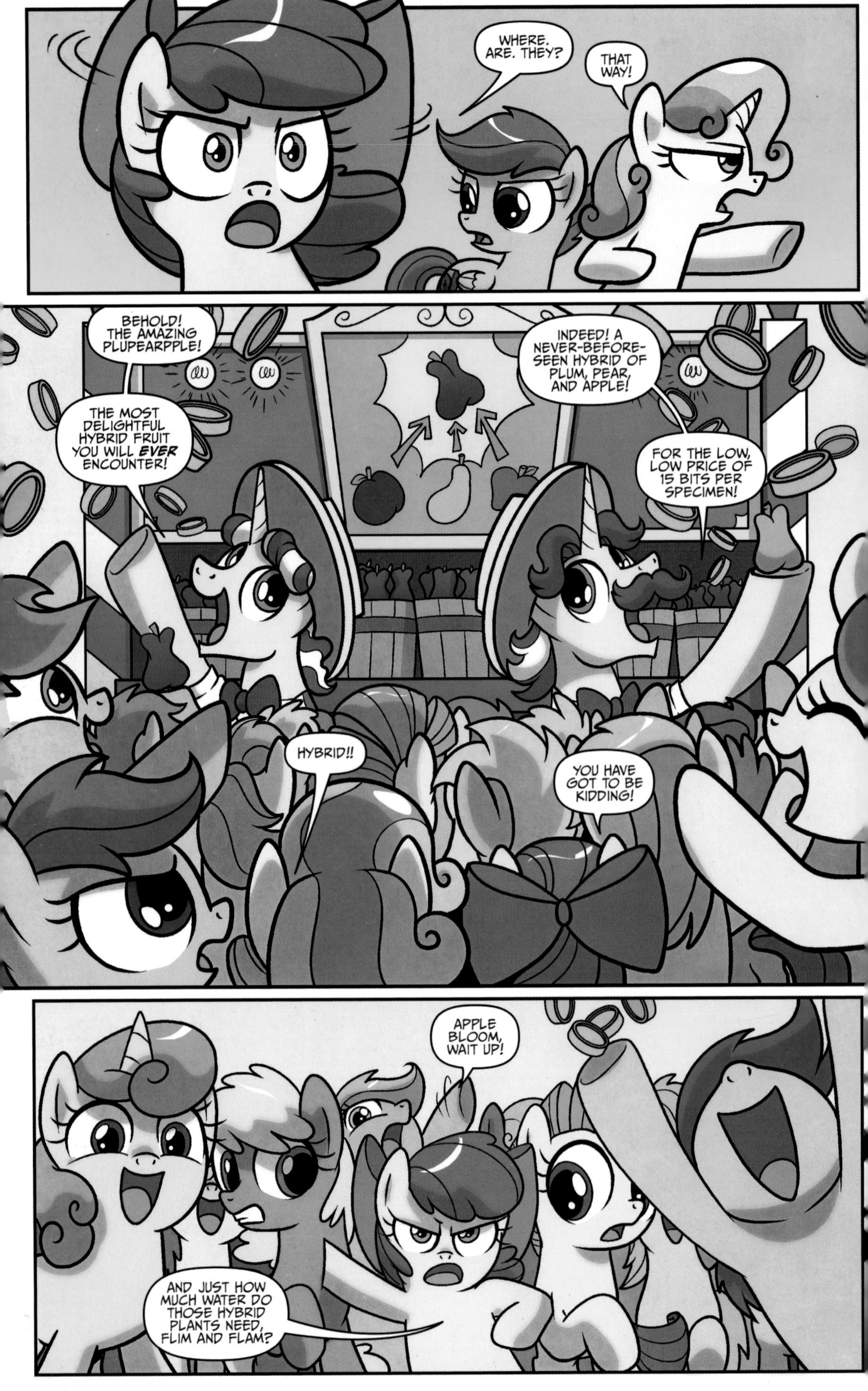

WHERE. ARE. THEY?
THAT WAY!
BEHOLD! THE AMAZING PLUPEARPPLE!
THE MOST DELIGHTFUL HYBRID FRUIT YOU WILL **EVER** ENCOUNTER!
INDEED! A NEVER-BEFORE-SEEN HYBRID OF PLUM, PEAR, AND APPLE!
FOR THE LOW, LOW PRICE OF 15 BITS PER SPECIMEN!
HYBRID!!
YOU HAVE GOT TO BE KIDDING!
APPLE BLOOM, WAIT UP!
AND JUST HOW MUCH WATER DO THOSE HYBRID PLANTS NEED, FLIM AND FLAM?

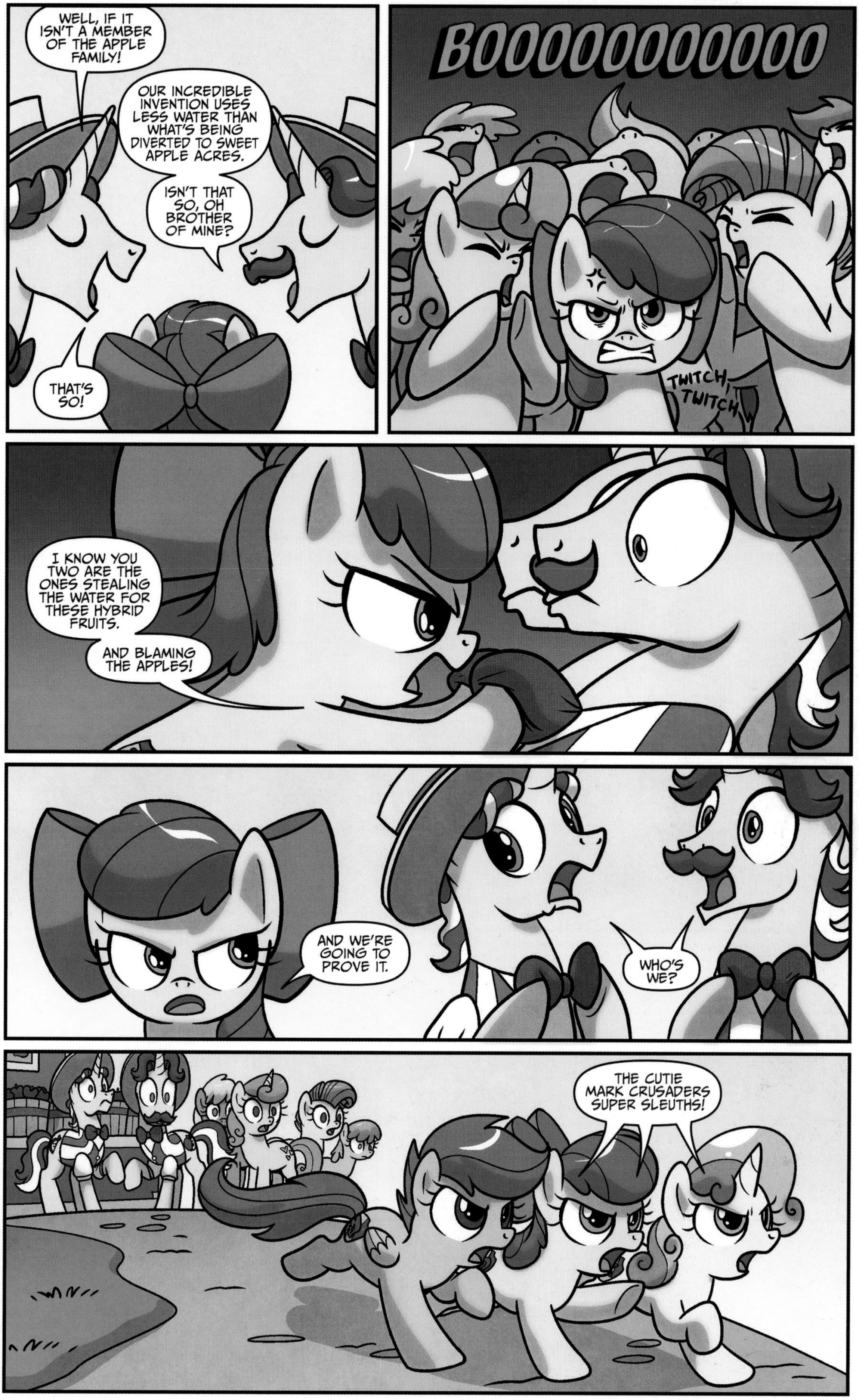
WELL, IF IT ISN'T A MEMBER OF THE APPLE FAMILY!
OUR INCREDIBLE INVENTION USES LESS WATER THAN WHAT'S BEING DIVERTED TO SWEET APPLE ACRES.
ISN'T THAT SO, OH BROTHER OF MINE?
THAT'S SO!
BOOOOOOOOOOO
TWITCH, TWITCH
I KNOW YOU TWO ARE THE ONES STEALING THE WATER FOR THESE HYBRID FRUITS.
AND BLAMING THE APPLES!
AND WE'RE GOING TO PROVE IT.
WHO'S WE?
THE CUTIE MARK CRUSADERS SUPER SLEUTHS!

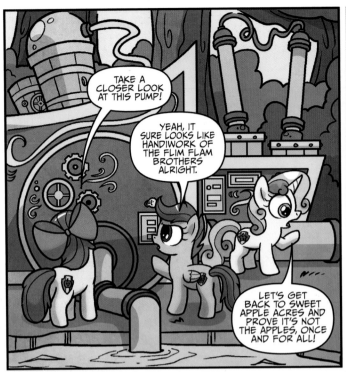

TAKE A CLOSER LOOK AT THIS PUMP!

YEAH, IT SURE LOOKS LIKE HANDIWORK OF THE FLIM FLAM BROTHERS ALRIGHT.

LET'S GET BACK TO SWEET APPLE ACRES AND PROVE IT'S NOT THE APPLES, ONCE AND FOR ALL!

AGREED!

C'MON, SLEUTHS, THOSE FLIM FLAM BROTHERS MUST HAVE THE WATER LEADING SOMEWHERE ELSE!

START CLEARING AWAY THESE LEAVES!

COME LOOK AT THIS!

THEY MUST HAVE BURIED THE REST OF THE PIPE TO MAKE IT LOOK LIKE IT STOPPED AT SWEET APPLE ACRES.

THIS IS IT!

LET'S SEE WHERE IT LEADS!

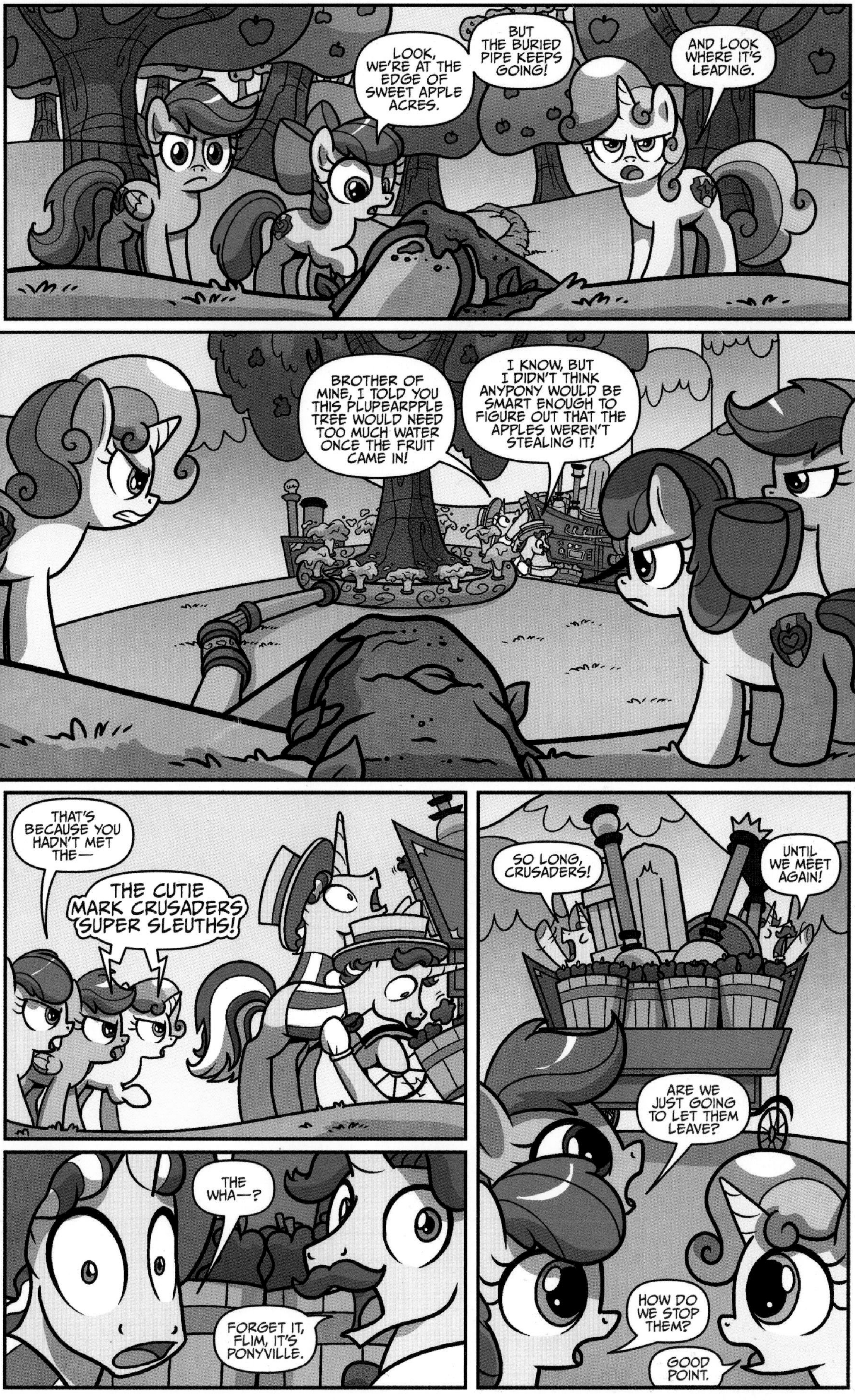
LOOK, WE'RE AT THE EDGE OF SWEET APPLE ACRES.
BUT THE BURIED PIPE KEEPS GOING!
AND LOOK WHERE IT'S LEADING.
BROTHER OF MINE, I TOLD YOU THIS PLUPEARPPLE TREE WOULD NEED TOO MUCH WATER ONCE THE FRUIT CAME IN!
I KNOW, BUT I DIDN'T THINK ANYPONY WOULD BE SMART ENOUGH TO FIGURE OUT THAT THE APPLES WEREN'T STEALING IT!
THAT'S BECAUSE YOU HADN'T MET THE—
THE CUTIE MARK CRUSADERS SUPER SLEUTHS!
THE WHA—?
FORGET IT, FLIM, IT'S PONYVILLE.
SO LONG, CRUSADERS!
UNTIL WE MEET AGAIN!
ARE WE JUST GOING TO LET THEM LEAVE?
HOW DO WE STOP THEM?
GOOD POINT.

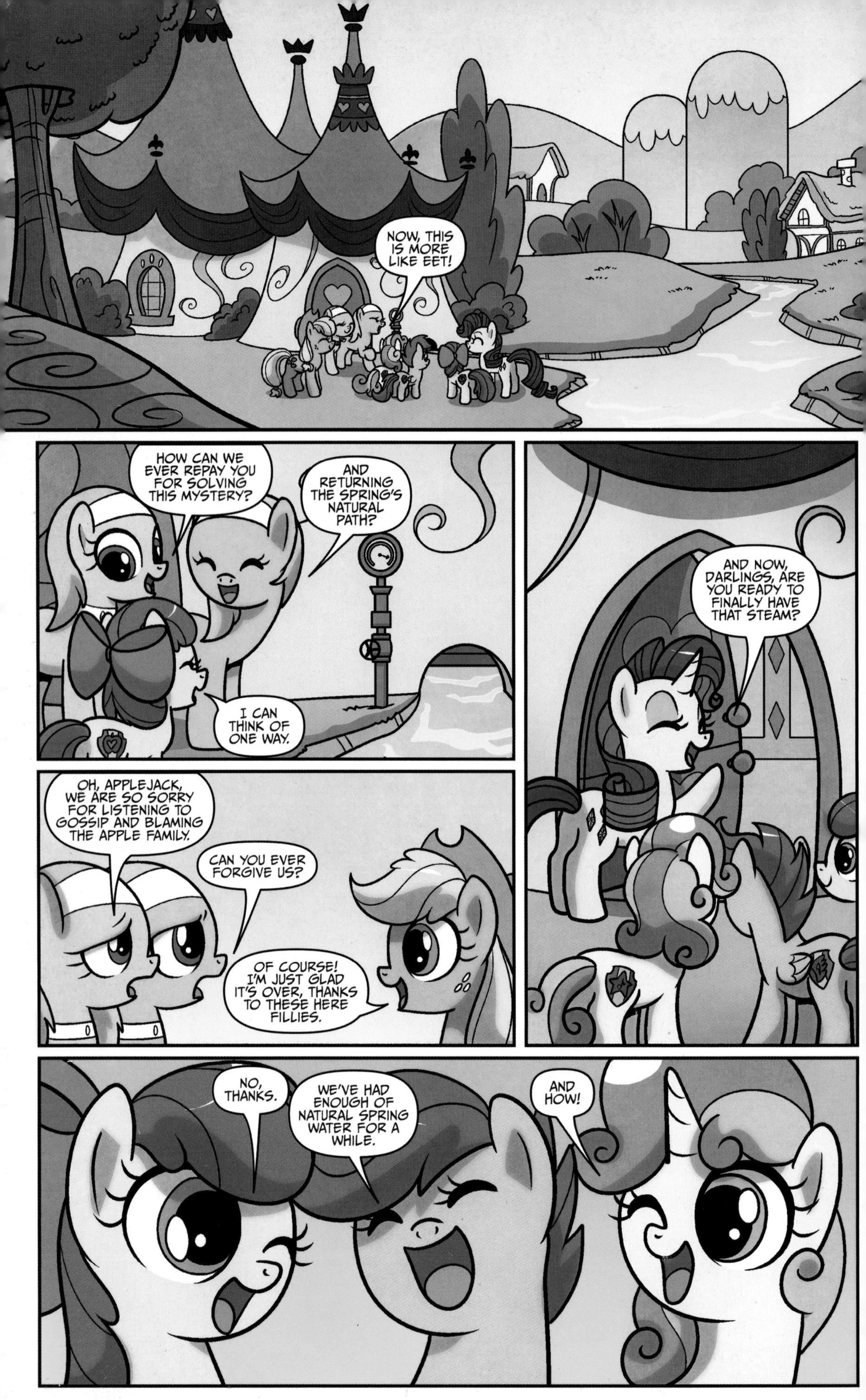
NOW, THIS IS MORE LIKE EET!
HOW CAN WE EVER REPAY YOU FOR SOLVING THIS MYSTERY?
AND RETURNING THE SPRING'S NATURAL PATH?
I CAN THINK OF ONE WAY.
AND NOW, DARLINGS, ARE YOU READY TO FINALLY HAVE THAT STEAM?
OH, APPLEJACK, WE ARE SO SORRY FOR LISTENING TO GOSSIP AND BLAMING THE APPLE FAMILY.
CAN YOU EVER FORGIVE US?
OF COURSE! I'M JUST GLAD IT'S OVER, THANKS TO THESE HERE FILLIES.
NO, THANKS.
WE'VE HAD ENOUGH OF NATURAL SPRING WATER FOR A WHILE.
AND HOW!

ART BY **PHILIP MURPHY**

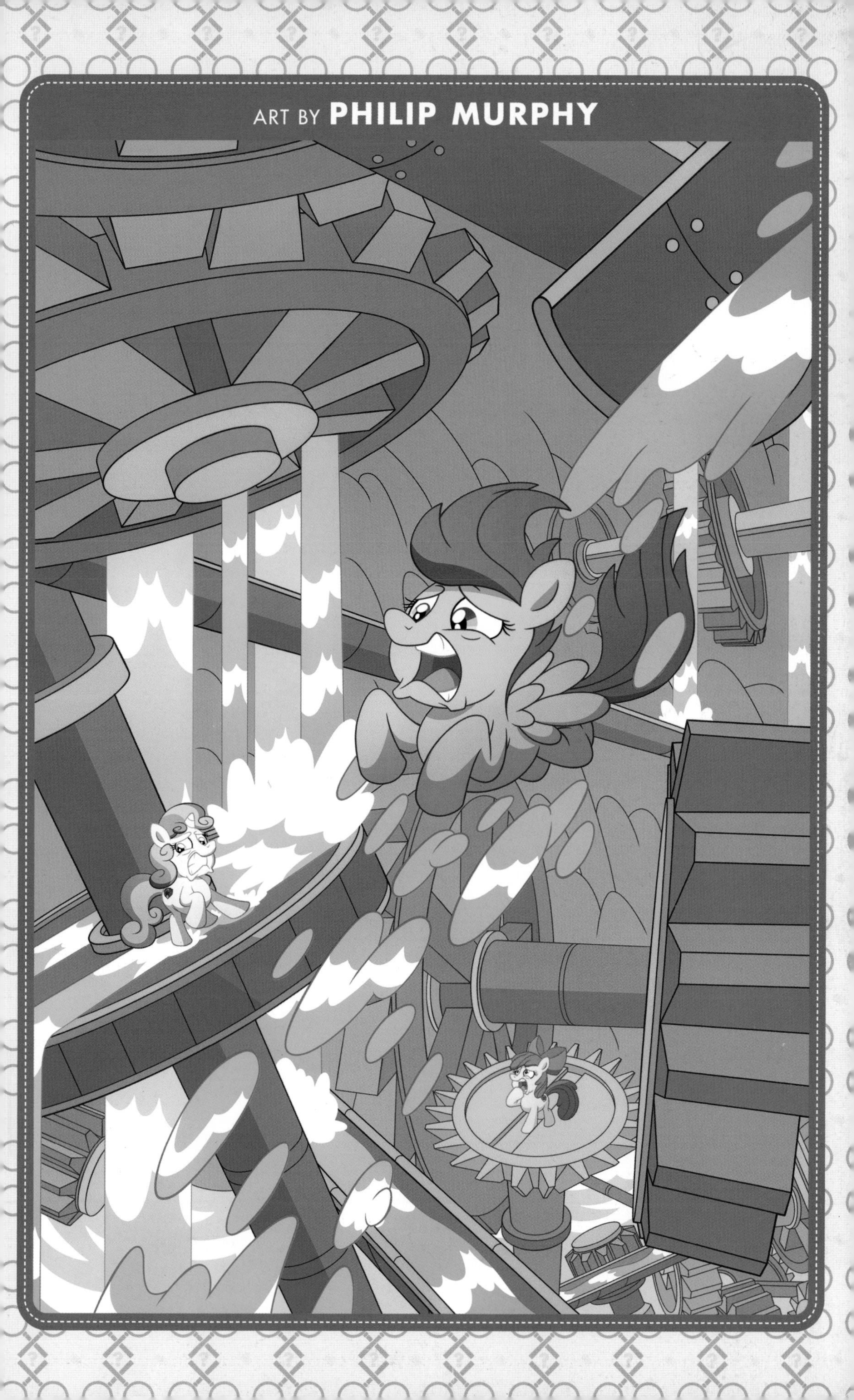

5 ART BY **AGNES GARBOWSKA**

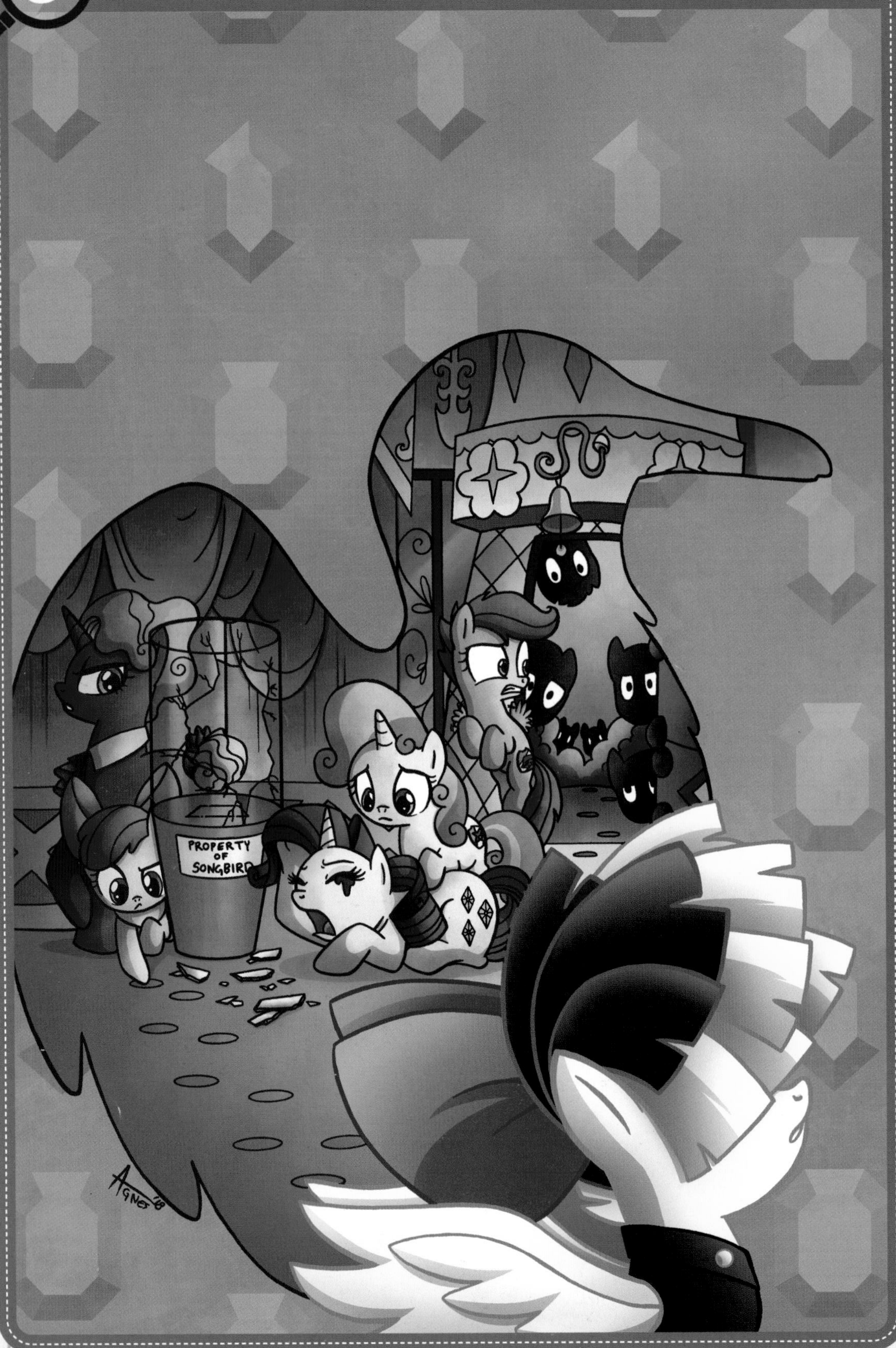
PROPERTY OF SONGBIRD

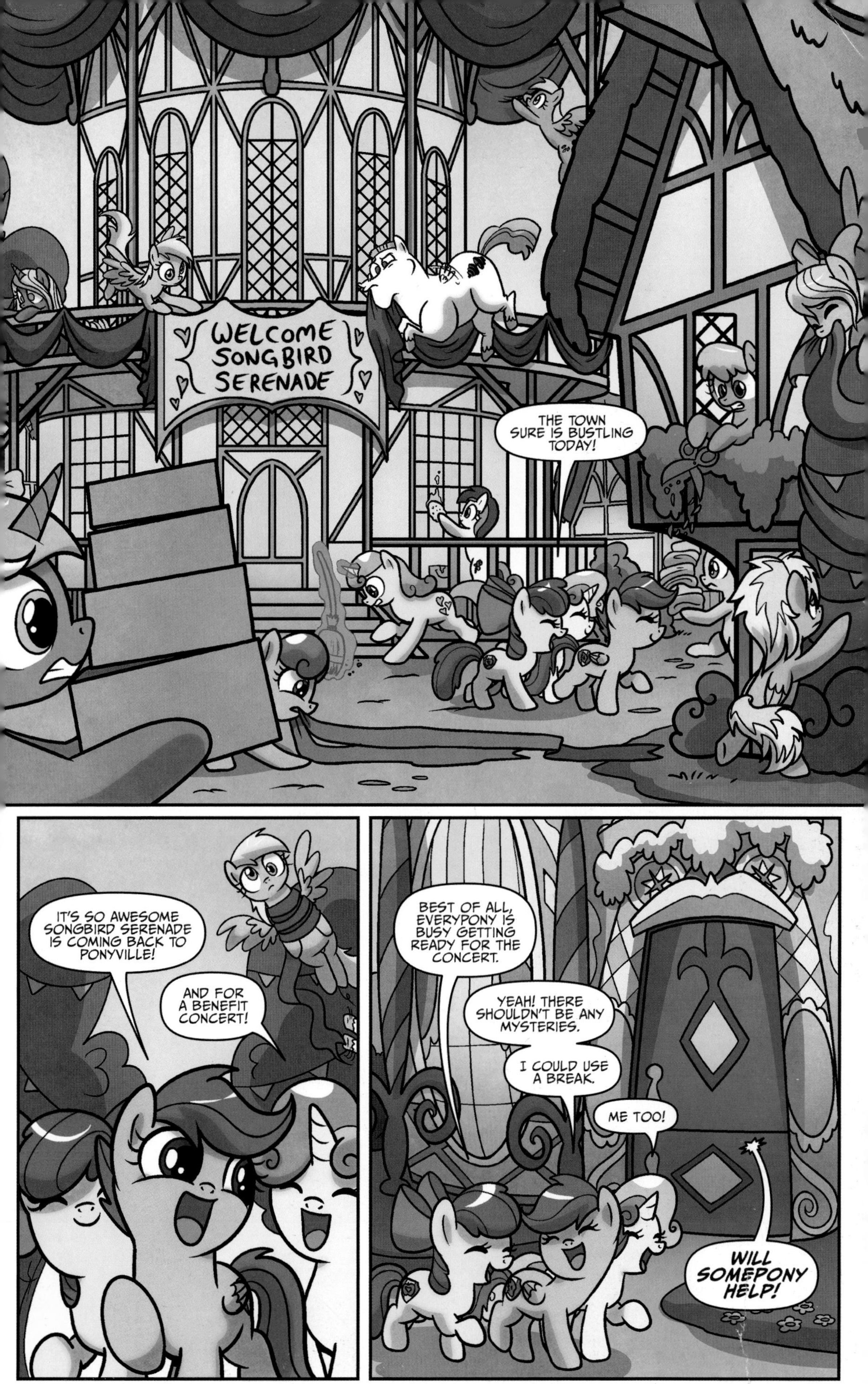
WELCOME SONGBIRD SERENADE
THE TOWN SURE IS BUSTLING TODAY!
IT'S SO AWESOME SONGBIRD SERENADE IS COMING BACK TO PONYVILLE!
AND FOR A BENEFIT CONCERT!
BEST OF ALL, EVERYPONY IS BUSY GETTING READY FOR THE CONCERT.
YEAH! THERE SHOULDN'T BE ANY MYSTERIES.
I COULD USE A BREAK.
ME TOO!
WILL SOMEPONY HELP!

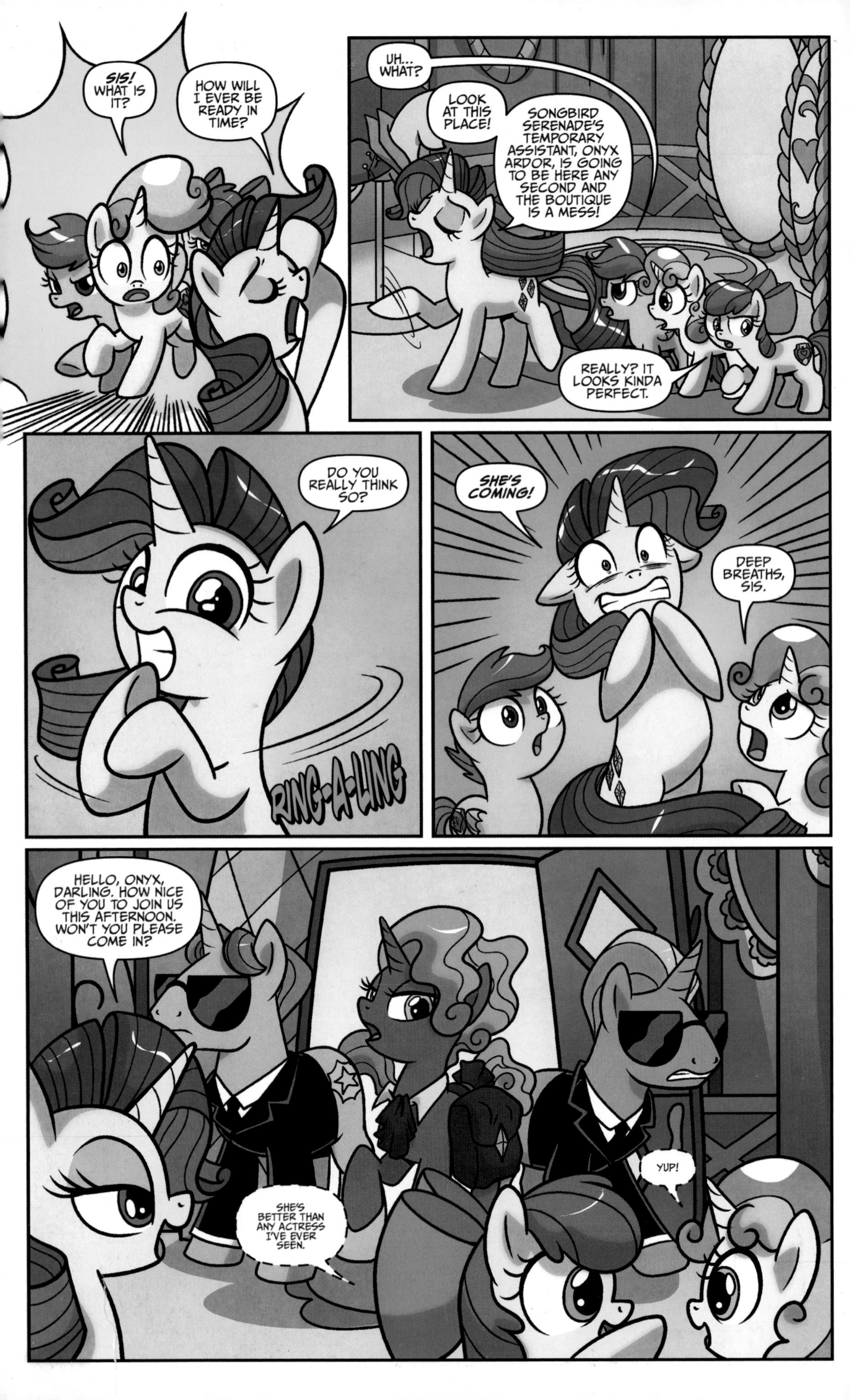
SIS! WHAT IS IT?
HOW WILL I EVER BE READY IN TIME?
UH... WHAT?
LOOK AT THIS PLACE!
SONGBIRD SERENADE'S TEMPORARY ASSISTANT, ONYX ARDOR, IS GOING TO BE HERE ANY SECOND AND THE BOUTIQUE IS A MESS!
REALLY? IT LOOKS KINDA PERFECT.
DO YOU REALLY THINK SO?
RING-A-LING
SHE'S COMING!
DEEP BREATHS, SIS.
HELLO, ONYX, DARLING. HOW NICE OF YOU TO JOIN US THIS AFTERNOON. WON'T YOU PLEASE COME IN?
SHE'S BETTER THAN ANY ACTRESS I'VE EVER SEEN.
YUP!

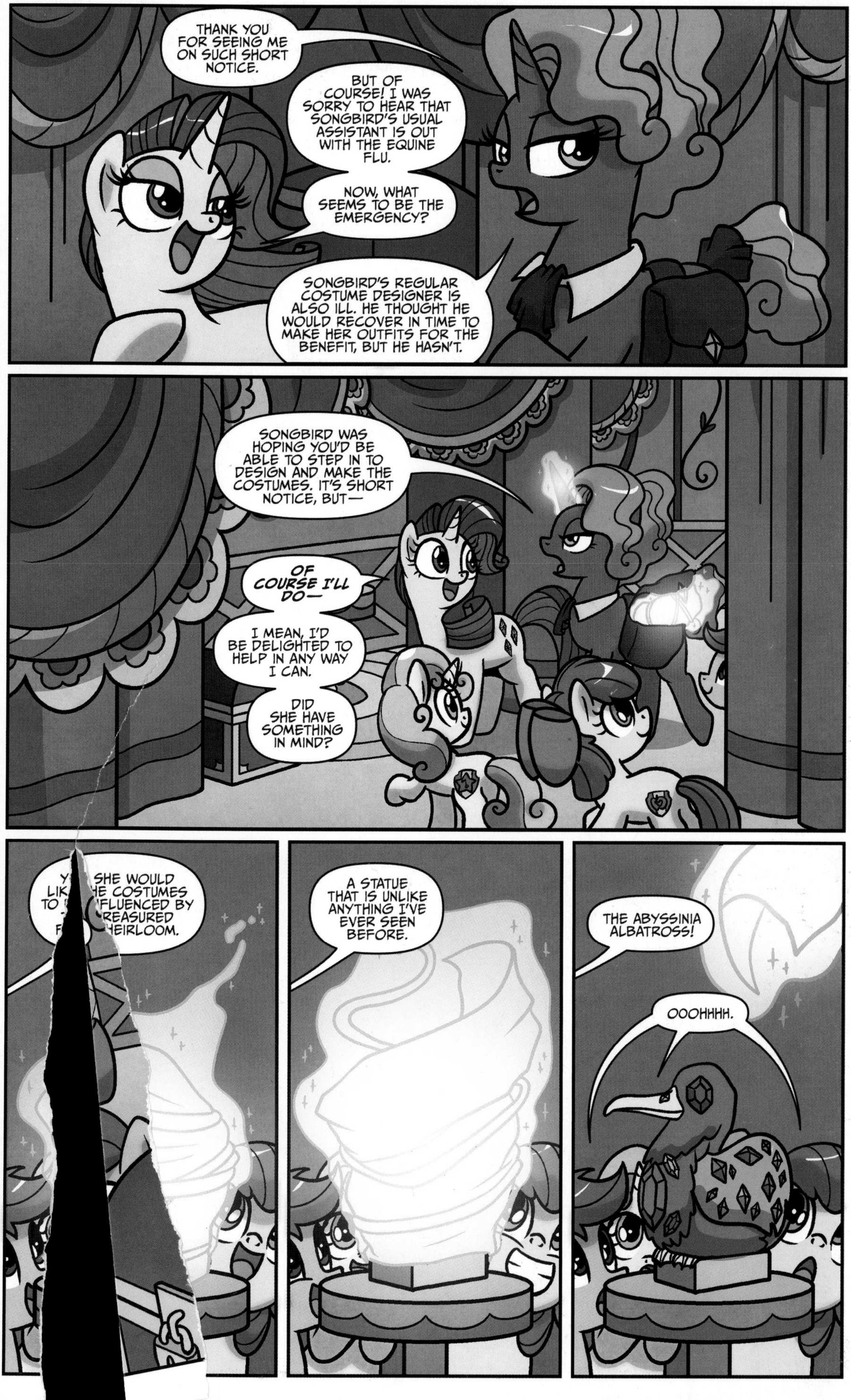
THANK YOU FOR SEEING ME ON SUCH SHORT NOTICE.
BUT OF COURSE! I WAS SORRY TO HEAR THAT SONGBIRD'S USUAL ASSISTANT IS OUT WITH THE EQUINE FLU.
NOW, WHAT SEEMS TO BE THE EMERGENCY?
SONGBIRD'S REGULAR COSTUME DESIGNER IS ALSO ILL. HE THOUGHT HE WOULD RECOVER IN TIME TO MAKE HER OUTFITS FOR THE BENEFIT, BUT HE HASN'T.
SONGBIRD WAS HOPING YOU'D BE ABLE TO STEP IN TO DESIGN AND MAKE THE COSTUMES. IT'S SHORT NOTICE, BUT—
OF COURSE I'LL DO—
I MEAN, I'D BE DELIGHTED TO HELP IN ANY WAY I CAN.
DID SHE HAVE SOMETHING IN MIND?
Y SHE WOULD LIK HE COSTUMES TO FLUENCED BY REASURED F HEIRLOOM.
A STATUE THAT IS UNLIKE ANYTHING I'VE EVER SEEN BEFORE.
THE ABYSSINIA ALBATROSS!
OOOHHHH.

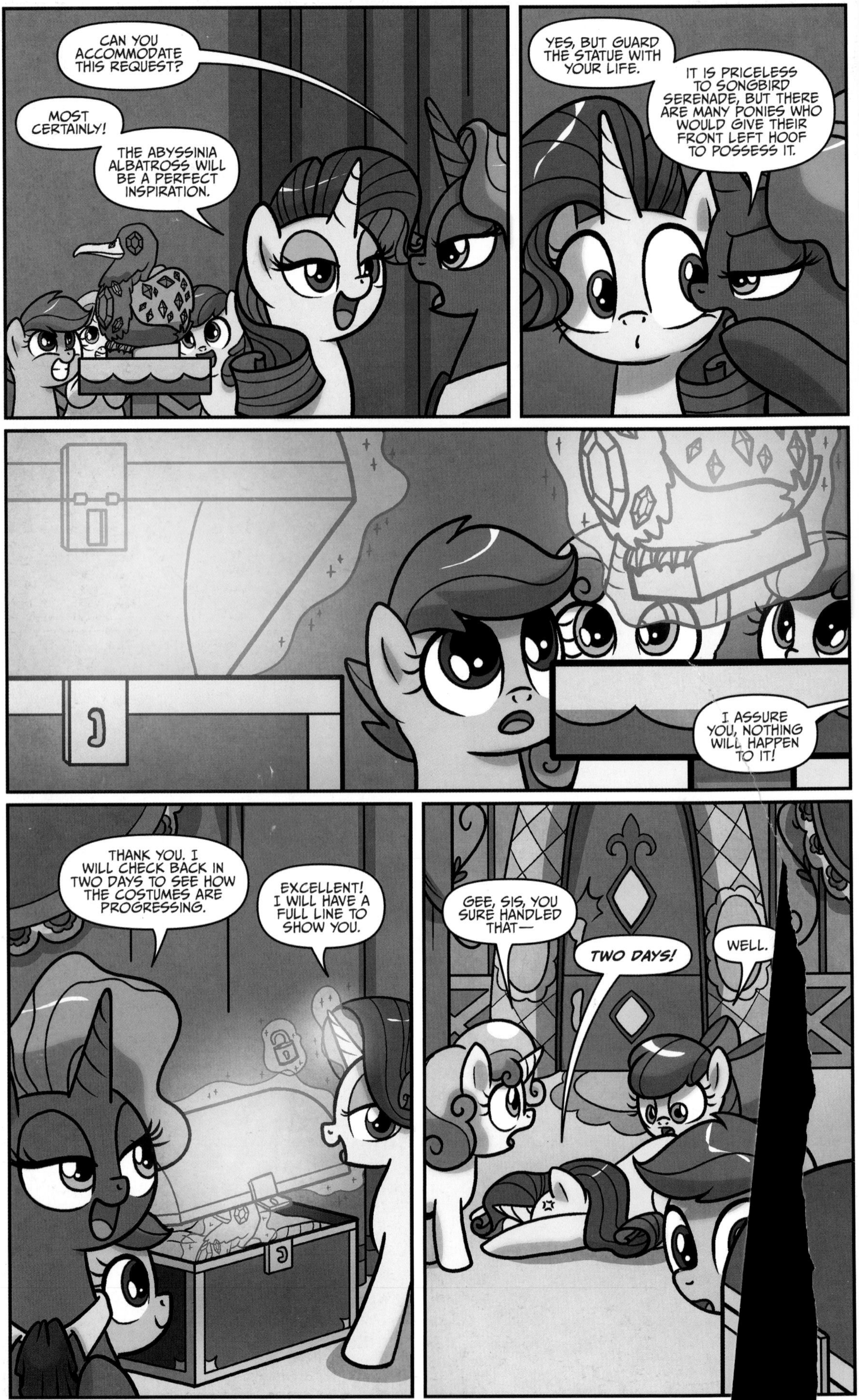
CAN YOU ACCOMMODATE THIS REQUEST?
MOST CERTAINLY!
THE ABYSSINIA ALBATROSS WILL BE A PERFECT INSPIRATION.
YES, BUT GUARD THE STATUE WITH YOUR LIFE.
IT IS PRICELESS TO SONGBIRD SERENADE, BUT THERE ARE MANY PONIES WHO WOULD GIVE THEIR FRONT LEFT HOOF TO POSSESS IT.
I ASSURE YOU, NOTHING WILL HAPPEN TO IT!
THANK YOU. I WILL CHECK BACK IN TWO DAYS TO SEE HOW THE COSTUMES ARE PROGRESSING.
EXCELLENT! I WILL HAVE A FULL LINE TO SHOW YOU.
GEE, SIS, YOU SURE HANDLED THAT—
TWO DAYS!
WELL.

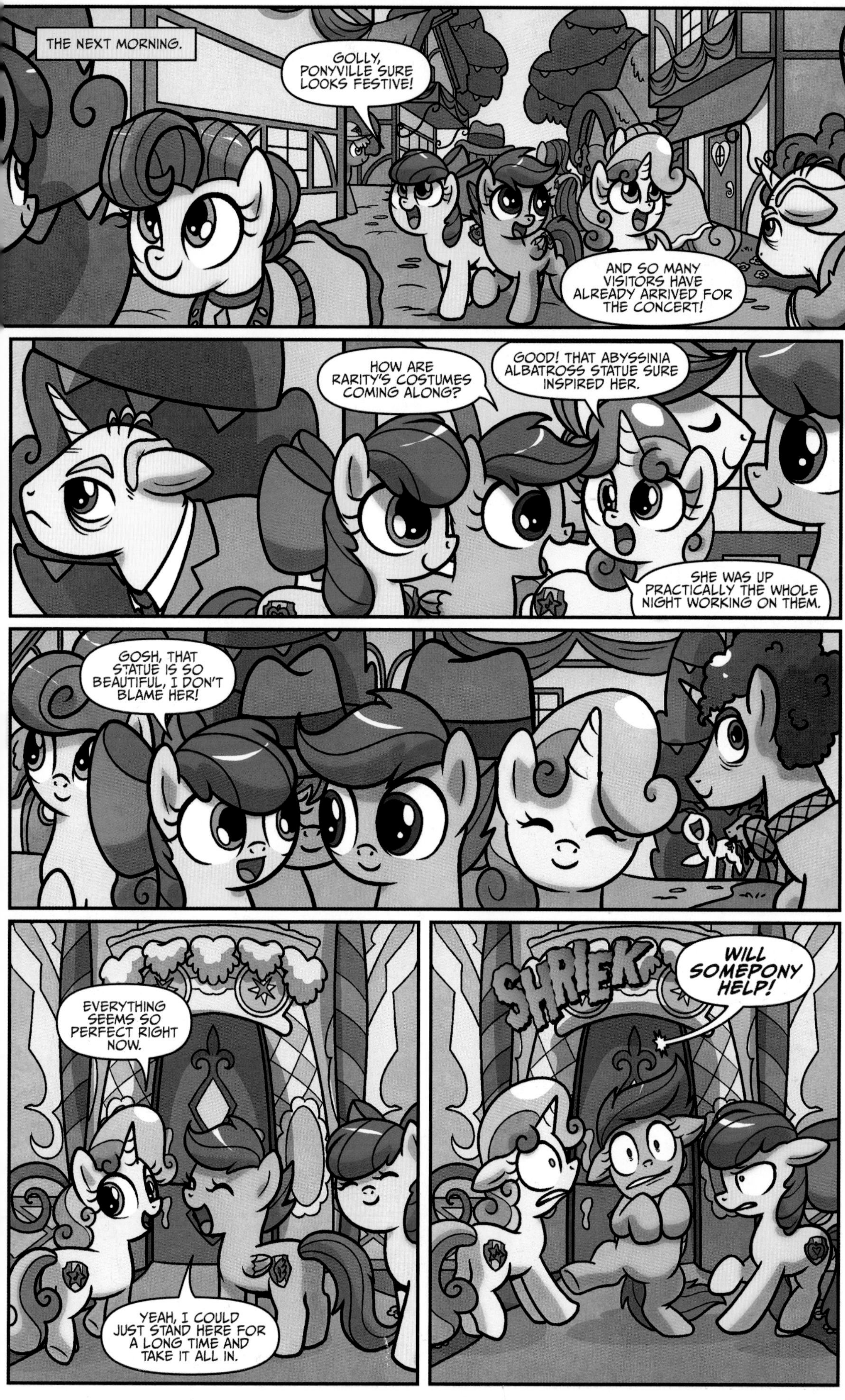
THE NEXT MORNING.
GOLLY, PONYVILLE SURE LOOKS FESTIVE!
AND SO MANY VISITORS HAVE ALREADY ARRIVED FOR THE CONCERT!
HOW ARE RARITY'S COSTUMES COMING ALONG?
GOOD! THAT ABYSSINIA ALBATROSS STATUE SURE INSPIRED HER.
SHE WAS UP PRACTICALLY THE WHOLE NIGHT WORKING ON THEM.
GOSH, THAT STATUE IS SO BEAUTIFUL, I DON'T BLAME HER!
EVERYTHING SEEMS SO PERFECT RIGHT NOW.
YEAH, I COULD JUST STAND HERE FOR A LONG TIME AND TAKE IT ALL IN.
SHRIEK
WILL SOMEPONY HELP!

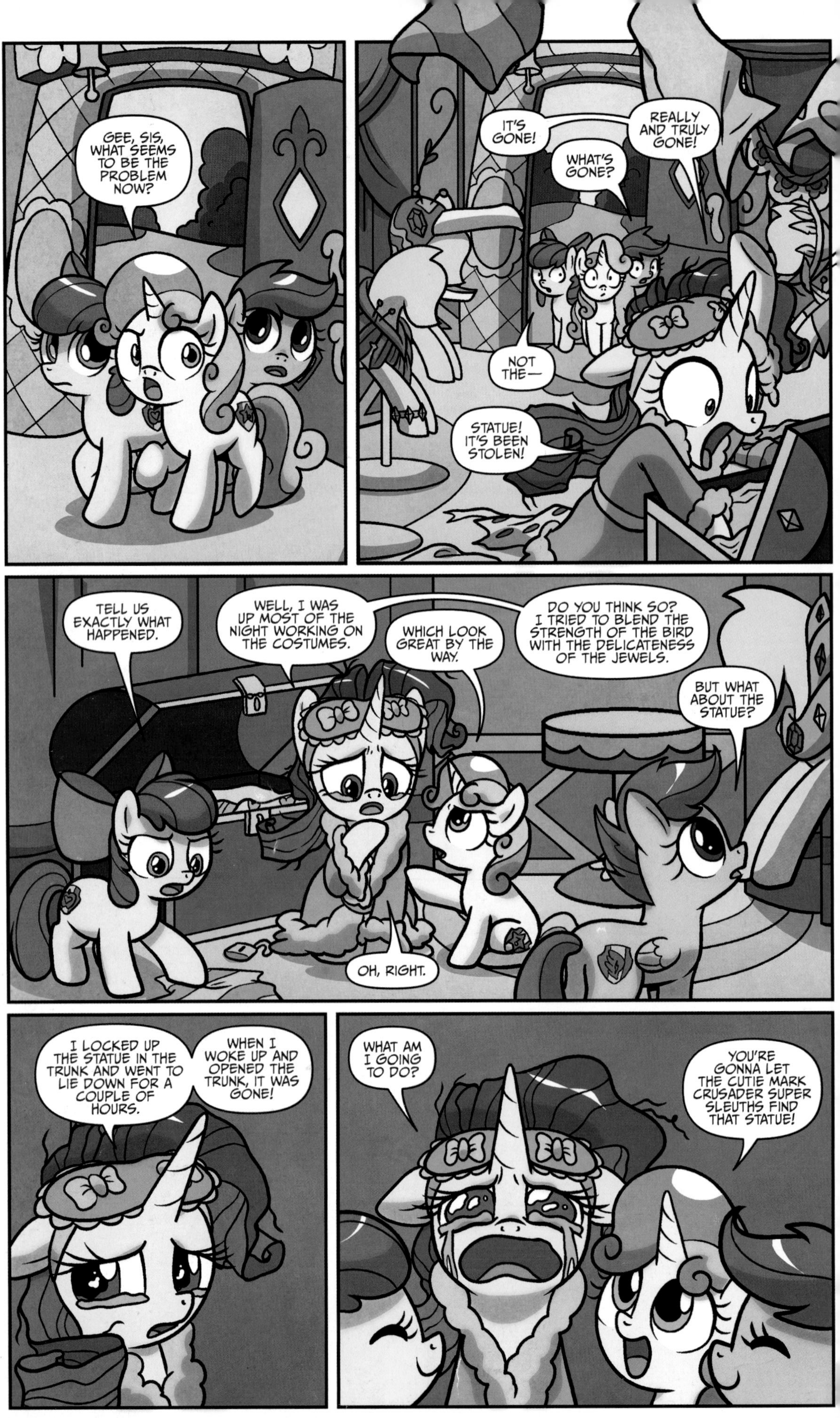
GEE, SIS, WHAT SEEMS TO BE THE PROBLEM NOW?
IT'S GONE!
REALLY AND TRULY GONE!
WHAT'S GONE?
NOT THE—
STATUE! IT'S BEEN STOLEN!
TELL US EXACTLY WHAT HAPPENED.
WELL, I WAS UP MOST OF THE NIGHT WORKING ON THE COSTUMES.
WHICH LOOK GREAT BY THE WAY.
DO YOU THINK SO? I TRIED TO BLEND THE STRENGTH OF THE BIRD WITH THE DELICATENESS OF THE JEWELS.
BUT WHAT ABOUT THE STATUE?
OH, RIGHT.
I LOCKED UP THE STATUE IN THE TRUNK AND WENT TO LIE DOWN FOR A COUPLE OF HOURS.
WHEN I WOKE UP AND OPENED THE TRUNK, IT WAS GONE!
WHAT AM I GOING TO DO?
YOU'RE GONNA LET THE CUTIE MARK CRUSADER SUPER SLEUTHS FIND THAT STATUE!

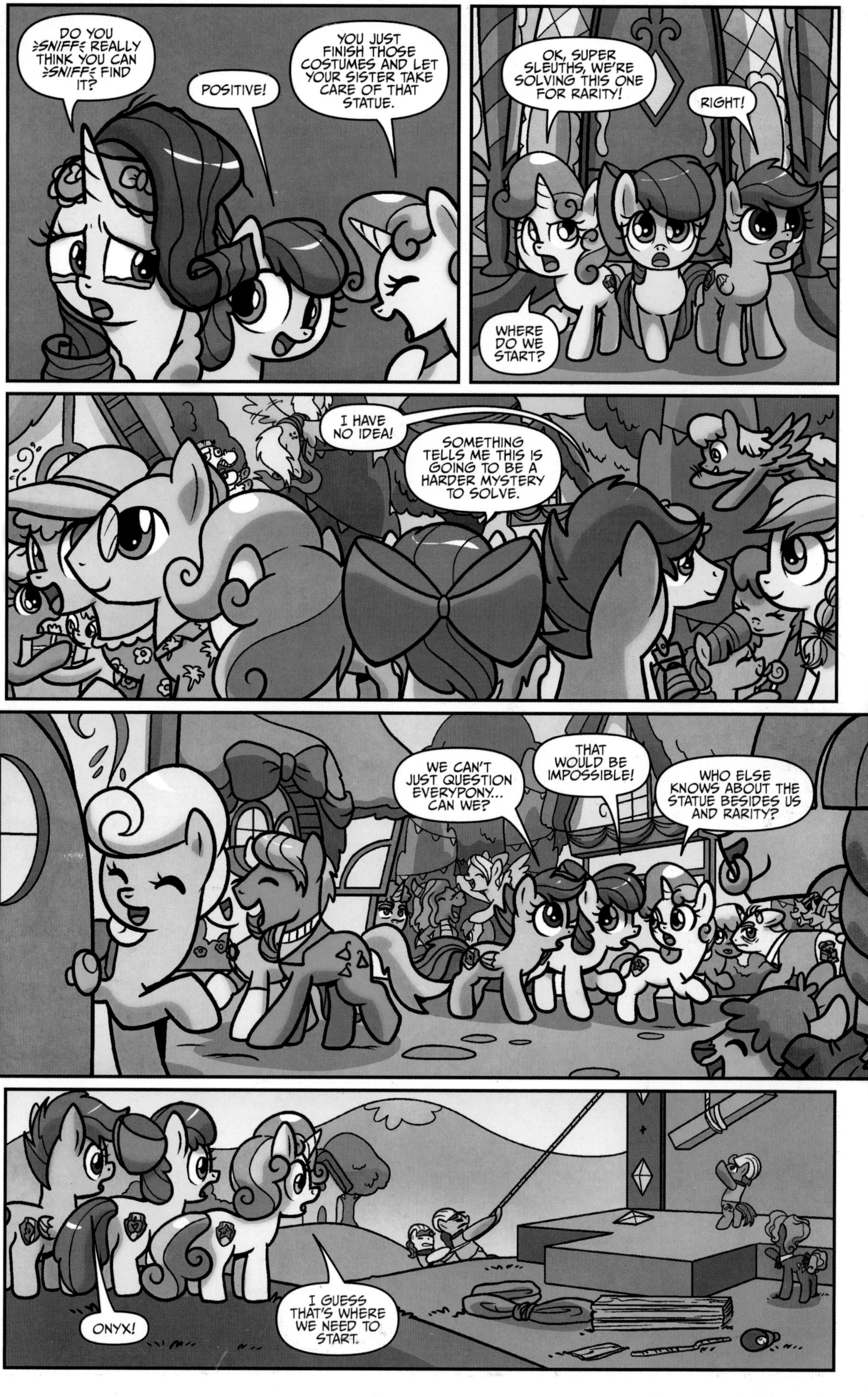
DO YOU ⋟SNIFF⋞ REALLY THINK YOU CAN ⋟SNIFF⋞ FIND IT?
POSITIVE!
YOU JUST FINISH THOSE COSTUMES AND LET YOUR SISTER TAKE CARE OF THAT STATUE.
OK, SUPER SLEUTHS, WE'RE SOLVING THIS ONE FOR RARITY!
RIGHT!
WHERE DO WE START?
I HAVE NO IDEA!
SOMETHING TELLS ME THIS IS GOING TO BE A HARDER MYSTERY TO SOLVE.
WE CAN'T JUST QUESTION EVERYPONY... CAN WE?
THAT WOULD BE IMPOSSIBLE!
WHO ELSE KNOWS ABOUT THE STATUE BESIDES US AND RARITY?
ONYX!
I GUESS THAT'S WHERE WE NEED TO START.

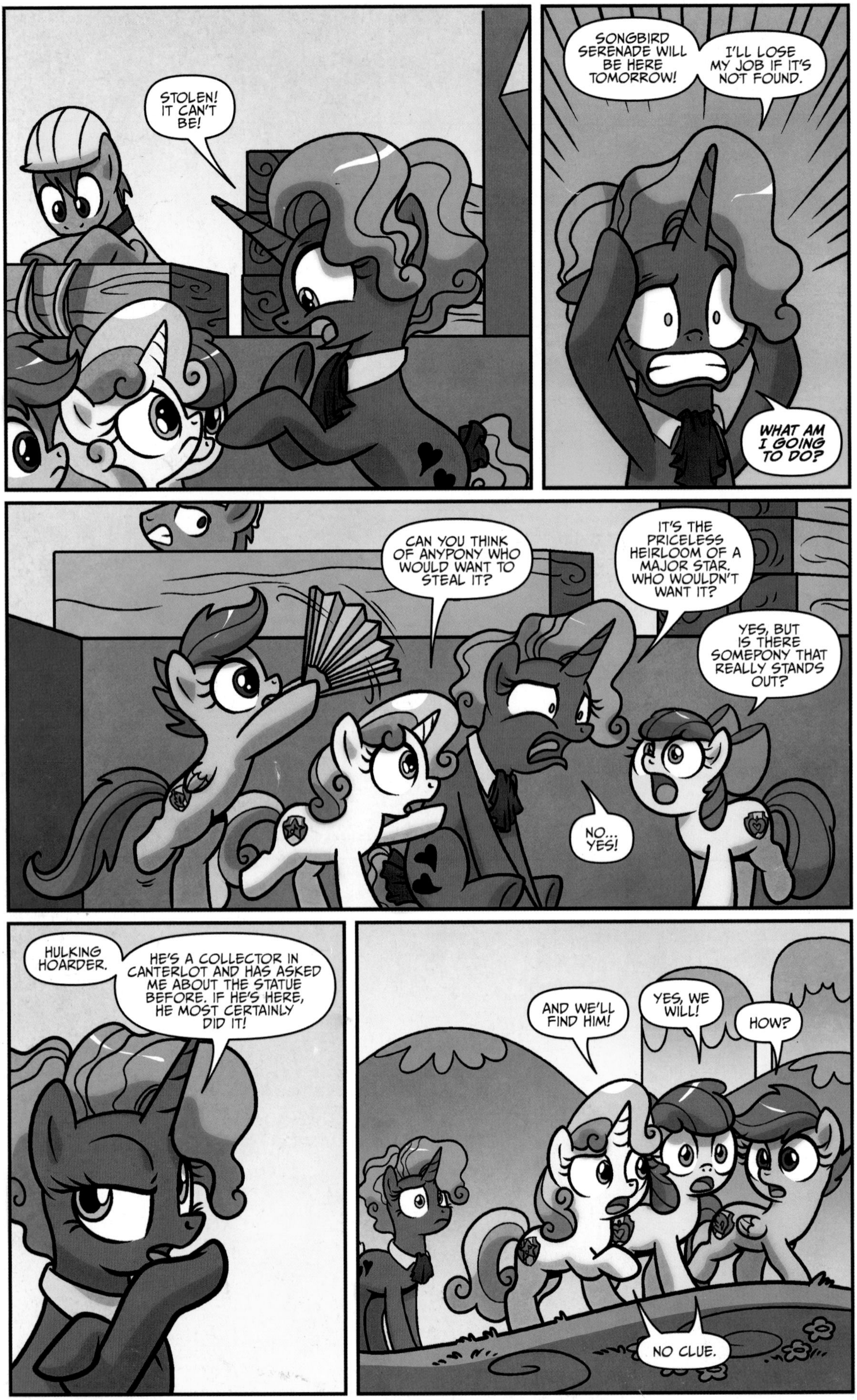
STOLEN! IT CAN'T BE!
SONGBIRD SERENADE WILL BE HERE TOMORROW!
I'LL LOSE MY JOB IF IT'S NOT FOUND.
WHAT AM I GOING TO DO?
CAN YOU THINK OF ANYPONY WHO WOULD WANT TO STEAL IT?
IT'S THE PRICELESS HEIRLOOM OF A MAJOR STAR. WHO WOULDN'T WANT IT?
YES, BUT IS THERE SOMEPONY THAT REALLY STANDS OUT?
NO... YES!
HULKING HOARDER.
HE'S A COLLECTOR IN CANTERLOT AND HAS ASKED ME ABOUT THE STATUE BEFORE. IF HE'S HERE, HE MOST CERTAINLY DID IT!
AND WE'LL FIND HIM!
YES, WE WILL!
HOW?
NO CLUE.

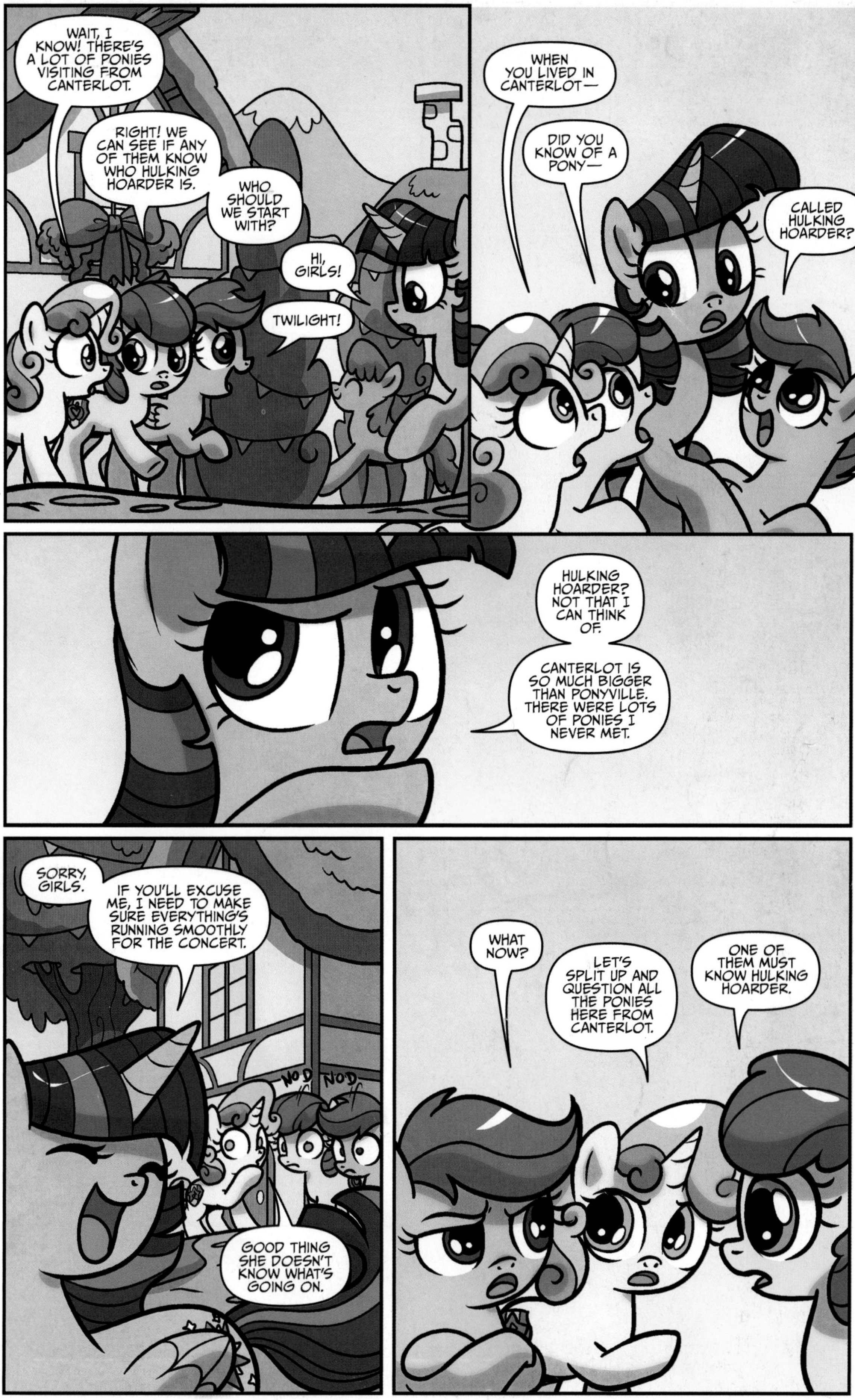
WAIT, I KNOW! THERE'S A LOT OF PONIES VISITING FROM CANTERLOT.
RIGHT! WE CAN SEE IF ANY OF THEM KNOW WHO HULKING HOARDER IS.
WHO SHOULD WE START WITH?
HI, GIRLS!
TWILIGHT!
WHEN YOU LIVED IN CANTERLOT—
DID YOU KNOW OF A PONY—
CALLED HULKING HOARDER?
HULKING HOARDER? NOT THAT I CAN THINK OF.
CANTERLOT IS SO MUCH BIGGER THAN PONYVILLE. THERE WERE LOTS OF PONIES I NEVER MET.
SORRY, GIRLS.
IF YOU'LL EXCUSE ME, I NEED TO MAKE SURE EVERYTHING'S RUNNING SMOOTHLY FOR THE CONCERT.
NOD
NOD
GOOD THING SHE DOESN'T KNOW WHAT'S GOING ON.
WHAT NOW?
LET'S SPLIT UP AND QUESTION ALL THE PONIES HERE FROM CANTERLOT.
ONE OF THEM MUST KNOW HULKING HOARDER.

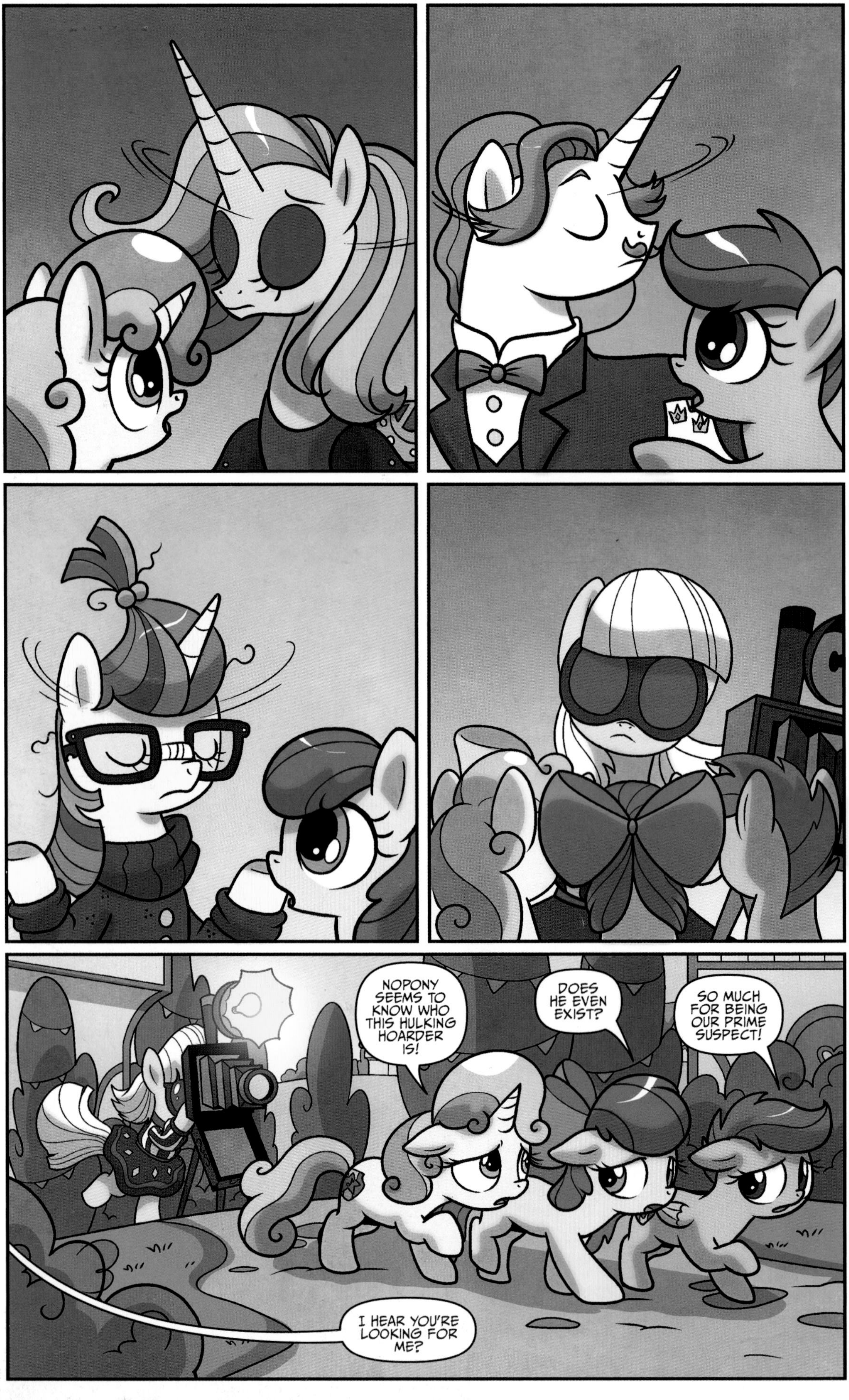
NOPONY SEEMS TO KNOW WHO THIS HULKING HOARDER IS!
DOES HE EVEN EXIST?
SO MUCH FOR BEING OUR PRIME SUSPECT!
I HEAR YOU'RE LOOKING FOR ME?

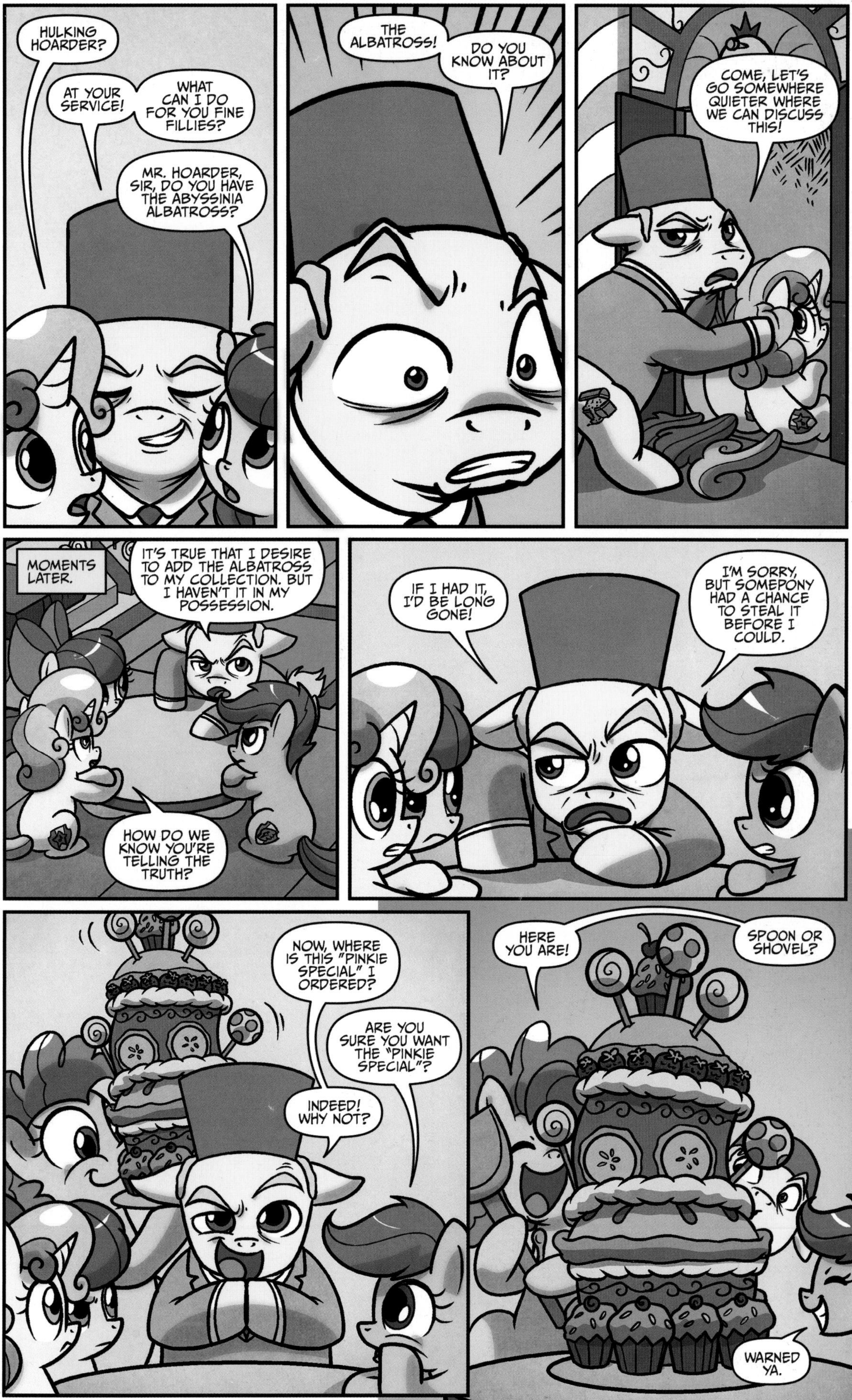
HULKING HOARDER?
AT YOUR SERVICE!
WHAT CAN I DO FOR YOU FINE FILLIES?
MR. HOARDER, SIR, DO YOU HAVE THE ABYSSINIA ALBATROSS?
THE ALBATROSS!
DO YOU KNOW ABOUT IT?
COME, LET'S GO SOMEWHERE QUIETER WHERE WE CAN DISCUSS THIS!
MOMENTS LATER.
IT'S TRUE THAT I DESIRE TO ADD THE ALBATROSS TO MY COLLECTION. BUT I HAVEN'T IT IN MY POSSESSION.
HOW DO WE KNOW YOU'RE TELLING THE TRUTH?
IF I HAD IT, I'D BE LONG GONE!
I'M SORRY, BUT SOMEPONY HAD A CHANCE TO STEAL IT BEFORE I COULD.
NOW, WHERE IS THIS "PINKIE SPECIAL" I ORDERED?
ARE YOU SURE YOU WANT THE "PINKIE SPECIAL"?
INDEED! WHY NOT?
HERE YOU ARE!
SPOON OR SHOVEL?
WARNED YA.

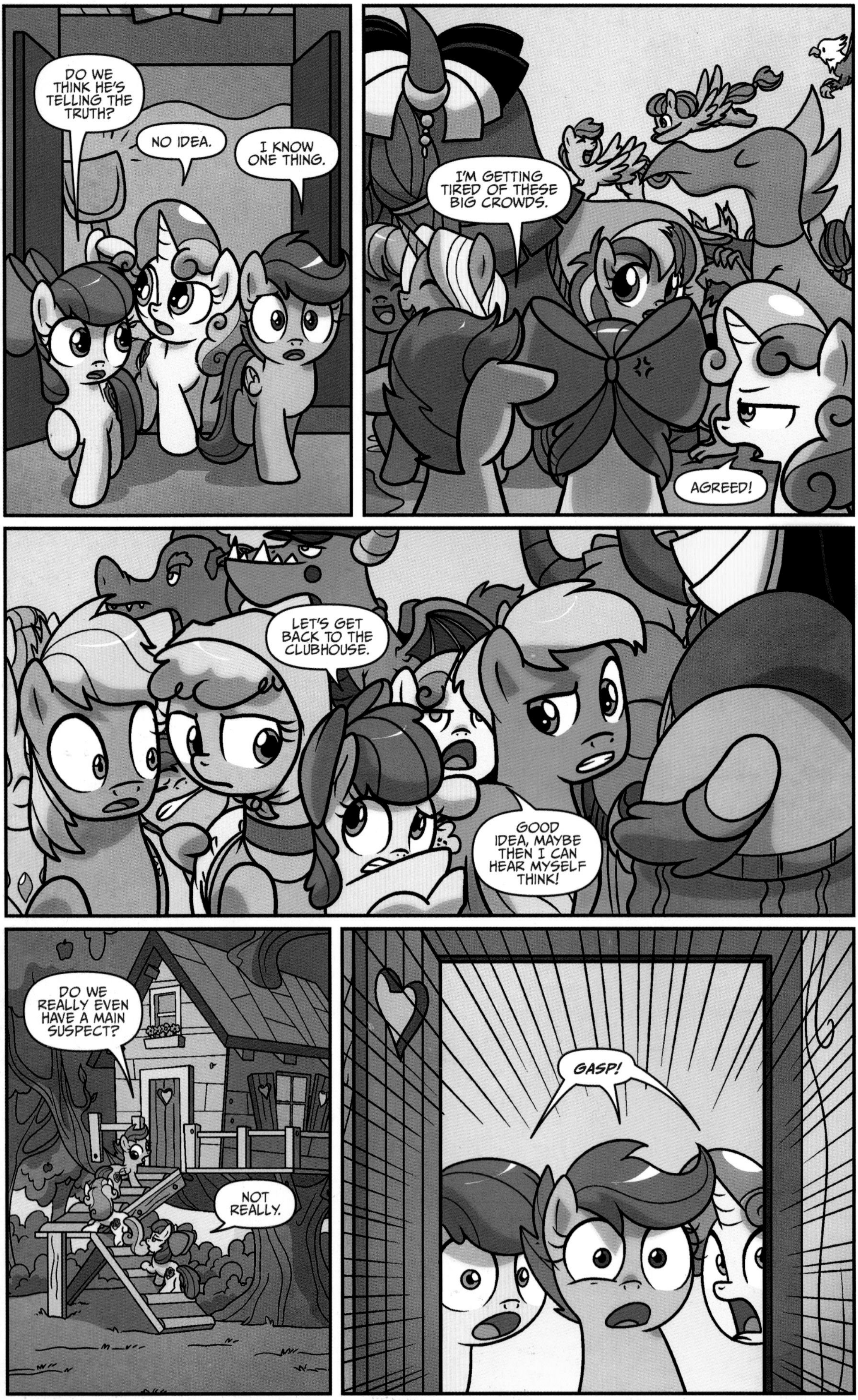
DO WE THINK HE'S TELLING THE TRUTH?
NO IDEA.
I KNOW ONE THING.
I'M GETTING TIRED OF THESE BIG CROWDS.
AGREED!
LET'S GET BACK TO THE CLUBHOUSE.
GOOD IDEA, MAYBE THEN I CAN HEAR MYSELF THINK!
DO WE REALLY EVEN HAVE A MAIN SUSPECT?
NOT REALLY.
GASP!

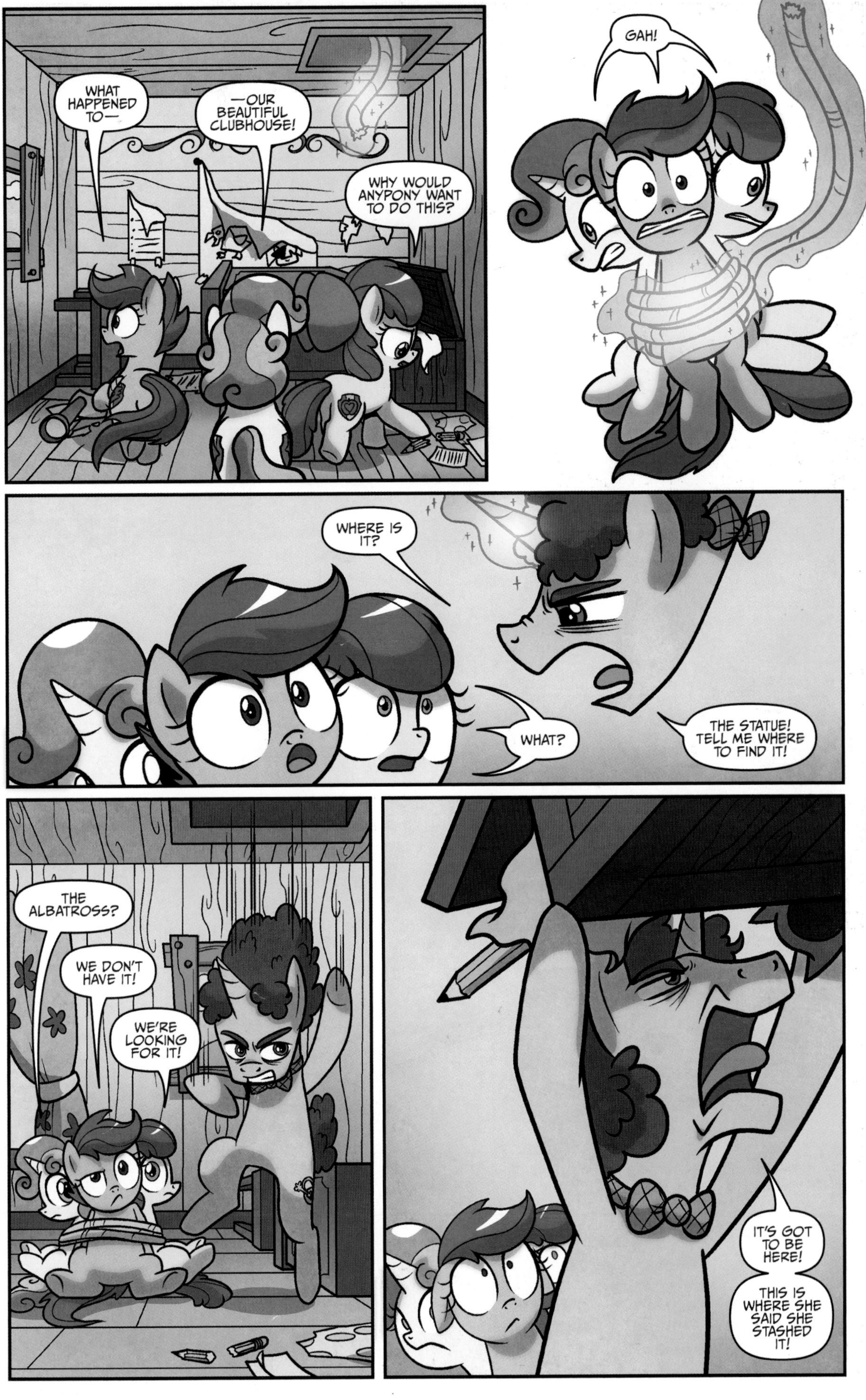
WHAT HAPPENED TO—
—OUR BEAUTIFUL CLUBHOUSE!
WHY WOULD ANYPONY WANT TO DO THIS?
GAH!
WHERE IS IT?
WHAT?
THE STATUE! TELL ME WHERE TO FIND IT!
THE ALBATROSS?
WE DON'T HAVE IT!
WE'RE LOOKING FOR IT!
IT'S GOT TO BE HERE!
THIS IS WHERE SHE SAID SHE STASHED IT!

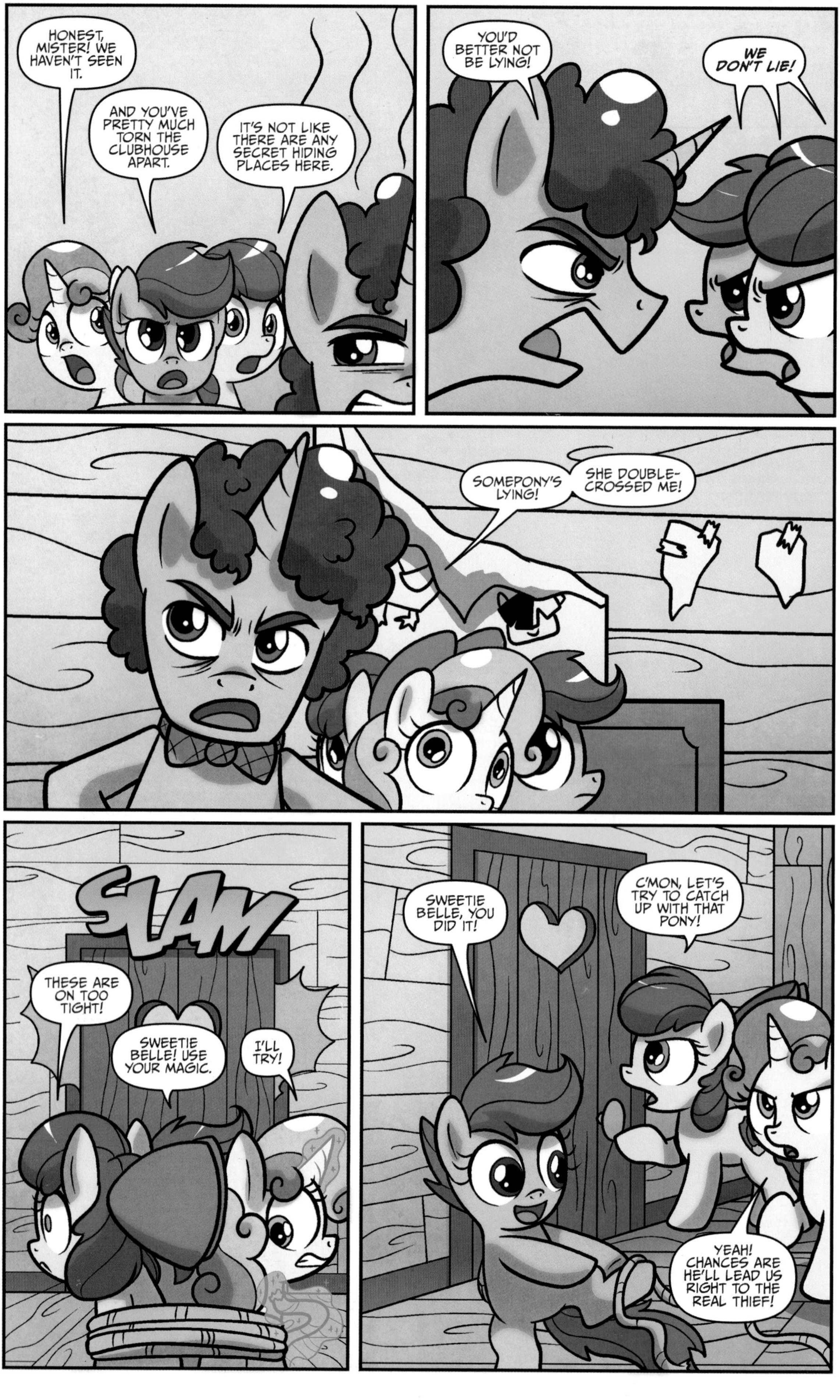
HONEST, MISTER! WE HAVEN'T SEEN IT.
AND YOU'VE PRETTY MUCH TORN THE CLUBHOUSE APART.
IT'S NOT LIKE THERE ARE ANY SECRET HIDING PLACES HERE.
YOU'D BETTER NOT BE LYING!
WE DON'T LIE!
SOMEPONY'S LYING!
SHE DOUBLE-CROSSED ME!
SLAM
THESE ARE ON TOO TIGHT!
SWEETIE BELLE! USE YOUR MAGIC.
I'LL TRY!
SWEETIE BELLE, YOU DID IT!
C'MON, LET'S TRY TO CATCH UP WITH THAT PONY!
YEAH! CHANCES ARE HE'LL LEAD US RIGHT TO THE REAL THIEF!

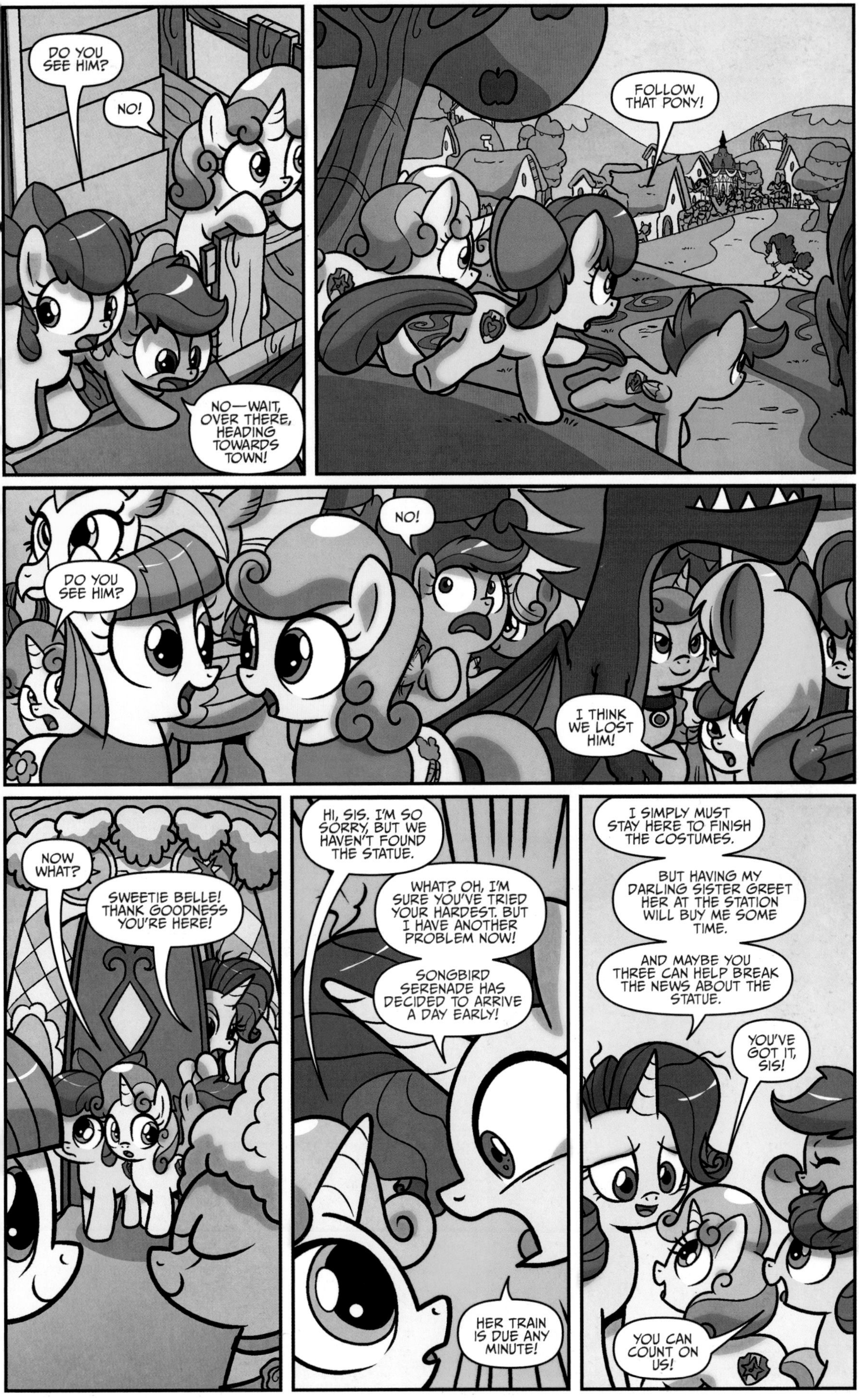
DO YOU SEE HIM?
NO!
NO—WAIT, OVER THERE, HEADING TOWARDS TOWN!
FOLLOW THAT PONY!
DO YOU SEE HIM?
NO!
I THINK WE LOST HIM!
NOW WHAT?
SWEETIE BELLE! THANK GOODNESS YOU'RE HERE!
HI, SIS. I'M SO SORRY, BUT WE HAVEN'T FOUND THE STATUE.
WHAT? OH, I'M SURE YOU'VE TRIED YOUR HARDEST. BUT I HAVE ANOTHER PROBLEM NOW!
SONGBIRD SERENADE HAS DECIDED TO ARRIVE A DAY EARLY!
HER TRAIN IS DUE ANY MINUTE!
I SIMPLY MUST STAY HERE TO FINISH THE COSTUMES.
BUT HAVING MY DARLING SISTER GREET HER AT THE STATION WILL BUY ME SOME TIME.
AND MAYBE YOU THREE CAN HELP BREAK THE NEWS ABOUT THE STATUE.
YOU'VE GOT IT, SIS!
YOU CAN COUNT ON US!

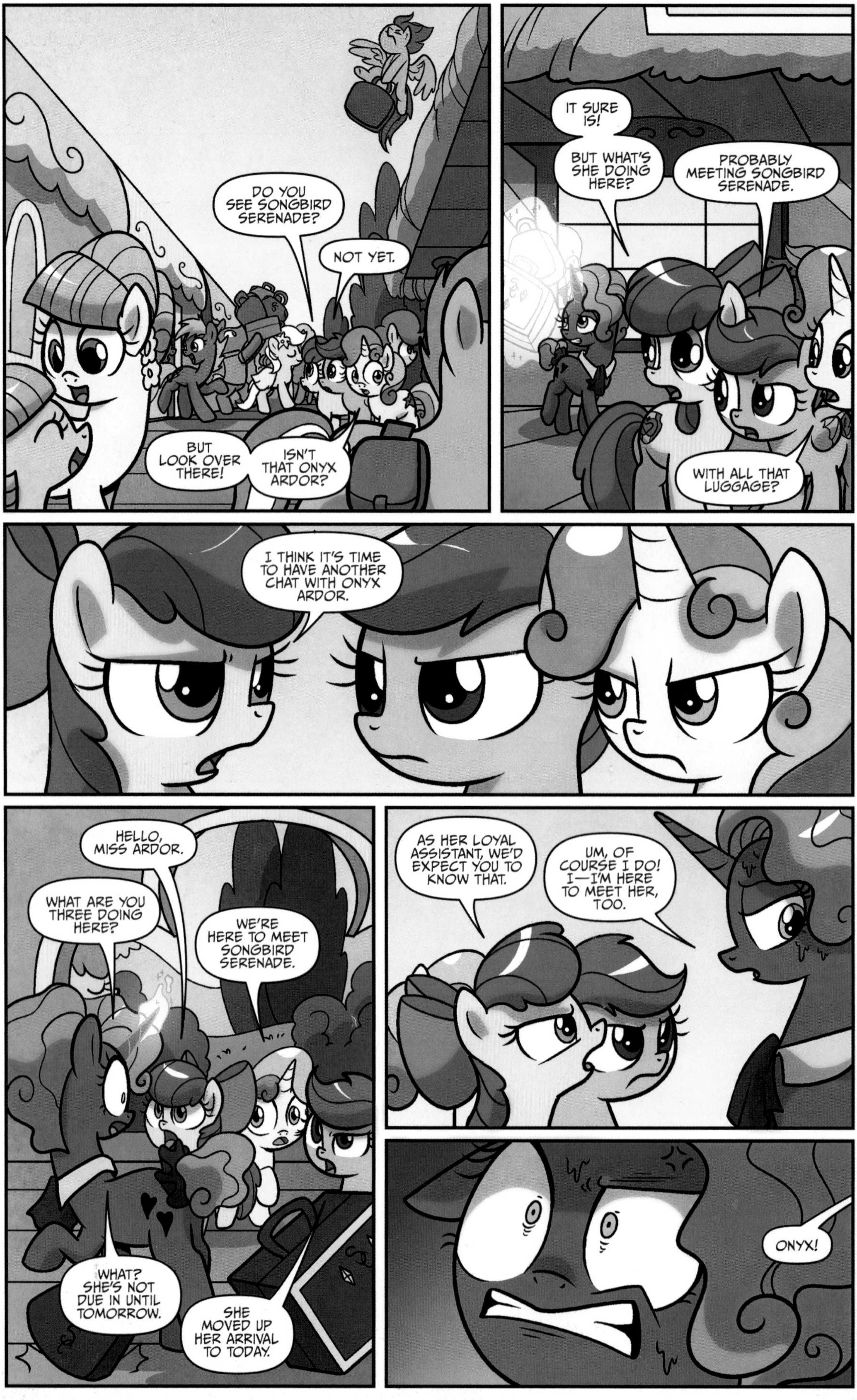
DO YOU SEE SONGBIRD SERENADE?
NOT YET.
BUT LOOK OVER THERE!
ISN'T THAT ONYX ARDOR?
IT SURE IS!
BUT WHAT'S SHE DOING HERE?
PROBABLY MEETING SONGBIRD SERENADE.
WITH ALL THAT LUGGAGE?
I THINK IT'S TIME TO HAVE ANOTHER CHAT WITH ONYX ARDOR.
HELLO, MISS ARDOR.
WHAT ARE YOU THREE DOING HERE?
WE'RE HERE TO MEET SONGBIRD SERENADE.
WHAT? SHE'S NOT DUE IN UNTIL TOMORROW.
SHE MOVED UP HER ARRIVAL TO TODAY.
AS HER LOYAL ASSISTANT, WE'D EXPECT YOU TO KNOW THAT.
UM, OF COURSE I DO! I—I'M HERE TO MEET HER, TOO.
ONYX!

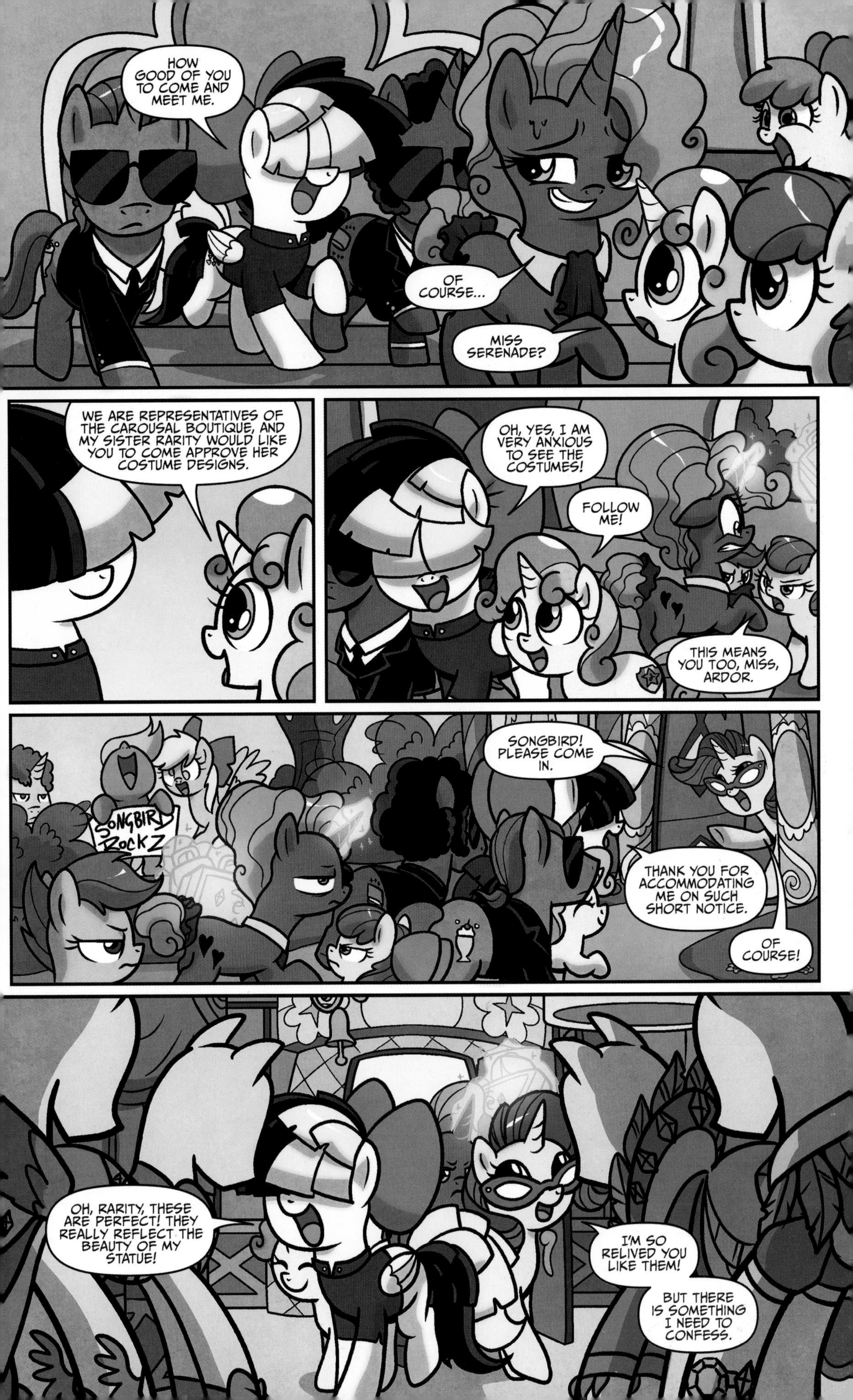
HOW GOOD OF YOU TO COME AND MEET ME.
OF COURSE...
MISS SERENADE?
WE ARE REPRESENTATIVES OF THE CAROUSAL BOUTIQUE, AND MY SISTER RARITY WOULD LIKE YOU TO COME APPROVE HER COSTUME DESIGNS.
OH, YES, I AM VERY ANXIOUS TO SEE THE COSTUMES!
FOLLOW ME!
THIS MEANS YOU TOO, MISS, ARDOR.
SONGBIRD ROCKZ
SONGBIRD! PLEASE COME IN.
THANK YOU FOR ACCOMMODATING ME ON SUCH SHORT NOTICE.
OF COURSE!
OH, RARITY, THESE ARE PERFECT! THEY REALLY REFLECT THE BEAUTY OF MY STATUE!
I'M SO RELIVED YOU LIKE THEM!
BUT THERE IS SOMETHING I NEED TO CONFESS.

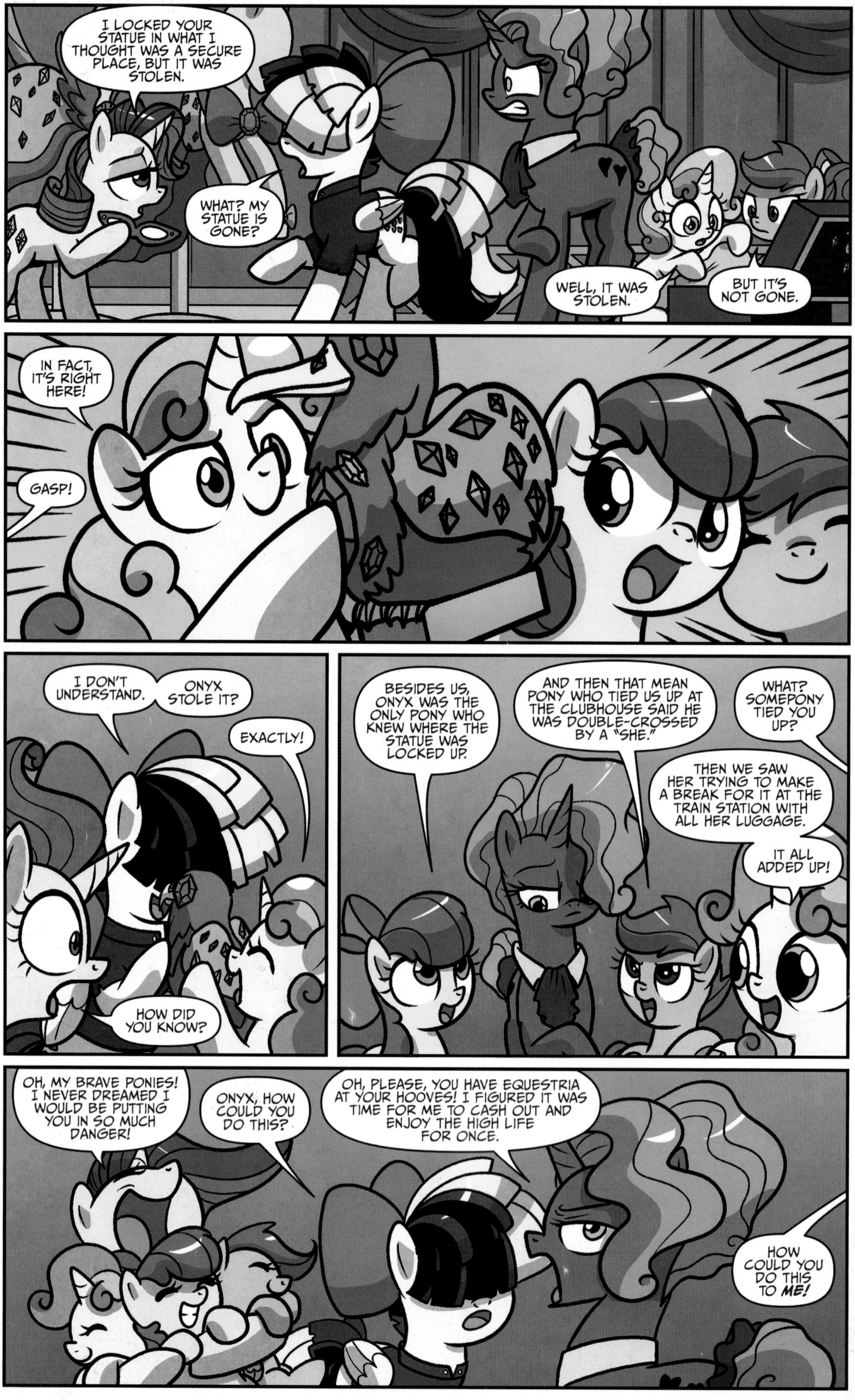
I LOCKED YOUR STATUE IN WHAT I THOUGHT WAS A SECURE PLACE, BUT IT WAS STOLEN.
WHAT? MY STATUE IS GONE?
WELL, IT WAS STOLEN.
BUT IT'S NOT GONE.
IN FACT, IT'S RIGHT HERE!
GASP!
I DON'T UNDERSTAND.
ONYX STOLE IT?
EXACTLY!
HOW DID YOU KNOW?
BESIDES US, ONYX WAS THE ONLY PONY WHO KNEW WHERE THE STATUE WAS LOCKED UP.
AND THEN THAT MEAN PONY WHO TIED US UP AT THE CLUBHOUSE SAID HE WAS DOUBLE-CROSSED BY A "SHE."
WHAT? SOMEPONY TIED YOU UP?
THEN WE SAW HER TRYING TO MAKE A BREAK FOR IT AT THE TRAIN STATION WITH ALL HER LUGGAGE.
IT ALL ADDED UP!
OH, MY BRAVE PONIES! I NEVER DREAMED I WOULD BE PUTTING YOU IN SO MUCH DANGER!
ONYX, HOW COULD YOU DO THIS?
OH, PLEASE, YOU HAVE EQUESTRIA AT YOUR HOOVES! I FIGURED IT WAS TIME FOR ME TO CASH OUT AND ENJOY THE HIGH LIFE FOR ONCE.
HOW COULD YOU DO THIS TO **ME!**

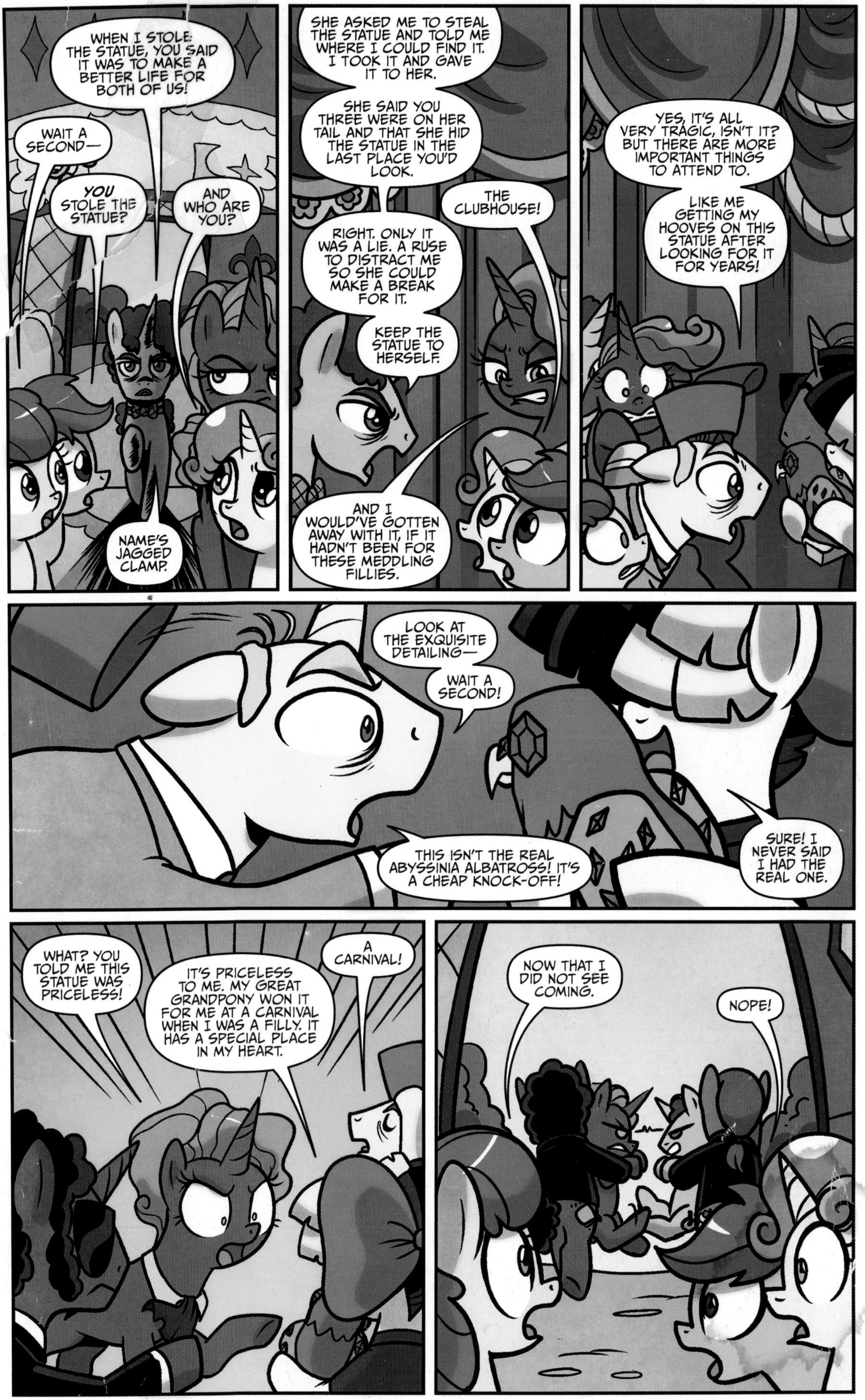

WHEN I STOLE THE STATUE, YOU SAID IT WAS TO MAKE A BETTER LIFE FOR BOTH OF US!
WAIT A SECOND—
YOU STOLE THE STATUE?
AND WHO ARE YOU?
NAME'S JAGGED CLAMP.
SHE ASKED ME TO STEAL THE STATUE AND TOLD ME WHERE I COULD FIND IT. I TOOK IT AND GAVE IT TO HER.
SHE SAID YOU THREE WERE ON HER TAIL AND THAT SHE HID THE STATUE IN THE LAST PLACE YOU'D LOOK.
THE CLUBHOUSE!
RIGHT. ONLY IT WAS A LIE. A RUSE TO DISTRACT ME SO SHE COULD MAKE A BREAK FOR IT.
KEEP THE STATUE TO HERSELF.
AND I WOULD'VE GOTTEN AWAY WITH IT, IF IT HADN'T BEEN FOR THESE MEDDLING FILLIES.
YES, IT'S ALL VERY TRAGIC, ISN'T IT? BUT THERE ARE MORE IMPORTANT THINGS TO ATTEND TO.
LIKE ME GETTING MY HOOVES ON THIS STATUE AFTER LOOKING FOR IT FOR YEARS!
LOOK AT THE EXQUISITE DETAILING—
WAIT A SECOND!
THIS ISN'T THE REAL ABYSSINIA ALBATROSS! IT'S A CHEAP KNOCK-OFF!
SURE! I NEVER SAID I HAD THE REAL ONE.
WHAT? YOU TOLD ME THIS STATUE WAS PRICELESS!
IT'S PRICELESS TO ME. MY GREAT GRANDPONY WON IT FOR ME AT A CARNIVAL WHEN I WAS A FILLY. IT HAS A SPECIAL PLACE IN MY HEART.
A CARNIVAL!
NOW THAT I DID NOT SEE COMING.
NOPE!

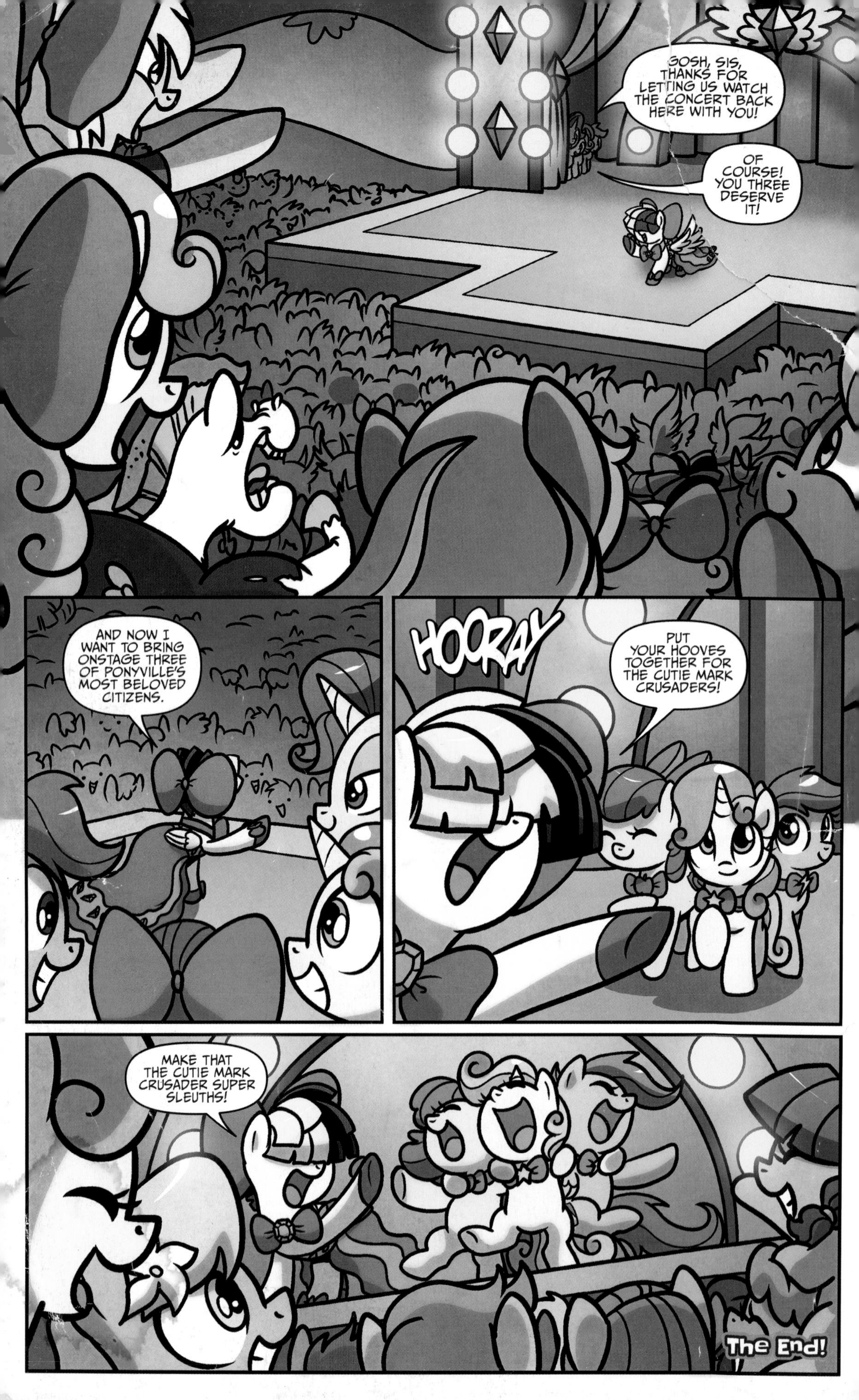
GOSH, SIS, THANKS FOR LETTING US WATCH THE CONCERT BACK HERE WITH YOU!
OF COURSE! YOU THREE DESERVE IT!
AND NOW I WANT TO BRING ONSTAGE THREE OF PONYVILLE'S MOST BELOVED CITIZENS.
HOORAY
PUT YOUR HOOVES TOGETHER FOR THE CUTIE MARK CRUSADERS!
MAKE THAT THE CUTIE MARK CRUSADER SUPER SLEUTHS!
The End!

ART BY **PHILIP MURPHY**

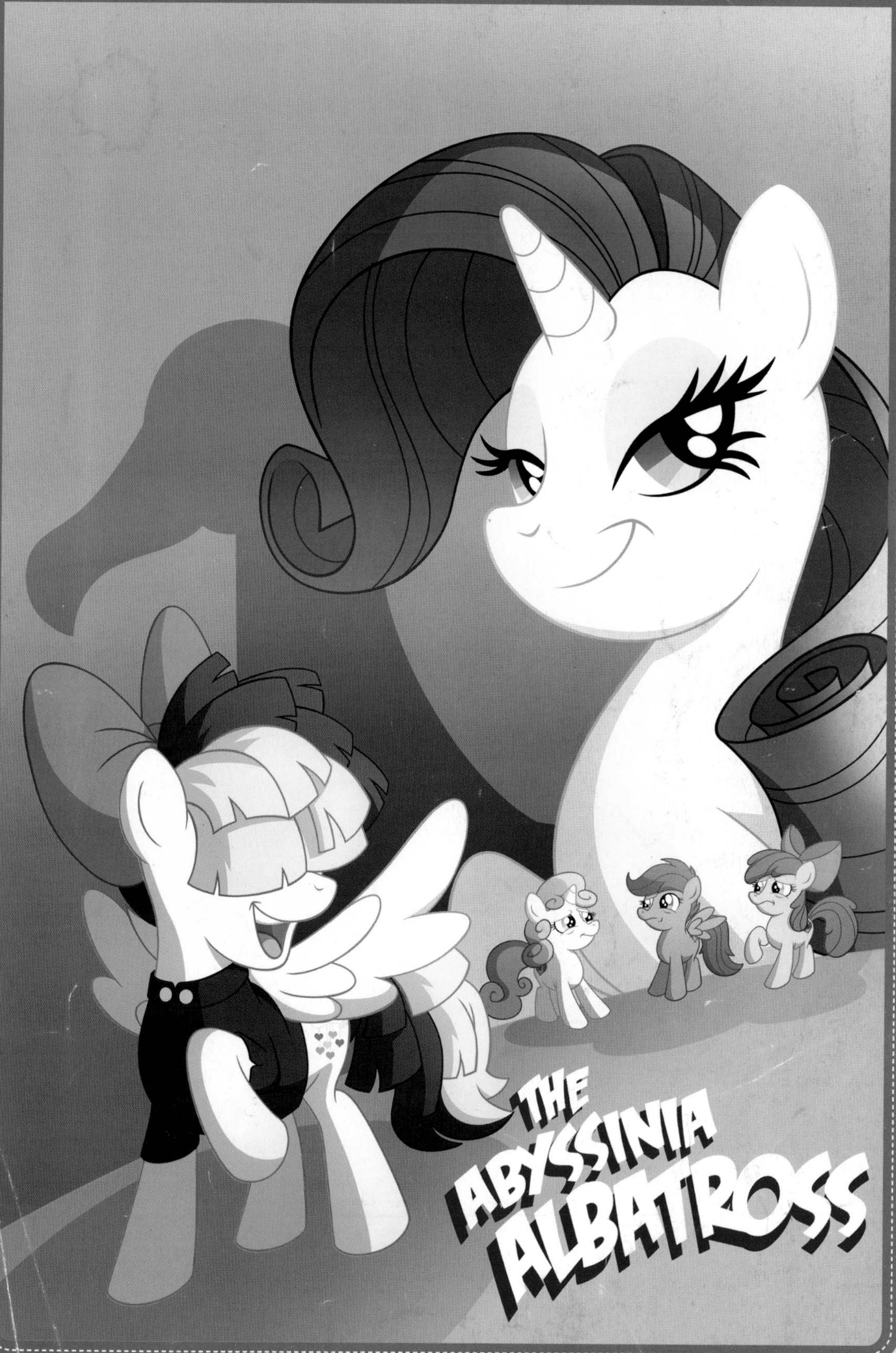
THE
ABYSSINIA
ALBATROSS

ART BY **JAY FOSGITT**

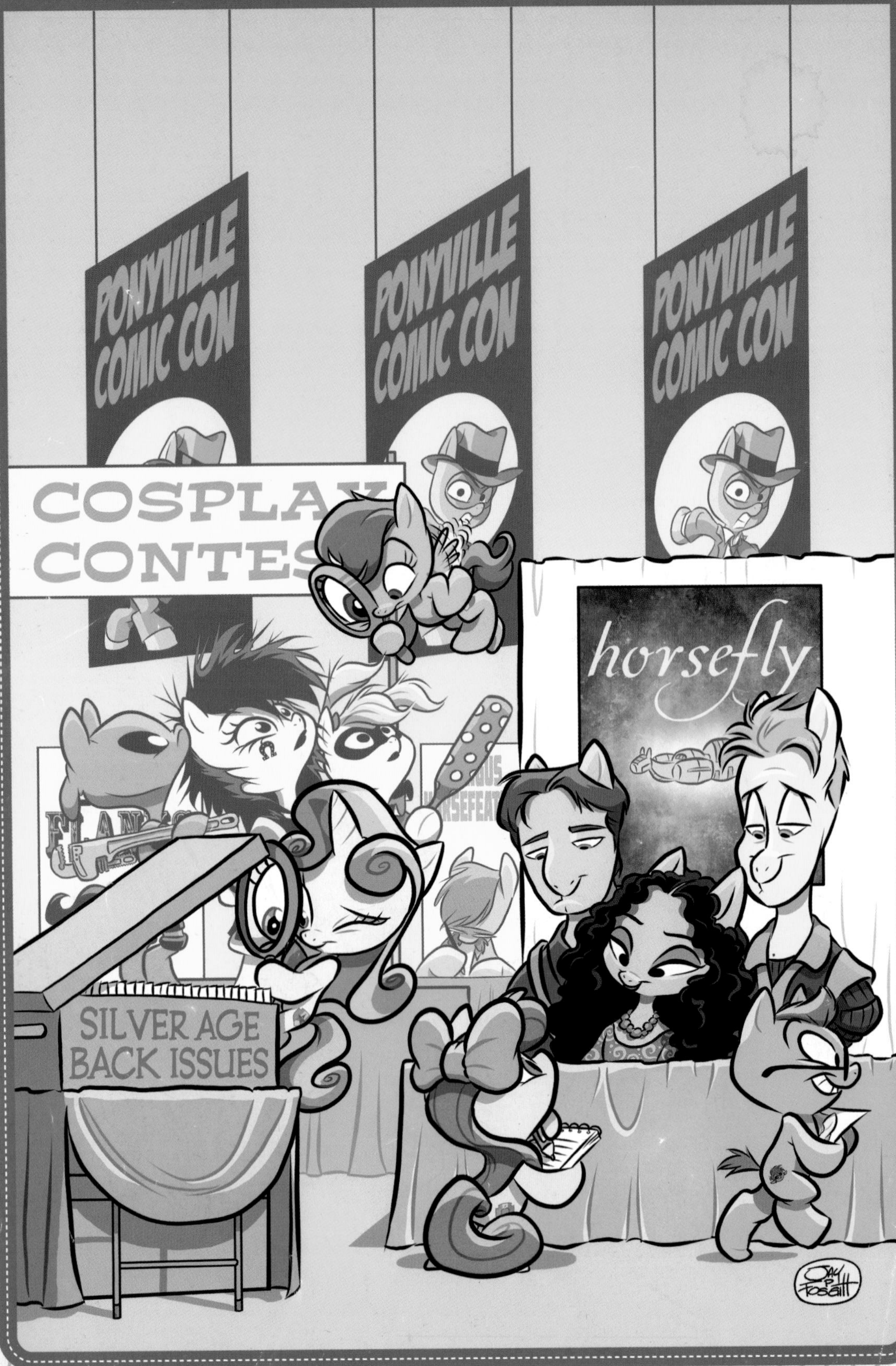

PONYVILLE COMIC CON
PONYVILLE COMIC CON
PONYVILLE COMIC CON
COSPLAY CONTES
horsefly
SILVER AGE BACK ISSUES

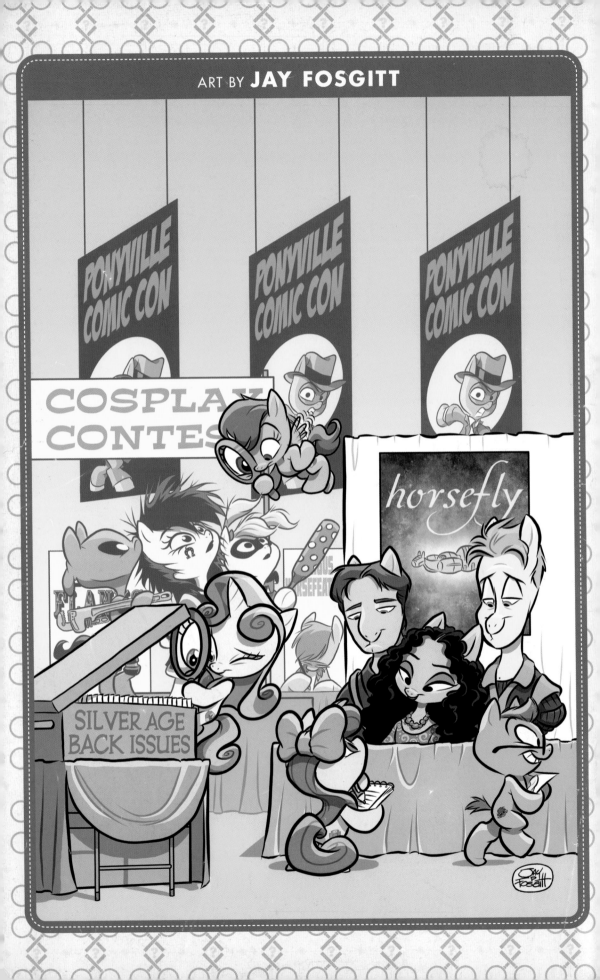

ART BY **TIM SHINN**

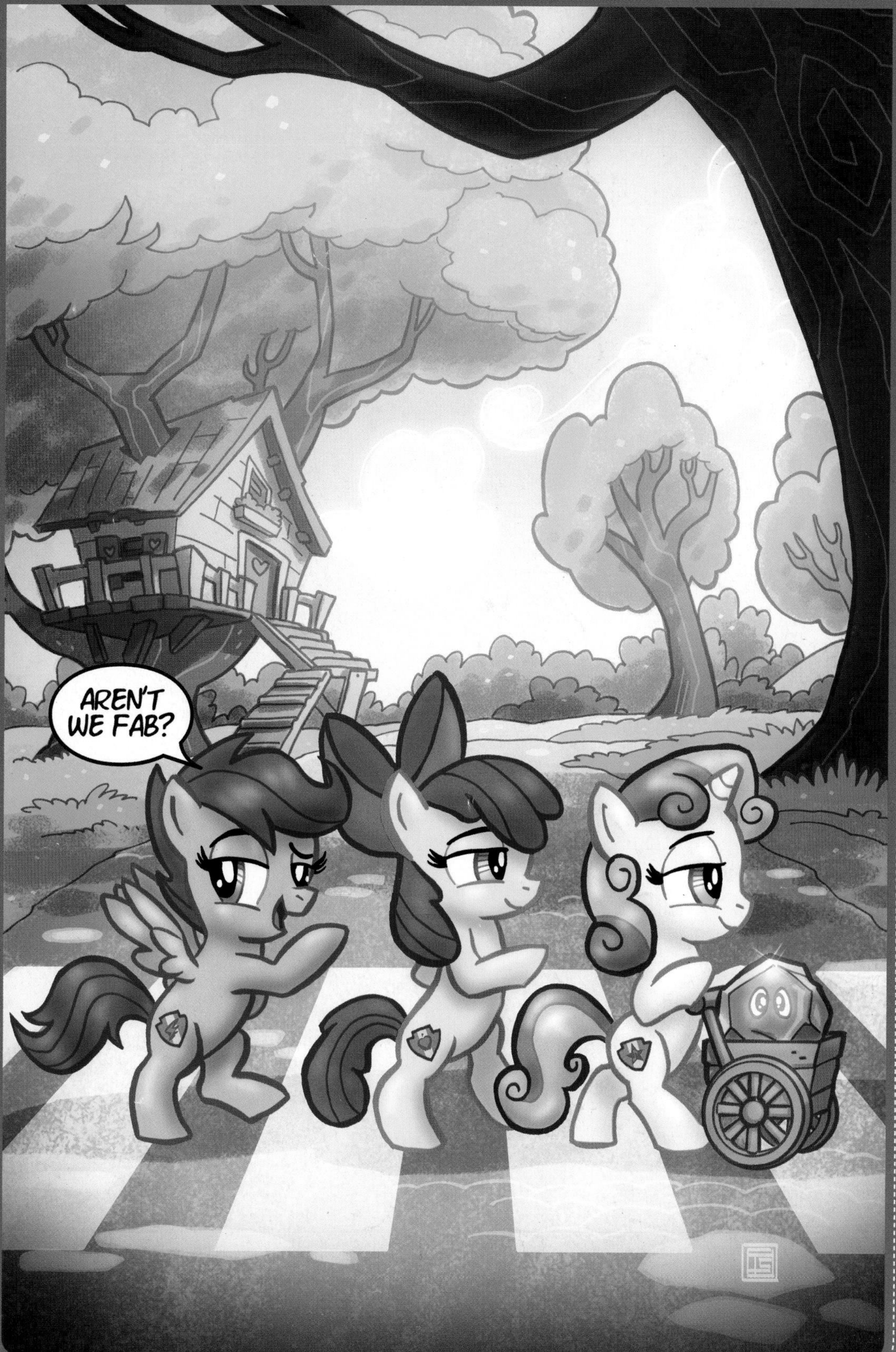
AREN'T WE FAB?

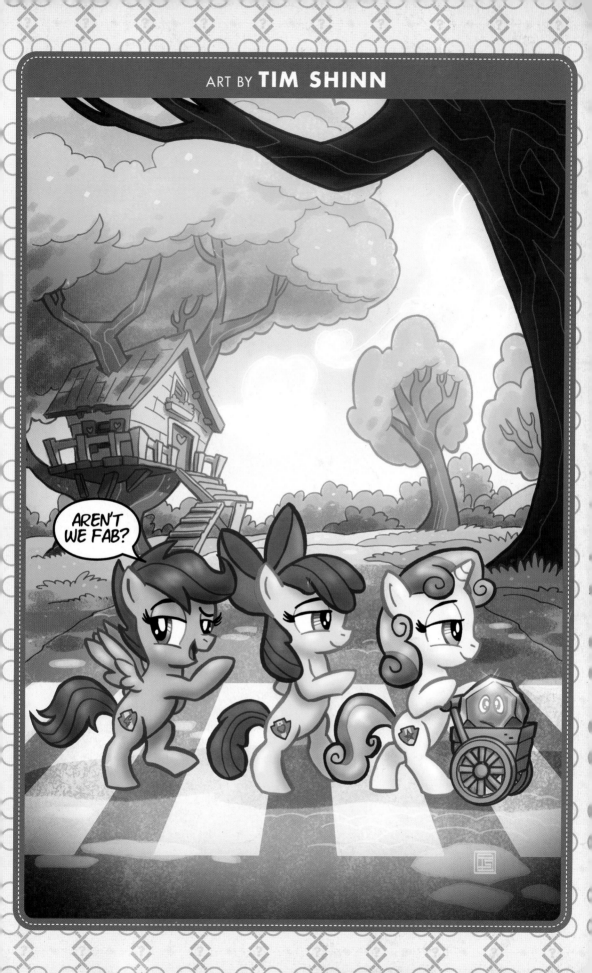

ART BY **ANDY PRICE**

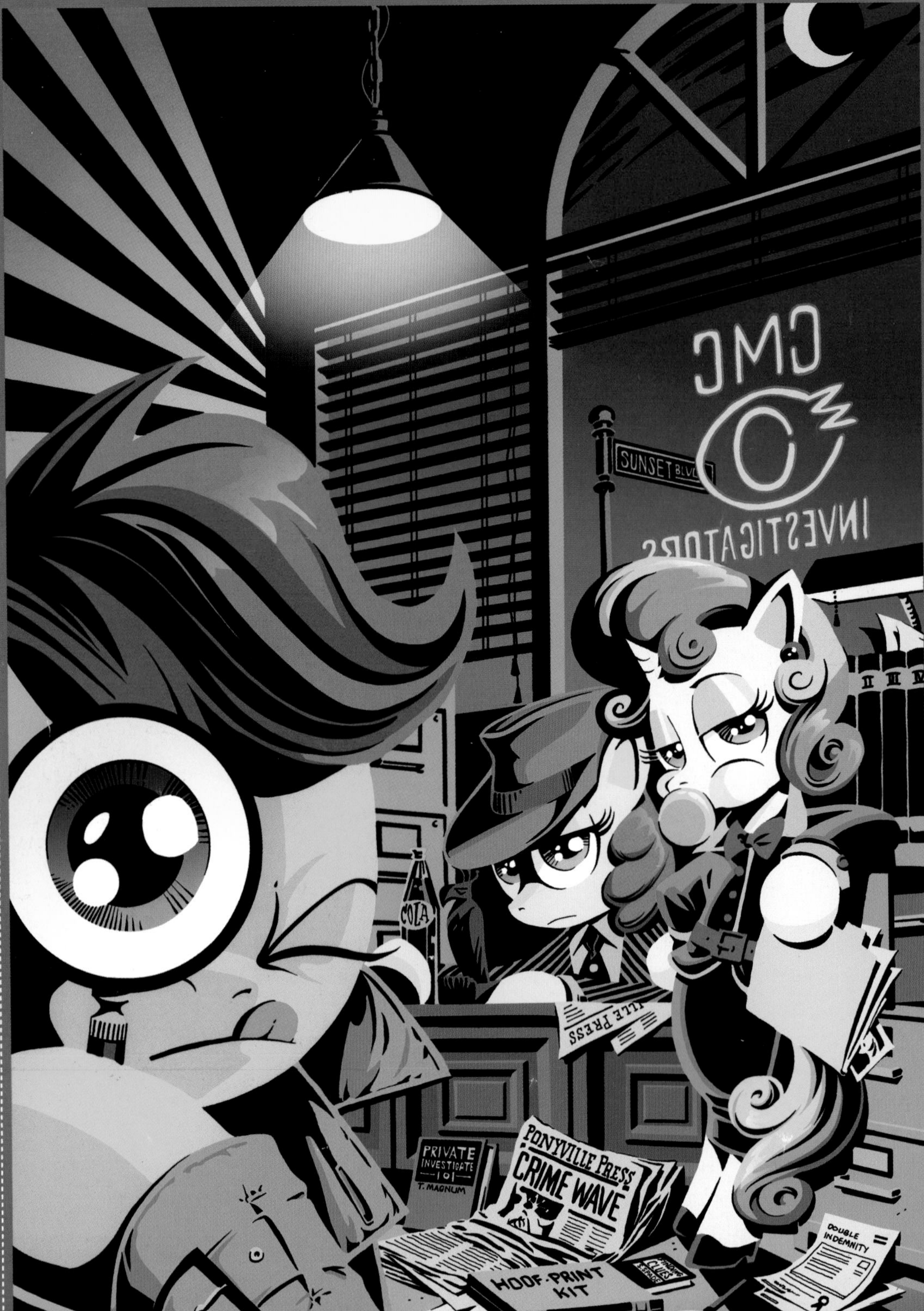

ART BY **ABIGAIL STARLING**

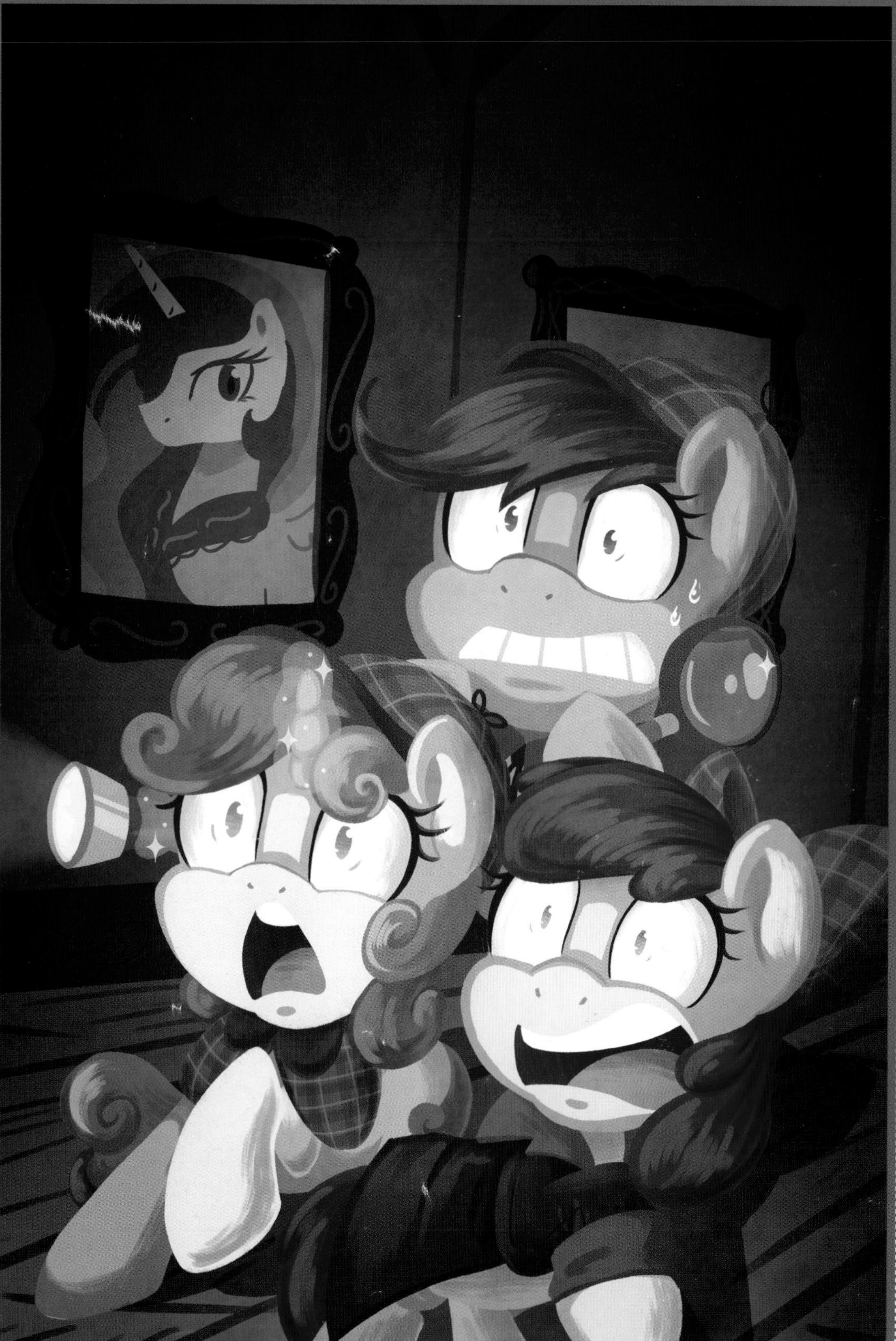

ART BY **JUSTYNA BABINSKA**

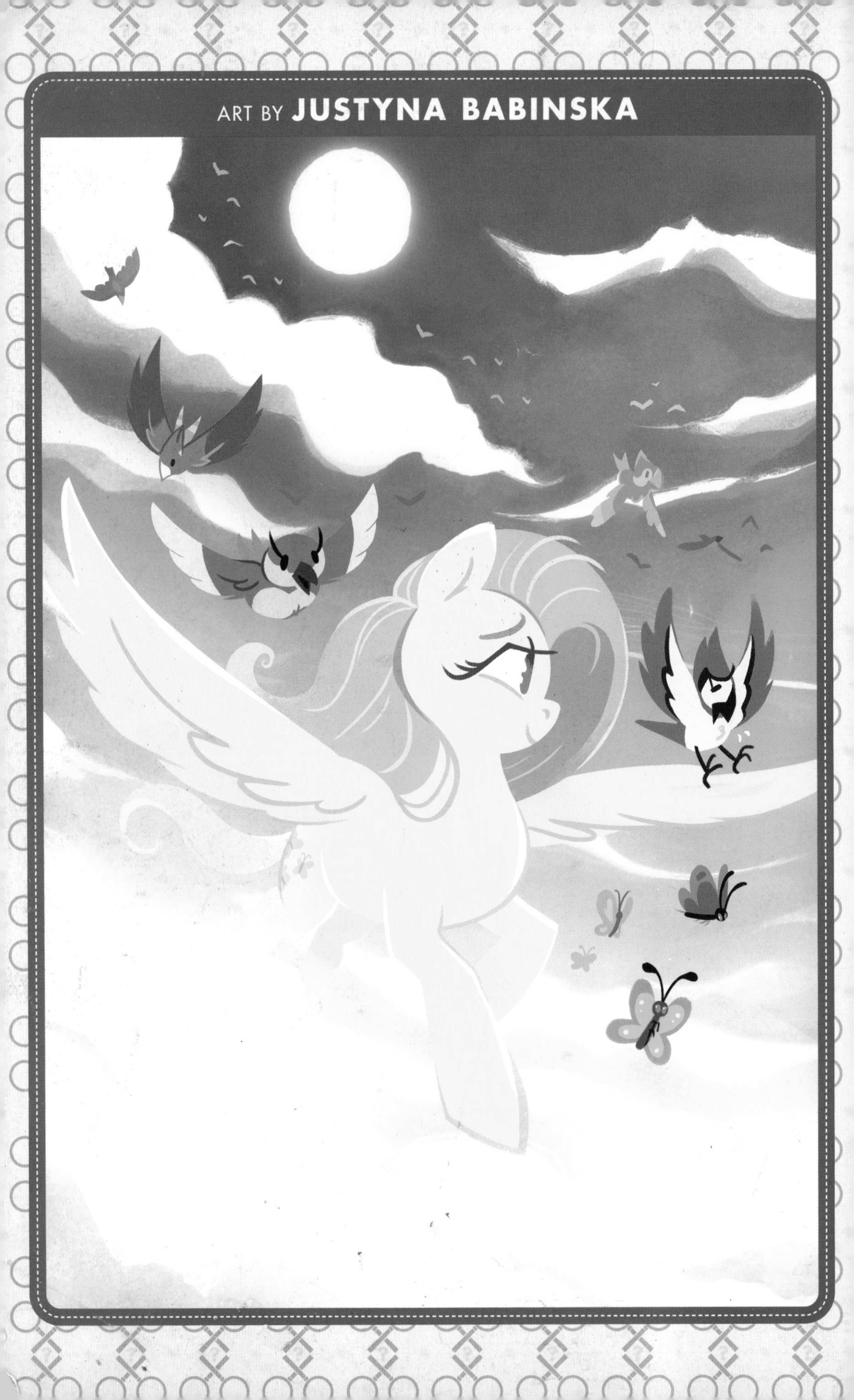

ART BY **TRISH FORSTNER**

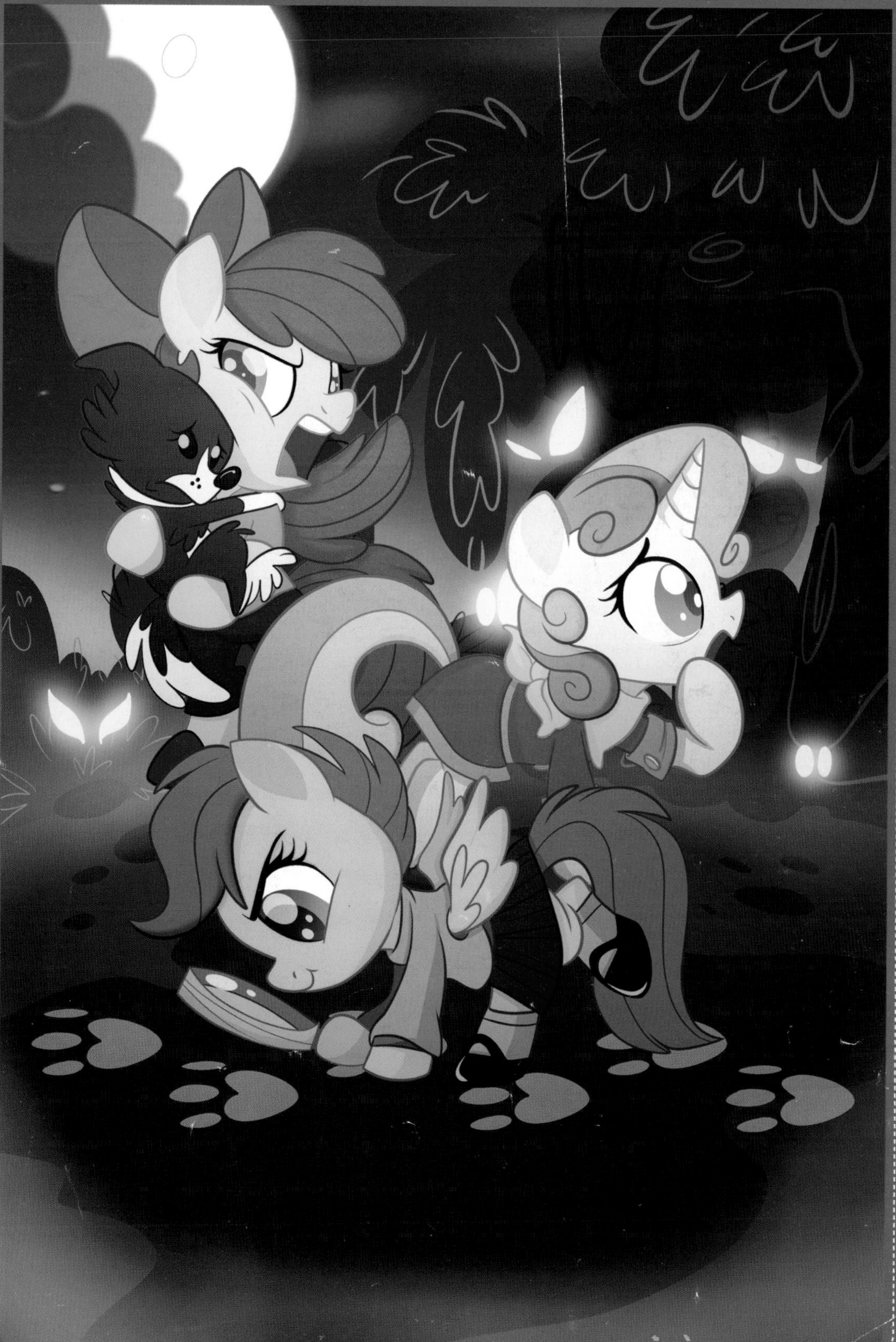

ART BY **KONRAD KACHEL**

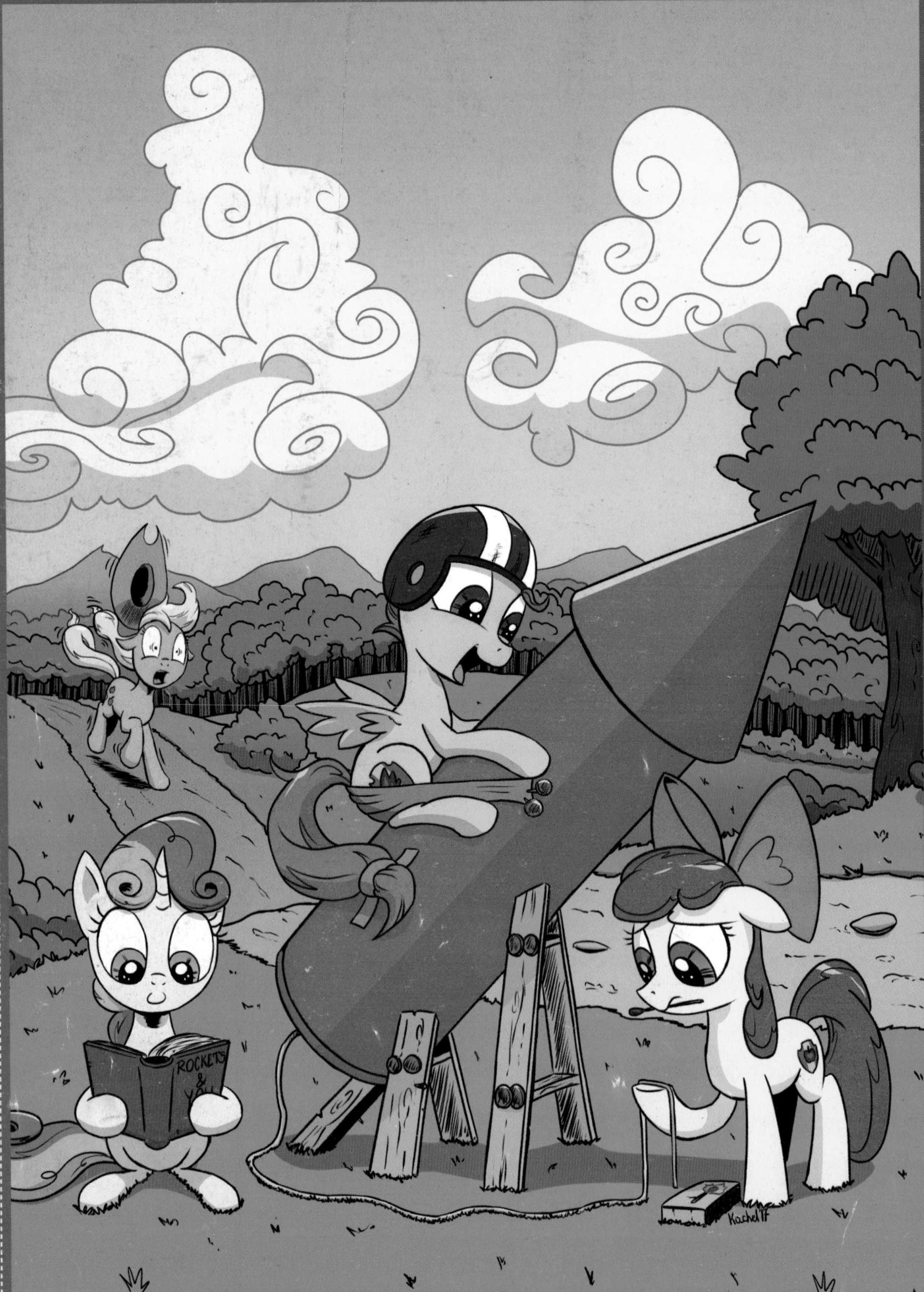
ROCKETS
&